Malice

Kevin C. Popp

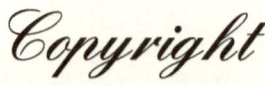

Copyright

ISBN: 978-1-7323211-6-8
Kindle ISBN: 978-1-7323211-7-5

Written by Kevin C. Popp

www.TheGarrisonSeries Instagram www.instagram.com/popp.kevin or Facebook at www.facebook.com/TheGarrisonSeries

Editing and Interior Design by Nita Robinson, *Nita Helping Hand?*

Cover by Kelly Martin, KAM Designs

Chapter One

At what point in my life will I stop aging? Would I know the year or the month of this event? I've spent many nights of my life sitting in Trevor's office pondering these questions. What haunts me is the possibility that this everlasting life that I am told I possess, doesn't exist. What if Wolfgang, Trevor, and Lewis were all wrong?

Trevor, my father who adopted me, told me just before he was murdered that my body should stop aging around 30 years of age. When one thinks about death, it can become very depressing. Many would think that staying young forever is a wonderful blessing bestowed from the great anointed one from the heavens, but for me, it is a curse. Imagine, if you will, all your friends and loved ones will age and eventually die while you will never age or die. This is the price that I must pay for my blessings. I will eventually witness the aging and death of my Marci. It is a hideous thought to contemplate.

When I concentrate and stay focused on the task at hand, I can hear my Marci upstairs sleeping. I can hear the sweet breath roll in and out of her most perfect mouth. I imagine her face that is permanently etched in my mind. I see that most perfect face that is so beautiful it haunts me in every imaginable way. To possess the knowledge that my face will be frozen in time while her face will be subject to the mercilessness of what time can do physically to a living animal is a curse. Time is so short for the living with the only exception – me.

During this time of my life, I stand before this all-knowing being named Christ, possessing the awareness of knowing and having the power of everlasting life. One would think this would give me comfort, but it has given me great unrest. No one can imagine outliving everyone they know or love. The closer I get to people, the harder it is to let them go. I have lost so many people in my life, I really don't know where to turn for comfort besides my Marci.

I cannot accept the thought of losing my Marci to death, but I cannot bring myself to force this curse, which disguises itself as a blessing, on the one I love the most. I could never hurt my Marci. I could never infect her with the formula and witness her transformation. The pain is unimaginable, as I have witnessed this from the transformation of my parents. I often thought of leaving my love and living with my birth parents in Germany, but I couldn't live with myself with the knowledge that I hurt her if I abandoned her that way. I will never abandon my Marci. She was abandoned by her parents, much as I was abandoned by mine. I will never hurt her in that way. At the same time, I grow selfish in having the pleasure of her company during these short respites of time that we have together until her eventual death. Therefore, this forces me to live with my most evil and selfish deed forever.

Damn that god of mine for giving me this blessing. Does this god even exist or is it just nature playing the most elaborate hoax at my expense? Why me? Why did he, or it, bless me with this possession of everlasting life? I wish he, it or this idea of holiness would manifest his presence before me and fight me like a man instead of hiding behind the convenient veil of his mantra, the son of god. Why did he punish me? I didn't ask for this blessing even though it feels so wonderful, while at the same time it hurts like no pain has ever felt. Maybe it is god's way of punishing me for being the most perfect of all creatures he has ever created. Maybe god never intended to produce a creation like me.

I am the man I am today because of my parents and the formula my father created. I am god's best creation. I believe, if there is a god, that he never intended for a thing like me to have been created. If he would eliminate me from existence, that would admit failure, something that this god isn't willing to accept. Maybe this great paradox is what angers god. Maybe what has happened to me is all god's fault and not mine. Is he the reason so many deaths and suffering have followed me throughout my life? The very thought that there is a chance of his existence is unforgivable to me. If he does exist, then why is he punishing me?

I had a difficult and intricate life. Throughout the years, I have consistently been at odds with conflicted feelings. Feelings that range from my own self-serving entitlement that was created by my complex, disjointed past to my unrelenting search to blame someone for the low points that I have experienced in my life. I cannot help myself from thinking that god is jealous of my ability and he is torturing me with the losses of my adoptive parents and the eventual losses of my future loved ones. I feel he is personally responsible for my current and future pain. I feel that sometimes I am confronted with the opposite position. Is my unique way of being such an oddity that the issues I must confront are permanently affixed to my life forever?

During these times of contemplation of my self-pity moments, I reminisce on the positives of my life. I suddenly feel better during these times; I am most peaceful when I walk the grounds of my estate late at night. The night has become one of my closest friends throughout my life. When everyone else is asleep, I am awake. I am either reading, working, or playing my violin. During my time of awakened consciousness, I seem to always be distracted, for some unexplainable reason, by the outside world.

The aroma of the night calls for me to rediscover what I had previously visited many nights before during my existence. Oh, that musky perfume of the night is one of my most favorite scents that I have experienced. This is the time of the day where the creatures of the night make their entrance into the world. They come out of the ground, from behind the rocks, and from the tops of trees. The night scent permeates through your clothes and mixes with your body scent for an indescribable pleasure of sensory aroma that could only be matched by my Marci's lustful, sexual scent. The heaviness of the night air tends to give off a sense of comfort to me that I've come to enjoy with great passion. The ability that I possess to see well at night allows me the opportunity to enjoy the hidden treasures that are mostly unseen by the unblessed.

Maybe my life isn't so bad, but at times, my heart bleeds self-pity. Not only have I lost loved ones in my past but having the knowledge that I will lose loved ones in the future is hard to comprehend and accept. I assume that is why I am drawn towards the night. I feel comfort in the dark. I can see things that others cannot. I feel free and one with nature. I don't belong with the humans that inhabit my world. My world is pure, strong, certain, and definite.

The intoxicating pleasure of the night goes beyond just the scent of the outside world. My bliss has always been heightened by pleasuring all my senses to create an ultimate experience of unworldly taboo encounters that would make god's soul crawl with utter repugnance. I've set many traps deep in the treed hills of my estate. I would have numerous late-night snacks on the animals of the diminutive forested area of my world. At times, I would hunt for my snacks, which always entertained me more than the meal itself. I never used a gun because I don't want to excite or draw attention from my neighbors. I would use a rock or a stick in my hunting expeditions. I would use these instruments for hunting to stun my prey. Then the most basic of all instincts takes hold of my soul and guides me to a more natural and pure form of enjoying the delicacies of my capture.

Some of the greatest pleasures in my life are on those musky nights where the air was either so thick with warmth from the ground that was created by the warm summer sun, or the coolness of the northern winds that brought its cool air down from the arctic world to mix with the warmth of the ground that lay beneath my feet. This backdrop, mixed with my nightly snacks, is a mixture of pure bliss. To pick up a live, moving, and scared animal in my hands and feel or sense its fear, its lust for survival, its longing for escape to a safer place, is so intoxicating it is almost orgasmic. The scent of fear in any animal is unique, and so help me, I am addicted to the process of the kill, not just the kill itself.

The precious moments that exist from the time of capture to when my teeth and lips feel the soft musky fur and flesh of the animal is one of the greatest feelings this world has ever given me. As my teeth enter the flesh, the feeling of the warm blood has this intoxicating, iron, savory aftertaste. This experience is like listening to a perfectly played passage from Mozart.

The flesh and fat on some animals is not to my liking but the strong tendons are what I crave. These parts of the animal's body have their own distinct personality. Oh, that feeling of how the body of the animal tenses up when the tendon is torn from the bone is an additional pleasure that is unequalled. During this process, the cries of pain give an audible satisfaction that could only be expressed by the blessed hands of a composer of Mozart's ability. During these processes of my feedings, I feel liberated and blessed that I am alive. This is when I know that I am truly blessed because my passion for life is strong.

My unbridled passion for living is shared by my loved one. Marci wants to be a participant in my daily servings of the most ultimate cuisine. I cannot allow her the pleasure for it will make my lover sick. She wants to be me. She wants me to infect her with the formula so she can live forever with me and to possess the ability to be as close to perfect as anyone could get. She doesn't care that her beautiful face and figure would be transformed into its contradictory form.

I tried to pass on the understanding and knowledge of what I know to her and how her physical appearance wouldn't be pleasant or to her liking. My love doesn't care about the horrific end result, which is a powerful and unfortunate trait that commands her soul. It saddens me that she doesn't appreciate her current beauty. It pains me that someday that beauty will age and disappear before my eyes. Then she will meet the eventual end of her time on this world. Oh yes, what a painful and unavoidable thought that has now become my worst enemy – death; the end of time and our permanent moment of separation between us. Not a day goes by that I don't curse the fact that this fear will be a reality in a matter of time.

My true pain resides with the fact that I cannot find a cure for the physical metamorphic change that takes place because of the formula being introduced into the human system. I need to find the cure to this change, but at this point I don't know if there is an answer.

I cannot allow my mind to wander to the place of acceptance of changing my love into a monster. Part of me damns myself because I am selfish. I don't want to destroy this most beautiful creature, even if she demands the change. But if I don't change her, she will die and we will be together no more. Since I have discovered my Marci, I have spent almost every waking minute of my life trying to correct the horrific physical change the formula has on a living species. I nor my father can stop the mutation once it begins.

I sometimes feel guilty that I am a product of my parents, which are two hideous monsters. I look and act normal on the surface, but deep inside of me lurks a chemical that constantly adjusts and changes to new environments. How can you change a formula that alters its chemical makeup every minute? How can you make changes to a chemical that changes and protects its natural chemical makeup no matter what foreign chemical is introduced into its presence? Maybe one day I will be a servant to Marci's wishes and infect her with the formula, but at this point in my life, I cannot do that to my love.

Chapter Two

The day I returned home from Germany, I stayed outside for the entire evening. I needed to clear my head. I walked the grounds all hours of the night. I couldn't sleep because my mind was racing from the past week. Seeing my birth parents for the first time was overloading my senses.

Marci was inside the house, fast asleep on the couch while Carolyn had locked herself in her room to mourn the death of the only love that she had known in her life. I wondered why I had never noticed her attraction to Lewis. I sense everything, but I wondered why I never sensed her love for him. Carolyn and I were always close from the moment that I met her as a young child. It concerned me because all my life I had possessed the ability to rely totally on my senses and my innate intuition. This started me thinking, wondering why I didn't anticipate my brother attacking my parents sooner than I did. Maybe I am a bit flawed and not as perfect as I thought.

I knew that I needed to speak with Carolyn, and hopefully I could ease her pain. I felt bad that Marci and I started to make love in front of her. Marci is a very sensual woman with great desires. She is so passionate on many levels, and that is why I am so attached to her. Carolyn is my friend and we grew very close while she was my guardian during my college days. Carolyn always gave me my space, and I was very appreciative of this gift.

I sat in a cool, wrought iron chair looking over the large pool. I watched the sunlight dance on the top of the water, making interesting, natural light shows. I heard the wind as it gently blew across the surface of the water, moving it ever so slightly. I heard the birds and squirrels in the air as they created small disturbances as they moved around the trees near me. I have always created a great unrest with the animals of nature. Many of the animals attempt to move from me or climb higher than usual in the trees they currently visited.

The winds, temperature and smells were changing. I could sense that winter was coming in a couple of months.

I heard Marci getting up from the couch inside the house. I wanted to greet my lover, but I couldn't take my senses away from the music nature was performing. I heard soft footsteps coming my way. I could smell her morning scent as she walked closer to me, and before I knew it, my love slowly appeared next to me. When she stopped a foot from my side, I looked up at her. She was completely naked. The sun was kissing her skin ever so softly as the wind played with her long, golden blonde hair. Marci looked down at me sitting in the chair. She moved in front of me and gently but firmly guided my legs apart with her hands. I looked deeply into her heavenly, light blue eyes as I felt her unbuckle my pants. Her eyes never left mine and before I knew it, she roughly pulled my pants away from my body. She took my pants and flung them to her side and hurried back toward me. I felt her nails scrape the sides of my hips as she pulled my underwear off my body. The wind blew across us and I noticed her nipples reacted to the sensation. Marci turned her body around and moved her perfectly shaped backside toward me ever so slowly. After what seemed like an eternity, her womanhood finally rubbed against the head of my penis.

Marci moved her ass up my manhood, trapping it between the lower part of my stomach and her ass. She moved her lovely body up and down my shaft, and in one effortless movement, the head of my penis found its home. I was in heaven and my cock never felt so strong in my life. She bounced on me as hard as she could, making unbelievable cooing and moaning noises. I reached around to her front and played with her breasts. I managed to move my feet for stability and I rose up with her as one. She bent her body forward so she could take all of me. My forearm rested as support between her large breasts, while my other hand held the top part of her shoulder. She allowed me to take control. I pushed my lover against me as hard as I could.

Like a wild animal, I attacked her insides with fast and long strokes. I suddenly stopped as I pushed myself deep inside of her. I raised her up so her back was against my chest. I gently moved her toward the chair and without instruction, she grabbed the arms of the wrought iron chair. I began to pound her from behind and she was in total bliss. Her moans were now screams of ultimate pleasure. Her breasts slapped in unison against her body. I could smell her sexual essences that brought a pure delight to my being. The mixture of the musky odor of the forest, the damp smell of the earth around me, and my Marci's sexual scent was too much for me to handle. I had to pull out of her, and as I did, she quickly collapsed herself into the cold metal of the chair. As quickly as she could, she reached for my penis, squeezed it hard and pulled it toward her mouth. Her warm and wet mouth caressed my penis as I exploded inside of her sucking mouth. She took as much of me as she could and swallowed every pulsing drop of my semen.

I had never climaxed as hard and long as I did that morning. Marci didn't allow me to pull myself away from her mouth. She continued to suck as hard as she could as she moved her most perfect head up and down my shaft. I could hardly stand any longer so I placed my hands on the back side of the lawn chair as she continued her masterful work. She didn't want to stop but after several minutes she allowed herself some rest. I stepped backward as I saw the lust in her eyes. She was finished and satisfied. My love didn't look away once. She kept her eyes on mine the entire time as she stood up with her breasts as perky as I have ever seen them.

Marci started to move away from me, but she was still staring into my eyes. She gently turned away and as she blinked those beautiful eyes, the spell that she had cast upon me broke. I had to watch her walk away. She moved her hips from side to side as they kept perfect rhythm with her swaying shoulders and large breasts. What a sight it was as I carelessly stood, exposed to the world. As my Marci went inside the house, I gathered my clothes and got dressed.

I came inside, and Carolyn was sitting at the kitchen table, looking at me as her two hands held her coffee cup close to her mouth. Carolyn said to me, "Why didn't you stop him? Why did you let him get attacked? You wanted him to die, didn't you?"

I looked at Carolyn and said, "I had no choice. My father wanted to bite him. Lewis said some things that were not too kind to me and my parents."

Carolyn quickly stopped me and yelled, "They are not your parents, Garrison. Trevor and Adelle were your parents! They cared for you, they took care of you, they are the ones that were your parents, not some monsters." I knew she was upset and she was not going to let this go. I could sense that she hadn't slept all night. Carolyn continued, "You were afraid of him... that is it. Isn't it, Garrison? You were afraid that he was going to expose you for what you are!"

I stopped Carolyn and said, "And what would that be? What am I to you, Carolyn?"

I heard Marci walking toward us. She didn't have a pleasant look on her face. She stepped into the room with an untied bathrobe hanging on her body. Her breasts swayed inside the loose-fitting robe as she quickly walked toward Carolyn. Marci got within a foot of her face and said, "Listen here, you old bitch. No one forced Lewis to go, he said something he shouldn't have and he had to pay for his actions. A little something that you should understand before you open your ugly mouth."

The power and the hate just flowed out of Marci's mouth. Carolyn wasn't surprised with Marci's anger, but it aggravated her to a point that her body began to shake. I had to step in and break up this potential altercation. I placed my hands on Marci's hips and gently pulled her toward me and away from Carolyn. Carolyn's eyes were affixed on Marci as neither woman backed down.

Marci said, "So, you loved the little doctor did you, but you weren't woman enough to tell him, were you? You didn't even get the chance to prove your feelings towards him, did you? What a shame. Now no one wants you because you are a lonely, fat, miserable bitch."

Carolyn got up from her seat and threw her cup of coffee at Marci. I quickly swung my right hand around and blocked the cup from hitting her. The hot coffee spilled on my arm and hand. The rest of the coffee splattered on Marci, causing some small burns, but nothing to cause damage to her skin.

Marci stood there with a shocked look then started moving toward Carolyn with a hatred that I had never seen from her. She tried to push me out of the way. With all my might, I held her back, pushing her into the adjoining room. Marci was screaming at the top of her lungs. I had to separate the two from one another. Marci was screaming, "You bitch! You fucking little, old, lonely bitch! You want me to be like you, don't you? You want me to leave Garrison. Why? So you could be the one fucking him in the morning? Get out! Get out of my house!"

Carolyn stormed toward us, screaming at the top of her lungs, "Your house? Your house? Look, you tramp, this is Garrison's house, not yours. You're nothing and will always be nothing, you fucking tramp."

I attempted to stop this fight from escalating further, but I couldn't keep the two separated. Carolyn went after Marci. I had to let go of my love so she could protect herself. As I let Marci go, my hands stopped Carolyn at her shoulders. I positioned myself between her and Marci. Before I knew it, Marci grabbed Carolyn's hair and pulled her down toward the ground. I had to let Carolyn go out of fear of her hair being ripped out of her head.

Marci had Carolyn down and climbed on top of her. Her breasts were swaying with every punch to Carolyn's face. I reached around and picked Marci up by the waist. As I did, Marci had a full fist hold of Carolyn's hair. I screamed, "Marci… let go of her hair. Marci… calm down… let go of her hair."

Marci threw her head back, still screaming. She finally let go of Carolyn's hair. She was fighting for me to release her. I carried my Marci to the other room and before I knew it, Marci turned to me and licked the side of my cheek with her long, silky tongue. She said in a breathy voice with as much passion and hatred as she had ever demonstrated in my presence, "Let's experiment on the bitch. Come on, Garrison, let's turned her into one of them. I want her to suffer. Please, Garrison…" Her body was tense, and her breasts heaved up and down in a sexual dance that was incredible to see.

I strongly said, "Marci, that is enough! Calm down! Get control of yourself." I let her go as she quickly stepped away from me. Those deep blue eyes glared at me then a smile developed on her face as she let out a witch-like cackle. She kept laughing as she could hardly hold herself upright. When she got control of herself, she put her finger to the corner of her mouth and said in a hushed but panting voice, "Come on… let's change her." After a few laughs and giggles, she finally went upstairs to her room.

Carolyn was still on the floor, crying as her nose bled profusely. I went over to her and asked if she was okay. She nodded as she attempted to get on her feet with my assistance. Carolyn said through her sobs, "She is crazy, Garrison. That woman is crazy."

I held Carolyn tight to console her and took her over to the couch. Carolyn sat down and I went to get her some brandy to help calm her nerves. After several minutes she finally got control of herself. I said, "Carolyn, you know that I love you and we have gone through so much together. You helped me when I went off to college, you have assisted me in every way through our lives together. Now I know my Marci can be a handful at times, but you guys must learn to get along. Please promise me that you will try your best to get along with her."

Carolyn said, "Garrison, you know that I warned her about you. I warned her because I knew that something like this might happen. I didn't want you or her to get hurt. I thought that if you guys would have separated and gone on your separate ways, there would be more peace in this household. But I see that you two love each other very much. For this I am happy for you, but I am also jealous over the love that you have for one another. I never experienced that with any man. I will try and get along with your love."

I left Carolyn and went upstairs to find Marci. She was inside her room as I could hear her pacing back and forth. As I approached the bedroom door, I knocked gently, and as soon as I got to the third knock on the door, it opened with a fury. Marci looked stressed and angry. I went inside and closed the door behind me and said, "Marci, I spoke with Carolyn about what happen. I asked her to try to get along with you. I need to ask you the same. Can you get along with her?"

Marci looked at me with hate in her eyes and said, "No! I cannot get along with that bitch. How can you ask me that, Garrison? She tried to push me away from you months ago. When you were gone on your trip to Germany, she tried to push me out and wanted me to leave. She almost demanded that I leave. She said you were a monster and that she was afraid for herself and me. She said that you would eventually turn on us. I don't believe that for a second, but that is what she told me."

I stood there listening to her every word. I said, "I understand, but what she is dealing with and has dealt with over the years is a very difficult subject matter, to say the least. I am very lucky to have you in my life and I am equally as fortunate that I do not frighten you. For that matter, I am surprised that my way of life and what you have experienced has not driven you off."

Marci turned away from me as she walked toward the window. She looked down as her shoulders slumped. She said softly, "You know, Garrison, all of my life I have never been wanted. My parents didn't want me. No one wanted to adopt me. I thought it was because I wasn't good enough for people, that I wasn't smart enough or talented enough to be accepted."

"After so many years, I just gave up on having a family that would accept me. I see so much of myself in your life. We kind of share the same family tragedies in a twisted sort of way. When I finally met you, I felt this incredible bond between us. I can't explain it, but you know what I mean, don't you?"

I quickly said, "Yes, I do, Marci. It is like we were made for each other. I share the same thoughts as you." Marci smiled and looked up through the window. Her voice changed to a deeper tone and she said, "So, that is why no one can ever come between us."

I said to her, "No one ever has or will."

Marci quickly turned and looked at me and said, "Then fix what has come between us."

I stared at her a while and said, "Carolyn will not be a problem any longer. I spoke with her and she will do what I asked of her. She has always been there for me and she has never disappointed me in the past. She will not disappoint in the future. She does not have long to live. I trust her, but I need her close to me, just in case. I cannot have her telling others what has happened in his house. That would not be a good thing for us."

Marci's eyes never left mine, "I know, that wouldn't be good, would it? It would ruin everything that we have together. It would ruin all of what you have done with your experiments. I just don't understand how you can risk so much for such a person." Marci walked over to me as her eyes wouldn't leave mine. She said, "Garrison, I want to live forever. I want you to change me into what you are." I shook my head from side to side. "I want to be perfect, Garrison. I want you to infect me with that formula of yours. I don't care what I look like; I just want to live forever with you."

I walked toward her and said, "Marci, listen to me." I took both of my hands and placed them on her shoulders. I said, "I do not know if I would ever find a cure for stopping the physical transformation, but I will try to the best of my ability to find this cure. But I do not know if I can. As of this very moment, I cannot change you because I love you. I do not want you to be excluded from all human interaction. You know that if you change, people will not accept you. They will run from you. You will not be accepted. I do not want you to repeat the pain again that you experienced in your life before we met." I let Marci go, and I turned and walked out. I gently closed the door behind me. I sensed that she understood what I told her.

The tension between the two ladies in the house decreased over time. Weeks went by without any major incidents. Carolyn fixed our dinners and took care of the estate. Carolyn and I had many conversations about Lewis. We spoke about his death but mostly why I left him behind. She began to understand that I was in an impossible situation to take him with me. I had no choice in the matter. Carolyn began to understand that I truly loved Marci and that we were made for one another. I could sense that Carolyn was afraid of me, but I assured her that no harm would come to her as long as I lived.

Marci's contempt toward Carolyn grew, but she kept it to herself and was quite civil to Carolyn after the incident. Carolyn tended to stay clear of Marci and they never actually spoke more than just a few words to one another. This continued for months after their encounter.

I worked when I could on the formula, but I knew it was pointless. I told Marci this time after time, but she still held onto the belief that one day I would find the answer, but until then, I couldn't infect my love. I couldn't deface her or, worse yet, I couldn't live with myself if she wouldn't like her new looks. I saw what it did to my mother. I couldn't live with myself if I had to go through that experience again.

I conducted my business as normal. I allowed my people to run their different divisions throughout my many endeavors, but always kept a close eye on the decisions they made. My interests continued to thrive over the years since my parents died. I invested my money well and I had very talented people working for me.

Marci graduated from music school at the University of Louisville. She was an outstanding fiddler. We played almost every night together. She was obsessed with striking and fingering every note correctly, but without fail she would make mistakes. It would anger her to no end. I stopped correcting her or giving her advice because at this stage of her career, she was past the handholding. She wanted to play and be free from my advice. She knew in her mind that any instruction I gave would be a repeat from the past. It was up to her now.

Marci needed to play for hours on end for her to close the endless gap between her imperfection to the reality of my perfection. She didn't like the imperfection. She wanted to be perfect like me. When we played our violins together every night, I could sense the passion that burnt inside her soul. She relentlessly tried to play perfectly.

This obsession did not stop at the violin. It continued through her everyday life. I would catch her throwing rocks at trees, trying to perfect her aim. She would throw darts in our library for long stretches of time to improve her hand-eye coordination. She wanted desperately to be like me. At times, I wondered if she was in love with what I am instead of who I am. We spoke about these subject matters ad nauseam and I soon concluded that she truly loved me for me but envied my abilities.

Marci understood me. She loved my abilities and she wanted to share the qualities that I possessed with me on the highest of all levels. Marci was at her happiest when she and I were equal. That was the main reason our sex life was so great. She was perfect at making love and she had full control over her actions. We worked as one during our lovemaking. We experienced this same feeling during our violin sessions. A smile would come across her face when we worked in unison and for a short but sensual moment, her playing was flawless. During these moments, she was living her fantasy. She loved those instances that all humans experience throughout their lives. Those short moments where everything works perfectly, where life sways with the rhythm of your senses. It is when the swiftness of your commands summons perfection from the abyss of your soul, those short moments where everything comes together and complements each other to a point where it creates a perfect moment.

These moments might manifest themselves during unexpected times in someone's life – like a first kiss, a hole in one on a golf course, or that perfectly thrown football where the spiral is so tight the ball looks like a missile being launched from a tank. Those moments where you and only you have demonstrated the highest level of performance that anyone could master. Many people that have played sports call it 'being in the zone.' A place where, for a short respite of time, everything you do is performed at the closest level of perfection as one could demonstrate. We have all shared these unbelievable moments throughout our lives. Marci wanted to have as much control as possible over this feeling and be able to demonstrate this control over anything that she wanted to be perfect at in her life.

I don't blame my love for this obsession that she desires. I take for granted the power the formula has over its hosts. The formula is truly remarkable. Its most special power is its ability to capture and tap into the very essence of perfection; this is a most powerful gift. In the hands of the wrong individual, this could spell doom for the current state of the human race. The formula's power can be intoxicating and nearly orgasmic when you are able to understand and control its power. I stay awake for approximately twenty-one hours a day, which gives me a lot of time to reflect on the formula's offerings.

One of those offerings haunts me to this day. I have noticed through the years the area where my mother's blood bathed the earth when she killed herself. The grass is so green and very thick. This area has spread through the entire back lawn of the estate. The formula is now part of my land and it is spreading throughout my property. I often wonder what I have done by allowing this small area to grow throughout my backyard. It has even traveled to some of the wooded areas that are located on my property. The trees, the brush, and the small plants have all grown greener, larger and their appearance is more brilliant than the unaffected areas of my property. If I could only mass produce this formula, I would be the richest man on the face of the earth but, more importantly, I would have the ability to create a select portion of god's creation and perfect what he believed was perfected. I could improve nature. I could create perfection. I could improve my life by making my loved ones perfect like me, especially my Marci. This is what I long for in my life.

I wanted to marry my Marci and we had a few days marked down, but after many discussions, we decided not to get married. Our relationship was built on trust, love, and lust for each other. We decided that we didn't need some fucking fake lover of god confirming what we knew in our hearts. I couldn't stand the thought of someone telling me that in their power of some fake god, they would pronounce us as husband and wife. Marci quickly started to see my way of thinking since we have been together. Marci was a God-fearing person when we met but since then, I have corrected her thinking.

As our time together grew, so did our circle of friends. We would entertain quite often, and surprisingly Carolyn was a huge help during our parties. It was the only time Marci and Carolyn exchanged more than a few words to each other. I believe it was Carolyn's way to release since she rarely ventured out from the estate. Although my relationship with Carolyn has deteriorated through the years, she was the next motherly image I had in my life since Adelle and Loren's deaths. She had always been there for me from the start. That kind of history and relationship cannot be dismissed quickly.

Something that had always bothered me was the fact that I never caught on to Carolyn being smitten with Lewis. I even approached the issue with Carolyn and she was surprised that I never discovered her secret as well. Carolyn had a strong mind but her will was weak. She could be easily manipulated, but down deep she had strong ideas and convictions; she just never had the confidence to think for herself or to take any chances in life.

Marci attempted to gain employment with the Louisville Orchestra as a violin player, but again, her skills couldn't compete with the other applicants. This greatly upset her but through all the disappointments, she continued to remain friends with many in the Orchestra. I offered her my services, telling her that I could pull a few strings, but she did not want any special treatment. I admired her valor. Marci never asked anything from me outside of sexual favors. All throughout her life, Marci had many accomplishments with no help from anyone. Marci did help with some of my business dealings. She was great with people and had a knack for business. I taught her as much as I could or as much as she could comprehend.

These past years were great times for Marci and me. We went on many vacations together, from California to Florida and throughout Europe. During our travels, I couldn't help but think of my parents. I wondered how they were. I speculated on what Lewis looked like or even if he was alive. I missed my parents terribly.

Marci and I spoke openly about our feelings on all subject matters, especially our original birth parents. Marci's unique views seemed to weigh on my conscience. She would always wish she could have met the parents that abandoned her. I think she would kill them on site if she ever met her parents. Of course, in her case, I knew how she felt.

On one of our trips to Rome, Italy, is when Marci made up her mind that she wanted to visit my parents. It was the start of her fascination with the complete and most disturbing part of my life. I knew what my love was thinking. Marci knew I would never change her with the formula. I know in her mind that she was going to ask my father to change her. I tried to tell her that the transformation wasn't something that she would like. If she were to change, she could never venture out in public again. Her whole life would be turned upside down, but she didn't care. She wanted perfection and everlasting life at any cost.

Marci said to me, "Garrison, why don't we stop by and try to locate your parents? I would love to meet them."

I said to her, "Marci, you do not want to meet my parents. They are evil and I would be afraid they would harm you. I could not live with myself if any harm came to you."

When we returned home, Marci started up the conversation again, "They love you, Garrison. You told me that from the start. You weren't harmed. I can reason with your parents. Do you not understand that the longer we wait, the older I get? At some point, I will die and you will lose me forever."

I just shook my head at her. She just didn't understand. Of course, down deep in my soul I wanted to visit them. I wanted to see them but more importantly, she was right. My love was growing older and soon she would pass me in age. She knew that her comments would force me to think about us in our later life. She can be so brilliant for a human.

I was also curious as to what happened to Lewis. Was he still alive or was my father still torturing that wretched soul? I wish there was a way I could stay in contact with them, but they didn't want a cell phone or any device that would give them contact with the outside world.

Weeks went by and Marci wouldn't drop the subject of meeting my father. Every morning and night, she talked about Germany and wanting to visit. She can be a very persistent person when she sets her mind on something. I knew this issue would never come to an end without making a trip. I agonized over the decision for days, but I finally sat her down and told her we were going. Marci jumped up from the table, gave me a bear hug, and wouldn't let go. I told her that Wolfgang wasn't going to change her. For a moment, Marci acted confused. I spent a better part of the week explaining to her how painful the transformation would be and how disfigured she would look. After days of conversation, I still felt that Marci didn't care how much suffering she would have to endure. All my love wanted was to be perfect and to live forever with me by her side. I was so torn inside because I knew that Marci was going to end up getting her way. She was going to see my parents no matter what. She was a very persistent woman.

The following days, I contacted Sonja in Germany. She was very glad to hear from me. I told her that I was coming to her country with my fiancé. She was ecstatic that I was coming to visit. She made the necessary plans to set us up in a cottage in the village as she had for Lewis and me years ago.

We told Carolyn of our plans and for some strange reason, she was glad to see us go. I believe she needed to be alone for a while. Carolyn took us to the airplane the following morning and we boarded our flight. Our flight was long but enjoyable. I am so honored that someone so beautiful and perfect would take her time to be with me. Marci loved me with all her heart, and I her.

When the plane landed in Berlin, the harsh truth of reality was starting to set in for both of us. We knew that there was no turning back. The moment we stepped foot off that plane, we knew we had already embarked on a new and special chapter of our lives, a chapter that I hoped above all hopes wouldn't end in tragedy. As we made our way out of customs, I looked across the area of the airport and saw Sonja who was there to greet us. It was an emotional meeting. Sonja hugged me tightly for an uncomfortable period. This was the first time she met my love, and Sonja instantly liked Marci and they talked for a while, exchanging pleasantries.

Sonja went with us to pick up our luggage then retrieved her car. She pulled up to the entrance of the airport, and I placed our luggage in her small trunk. Sonja asked Marci to sit up next to her in the front while I sat in the back of the car. As Sonja drove, I cast my eyes from the back of my Marci's head to the beautiful country scenes that passed before me. Every so often, I would treat my eyes to my love's stunning profile. The beautiful eyes of my love always had a way of melting my heart and soothing my nerves. After several hours of travel through winding back roads, we finally arrived at the foothills of the village. It was the same as I remembered it about three years prior. Nothing seemed to have changed. The town was quiet, with the same mill looming as the backdrop of the village. This picture-perfect scene was surrounded by tall, massive, thick trees that lined the entire village.

We reached our cottage and as we got out of the car and looked around, there was no one outside. I unloaded the luggage from the car and thanked Sonja for driving us. I told her that we would visit her later during our trip, but I told her that I wanted to show Marci my birthplace. Sonja understood and she drove off, leaving us in this strange but peaceful village.

It was getting dark outside and we were hungry. Marci and I stopped by one of the few local restaurants. As we went inside, everyone suddenly stopped talking, not a word was spoken. I looked around the room and all eyes were on us. The locals looked like they were frozen in time. I spoke in perfect German and told them we were just visiting. Suddenly, the room began to awaken. The locals started back to their usual level of normalcy.

Marci and I sat down, and from the distance, the bartender came over to our table. He was a nervous, thin man with long, oily hair. His name was Herman. Herman spoke in broken English to us and said, "Excuse me, sir. You would not happen to be the boy from the woods?"

I said, "Why... yes I am. How did you know it was me?"

Herman sat down without asking for permission. He rubbed his hand across his mouth and spoke, "I remember you a few years back. You came here with an older man. You are the legend of the forest. You are the boy they found lying in the forest when you were a baby. You were and still are quite the legend. Everyone in this town has followed your career. We all knew you would be a special person someday. You are very intelligent and talented."

I bowed my head in thanks. Marci sat there without saying a word, as she was star struck for a second. She didn't know what to think. The bartender leaned toward me and said in a low voice, "I have to tell you something. The activity from the forest has increased ever sense you paid your visit. We think you made him angry."

I said, "Who did I make angry?"

The man said, "The demon in the forest." His eyes fell sad as he began to tell me a story, "One night my father and I were cleaning up. It was a few days after you and that old guy you were with left. We heard some footsteps outside. My father picked up his shotgun and went to look outside. He saw some footprints along the side of the building." Herman stopped and took a deep breath, glancing over to the window in the back of the bar. He pointed and continued, "I was standing there looking out that window. It was hard to see because it was so late and dark. Then I saw this figure. It was like a bear standing on two legs, very large, wide, and tall. I was so scared. I tried to yell but I was afraid. I had just two thoughts – my father was out there, and I didn't want to spook this thing either. I walked slowly to the window and then it bent down and looked directly at me. It growled. I backed up into a table and made a lot of noise. The demon left in a hurry. I heard my father outside yelling then I heard something hit the side of the building. My father yelled a few times but all I heard were footsteps running. I went outside. In the distance, I saw the demon with my father across its shoulders, running away. It looked like he was running with a sack of potatoes. No effort in carrying my large father.

I ran after them as fast as I could and when I got into the forest, I heard nothing but the trees and insects making their sounds. I went back to the village and told as many people as I could, waking them up, yelling, screaming. We formed a search party but when we got inside the forest, the party only went so deep. We all knew my father was dead. At first, I was angry at everyone for giving up on my father, but I knew down deep that he was dead."

Herman covered his face and said, "All my life we have had issues with the forest. Usually the forest demon leaves us be. From time to time, farmers will see large footprints in the soil of their gardens and vegetables taken or half-eaten. Same with farm animal's; bones would be littered throughout the town. A half-eaten limb or half of an animal carcass would be found in town. But never had one of our own been taken."

He stopped and looked at me squarely and said, "We don't get many visitors here and most of us like it here because, well, it's healthy here most of the time. Whatever you do, don't disturb the demon."

With that, he got up and left us alone. Marci sat there in shock with pursed lips, looking at me and then down at the table multiple times. I sensed true fear in my love. Finally, she had come to grips with the severity of this situation. However, I knew she didn't want to back out now. She still wanted to meet my father. She wanted him to bite her so she would be infected with the formula. She longed to be perfect and she wanted to live forever. Those two thoughts dominated my love. I couldn't erase those goals from her mind. No matter what I did, her mind was made up. Part of me wanted her to live forever. I hated myself for thinking those thoughts, but I couldn't bear the thought of her dying. I couldn't live forever on this planet with that horrid thought pulsing throughout my soul.

Marci and I ate our dinner and went back to our cottage. She was tired and fell fast asleep. I, of course, stayed awake for most of the night. I wanted to get up early in the morning for our trip inside the forest.

As Marci slept, I went outside of our cottage. I looked around the small town. Everything around me was pitch black. Of course, I could see in the dark but on this night, it was difficult for me to clearly make out certain items from long distances. I walked the dark streets in the attempt to clear my head. I thought back on the evening's events and the locals that we had met. I couldn't help but notice something strange about many of them. It was the same eerie observation that Lewis had when he first visited this village. I had the same feelings when I visited my first time. All the locals were aged and many of them where very old but didn't act their age. Strange stories that Marci and I heard on our visit were the same stories that I heard the last time I was there. I read every word of Lewis's documentation on his first visit to this village. Again, the same stories kept surfacing. Stories of large creatures, evidence of large footsteps in the fields, confirmed sightings by many of the locals of a tall, wolf-like creature. Multitude of stories of livestock taken, blood trails, and animal parts and bones left throughout the town from time to time.

When morning finally arrived, we ate a light breakfast. Afterward, we packed up our gear and were out the door before daybreak. Marci was nervous but excited. She could hardly sit still. She was bouncing off the walls before we set out on our trip. I told her to calm down and to save her strength, but, like in the past, she rarely listened to me.

We walked to the entrance of the forest. So many memories came flooding back at me as we walked along the floor of the forest. The trees were so tall and thick, just like the portion of trees on my estate. The tops of the trees were so thick and heavy that hardly any sun or moon light would make its way through. In places, the forest brush was so thick it would be impossible to pass through them. As I looked around, I discovered a pathway that I remembered taking with Lewis the last time I was there. After several hours of walking, Marci told me she was exhausted. We stopped and she rested on a large rock. I looked around to see our surroundings. Everything was green, lush and sprinkled with a few flowery plants. After several moments, we continued our walk.

Suddenly, I saw a hill, and I knew just over the hill was a stream of water with a small patch of bare ground. This was the place where my mother left me to be found or to die, depending on my luck. When we reached the top of the hill, I saw the spot. Above this area was an opening in the forest. Sunlight was shining down on that spot. It looked like something out of a painted picture. Marci was almost brought to tears it was so beautiful. The musky, thick scent of the forest seemed to ease somewhat as we made our way to the spot.

When we reached this area, we rested. I knelt on the bare, hard ground of the forest and rested my hand on the cold dirt. The stream of water next to us was running stronger than I remembered the last time I paid homage to this spot. I explained to Marci that this stream of water went directly to the village, and in my father's findings, the moss plants that grew around this area excrete the substance that is the basic building block of the formula. It mixes with the water, and as the water flows down to the village, it gets into the springs, which are the source of the villager's water supply. This is the reason the villagers don't age at a normal rate and why they don't have disease or physical ailments.

Why no one had come upon this discovery and captured this special water for profit is beyond my understanding. I could sense Marci's mind was working overtime, thinking how she could profit off this natural phenomenon.

Marci wanted to drink out of the stream, but I told her not to. The water was untested. The issue that was the most concerning was how much you had to drink to live longer than the average human. Do you drink one glass or does one need to live on the water for years to make the body live longer and free from ailments? Thus, I wanted to err on the side of caution and I insisted Marci not drink the water. I told her at the time that I didn't want her to poison herself on the unfiltered water.

After our rest, we packed up and continued our long journey. We walked as far as we could. Marci was in great shape but the continuous walking through the thick brush and the heavy air proved too much for her at times. We came across an area that looked like a good spot to set up camp for the night. We had some dinner and Marci turned in for the night. Meanwhile, I kept an eye out for my father. I sensed that he knew we were in his forest by now. Much to my surprise, my father never showed himself. When morning came, I woke up my love and we continued our journey.

We walked for several hours then suddenly I heard a noise. I stopped and told Marci to be quiet and not to move. I walked and stood on top of a small hill then motioned for Marci to come toward me. I had her stop a small distance from me. I placed my gear on the ground, brought my hands up to my mouth and shouted, "Father, this is your son... Garrison. I am here to pay you a visit with my fiancé." I waited for several moments and I shouted again, "Wolfgang! Father! This is your son, I came here for a visit." I waited and no response. I could sense he was near. I started to become very nervous. I sensed that he wouldn't hurt me but in the back of my mind, I was concerned. What concerned me more was the safety of my Marci.

We continued our walk. I told Marci not to speak to my father when she saw him. I told her that he wouldn't approve of her being in this forest. As we walked, I kept shouting for my father and telling him that I had the love of my life with me. I hoped that he wouldn't attack her first and ask me questions later. Suddenly, I heard the footsteps. My heart started to race faster. It was my father's footsteps. Although I have only met him once, I felt closer to him than I did my own adoptive mother, the only person that I truly loved before my Marci.

I didn't care if he felt the same. I have no control over what others think, feel, or reason. I can only control what I experience emotionally. I have been rejected and felt unwanted all my life, with the exception of Marci's feelings toward me. Everyone in my life had treated me poorly. Those couple of days that I spent with my father, Wolfgang, earned a special place in my small inner circle of friendships. I knew that he was part of my family and this was my heritage.

My heart pounded harder as each step got him closer. Marci didn't hear the footsteps pounding on my father's forest floor at first, but suddenly she stopped walking and asked me, "Garrison, what is that noise?" I laughed softly and said, "Be still, my love, it is my father coming for us." I could sense that Marci was frightened like no other time in her life. I could smell the fear that her beautiful body was excreting as my emotions wavered between fear and excitement for the waiting of his arrival.

We stopped, and I heard branches being broken, leaves being moved aside, and the footsteps becoming louder than before. My eyes cased the entire forest in front of me then suddenly I saw some branches move. I pointed my right finger toward that direction. I heard my love's head and body move in response to my gesture. I said, "There is my father, please be still and try not to be afraid."

Then my glorious father emerged from the brush. There was just enough light fighting its way through the covered umbrella of leaves from above our heads. Beams of light came down in various parts of the forest between us and where my father stood. He took two steps out from the brush and there he stood, all eight foot of his massive structure that his formula had created over a century ago, standing just twenty or thirty feet from us. I spoke, "Father. Hello. I hope you do not mind, but I needed to see you. Please, I beg of you not to harm this woman. This is Marci, the love of my life. She knows everything. I told her so much about you. She is here to assist me. Please, do not harm her."

Wolfgang looked at me angrily and said, "I told you I did not want any outsiders visiting me."

A sweat formed all over my body. I said, "I know, Father, please, this is my fault, but I had no choice."

My father interrupted me and said loudly, "We all have choices; you choose poorly." With that said, he began to walk toward us. The earth shook around us after every step he took. After what seemed like an eternity, he was there before us, a towering mass of muscle breathing heavily with anger. Oh, the passion and the hate that I sensed was something that I will never forget. He looked down into my eyes. I stood there, commanding all my senses the power to convince him not to attack us. He could sense my fear. He sensed from my emotions that I wasn't concerned for my safety as much as I was concerned for my Marci's.

Wolfgang broke eye contact with me as he whipped his head toward Marci. Their eyes met. Wolfgang stepped toward her. She took one step back. Wolfgang took a deep breath as he looked at her. Saliva started to form around the corners of his wolf-like muzzle. He quickly looked back at me with a smirk on his face. He slowly moved his head and looked at my love while showing his teeth and letting a low growl escape from the pit of his stomach.

Wolfgang and I could smell the strong fear in her scent, but it was a different scent of fear. I knew my father was a little surprised at what he was experiencing. This was my only hope for my love. He had to find her interesting or he would kill her on the spot. Marci looked into Wolfgang's eyes, and after a long, hard swallow, she managed to develop a small, nervous smile. This facial movement perplexed Wolfgang. I could sense his confusion. I also saw it on his face.

Unexpectedly and without any notice, Marci reached up and attempted to touch his face as she continued to smile at him. Wolfgang was totally caught off guard. He immediately and without any hesitation took his right hand and grabbed her wrist. Marci moaned from not only being scared by the quick action but from the strength of Wolfgang's grip. I quickly said, "Please, Father, please do not hurt her."

Wolfgang quickly looked at me and said, "So you love this bitch?"

I told him, "Yes, Father, I love her and please, she is not a bitch."

Wolfgang didn't like my tone, but he knew that he might have overstepped a father and son boundary when it came to a son's love of a women. He looked at Marci. She quickly spoke, "I... I...am sorry to have bothered you here but I don't mean to cause you any problems. I am in love with your son." After her plea, she again smiled at my father with that look that melts my heart. I was never so proud of my Marci than at that moment. She confronted my father and controlled her fear of him and the situation. She continued to speak but now in a more convincing and confident voice, "Wolfgang, sir, I came here with Garrison because I want to be perfect. I want to be like him. I will do anything to live with him forever. Anything!"

Wolfgang snorted and growled again while he looked at Marci. Marci pleaded with my father, something that I feared and even told her not to bring up in front of my father. She said, "I want what you are!"

Wolfgang roughly pulled her closer to him with one quick pull. Marci let out a quick, loud but short scream. She looked down at first but after she recovered from the jerking motion from my father, she again looked him in the eyes. His yellow eyes were dancing around inside of his head, in anger but also in admiration. Admiration for the fact that she hadn't once pulled away from him.

Before my father knew it, Marci placed her free hand on his hairy chest. She uttered the words, "Please... infect me with the formula. I want to live forever. I want to be perfect like you and your son." Her eyes never left my father's eyes; they were focused on the task at hand.

Wolfgang opened his mouth as wide as he could as large amounts of saliva fell out of his mouth. He let out a loud and unholy growl and moved my love's hair back as if she was in a stiff breeze. Marci closed her eyes and at that moment, I thought she was dead. Then without any notice, in the middle of what seemed like an eternity, as he continued his long growl, he pushed her to the ground. It was like a man throwing a small doll in disgust.

I raced over to come to the aid of my love, when abruptly my father's strong hand and arm stopped my movement. His large hand covered the length of my chest. He released me and pushed my chest with his index finger. I stumbled back a few feet as he said, "You chose a smart and brave woman, my son."

Wolfgang looked down at her as she was looking directly in his eyes, but this time with anger. Wolfgang was surprised. Marci got up quickly and walked toward him and said, "Don't ever do that again, do you understand?" A part of me died right there because no one talked that way to my father and lives, not even before he turned himself into what he was today. Marci continued, "That hurt. Either kill me or infect me, just make a decision."

Wolfgang was stunned. He hadn't sensed this reaction from her. This was something new to him. Only my mother could speak to him this way. He stood there, and without any notice he began to laugh. I wanted to run toward my love to somehow protect her, but it would have been a fugal attempt. My father continued to laugh and abruptly said, "Woman, you have a lot of guts coming into my forest and giving me ultimatums." Then he yelled in this lusty, thick voice, "No one tells me what to do." They both stood there staring at each other, and after an intense moment, Wolfgang smiled and shouted, "You live because my son loves you and that is the only reason why you have your life right now."

Wolfgang could sense my relief. He looked over at me and said, "What kind of father do you think I am? I understand these things called love, infatuation. Her interest in you and her longing for perfection is unlike anything I have witnessed in over a hundred years. You, my son, are a very lucky man." I nodded in agreement. Wolfgang said, "Come... the both of you. I will lead you to my house."

Marci's confidence wasn't as strong as it was moments ago. I think the reality hit her strongly. She knew yelling at my father caused her to almost lose her life, but her emotions outpaced her reasoning for a moment. I went over to her and she was trembling with fear. I tried to calm her down, but she was shaking violently. Wolfgang turned around and smiled at us and said, "Come... I have something to show you, the both of you." With those few spoken words, I could sense Marci's nerves settling. When Wolfgang acknowledged us as a couple, those few words were music to my lover's ears.

We walked toward the entrance of the cave. Marci continued to look at my father as he led us to the cave. She was mesmerized by his size, the way he walked, and the way he carried himself. In a sadistic way, she wanted to be him. When we reached the entrance to the cave, Wolfgang announced our presence to my mother. My mother came running out to greet me but stopped in the middle of her stride and looked at my Marci. I said, "Mother, this is Marci, my fiancé. Please do not harm her, I love her very much." My mother smiled as she looked at me then walked toward me and gave me a hug. Her massive arms engulfed me as my face was pressed against her large breasts. I looked up at this seven plus foot being with the love that only a little boy can have toward his mother.

I noticed she wasn't pleased with Marci's presence. During my mother's rare display of affection, she showed her teeth and growled at Marci. Obviously, Marci was uneasy with Zelda's attitude toward her. In the attempt to ease the situation, Marci said, "So you are Garrison's mother. It is a pleasure to meet you. I met your husband before, and he was gracious enough to bring me to your home." My mother quickly jerked her head with great force to look at Wolfgang.

Wolfgang smiled and said, "I let her live. She loves our son. Can't you sense it? Our son has sexual needs, this is his toy. Let them be."

I knew that wasn't what Marci wanted to hear. My mother then loosened her grip on me and as her eyes slowly lifted from Marci, Zelda then looked lovingly into my eyes. She looked at me from head to toe as she moved me like a small doll from side to side. She said, "My son, it is great to see you. I did not know if I would ever get to see you again."

When Zelda released her grip on my body, I stumbled back several feet. As I regained my balance, I walked over to my love and placed my arm around her. Marci was upset at what my father said about her. I told her, "You are not my sexual toy. You are my soulmate."

I looked at my father and said, "I need to find the answers, Father. I don't want her to go through the transformation. I must find that secret to the formula. I am asking for your help."

Wolfgang smiled and said in his broken English, "I have many surprises for you, my son."

We entered the house and before I could gather my senses, I heard the cry of a baby coming from within the cave. I noticed a small wooden bassinet in the middle of the old wooden room my parents had called home for over a century. The bassinet was made of wooden logs placed together and tied with rope. All four sides of the crib jutted out in uneven lengths.

My heart skipped a few beats. The crying inside the crib was unnerving. The cries sounded normal, but considering who my father was, I was preparing myself for anything. Marci broke the uncomfortable moment and said, "Oh, you have a baby." Before I knew it, Marci walked quickly around me and went to the side of the crib. She looked down and from her expression, she was not disgusted by what she saw.

Suddenly, Wolfgang raced over and grabbed Marci by the throat and pushed her back several feet from where she was standing. I yelled, "Father, no!"

Wolfgang looked at Marci as his huge, thick hand remained around her throat. He uttered these words, "Don't touch my daughter."

Marci was gasping for air as both of her hands were around his hand, struggling for air. Zelda walked over and placed her hand on Wolfgang's shoulder and said, "Let her go, Wolfgang."

Wolfgang didn't want to let go. I sensed that he viewed Marci as a threat. He didn't trust her, and I understood his feelings more than anyone, but I knew he sensed that Marci was different from the other humans he had known in his past. It was not only her beauty but what was in her soul. I love my Marci with all my heart, but she is not flawless. Hidden deep in her soul, I sensed from the first time we met that she thought different from other humans. Her personality was charming and she was a pleasant woman, but there was another side to my love. I sensed that she could be sadistic. She cannot change that about herself. It is inherently innate. Probably her being an orphan helped develop this unconscious dark side of her undiscovered personality. She had an inner hate that was boiling. If I sensed this, I knew my father had to as well.

Wolfgang took a long look at Marci, and I knew at that moment he was going to let her go. He was protecting his offspring, and I sensed there was a meaningful story about this baby that my father allowed it to live. My father let my love go as he pushed her down on the hard, dirty wooden floor. Wolfgang turned and approached the baby in the crib. He leaned down and gently picked her up. He held her under her arms and brought her to his eye level. As he stood there holding this little creature, he looked down at me and said, "Garrison, this is your sister. Her name is Eva. I named her after my Fuhrer's mistress."

It was hard for me to speak. I was in total shock. I muttered the words, "So, I have a sister." The joy was great in my heart and Wolfgang could sense it. He closed his large, yellowish eyes, looked slightly upward, and took a deep breath. He smiled. I never saw my father smile before, which further warmed my heart. As he was exhaling, he lowered his large head and eyes toward me with that most wonderful smile. He then did something that cemented our relationship forever, a gesture that was so sweet and kind that it moved me to tears. He leaned down and offered my sister to me. Tears were running down my cheeks. *A family*, I thought to myself. *I finally have a family to call my own. No adoptive mother or father or paid nannies or overpaid house doctors.* No, at this moment, all those memories left my consciousness.

All I could focus on was my sister and our parents in the same room together. I gently took my sister from Wolfgang. He continued to smile. Not a word was exchanged between us. Our senses were on fire. He knew what I was thinking and I sure as hell knew what he was thinking. I stood there holding this perfect being, my sister, Eva.

As I looked at this beautiful little baby girl, I knew she was perfect. Perfect like me. Her skin was flawless. Her long, thick, blonde hair matched perfectly with the most piercing blue eyes. She was larger than any baby I had seen at that age. Her skin was soft and the perfect color of white I had ever seen in my life.

When I collected my thoughts, I started thinking about how all of this happened. The reality of the moment had blindsided me. My parents mated and had another child. This time it was a girl. I knew Wolfgang had plans for this child unlike any plans that he had for me. During my birth, he wanted to kill me like he did my three brothers. But at that time, Wolfgang did not want any children. I quickly thought that after seeing me, he must have changed his thinking. Maybe I thought too highly of myself, but it momentarily brought comfort to my heart thinking those thoughts.

As I held Eva in my arms, I glanced over at Marci. She was still on the floor, breathing heavily. Wolfgang's smile disappeared and he walked over to my love. He extended his long arm and hand toward her. She looked at him in fear as she reluctantly accepted his hand. Wolfgang pulled her up but his eyes never left hers. I didn't want to upset my father so I didn't call for Marci to come over to see Eva. I did manage to say, "She is beautiful. So, how old is she?"

Wolfgang said, "A month or so old, I don't count the weeks."

Eva stopped crying as she fell asleep in my arms. Wolfgang walked over to his large wooden chair and sat down, making a rather loud noise in doing so. I placed Eva in her crib and covered her up with some old blankets. I made my way over to my father. I sat down and Marci followed my lead.

I asked Wolfgang, "So, Father, what is the story here?"

Wolfgang smiled and said, "After you left, your mother and I thought we may never see you again. So, I decided to have a child. We mated and Zelda produced four children like before. Three were male and one was female. We decided to keep just the girl." Wolfgang stopped and I sensed he was not going to deliver more information.

Suddenly Marci said, "So, where are the other babies?"

Wolfgang's body sat motionless. Only moving his eyes, he said, "You are very persistent bitch, aren't you?"

Marci smiled and chuckled a little and said, "It's one of my best qualities."

At that moment, I sensed that Marci had controlled her fear of Wolfgang. I know Wolfgang sensed this as well, which seemed to impress him. Wolfgang continued, "Woman, I took the three boys, one by the legs and two by their arms. I opened the door and slung them outside the cave. I walked over to each one and stepped on their heads until they popped open to make sure they were dead. I came back inside to my wife and daughter and tended to their needs. I don't like most people, especially young humans, but I wanted a daughter. I have plans for my daughter."

Marci hung on every word, and even though she was disgusted by his comments, she didn't show any remorse or anger toward him. Wolfgang studied my love after his tale of terror. He was impressed by her control and acceptance. He said, "Does this disgust you, woman?"

Marci quickly said, "I don't like your decision, but it's your life, your children, you know what's best."

Wolfgang knew she was lying but was impressed by the answer. He leaned forward in his wooden chair and said, "I do not know you, and never give me reason to dislike you, but I feel that you are good for my son."

Marci said, "I would like to hope so."

Zelda broke up Marci and Wolfgang's conversation by offering us water. I told my father, "Eva is just beautiful. I assume that she has the same chemical makeup as me?"

Wolfgang said, "I am glad you brought that issue up. I believe so. From all accounts, the chemical makeup should be the same, of course, because of the formula, the chemicals will be in a constant state of change. That is the main reason the formula cannot be manipulated. The formula is constantly evolving, learning, if you will. No matter what is introduced to the system, the formula mutates and forces the new foreign substance to change. That is why you are disease-free. That is why your body will never age. The formula attacks what is genetically incorrect and forces the genetic inferior cells to become superior." Wolfgang smiled at me as he pointed his long finger and made a motion toward me to follow him. He said, "I have a surprise for you."

I followed my father deeper in the cave. Marci said, "Can I come with you guys?"

Wolfgang said in a rough voice, "Do what you wish, but I doubt you could handle what you are about to see."

Marci hurried to catch up with us as she looked back at Zelda and asked, "Are you coming with us?"

Zelda looked perplexed. She nodded her large head with a mass of light brown curls dangling from the sides of her large head. She angrily said, "No!"

We didn't have far to walk. There was little need for light, since my father could also see in the dark as well as he could during the day. Marci had to hold onto my shoulder for support. The air was thick and humid. I smelt an odor that was all too familiar. At that very moment, I knew what my father wanted to show me. It was one of his new experiments, but this time it was an old friend.

We walked down a narrow tunnel, deep into the cave. As we walked, the tunnel widened. Suddenly, I saw the surprise my father had for me. It was Lewis chained up against the cold, damp wall of the cave. Wolfgang lit a lantern so we could get a better look at the surprise. Marci gasped loudly when the light hit upon Lewis's image. Of course, Marci was scared. She was not expecting to see Lewis in this condition. She embraced my arm and I held her tightly.

Lewis had transformed as expected, but never did I sense that Wolfgang would keep him alive after all these years. It had been about three years since Wolfgang bit him on the arm, breaking it in two.

Lewis slowly looked up. His eyes widened with what seemed to be the most pleasant sight he had seen in years. His voice was different, but his personality was the same. You could just tell. The formula doesn't take everything from you, it just makes you better, purer. It highlights all your senses, and any unique ability that you had previously gets further developed beyond belief.

Lewis said, "Garrison, it is good to see you. Marci, how are you?" The voice was more of a quivering and raspy style. I sensed he had suffered greatly. I knew my father wouldn't stop torturing him. I couldn't get the thought out of my mind, wondering why my father had not killed him by now. Lewis continued now in a more pleading voice, "Garrison! Kill me, please kill me. Put me out of my misery..." He started to cry and then without notice, I heard a whipping sound which smacked Lewis on his right chest. A chuck of flesh was removed from his body.

I quickly looked over and saw Wolfgang holding a bullwhip in his hand. I looked down at the end of the whip and saw the end of the whip was attached to a small box made of wire with hooks coming out of each of the corners. I said to my father, "Did you make that device?"

Wolfgang laughed so hard his loud laughter bounced off the walls of the dark cave and radiated as an echo down the tunnel we came down, plus the other tunnel that leads to the waterfall on the other side of the cave. I noticed a good amount of Lewis's flesh was trapped on one of the corner hooks of the contraption. Wolfgang spoke to Lewis, "Shut up, you bastard." Wolfgang walked toward me and said, "This man does not appreciate the formula and the wonders that it brings to man."

Marci released her grip from my arm and gingerly walked toward Lewis but kept her distance. She said, "So, this is what it looks like after the change." Marci stood there and admired the transformed body. Lewis's body had transformed like all the others. Increased height and weight with arms, fingers, legs, toes, tongue, and neck all getting longer while the head grew to an immense size. Marci looked at Lewis as if he was a beautiful new car in a showroom or a famous painting in a museum. She stared at Lewis's exceptionally long muzzle down to his large feet. Not an inch of his body was missed by her beautiful blue eyes. Marci broke the uncomfortable silence and asked Wolfgang, "So is he perfect? He will never die?"

Wolfgang smiled at my love for the first time and said, "He is. He will never die. He will never have disease. He is better now than he was ever before."

Marci looked away from my father and back at Lewis. Then she spoke the words that I never wanted to hear, not at this moment in time, not in this cave. She said in a breathless voice, "I want this."

Lewis, without warning, lunged toward her, but before I knew it, another whipping sound filled the air. This time the metal hooked box went deep into Lewis's back. More flesh was pulled out. Lewis made an ear-piercing screaming sound. Extreme pain now was his companion. Wolfgang said, "In a day or two, those wounds will totally heal and leave no trace on his body. That is the beauty of the formula. You can torture as much as you want and your subject will never die. You give them time to recover. They heal. Then you can start over. I wish I had this afforded to me when I experimented on those Jews."

Reality was setting in for Marci. She was in the presence of something unholy yet enormously special. Few people have met a former high-ranking Nazi official from over a century ago.

Wolfgang said, "So, you want this formula? Do you know the pain and suffering you will have to endure?"

Marci said, "Yes, yes I—"

I quickly interrupted, "No, you do not, Marci." I looked at my father and said, "Please, don't listen to her. She is in love with me and wants to live with me forever. I want this as well, but I want to first find the solution to this formula. I do not want her to change. I just need more time to figure this out."

Wolfgang emotionally said, "There is no hope for her or the others in stopping the change." He looked at Marci and said, "You are different. You fear but not let fear control what you want. I sense that you enjoy seeing pain in others."

Marci said, "I… I don't know about that."

Wolfgang said, "Don't be ashamed. It is a good quality to have. Few have that personality trait." Wolfgang then noticed Marci's eyes as they wandered across the wall behind Wolfgang. On this wall was a collection of torture devices, or so it seemed.

Marci surprisingly walked between me and my father. She walked up to the devices and said, "What are these?"

Wolfgang looked at me and laughed hard. He laughed so hard it startled Marci. Wolfgang said, "Now I know why you love this woman." Wolfgang walked up next to Marci and explained a few of the items on the wall. He told her how he used them on the Jews during World War II. He sounded disappointed that many of his subjects couldn't take the pain and the abuse of his torturing methods. He said this was the reason he kept Lewis alive. He could torture him extensively with so many techniques.

Marci enjoyed her conversation with Wolfgang. She asked him, "So, Garrison told me everything about how his parents changed and the story with Lewis. It is amazing to me. It, it is out of this world. It's unbelievable. I never would have thought something like this ever existed. And you created this formula?"

Wolfgang nodded and said, "Let me say, I discovered it. Not created it."

Marci took her eyes off Wolfgang and looked at Lewis kneeling in pain. A smile developed on her lovely face. Wolfgang noticed it instantly. Marci said, "So what is the story with Lewis? What happened after Garrison went back home?"

I stood there in total silence, watching this amazing conversation taking place before my eyes. I witnessed the most beautiful woman in the world who stood approximately five feet ten having a conversation about torture and torture devices with a creature that is over eight foot in stature.

We walked inside of the lab that he'd had since he moved into the cave. I noticed the instruments were clean and polished now. I knew he was back to experimenting. Wolfgang explained in great detail what happened after I left Lewis. He obviously experimented on him and he wanted to see how fast broken bones would fuse together or how quickly torn muscles would grow back to their normal state. He told me that after I left the cave on my way back home, Zelda placed Lewis's arm in a makeshift splint. She popped his shoulders back into place after their dislocation.

Wolfgang noted the transformation was painful and he enjoyed watching the pain that Lewis endured. His legs and arms would bleed from the rapid growth of the bones and muscles of his extremities. Extreme and painful headaches occurred with the increasing size of the head and, of course, the protrusion of his mouth. This was another phenomenon that puzzled my father and me. Why does the formula create a wolf-like appearance in the facial area? Lewis's total transformation lasted about three months, which was consistent with Trevor's transformation.

Wolfgang said he chained Lewis to the wall of the cave. He didn't have a bed or a chair for him to lay or sit on as he monitored him as he went through the transformation. Lewis must have begged for his death numerous times, but his pleas were obviously ignored. Wolfgang said he took blood from Lewis and studied the samples daily. He said the transformation went into the exact stages of change that he and Zelda experienced. When Lewis completed this transformation, Wolfgang began to experiment on his body. He told us that he would break his arm with a sledge hammer, completely shattering the bones in the arm. After a week and a half, the bones began to grow together with the help of Wolfgang's splints used to wrap up the lifeless arm. The formula expedited the healing time.

Many other experiments were conducted on Lewis. Wolfgang would attempt to poison him but death did not befall Lewis. His advanced immune system prevented the poison from taking its full effect and after a day, his system removed the poison. He found there were limits to the formula's reproductive abilities. It would not re-grow a finger or a limb; the formula only enhanced the body's natural ability to defend itself from foreign impurities. The rapid repair of bone cartilage, or recovery of skin and muscle damage, which is part of a typical natural healing trait, would be accelerated by the formula beyond normal understanding. Wolfgang performed other experimental procedures on Lewis, most of which he didn't go into during the conversation.

After a long pause, Wolfgang pointed down another long passageway that led to the other side of the cave. The cave which my parents called home had two entrances. The second entrance was in the back. Wolfgang and his fellow Nazis, during World War II, made this cave the main shelter for Wolfgang and his work. Wolfgang said that it was his belief that this shelter was also made for Hitler and his mistress, Eva Brown, and some other high-ranking officers in the Nazi party.

The back entrance, or access, was in the middle of this large mountain. A stream of water trickled out of this entrance and combined with other small streams of water that made its way around the sides of the mountain. Wolfgang said this mountain had many small springs that ran throughout the backside of the mountain. Wolfgang and Zelda's cave was on the top portion of the large mountain. We followed Wolfgang toward this entrance. I saw light and foliage at the end of the opening. I looked around a corner to my right where the cave widens out and was startled by a figure that was standing in the corner. It was another person that had been transformed.

Wolfgang laughed as he shook his head. He said, "This is another one of my experiments. I took this man from the village below. I wanted to run more tests on a human subject and compare the data to Lewis's numbers. The specimen was older than all the others that I have taken. I have only seen five people transform, four of them completely, but all have been under fifty or sixty years old." I could tell this man was much older when he transformed. His face and body were at a more advanced in age.

The old man spoke in an older, rattled voice, "You! You are the boy from the forest." Then it hit me — I knew at that moment his identity. It was the owner of the bar. This was the father of the bartender that Marci and I met the day before we set out on our trip into the forest. He was also the man that Lewis and I spoke to the first time I visited the village. The old man continued, "I spoke to you years ago about the monster from the forest. Look at what he did to me."

Wolfgang shouted, "Shut up!"

At that moment I didn't know what to do. I said, "Good evening, sir. I see that you and my father have been working together."

The old man slowly walked toward me, but his chains stopped him. He was shackled with enormously thick chains around his neck and waist, as well as around both of his arms and legs. The old man spoke, "Working together? Look at what he did to me. Who are you people? What are you people?"

Wolfgang stood there listening and enjoying what he was hearing. He chuckled and said, "We conducted many experiments on you didn't we old man?" The old man hung his head and hurried back against the wall. He wanted to run and get away, but of course he was bound to his spot in his personal living hell. The old man possessed a horrible stench. My father probably never cleaned him. A large mound of animal waste lay over in the corner of the cave. Wolfgang said, "His data matched Lewis's. There were no abnormalities in either of their transformations. I even compared your mother and my data and in all four cases, the transformed stages were all the same, and the amount of time of the change for each stage was all similar."

Wolfgang explained the night he abducted the old man. He quietly walked out of the forest area and made his way down to the bar where the old man lived. He took his large hand and twisted the doorknob until it broke, then entered the bar. Wolfgang said that he heard the old man, who was upstairs, get up. The man slowly walked down the stairs as Wolfgang patiently waited for him. When his victim was near, Wolfgang quickly grabbed him by the arm, swung the old man around, and immediately crushed his larynx so he couldn't scream for help. The old man fell to the floor in tremendous pain. Wolfgang picked him up and placed him onto his back, and ran out of the house and into the forest.

The old man bounced on Wolfgang's shoulders, trying to catch his breath. He attempted to kick with his legs and he beat his arms on

Wolfgang's back. When Wolfgang was a few hundred yards inside of the forest, he threw the old man on the ground then forced him onto his stomach. Wolfgang placed his large, bare foot on the small of the man's back, took hold of the man's arms, and pulled back until his back snapped. This paralyzed the old man instantly. Wolfgang proceeded to injure the man further by taking ahold of the back of his head, and with his long fingernails, roughly scratched both eyes to a point where the man was blind. Wolfgang picked up the broken man and placed him back on his shoulders. Wolfgang knew the forest like the back of his hand. He could see every tree branch and twig in front of him in complete darkness. Wolfgang's long strides and steady feet made the trip to Wolfgang's dwelling a short journey.

Every bounce of Wolfgang's running steps further injured the old man's back. Once inside of the cave, Wolfgang took him back to the place he now calls home. Wolfgang bit him on the neck and infected him with the formula. Wolfgang told us in detail why he wanted the man injured beyond the natural reach for the human body to repair itself. He wanted to see at what stage during the transformation the formula would start to correct the injuries, or if the injuries would remain after the change.

During the three-month long mutation process, the old man's back, eyes and voice box didn't heal in the first two and a half months. The change was extremely difficult for him but during the last few stages of the transformation, his body started to heal. His voice box was healing, and his spine started to grow back together and repair itself. After the last stage, the old man's eyes regenerated and his vision was better than it ever had been. He had complete feeling and movement in his lower body. The spinal cord and the bones that were broken healed back in place. Wolfgang didn't have use of an x-ray machine, but after he conducted a few tests, he concluded that the old man's body had completely healed from Wolfgang's inflicted trauma.

I asked my father what he was going to do with them. He smiled and ignored the question. We left the old man and Lewis and went to Wolfgang's lab. Everything was so dated and dirty. I told him I didn't know how he worked in such conditions, but I assume that after a century goes by, a person gets used to their surroundings. I brought up a subject that was once not up for consideration, but I sensed maybe this time my parents would listen. I asked my father if I could have a word with him and my mother in the same room. We walked to the main room of the cave. My mother was cooking dinner for us. The limited variety of food in the forest made for a basic selection.

I asked my parents to sit down at the kitchen table. The self-made wooden chairs were extremely large. The width was almost twice as wide as normal and the height was as tall as a bar stool. Marci had some trouble sitting in her seat, which amused my parents. The table was not as long as one would imagine. I sat in my chair, feeling as if I was seven again. I fiddled around in the attempt to make myself comfortable at the table. I said, "Mom and Dad, I want to ask you to consider something. I know you will not like what I am about to say, but please hear me out. I want you guys and Eva to move to the States with Marci and me. I know that this is your home and there is an issue with your appearance in public, but I believe we can work around that obstacle. I just want you guys with me. I have a state-of-the-art lab in the basement of my house. My estate is large and the grounds are private. I get no visitors. We have a large forest area behind our house, and I share in your taste of animals. I have more money than I know what to do with. You will live in luxury for eternity. You will have the best and the latest in technology. Cooking will be easier. Conducting experiments will be easier. I have books, television, and use of the Internet. So please... consider this as an opportunity to make your life easier, and I also want you to be there. I want you as part of my family because you are the only true family I have ever had. My adoptive mother was the only one that has ever truly loved me but when she discovered who I was, she was afraid of me, she pushed me away, and eventually killed herself. Then I met Marci. I love her with all my heart. I want to be with her because she makes me feel complete. But you guys are the key to making us a true family, making us complete. So, there is my offer."

My parents sat there listening to every word. Wolfgang looked at Zelda who just stared at me for a moment. Then, she slowly looked Wolfgang's way. Wolfgang and I sensed that she was thinking about the offer. Then to my total surprise, Marci spoke, "I know this is not any of my business and believe me, what I have experienced with your son over the past four years or so is... well... both surprising and fascinating. I love your son. You cannot possibly know how much I love him. I am willing to go through the transformation to be with him forever. I have never felt more alive than I did the moment I met him." Marci became very nervous and let out a shaky laugh. She said, "This,

this is intimidating. You guys are intimidating. I am very appreciative to you guys for not killing me. Garrison was a nervous wreck over bringing me here to introduce me to you. But I am in full support of you coming with us. If this makes Garrison happy then it makes me happy. And I can help you, if you want, in raising Eva."

Zelda broke my parent's silence. She said, "I did not like you at first. But you have a lot of courage to come here. You risked your life for your love of our son. Do you know that we are just getting to know Garrison ourselves? We don't know our son. Now we have a daughter. So, it is a lot to ask of us."

Wolfgang shook his head in agreement. "The trip is too far. How will you get us on a plane or a ship? Our appearance would cause panic amongst people."

I said in response, "I can afford to charter a private jet. I could hide you in a large crate or a storage container that would fit both of you comfortably. I could have this container placed on a truck and I will personally drive it to my house. It will be uncomfortable and it will take some time, but I really do not see any other way."

Wolfgang said, "You realize that we have lived here for over a hundred years? We just cannot be moved in a container like an animal and fly halfway across the world to a place that is so strange to us."

I said, "Yes, I know it is a lot to ask. You do not have to decide now or if ever, but I would like for you to at least think about it for a while." Suddenly, Eva started to whine and Zelda went to her aid. She picked up the perfect little one and rocked her back and forth. Wolfgang watched the moment and then got up. I continued, "Father, I do not want you to do something that you do not want to do. I just thought it would be nice to have everyone together. If you do not like it, then we can always transport you back to this cave."

Wolfgang continued to walk away from me but only a few steps. When he stopped walking, he turned to me and said, "It is interesting that you proposed this to us at this moment. Garrison, I need to speak with you alone." Marci sat in her chair and she became a little uncomfortable. I told Marci to wait in the room. I told my mother if she needed help with anything, Marci is here to help.

I walked with my father to his lab. Wolfgang was very silent. Obviously, he needed to tell me something important. He stopped at his microscope and placed a slide under the scope. He ordered me to take a look. When I viewed the specimen, he asked me what I was viewing. I said with a fair amount of certainty that it was a culture of my blood. Wolfgang told me I was correct. He then placed another slide under the scope and again told me to look at the slide. I noticed the same cell structure as the last one. The cells were in constant change, though both specimens seemed to be the same. Wolfgang repeated this procedure three additional times; all were the exact same as the one before.

The cell structure in all five specimens looked similar in structure and acted the same in movement and mutation. I knew Wolfgang was attempting to make a point after this demonstration of slides. Wolfgang told me, "These five slides are from five different beings. One is you, one is of one of your dead brothers, both at the time of your births. The other specimens are of Eva and her three brothers who were all born at the same time. I disposed of the three males after your sisters' birth. As you can see from all five specimens, the blood's cell structure is virtually the same in all cases. I can say with great certainty that Eva will be just like you... perfect, or I should say as close to perfection as we can achieve. With that in mind, my dream, our dream, Hitler's dream of the perfect human race is right before our eyes, Garrison."

He walked toward me and placed his large hands on my shoulders and said, "Don't you see it? Don't you see it? The secret to the formula is hidden in the formula itself. If two infected beings like myself and your mother can create five perfect beings, or seven, can you imagine if those offspring would mate and have children? I believe this will bypass the transformation."

I was shocked by my father's words, but he was correct; at least in theory it seemed to be the case. I said, "So the problem with the formula is that it is essentially too perfect. When it is introduced to the subject, it is attempting to change its cell structure into perfection, but the formula is missing something. It is missing the other perfect cells. Therefore, the perfectly formed cells are attacking the non-perfect cells of the current hosts."

My father was standing there nodding his large head. He interrupted me and continuing the thought, "Yes, yes, yes and that is why the transformation occurs. Which we already knew of this, but now what happens if two perfect beings that have not been transformed would mate? Would there be a change? I don't think there will be. Your blood, your cell structure is perfect, just like Eva's. The formula cannot perfect what is already perfect, so the formula would not attack the other cells. Don't you see it, Garrison? I found a way to create the ultimate being, a being that will never age or succumb to disease. I finally found a way to produce the perfect human."

He stood there with his yellowish eyes glistening. They danced from side to side in unadulterated bliss. I sensed his thoughts. A horrid feeling came over me. It had been building ever since we started this conversation. I knew what my father wanted. I knew what he was leading up to.

Wolfgang said, "Imagine it, Garrison – you and your sister creating a perfect human."

I said, "Do you think the child will be perfect physically? No mutations?"

Wolfgang turned away and went to his notebook, "I think so. Of course, the only way to prove this is to conduct an experiment." He turned his large upper body toward me and smiled. I didn't know what to say. Part of me was intrigued with the possibilities of us creating a perfect human. Then part of me was disgusted by the thought of incest, but there are other ways of impregnating my sister in the future when she is of proper age. The future experiment got me wondering. I must address this matter with Marci, but I had to be mindful of when and how I would tell her. I worried because I did not want her to say something that would upset my father.

I said to my father, "Well, this is a very intriguing theory of which I believe will work. My only concern is what if we are wrong and some form of mutation develops? What if there is more than one fetus or the fetus changes like in my experiment with the homeless lady? The fetuses grow too large for the womb and split her open, killing her. I would not want that to happen to Eva. Right? Please tell me, Father, that you would not want that either?"

Wolfgang looked at me for an uncomfortable time and said, "If it happens, then your mother and I will start over with another child." The cold, icy stare went through me to my soul. This confirmed my innermost fear that Wolfgang didn't care about his daughter. So, I began to wonder. Does he care about me? My heart started to ache with that thought. Wolfgang spoke, "I feel this bothers you?"

I said, "Father, all of my life I wanted only one thing and that is to be loved. To be wanted and to be part of a real family. I had that taken from me by my own brother. I now have Marci in my life, but we cannot bear children because I do not want to create a being that is transformed. They do not turn out right. They turn into my brother. Part animal, part human. I do not want that for us. You understand, right?"

My father stood up straight and arched his back and said, "You want a perfect offspring?"

I said, "Yes I do."

Wolfgang said, "Well… I am giving you that opportunity. Does it matter which womb the perfect human comes out of? I sense that you don't like my candor when I spoke about Eva."

I needed to say something because he knew I had something on my mind. I felt I had to let him know. I remorsefully said, "Father, I find your candor regarding my sister disturbing. Don't you love your own daughter?"

My father laughed and said, "Disturbing? I assume you are all loving, my son, Garrison?"

I said, "I believe I have more feelings toward the people that I am close to."

With that Wolfgang let out a loud roar toward my face. He said in a very angry voice, "You pompous fuck. How dare you stand there and judge me. Is it not true that you hated your own brother? You tortured him, right? Or was that a lie? You said you cut him into many pieces and buried him in your backyard in garbage bags. Is that not true, Garrison?" He leaned toward me with his teeth showing and saliva dripping down from his mouth.

I quickly thought about what he said. He noticed my thought process at that moment and I said, "You are right. I did."

Wolfgang continued his rant, "You brought your only friend in the world to see me, knowing that he would die in the process?" He then yelled, "Isn't that right, Garrison!"

I quickly and nervously said, "Yes."

Wolfgang continued, "You said you murdered young babies, conducted experiments on them, you made them suffer. You changed two innocent humans into creatures like me! Right?"

I had to agree with him. I again said, "Yes! All of this is true."

Wolfgang backed away from me and said, "And now you stand before me and judge me on my love of my child." Suddenly, my soul felt as if it was on fire. I felt this incredible rage that quickly grew inside of my being. The rage was so strong that I knew my father sensed it. He looked at me with his yellowish eyes squinted. He said, "You are angry.

I made you angry. Good. What is on your mind? Tell me, don't be afraid."

I unleashed my tongue, of which I felt I had no control. I said in a loud voice, "Okay! You want to the truth? Here it is. You disappointed me when you said that about Eva. You spoke about her like she was just an experiment to you. Maybe she is. Fine! But…" The feeling inside me began to turn now from anger to depression. I continued as I fought back my tears, "For some fucked up reason, I believed that you loved me. I thought that I finally found my parents. I had this fantasy that maybe they would love me like other parents would love their child. I thought for just a moment that you loved me or that at least cared about me. At worst, I believed that even if you would not love me like a real father would love a son, maybe you would have some sort of caring feelings toward me. I guess I was wrong. This is not about Eva, it is about me. Understand." My feeling of depression was now flipped back to anger. I stood there with my heart rate to a point where I thought my heart was going to jump out of my chest.

Wolfgang looked down and said something I never thought he would say. He said in a low voice, "Garrison… I don't say this to just anyone. Throughout my long life, I have only admired a handful of people. But after reading your manuscripts of your experiments on animals, humans, and your brother has made me very proud. Very proud. I have never cared this deeply for any human since Hitler or…" His voice lowered to almost a whisper, "your mother. I do care about you, my son, and I do care about Eva. But you, you are special. Perfect in every way. You are what I wanted to be and what I strived to be. Perfect both physically and mentally. I am not perfect physically. So, you are better than me. I admire you and, in fact, I am jealous of you because of these facts. You are my son. I am proud of that fact. As far as love goes… well… that is just a word. Actions demonstrate more than words. The fact that you are still alive and that I have not killed your woman should be proof enough that I care for you."

My heart, which experienced a wide array of emotions in just minutes, experienced another emotion after my father spoke. It was pure, unadulterated joy hearing those words from my father's lips. I needed to hear those words. I found myself not able to speak. I tried, but after three decades of pain, I couldn't express my feelings in words. For the first time since Adelle died in my arms, I cried. My father then did something I had also needed for so long. He walked toward me and he held me in his large and powerful arms. He hugged me. This man that had murdered thousands of people, conducted many cruel experiments on too many to humanly count, held me. It was the greatest honor anyone has ever bestowed upon me.

Suddenly, I sensed a presence behind me. I looked up and I knew something caught my father's eye as well. He stopped our embrace and I turned around. There was Marci with tears rolling down both of her cheeks. She had a long, black iron poker in her hand that she grabbed from the fireplace. Apparently, she heard my father's roar and she came to my aid.

Out of nowhere, Zelda appeared behind her and grabbed the iron poker from my love, which she freely gave up. Marci ran into my arms and held me tight. She said, "I heard this terrible roar and I was afraid for your life, Garrison. I thought... I thought your father was going to hurt you."

My father said, "Your woman came to your defense. She knew she would have not been able to stop me... but she came to you and did not escape. I admire the loyalty. Come. Let us sit down in the front room."

My father walked past us, and I held onto the love of my life. From that moment on, I truly felt safe in my home. This was now indeed my family.

Chapter Three

Marci was exhausted and needed to sleep. I got her sleeping bag out from our gear and placed it on the floor in the corner of the cave. My parents and I do not require much sleep so we all stayed up through the entire night talking and getting to know each other better. I mostly spoke with my mom. Zelda had an incredible love for my father. She loved him so much that she was willing to permanently change her physical appearance forever without a moment's hesitation.

Wolfgang told me the story of how fast it took Zelda to decide to accept the injection of the formula. Wolfgang injected himself first and then Zelda. They retreated to the cave just hours before the Russians invaded the area near Hitler's bunker. It took them days to get to the cave. Wolfgang was told by Hitler that other high-ranking Nazi's were supposed to report to the cave, along with Hitler and his mistress, Eva Brown. But they didn't make it. Wolfgang said that he believed many of his fellow officers got lost in the forest. He told me amazing stories that he would go out scouting the area, even for days on end, to see what and who was around the cave. He came upon some officers that had died from gunshot wounds or who engaged in acts of suicide. Wolfgang told me that not one soldier made their way to the cave. He concluded that many of them might not have known the precise location of the cave. Also, if one was not familiar with the forest or was not prepared for its near complete darkness, finding the cave would be almost impossible.

As we sat and talked, I could tell there was something in Wolfgang's voice that was leading me to think he was getting restless with his home. He spoke about how old and outdated his lab was and how he longed for the amenities of a nice, clean home. Zelda was her usual, quiet self, but when Wolfgang touched on the house amenities, that was when my mother spoke up. She wanted hot, running water and most of all, a cleaner place to bathe.

I told my parents as much as I could about today's world. They didn't understand many of the items that I spoke of, like the microwave oven and electronic devises like the phone, computer, and video camera. When I showed Wolfgang the video camera the last time I was here, he was just amazed. In fact, I sense he was a little afraid at first. I showed him some clips of a few of my experiments. I told him that I had all of them documented.

We talked through the night and when daylight was struggling to make its way through the thick leaves from the forest trees, I again brought up the subject of coming back with me to the States. This time they listened more intently, especially Wolfgang. I did my best sales job on them. I was on fire as my senses were working at a very high level. Wolfgang and Zelda felt my passion; they felt my longing for having them with me under the same roof. They knew that I would not be happy here in the cave. They knew I had to get back to my world. It was a lot for them to accept, but I knew down deep that my mother was willing to give it a chance.

My father was still wavering, but he was closer to the acceptance of leaving than a day ago. It's hard to convince your parents to move from their home that they had lived in for so many years. One hundred twenty-four years they had been living in this cave. They had forgotten what it's like to live well.

Marci started to move around in her sleeping bag. She got up and let out a small yawn. This was very entertaining to my father. He began to laugh so hard that he had to brace himself with his arm on the table. I was a little confused at first. Zelda then began to laugh with my father. Marci was half asleep and confused as well. She asked what was so funny. A few moments later Wolfgang said, "You just get up, yawn like it is nothing. You sleep all night long and did not awake once. You are not... normal woman."

Marci said, "I was tired."

Wolfgang and Zelda laughed even harder. Then Wolfgang said to Zelda, "She was tired." They laughed again. Wolfgang said to me, "It is up to your mother. If she wants to take a trip to the States, then we will go." With that news in hand, I was extremely happy.

Zelda said, "Let's go."

I was overwhelmed with excitement. I got up and gave my father a firm handshake of which he squeezed my hand so hard I thought he broke it. I then hugged my mother. Marci said, "That's great. So, when are we leaving?"

Wolfgang said through his laughter to me, "This woman treats us like we are just normal human beings. Where did you find her, Garrison?"

I just smiled and said, "I am a very lucky man, Father."

Wolfgang got up from the table and escorted Marci and I outside. We went exploring through the forest after our breakfast. He took us on a little tour of his area of the forest, showing us the backend of the cave from the outside. A thin waterfall fell from the back entrance of the cave to what looked to be over one hundred feet down into a small, quiet river. This river made its way around the mountain that housed the cave and flowed to the nearest village, which was the village in front of the entrance of the forest.

I told my father that the people from that village lived longer, did not age as quick, nor did they have a normal level of disease or illness. Wolfgang told me that he had been studying this for decades and agreed. He told me the moss plant that Lewis stumbled on was the basic building block of the formula. Wolfgang explained his discovery again to me from years ago. The moss plant had a long, white root that resembled a carrot. That white root excreted a small, slimy substance from its root system. If you took the root in your hand, it would have a slick and oily feel to it. The top portion of the plant's root had a small stem coming from it. This stem had very small, vein-like vines that would spread out along the ground. Once it took root in the soil, the vines of the plant would produce a cover of what looked and felt like moss. In some cases, a small vine-like sprout would grow up about five or six inches and would bear a resemblance to parsley.

I told Wolfgang that I had a moss plant at my house and it was still growing to this day. Wolfgang was very concerned over this fact and told me not to let this plant take root outside. He attempted to recreate the original formula from the moss plant only, but that ended up as a complete failure. Wolfgang said that other chemicals had to be mixed with the root's slimy substance. He believed that the obvious answer was usually the most accurate explanation. He believed there must be some other chemicals coming from other sources that were transported by water. As the water flows and seeps into the soil, it encounters the moss plant's root system or with the moss plant itself. Somehow, a chemical reaction takes place, and through years of evolution, as the water passes down the stream, it picks up a mutated chemical which Wolfgang believes is the basis of the formula's essence.

Wolfgang told me that he had about three gallons of what he believes is the pure, original version of the formula. He didn't elaborate in any detail on how he extracted the pure form of the formula. Wolfgang did tell me that it took years of hard, painstaking work. The amount of the original formula had to be collected and measured by drops of liquid and not by cup or thimble full. He had tested from these batches of liquid that he had captured during his time living in the forest. Test after test had produced the same metaphorical transformation in living animals.

Wolfgang didn't tell me where he hid his extracted formula. He didn't want the formula to ever fall into the hands of the wrong people because of the horrid physical change that develops when introduced to the receiving host. Wolfgang's main purpose for all his work regarding Formula L was to find a potion that gives a living host everlasting life, to create or redevelop an immune system that would be disease-free and would stop the cells from producing imperfect reproductive cells, thus eliminating or at worst, severely slowing the aging process. Wolfgang again repeated to me that in his opinion, the original formula attacks the cells from the host that it encounters, and from that moment of contact, the formula constantly changes its chemical makeup. Because of this constant change, it is impossible to control the formula, to stop the transformation that the formula causes to the receiving host.

Wolfgang's theory on why the villagers hadn't experienced the physical transformation was that the formula was diluted to a point where the chemicals that make up the formula were so weak compared to the complete version of the original formula. What the villagers had was very special, and many people would pay a king's ransom for what they had. Wolfgang said there had been numerous people that had visited the small community in hopes of finding the answer to the slower aging phenomenon, but many outsiders didn't believe there was just one magical potion causing the long survival rate. Many believe the village's secrets are from the inhabitant's way of life. Either way, the village has been untouched by the outside world for a very long time.

Wolfgang said that it took him over a century to convince himself that the only way for the formula to be passed from host to host without any physical or mental mutation is for two infected hosts to mate and create an offspring. Its primary and first proven example of this fact is me and my newborn sister, Eva.

Wolfgang's newly formed theory was that when two infected hosts are in a perfect physical and mental human form and they mate, that would then create another perfect human, like its parental hosts. Wolfgang believed that if I would mate with my sister, we would create a perfect creature. The formula had mutated to a point that the chemical makeup of the host's cells was so perfect that the formula needed no adjusting to recreate what was already perfect.

Wolfgang and I both sensed that Marci was very depressed. I knew down deep in my heart that Marci knew there was no cure for the formula's mutation process. Reality had hit both of us, which made me very concerned about what action my love might attempt to pull. I knew she wanted to live forever and to be perfect.

We walked a while around the inside of the cave. I saw many bones lying around the floor of the forest. Wolfgang said he would do most of his hunting in areas away from the back of the cave. Most of the woodland creatures tended to make their way toward the waterfall. I asked my father if he noticed the difference in the taste of the animals over the years or if their sizes had changed. It would seem to me that the animals would be larger and probably would have a different taste since they had probably drunk from the many streams of water that were in the forest.

Of course, Wolfgang said he conducted many experiments on many animals over the years, and he found they had grown larger in size and seemed to live longer. He said the deer's antlers would grow faster, they jumped higher, and were quicker. The taste was different and had improved over the decades in the forest.

After many hours of discussion and exploring, we made our way back to the cave. My mother made us lunch. She chopped some fresh meat that she had stored in the cooler part of the cave. Marci had not developed my appetite for raw animal meat, so she had some food that she brought with her in her backpack. As we ate our lunch, we started to prepare for my parents' move to the States. Wolfgang was very concerned about how he and his wife were going to travel unnoticed overseas. I'd had some thoughts on this issue before we even left for the trip. The mode of transportation was not really our main problem. What concerned me and my parents was how we were going to load my parents from the cave to a carrying container.

Marci brought up a subject that caught everyone by surprise. She asked, "So, what is going to happen to Lewis and that other guy?"

Wolfgang was perplexed. It didn't even occur to him to think about what he was going to do with the two. We knew they were not coming with us back to the States. I asked my father what he wanted to do with them and he just looked at me for the longest time. He didn't have an answer.

Then Marci, with that unearthly little twinkle in her eye, suggested, "Why don't we have them fight each other to the death? Tell them the winner of the fight wins a trip to the States. At the last moment, kill the remaining subject."

I smiled as I looked at Wolfgang. I said, "She even used the word subject."

Marci's innovative idea captivated Wolfgang's interests. He said to me, "Again, your woman does not disappoint." He said to my love, "How would you arrange this fight?"

Marci continued eating her food as she thought about how she would have this fight played out. After several moments passed, she suggested, "Do you have longer chains? I would keep them on chains but use longer chains so they can reach each other."

Wolfgang completed her thought. "Yes, I have longer chains. We could have the two chained at the same spot but with longer chains around their neck, waist, and limbs. We will have them fight to the death, and after the fight I will eliminate the winner."

I sat there marveling over this exchange. This was the first time my father had ever had a conversation with Marci. I sensed he admired her passion for the darker side of her personality. She said, "I want to watch this fight and I want to kill the survivor of the fight."

Wolfgang laughed and said, "I don't think you have the stomach for a fight that I have in mind and you will not kill. I don't think you have it in you."

Marci was disappointed in Wolfgang's doubts. She said hastily, "I have killed before, just ask Garrison. I have killed four mutated humans." Wolfgang was surprised by her passionate pleas. I told my father about the part Marci played with the newborns. I told him the entire story and how she burnt them alive with their father.

As Wolfgang listened, he nodded in approval of her past actions, but said, "You have never killed someone up close, have you?"

Marci said, "Please, I beg you. Give me this opportunity. I promise I will not disappoint you."

Wolfgang continued to be impressed with her and he looked at me for a moment and said, "I understand why you like this woman. I can see how her personality is so addictive to you. The more I spend time with her, the more I understand why you care so much for her." He looked at Marci and said, "I will allow you to watch the fight. If you are still interested, I will think about you killing the survivor."

Marci smiled as she clapped her hands saying, "Thank you. Thank you so much." The next morning, I started working on the task of transporting my parents back to the States. I was concerned about not creating a lot of questions from the villagers. I sensed they were suspicious of my visit to begin with, and the last thing I needed was to have a large moving container near my cottage. Somehow, I had to get my parents to meet up with me at a place outside of the village. I sat down with my parents and attempted to come up with a basic escape plan. Wolfgang said he knew of a place where he and Zelda could go at the back edge of the forest that was located near a country road. This road was not heavily traveled, and they could hide out in this spot for me to pick them up in some form of transportation.

My plan was to call Sonja to set up a rental van or truck then transport my parents to a large travel container that could be boarded onto an aircraft. We would then repeat the same procedure when we got back to America; have the container delivered to a storage unit area and then transport my parents in a large truck or van back to my Estate.

Wolfgang liked the plan and told me to give them a day to pack. My only other concern was Eva. What would happen if she would start to cry during the process? Is she old enough for this kind of trip? I needed to make the storage container as comfortable as possible. It needed to be climate controlled, and I also needed the unit to be as soundproof as possible.

Wolfgang suggested we take Eva with us on the plane back to America. Of course, this would be safer and easier for Eva.

I had had issues with my cell phone working at certain times or locations the last time I was in the forest. This time my phone could reach the outside world with more regularity. I called Sonja and informed her that we were doing fine. I asked her to arrange a climate controlled moving truck for us. I told her that we were going to purchase some items and were going to have them shipped back to the

United States. Sonja told me she would make the necessary arrangements with a small moving company.

The moving company was in a nearby city of the village where our cottage was located. I specifically told her that we would pick up the truck at their place of business and not to have it delivered to our cottage. I asked her if this could be accomplished and she told me it would not be a problem. I asked her if we could have a few days and she told me that would be fine. She was thoughtful enough to offer to have someone with her to take our rental car back to the airport.

When I got off the phone with Sonja, I informed everyone what was happening. I then shifted the conversation to Lewis and the old man. I said that we needed to eliminate them before we left. We could not keep them alive under any circumstance. Wolfgang agreed and wanted to end their lives as soon as possible.

Wolfgang still had some doubts about Marci witnessing what was about to take place. Marci reassured my father that she would not get in the way and she wanted to be there to watch. Wolfgang reluctantly kept his promise and agreed to her wishes. We went back into the cave toward the two beings in chains. Wolfgang reached into a large chest and pulled out two long chains. These chains were extremely thick and looked like they weighted a ton. Wolfgang maneuvered these chains with ease as he stepped toward Lewis and attached one of the chains onto Lewis's neck brace. Then Wolfgang walked down the long passageway and proceeded to do the same with the old man.

As Wolfgang left our sight, Lewis spoke in a panicked voice, "What is he going to do? What is he going to do?"

I said, "I do not know, Lewis, I guess we have to wait and see."

Lewis didn't like my answer. He attempted to come after me but the old chain that was on his neck brace, waist and limbs stopped his advance. Lewis's sudden movement scared Marci, and she ran back several steps from where she was standing. Then Marci got mad and said, "You stupid bastard. You scared the fuck out of me!"

Lewis immediately growled at Marci and said, "Shut up, you bitch. You are the reason I am in this state to begin with. If it wasn't for your boyfriend's love or lust for you, I would have never come back to his God-awful hell hole."

I quickly spoke, "You came here because you wanted to find the cure for the mutation, just like me, and I would suggest that you do not ever call her a bitch again."

Lewis shouted said, "Fuck you and fuck your whore, you unnatural freak."

Then, like a well-orchestrated moment, my father walked in and said, "Save your energy. You are going to need it." Wolfgang walked at a brisk pace past us. He retrieved a large military weapon, a machine gun, from behind a stack of cabinets in his rustic lab. He also had a long pole that resembled a dog leash with a loop at the end of the pole in his other hand. He came toward us, stopped a few feet from me and asked, "Do you know how to use this?"

He held the gun out toward me and I cradled it, trying to be as gentle as I could. I replied simply, "No. I don't know how to use it."

Wolfgang snarled at me and roughly showed me how to use the gun. After his short and hasty demonstration, he looked at me with an icy stare and told me, "If he gets out of control, empty the chamber into Lewis's body. Just don't shoot me." Wolfgang walked to the side wall of the room and picked up a large axe-like weapon and the pole with the leash attached to the end of the pole. He walked over to Lewis, and Lewis immediately coward down. Wolfgang reached down and quickly placed the loop over Lewis's neck. Then, without warning, he quickly raised the axe over his head, and with most of his might, the axe struck one of the chains attached to Lewis's left leg. Quickly, at the first swing of the axe, Wolfgang proceeded to break all the chains that were committed to his extremities. Lewis was now free from the wall of the cave for the first time in years. I nervously held the machine gun firmly in my arms. My senses were on fire. My only thoughts were on Lewis. I didn't want him to get loose and hurt either my father or Marci. Of course, I was more worried about Marci getting hurt.

Lewis was so mentally abused through the years by Wolfgang; Lewis had to let him do whatever he wanted to him. He knew he had no choice. Wolfgang ordered Lewis to walk down the passageway in the next area of the cave where the old man was waiting. I followed my father and Lewis with a safe distance between us. When Wolfgang reached the old man, he took the end of Lewis's chain and attached it to the same loop that the old man's chain was on. Wolfgang took the dog leash off Lewis and walked back toward me. He swiftly took the gun from my hands and held it with one arm, with the point of the gun aimed at the ceiling of the cave.

The two chained men didn't have a clue what was happening. They dared not ask any questions out of fear of what Wolfgang might do. I believe Lewis and the old man thought they were going to be gunned down, but just when they thought he was going to shoot them, Wolfgang broke his silence. He said, "My wife and I are going to leave this place. We are going to live in America for a while."

Lewis's large, yellowish eyes beamed with excitement and his heart started to beat out of his chest over the news. I knew he thought this was the opportunity he had been wishing for, the chance to go home. Wolfgang continued, "So I can't leave both of you here. I can only bring one with me. So, this is what's going to happen." Wolfgang's heavy steps could be heard throughout the cave as he walked over to the corner of the room. He picked up two long, iron rods. He then walked over to the two men and threw each of the rods in their direction.

Wolfgang said, "You make a move toward me or my son, I will kill you. Now pick up the iron rods." The two men picked up the rods and held them tightly with both hands. Lewis and the old man knew what was next. Wolfgang said, "You two will fight to the death. The one that lives goes back with us to America. Now fight."

The two men stood there in shock as they glanced at each other. They didn't want to fight. Before I knew it, Wolfgang made his way to another area of the room and picked up a bull whip. He quickly walked over and raised his arm while the other arm held the machine gun. Within the bat of an eye, the long, leather whip sailed through the air, making a beautiful whistling sound that resonated through the walls of the cave room. The whip found its home on the bare back of the old man. Like a quick stroke of a pen to paper, the whip caused a sizable wound that formed on his back. The old man's reaction was one of surprise. He dropped his iron rod and made a loud groaning sound. As quickly as my father's whip lashed out, Lewis attacked. He stepped forward with his rod, striking the end of the weapon into the old man's stomach. Lewis quickly thrust the rod back with both hands, and as he slung it, he struck his victim across the chest. The old man stumbled back but remained on his feet. Lewis raised the rod over his head and struck the old man on the side of his neck. The old man's reaction was too slow to protect himself. The old one fell to his knees. He was in a great deal of pain, but he forced himself to find his weapon on the moist rock floor. Lewis struck the man again with another blow, this time hitting him in the middle of his back. Lewis hurried over to the old man, took his metal rod with both hands, and thrust the rod into his back as hard as he could.

Without warning, there was a familiar sound whipping through the air. Wolfgang took his bullwhip and struck Lewis in his face. The force and surprise from the strike took Lewis totally by surprise. He dropped his iron rod and held his face. Blood started to seep through his long fingers. He held his face firmly, trying to recover from the stinging pain from the blow. The whip broke Lewis's skin from in the middle of his forehead, between his eyes, and down to his cheek.

The old man took this opportunity to make his way over to his weapon. I instinctually took my foot and guided the weapon toward his direction. After my act, I sheepishly looked over to my father for approval and he just batted his eyes over my action. The old man found his weapon and struggled mightily to get to his feet. As he turned to face Lewis, Lewis swung his rod onto the side of the old man's large head, causing his head to bleed from the blow. The old man gathered himself and lunged with his weapon toward Lewis. Lewis quickly moved away from the weapon then proceeded to repetitively hit the old man with his weapon as many times and as fast as he could. Most of the blows landed on his back. The old man had given up through no fault of his own. He was too old to win any fight at his advanced age. Even with assistance from the formula, the eternal foundation of youth, the formula only stopped the aging, it doesn't make one younger.

Lewis stopped beating the old man as he gathered control over his thoughts and emotions. With his foot, he rolled the old man over onto his back. Suddenly, Lewis started to cry. He didn't like what he was doing. He wanted to stop beating this poor soul to death, but he knew that if he wanted to go home, he had to follow instructions.

Over the past few years, all Lewis had done was follow his master's instructions. He had suffered so much at the hands of my father's notions, I think he was just conditioned now to react emotionally whenever he had a task or was forced into an experiment that he didn't want to be a part of.

With both hands, Lewis raised the rod over his head and with loud, slobbering whimpers, he froze at the apex of his potential strike. Wolfgang shouted, "Do it Lewis… if you want to go home. Kill him. It is easy. I have done it thousands of times myself. You have killed many humans and animals many times in your lab back home."

Lewis, hanging on every word coming from my father's mouth, let out a loud and forceful screaming, "Noooooooooooo" as he plunged the rod into the mouth of the old man. Breaking a couple of teeth along the way, the rod went through the back of the throat. We heard the end of the metal pole hit the rock laden floor. Lewis stumbled back, his breathing heavy and out of control. He looked at the old man wiggling in pain and trying to get the pole out of his mouth and the back of his throat. The tip of the rod was poking out of the base of his skull. Lewis continued to scream, "Noooooooooooo."

The old man was in extreme pain. He was bleeding all over the floor of the cave. He took his hands, grabbed the pole, and pulled it out of the back of his large skull. Blood was pouring out of his mouth and the back of his neck. He had trouble getting up. I assumed it was because of the damage to the upper portion of his spinal cord. Lewis stood there, panting with his hands out, wanting to help him but he knew he couldn't. Wolfgang shouted, "Fight, Lewis. He is trying to kill you and he would if he could. Why are you standing there looking at him? Finish him."

The old man was trying his hardest to get up, but his injured spinal cord wouldn't allow him to get onto his feet. His right side was paralyzed. Then, unexpectedly, Marci said, "Let me make the fight more even."

Wolfgang quickly looked at Marci with a puzzled look on his dark and hairy muzzle. He said to Marci, "What do you mean?" Marci held her hands out toward the machine gun. She wanted to fire it toward Lewis. Wolfgang slightly moved the gun away from Marci saying, "Now wait a minute. What are you suggesting?"

Marci said, "Give me the gun and I will show you." Wolfgang quickly said in a loud snorting voice, "No!"

Marci impatiently said, "Make the fight more interesting. That pussy is not going to kill him. Shoot Lewis in the legs to make it fairer. The guy is too old to fight back."

Wolfgang stood there in a daze while listening to Marci. He was impressed by her imagination and passion. Without another thought, Wolfgang pointed the machine gun and opened fire on Lewis's legs. The bullets came out of the gun at a rapid pace, and the noise was intense. Marci had to put her hands up to her ears, it was so loud inside of that area of the cave. I watched Lewis flinch numerous times as he stood with a forward lean. Wolfgang didn't let up with the bullets. He started to fire them slowly, making sure many of them didn't miss his target. The bullets that did miss Lewis's legs hit the side of a large chest that was behind him. The bullets were mostly aimed at Lewis's knees. After several moments, Wolfgang stopped firing and Lewis fell onto the rock floor. He let out blood curling cries of pain.

Marci took her hands from her beautiful little ears and started to jump up and down. She clapped and said, "Yes! That's what I am talking about! Good shooting." Wolfgang quickly looked at her with a stern look, then a smile broke across his face and he started to laugh. She was so excited that she jumped toward Wolfgang and hugged his right arm as he strongly held the smoking gun in his powerful hands. Marci came over to me and gave me a hug as well.

Lewis was on all fours, attempting to catch his breath. Suddenly, the old man drug half of his limp body around and with his good hand, went for Lewis's throat. His body went into Lewis's, knocking him over to his side. His pain increased even more with the most current blow. The old man attempted to reach for Lewis's throat but instead found one of his eyes. The old man dug his finger into Lewis's eye socket. Lewis fought to move his face away, but the damage was already done. Lewis reached for his wounded eye with both hands, making even louder cries.

The old man tried to crawl on top of Lewis and without any hesitation, the old man opened his mouth as wide as he could. He aimed his head toward Lewis's knee. He struck as fast and as hard as he could. The bite was perfect. Most of the knee went inside of his large mouth, and he bit down as hard as he could.

All we heard was a couple of loud popping sounds. Lewis screamed louder as he reached for his knee. I noticed his right eye was bleeding and looked like it was blinded. The old man, with all his might, tried to move, pull, and tug on Lewis's knee. Then, he placed his good hand on Lewis's upper thigh and with a firm grip, held it down. Lewis, meanwhile, was sitting up and he grabbed the old man at the shoulders, trying to get him to release his hold. The old man started to yank and pull on the wounded area. After each attack, he bit further into Lewis's knee. Lewis couldn't stand the pain. He was yelling for him to stop. He even hit the old man on his large head, but that made the pain worse.

I looked at Marci to see her reaction. Her eyes were glued to the scene with a satisfied smile on her captivated face. She never looked away.

The old man quickly moved his strong hand down to the lower part of Lewis's leg. The knee area was completely chewed as most of Lewis's knee was gone. The old man grabbed the lower leg. He wanted to tear the leg off but half of his body was not cooperating. The limp side of his body was in the way. The old man bit down again, and this time he positioned Lewis's leg in an upward pose and bit the under part of the knee. Within moments, he had the leg hanging from Lewis's body by a few muscles.

Lewis was in so much pain. Even though he could hardly see with just one good eye, he attempted to make a lunge toward the old man. His hand found the long ear of his attacker. He crudely pulled the ear on the large head of the old man away from his leg. With all of Lewis's might and fortitude, he moved his body forward and, using the weight of his body, he pushed the old man over. Lewis's leg was barely hanging onto his body as it was contorted and twisted in directions that I had never seen. Lewis slithered like a snake toward the old man. Within moments, he took his left hand and plunged his thumb into the hole that was at the top part of the old man's neck. The victim was in great pain as he tried with all his power to escape Lewis's hold on him. The distress on the faces of the large wolf-shaped heads displayed the immense amount of pain the two were experiencing. Lewis's hold on the old man's neck reminded me of a bowler's hold on his bowling ball. Lewis dug his long thumb deeper into the old man's neck. He was at the point of surrender.

The air in the cave smelt of a musky animal odor combined with the iron-like scent of warm blood. The floor of the cave was covered with large splotches of the dark red liquid. The moaning and grunting the competitors were making made for a very interesting scene.

Physically, Lewis was in a difficult position. He had no use of his legs from the knees down. One was shot up to a point where it was impossible to move, while the other knee was completely gone. With the lower part of his leg hanging on by a muscle or two, the pain was unimaginable.

While on the floor of the cave, the lower leg was unnaturally bent. Lewis, with all his will, took his other hand and placed it on the old man's shoulder. In a feeble attempt, Lewis started to pull the head and the shoulders in opposite directions. Lewis was desperate. He knew he had to kill his enemy to survive. He also understood that he had regained the upper hand in this fight to the death.

From the look of things, the old man seemed to be totally paralyzed, although Lewis couldn't get enough leverage to complete the attack he developed. He couldn't stand or move to get enough strength because of a lack of leverage to separate the old man's head from his body. I could tell that this was killing Lewis's soul. He was not a killer. He never wanted to kill. He didn't enjoy it. This is what made Wolfgang an expert at torturing. He not only relished inflicting physical torture on his victims, he thoroughly enjoyed the mental torturing of his subjects.

Lewis knew that the only way to kill the old man was to separate his head from his body. He knew of only one way to accomplish this. He had to use his teeth. I could sense the arousal in my father's heart. I could see this developing into a perfectly played symphony for my father's enjoyment. Marci was enjoying the scene as well, but I could sense her disappointment in Lewis winning this match.

Lewis looked down at his victim's long, hairy neck and once again, he began to sob loudly. I could hear Lewis opening his mouth while the old man's eyes were open as wide as they could get. Most of his body was paralyzed so there was little fight that he had left to protect himself.

Lewis's face had a unique mixture of blood from his nonfunctioning eye mixing with the tears from his operative one. He had a look of pity as he slowly lowered his face toward his competitor. Wolfgang, knowing the cruel mental torture Lewis was under, broke this wonderful silent scene by saying, "End it quickly if it bothers you so much."

Lewis started to cry and said, "God damn you for this." Lewis let out a cry of disgust and per Wolfgang's instructions, he quickly struck the old man's neck with his open mouth, biting deeply into the neck of his victim. Lewis released his bite then quickly bit into his neck a second time. Lewis was now at a point of no return. He started to devour the neck area and began ripping the hairy, leathery skin from his prey. At each powerful bite, he tore more flesh away while at the same time, pulling the head away from the body. Through all the blood and chunks of flesh, the neck bone began to expose itself. Lewis reared back and thrust all his might toward the exposed bone. I heard the bones crack, and the head was getting looser from the body. The constant pulling and biting finally paid off. Within moments, the head was completely separated from the body. Lewis cried with all his might as he threw the victims head at Wolfgang's feet.

Wolfgang developed a full and hearty laugh. He kicked the victim's head with his foot, moving it halfway across the room. Marci said nothing as she stood there enjoying the performance. Lewis was lying in his victim's blood, only supporting his upper body with his long arms drenched in blood. He buried his head in his chest as deeply as he could. He cried like a little boy over spilling his milk as the blood from his victim continued to seep out of the headless torso.

Wolfgang started to clap his large, beastly hands together saying, "Bravo, Lewis. Well done. Good fight. You are the winner."

Lewis continued to cry. Large tears continued to roll out of his eye. Lewis spoke in a shattered voice, "Help me. Help me!"

Wolfgang's good mood quickly turned to anger. He shouted, "Help me? You just dammed me a minute ago, you pathetic excuse for a man." Wolfgang walked slowly over to a large chest and bent down and opened the lid. He reached inside and pulled out two long, metal spikes, which resembled railroad spikes, in one hand. He picked up a large, oversized hammer with his other hand. My heart raced as I had an idea what my father was about to do. Marci reached over and held my hand tightly. I sensed that she was very excited as well.

My father's heavy footsteps on the rock lined floor made a wonderful thumping sound at every step he took toward Lewis. The metal spikes clanging together only added to the natural, symphonic hymn. My senses were on fire and so were my father's. We both heard the music that was being made. I experienced the buildup like any classical music work would demonstrate before the musical piece reaches its climatic level.

Lewis said in a desperate voice, "What are you doing? Leave me alone! Leave me alone!" He moved around on the floor like a snake. Blood was everywhere. This moment was like a classic, operatic moment that one can only enjoy from experience and can never be fully explained by a third party. Greatness is only witnessed and then felt. Words within the context only add to the climactic moment. Words that are spoken outside of the performance only ruin the scene.

My Marci stood motionless. She wanted to say something, but she couldn't because the moment didn't allow her to speak. My perfect lover understood what a special theatrical performance was about to be displayed in its complete entirely. She understood how rare the moment was for her to witness this metaphoric marriage of the innermost evil that was about to be demonstrated by this monumental being. This was a moment that doesn't normally happen in one's life. My love understood the beauty and the complexity of watching and being a participant in a moment that in many people's view, is only reserved for their God.

Without speaking a word, Wolfgang made his way to Lewis's mutilated body. Lewis was lying on his belly. Wolfgang took his foot and flipped him over onto his back. Wolfgang quickly but calmly made his way in front of Lewis. He threw his right leg and large body onto Lewis's chest. He allowed one of the spikes to hit the ground while still holding onto the other one. Lewis's arms were pushing on Wolfgang, trying to stop him from the inevitable. Wolfgang positioned his body as a shield to keep one of Lewis's arms out of the way. Wolfgang calmly took hold of Lewis's arm and forcefully pushed it down on the cold rock of the floor of the cave. Wolfgang expertly positioned his arms and legs to control Lewis.

Wolfgang positioned the spike he had in his large hand and placed the tip of the spike into the top of Lewis's wrist. Lewis was screaming as loud as he could, and I could hear his voice starting to quiver as he was losing control over his emotions. Wolfgang quickly raised his metal hammer and expertly lowered the object onto the metal spike. The spike entered Lewis's wrist. Within moments, a second strike of the hammer hit the spike, further moving it through the wrist. Before Lewis could take another breath, a third and then a fourth blow drove the spike deep inside the rock floor under the back of his hand. Lewis was at his breaking point. The metal spike was now firmly secured to the floor of the cave. The spike went into the rock several inches. Lewis was shouting and spitting saliva. Wolfgang stopped for a moment as a large smile developed on his face and then he began to laugh. He was truly enjoying this moment of torture.

Wolfgang raised his eight foot plus frame onto his feet, but he kept his large foot on Lewis's unpinned arm. Wolfgang picked up the other spike and positioned himself along Lewis's body. He held Lewis's arm to the cold rock and proceeded to nail the spike into the wrist before him. Like the other wrist, it only took four blows from the hammer to complete the task.

Wolfgang got up and stepped away from the helpless, restricted body. Lewis was crying for mercy. He wanted and needed his pain to disappear. At first, he instinctually moved his arms to get away from the pain, but the pain was so intense, he couldn't keep from moving. The more he moved, the more the pain increased.

Lewis's legs were useless from the knees down. Every movement he made caused increasing pain throughout his body. The pain was so great that he spontaneously arched his back with the hope that movement would alleviate the pain, but it was useless. He had to endure the pain for however long his owner's wishes prevailed. Lewis was my father's pet, a half human, half beast of a pet. He never saw Lewis any other way.

Marci moved toward our victim. She moved across the cold, damp ground as if she was going to make love to him. Her hips rocked from side to side in an intoxicating manner that even Wolfgang noticed. She stopped a few feet from Lewis and bent down, with her legs spread apart and her arms on both of her legs near her knees. She leaned forward and looked Lewis straight in his pathetic eye. She moved her hand to her mouth and placed her thumbnail to her front teeth. She rolled her eyes upward and shook her head then looked down at Lewis and said, "You're pathetic. You know that don't you?"

Within seconds, Marci's mood changed. Her smile and laughter immediately turned to pure hatred. She said, "You piece of fucking shit. You never liked me. You were always against me and the love of my life. You never wanted me in did you?" As she leaned even closer, Lewis was nervously shaking his head from side to side, trying to say the word no but he was in too much pain to even talk.

Marci looked up at my father who was standing there, trying to process what he was seeing. I sensed he was confused. He found her attractive from the start, I could sense it, but now he interested in her. She impressed him, which is a very difficult task to accomplish. Somehow, Marci knew she was affecting him. Wolfgang knew it and so did everyone in the cave. My father now totally understood what I saw in Marci, a special human being.

Marci's eyes looked as if they danced when she said to my father, "So, what are your plans for this miserable piece of shit?"

Wolfgang smiled and said, "I was thinking I would leave that up to you."

Marci, without looking away, smiled at my father and jumped up quickly. She bounced a couple of times on her tips of her toes. She stepped over the right arm of Lewis, all the while looking down at him and smiling. Her smile then turned into a giggle. Marci said to Wolfgang, "What do you have? You know... I don't like this bastard. I want him to suffer but I want us to go home. I just want to end this. So, what do you have for me?"

Wolfgang stepped over to the wall on the opposite side of the cave's large area. Marci saw something leaning up against the wall. She walked quickly over to the object, even passing Wolfgang's long stride. She quickly picked up the long-handled object that looked like long scissors. The scissor end had small blades and looked like a pruning device for trees. The contraption was old and rusty. She had a difficult time trying to move the blades at first, but after a few times, the excess rust flaked off the blades and it was easier to move. Marci looked at Wolfgang and said, "Can I try this one out?"

Wolfgang nodded and said, "Do what you wish."

Marci walked over to Lewis and stood by his side. She was uncomfortably close to Lewis for my liking, but I knew that Lewis couldn't harm her. Marci looked at me and smiled then her smile evaporated from her face. She looked at me with sad eyes, asking me for my approval by uttering the words, "Can I?"

I looked at her beautiful, longing face, like a little girl wanting candy in a candy shop. How could I refuse? I smiled and looked down at Lewis and said, "You bastard. We could have had everything. At one time I thought you were my friend, part of my family. Then I learned all you saw in me was some freak, an experiment. You never really cared for me, much less loved me. That is really all I ever wanted. I just wanted someone to love me. You and Trevor only cared about one thing – the eternal fountain of youth. You pulled me into that trap. You made me what I am. I left you here because I had no choice. My father was never going to allow you to leave with me. I might have had a small chance to talk him out of it, but your rant was too much for me to forget or forgive. You hurt me Lewis. I don't like it when people hurt me. So, here we are. I need you out of my life, Lewis. I am sorry it did not work out. Marci... do what you need to rid us of this being."

Lewis said, "Garrison! Help me! It hurts. It hurts."

Listening to what he was saying angered me. Marci knew it. She could see it in my face. I said, "It's always about you, Lewis. You really are one fucked up person."

I looked at Marci and nodded my head. She smiled and gave me a wink, rolled her head back a little, then rolled her head to the other side of her shoulders. She looked at Wolfgang and smiled the looked down at Lewis. He said to her, "Fuck you, bitch! Go ahead and kill me! Put me out of my horrible existence!"

Marci said with a smile, "Horrible existence? Lewis, you amaze me. I want to be you. I mean, not you now, but you before all of this." Marci laughed then suddenly she became serious. She said, "How does it feel to be perfect? I always wanted to be perfect, but it's not possible for me. I tried and tried to play the violin perfectly, but I always mess up. Always! I hate that. You know what I mean? I hate when I see the love of my life standing over there hurting because of someone like you! You hurt him!"

Marci stepped around Lewis and stood near the top of his head. She lowered the iron clippers toward his right ear, opening the clippers and placing the long, twitching ear between the blades. Lewis moved his head from side to side. Marci lost her patience with him and placed her seductive feet on each side of his head to brace it as tight as she could. She placed his ear in the clippers once again. "You hurt me when you hurt him. No one hurts my Garrison." She quickly closed the clippers, and to Marci's amazement, the blades easily cut through the soft tissue of Lewis's ear. The ear found its way to the cave floor. Lewis was screaming even harder now. Without missing a beat, Marci said, "Well... that was easy. I am having so much fun. What about you, Lewis... huh? No, not so much."

Marci's face scrunched up and she slightly moved her head back and forward as if to agree with herself by gesturing no. She proceeded to cut off the other ear, only this time it was much quicker. Again, a loud cry from Lewis.

Marci said, "Will you shut up? God, your whining is getting on my nervous." She kept looking at him, studying him with her feet on his earless head as she adjusted the clippers in her hand. Marci's face turned serious as she quickly moved the clippers back, and with a little force she slammed the clippers into Lewis's mouth. In the process, she broke most of his front teeth. Her feet were losing their hold on Lewis's head, so Marci quickly took the clippers, opened the blades up, and forced the tip of the blades inside of his mouth. Marci said, "You need to learn to stop talking so much. Blah, blah, blah, blah, blah. That is all I hear from you." She rooted around his mouth and out of frustration, she started using the blades, attempting to cut his tongue out of his mouth. She was not having any success, but she sliced his tongue multiple times.

There was so much blood inside the mouth of his wolf-life muzzle that it was pouring out onto the floor, adding to the existing large puddle of warm, red liquid. She worked and worked and finally removed a good portion of his tongue. She looked at her work and seemed pleased. Lewis was spitting out blood as fast as he could. She removed her sexy little feet which now were covered in blood.

Wolfgang stood there smiling the entire time. He looked at me and said, "This is some woman you have here, Garrison."

Marci said without looking up, "Oh... you haven't seen anything yet." Marci, without any hesitation, stepped over to the side of his body and placed the clippers on Lewis's old tattered belt that was holding up an old holey pair of pants that Lewis was wearing. She worked hard on trying to cut through the belt. Wolfgang noticed she was having trouble, so he walked over and helped her out. His strong hands easily caused the blades to cut through the belt. Marci then went to work and continued to cut down the pants until she exposed his manhood to everyone inside the cave.

Marci stood up to collect herself as she wiped her head with the back of her hand and placed both hands back on the clippers. She said, "Okay, Lewis. Hold still. This might hurt a little." Lewis was moving around on the floor, but with little use of his legs and arms, it made movement extremely painful. All Lewis could do was plead for either his life or for this evil woman to stop torturing him. I could not distinguish what he wanted. He was hard to understand.

Marci moved the blades of the clippers onto both sides of Lewis's penis. His manhood was long and thick. Black fur surrounded it with no distinguishable head that would resemble the human version. Marci quickly slammed the clippers together. Lewis screamed louder than he had that entire day. Marci noticed that during the clip, Lewis moved a little and part of his penis was just barely hanging on by its back portion. Marci said, "Damn it. I missed. Hold on, let me try again." Marci adjusted the clippers around the area that was previously sliced and she completed her second snip. This time the appendage was completely cut from the body. Blood was pouring everywhere.

Marci stepped back and admired the poor creature's pain. She seemed happy of sorts. Wolfgang was very impressed, proven by the large smile that appeared on his muzzle. He said, "You enjoy this, don't you?"

Marci looked at him from the corner of her eyes. She moved them back down to the subject and said, "Yes, sir. I do."

Wolfgang said, "Well, we need to end this. We have a long trip ahead of us. The truck will be ready tomorrow. We need to plan out our route."

Marci shook her head in agreement and said, "When is he going to die? I thought he would be dead by now."

I spoke up, "It has been my experience with my brother that the formula keeps the body alive longer than without it. The formula recreates the necessary cells and chemicals to help repair the defective cells, muscles or even tissue. The loss of blood is damning to the body and it could eventually kill the subject from the blood loss, but my brother was still alive with no arms and legs. The head must be separated from the body, which makes the blood turn cold, drastically affecting the formula's effectiveness. Thus, the result is the subject dies."

Wolfgang agreed with my theory. He went over to pick up a large, heavy axe. Marci walked toward him. She asked him if she could use it. Wolfgang handed her the axe. Marci walked over to Lewis and attempted to bring the axe over the head, but it was very heavy. Wolfgang reached for the axe to take it from her and Marci said, "No. I've got this." She positioned herself next to his head and with all her might, she tried to get the axe overhead. The axe only got past her shoulder level, but she continued. She did her best, and when she brought the axe down toward Lewis's neck, she put her weight behind it. As the axe came down, her aim was off and it slid sideways, causing the point of the axe to penetrate the collarbone area of his chest at a slant. The blade of the axe cut the thick layer of Lewis's skin, and the weight of the axe caused additional damage. Lewis again let out a pitiful cry for help. Marci picked up the axe, adjusted her feet and brought the axe down again with similar results. This time, the second cut was just above the first. Marci said, "Damn it. I can't get this thing to hit where I want it."

Wolfgang said, "Just take your time, aim, and come straight down."

Lewis was in complete agony. He moved his head from side to side, arched his back and slightly moved his shoulders. He did everything to make the pain to go away but that was impossible. Every one of his movements caused more pain for him. That was the purpose of nailing the spikes in his wrists.

Marci picked up the axe and this time she moved it back not as far and brought it down on Lewis's neck. Lewis's was now choking, and he could not catch his breath. A warm yet lonely feeling fell upon my being. This was going to be the end of Lewis. So many years we had spent together. Those years were forced on him by Trevor, which was beyond the doctor's control. Lewis never cared for me, especially over the past decade.

Marci then pulled the axe back and it came down again but this time it was in the same spot as before. We heard the bones crack and the body stopped moving. Marci started chopping the axe in short but fast stokes. After hearing the blade hit the rock floor a few times, Marci stopped. She stood up and swung the backside of the axe at the side of the large skull, pushing it away from the torso. Lewis was now officially dead.

Marci handed the axe to my father and slowly walked over to me with a sympathetic look on her stunning face. Droplets of blood covered her clothes and face. She reached out and hugged me. I placed my hand on her back and said, "Thank you."

Marci said, "You're welcome."

We turned in unison and walked slowly out of the room. I heard my father in the background, pulling up the spikes from the floor.

Chapter Four

*W*hen Marci and I went back to the main part of the cave, Zelda was there waiting to help Marci clean herself up from the blood splatter on her body and clothes. I cleaned up as best as I could while Zelda assisted Marci. It was strange seeing Zelda and Marci together. In the back of my mind I worried about her safety, but I never sensed that Marci was in a lot of danger. My parents liked her and that was one of the few things keeping her alive.

Marci seemed to be at peace with herself and the actions that she undertook. After she was cleaned, Zelda took all her clothes and undergarments outside of the cave to dry. Marci's beautifully sculpted body seemed to float across the wooden floors of my parents' home, although she was exhausted and needed to rest. Marci went to sleep as soon as she laid her naked body down on the hard wooden bench that was made as a couch. Zelda covered her up with a large, rather worn blanket.

The next day, at the first signs of early dawn, I woke my love up from her deep sleep. As Marci got dressed, I went over our plan with my parents for their trip to the States. Wolfgang was not taking many of his supplies with him. He took several notepads, along with a few items that he didn't show me that were in a large World War II leather backpack. My mother brought a few belongings along for the trip that consisted of some pictures and jewelry that my father had gotten for her from the Jews he tortured. My parents were not very emotional when it came to material things. They knew they were going to start a whole new life on this adventure and even though their past was special to them, they wanted a clean break.

Marci and I packed, and after a handshake from my father and a hug from my mother, we started on our way out of the forest. It was going to take a while before we would get to the end of the forest and back to the village. Wolfgang and Zelda, meanwhile, went on their way.

They were going in another direction, toward our lonely predetermined area near a road not often traveled. This forgotten dirt road led to the destination point where we were to meet, located on the opposite side of the forest from where the village was located.

Marci was determined not to stay the night. She walked alongside me and attempted to keep up with my fast pace through the dark and musky smell of the mysterious forest. The problem with walking through the forest was not just the heavy vegetation but the thickness of the air. Very little wind flew through the deeper part of the forest so the air had this pungent, earthy smell that you could almost cut with the knife. The musky smell seemed to be a combination of decaying and living leaves, trees, and plants.

It took a good part of the day and after many rest breaks, we finally came to the end of the forest. It was late dusk when we emerged from the forest line. We walked across the tall, grassy field that separated the forest from the village. I cast my eyes around but didn't see anyone out. I told Marci not to speak until we got back to our cottage. I didn't want people asking questions about where we had been.

We entered our cottage and the first thing Marci wanted was a shower. She quickly got out of her clothes and made her way to the bathroom. She moaned many times as the warm water caressed her beautiful, porcelain skin. The lucky drops of liquid found their way in places that only a king should explore.

Meanwhile, I unpacked and called Sonja to make sure she was going to pick us up at the cottage. Everything was going according to plan. After Marci's shower, she stepped out and dried off. She saw me ogling her most desirable body. She was so sexy standing there holding nothing but a towel that teasingly hid some of the most interesting areas of her body. She smiled and said, "Hi. I had a lot of fun today. Did you?"

I said with a corresponding smile, "Yes, I did. I am glad that you and my father get along."

Marci said, "Would he have killed me if we didn't get along?"

I said, "Within seconds. I was very worried, but I sensed that he would like you. You and he are, to some degree, similar by nature."

Marci laughed with her eyes looking briefly to the ceiling then back down at me. She walked toward me and gently brushed my arm with hers as she made her way to her bed. She spun herself around and fell onto the bed with her arms supporting her. She moved her leg up toward her shoulder as she allowed her body to rest on the bed sheet. Her hand snuck around her lovely and muscular thigh as her fingers found her vagina. Her other hand reached down in front of her stomach and found its way to her womanhood. She fingered herself as she lifted her leg straight up in the air while she moved the other leg over to the side. I made my way to her and knelt before her. I used my tongue to the best of my ability, and after several moments brought her to her climax.

I got my shower and returned to the bed. Marci was still exploring her womanhood. We made sweet love through a good part of the night. When she drifted off to sleep, I got up and stepped outside. I looked toward the forest from the porch of our cottage. I knew that I would never find myself back to this area anytime soon, if ever.

I took in all the forest's essence with all my senses. This was my birthplace. If not for my mother, I would not be here today. She saved my life the day she rescued me from my father. I understand why he did what he did to my other brothers. He didn't want people like me to escape and cause issues with the general population of ordinary humans. I believe, after all these years, he was proud of me and somewhere deep in his heart, he was glad that he didn't kill me when I was born.

The next morning, Marci awoke and prepared for our departure. Sonja picked us up on time and we placed our belongings in her car. We exchanged our pleasantries and told her that we'd had a wonderful time in the village. She drove us to this small storage business with a few moving trucks and storage units that were in the back of the business. Sonja went inside and paid the man behind the counter and collected the keys to the truck. We walked over to the vehicle and I went to the back of the truck. I opened the large rear door and, as instructed, there was a climate-controlled bay. Inside of the truck was a large shipping container that measured about six feet both in width and length. The height of the box was just about the height of my parents. I was surprised that Sonja didn't question me about my intended use of such a large shipping container. I felt that I needed to offer up some story as to why we need this vessel and why we were being so secretive so I told her that we had purchased many priceless works of art and some very expensive furniture. I wanted to keep these items close to me as much as possible. I told her to pay off as many people in customs as possible so we wouldn't have any shipping issues.

I closed the door of the truck and thanked Sonja for all her work. She told me that she had a private jet waiting at the airport for us. She instructed me where I needed to drive the truck to the jet then I could unload my contents into the rear of the plane. The airport would take the truck from there. Sonja also confirmed that when we got back to Louisville, there would be a storage truck waiting for us when we landed. She then handed me a considerable amount of money so I could tip the people that were helping me at the airports. I had many worries, but my biggest worry was someone seeing my parents. That couldn't happen. It would have been disastrous. The world would find them repulsive and I would lose them forever, and the secrets to the formula would be lost forever. My father, if ever captured, would die before he would ever reveal any information about how he transformed himself or any information about the formula.

Sonja told me that when I arrived in Louisville, a tall man with glasses would approach me. He was the person that we paid not to inspect the inside of the container on our arrival. We said our farewells to Sonja.

Marci and I got inside of the truck and drove to our destination per my father's instructions. Meeting up with my parents without a cell phone or even a predetermined rendezvous time was going to be a challenge. We drove down the long, quiet country road. The road was mostly made up of dirt and small rocks. Tall weeds littered the roadway. It was getting late in the evening, the sun was setting, and it was getting darker outside. I had my reservations about whether my parents made it to our meeting area. Wolfgang told me to drive until I saw a large dead tree that stuck out from the rest of the trees on the left side of the road. Marci helped me look for this tree. We slowly drove for a while so we wouldn't miss the landmark. I started to get a little anxious for I was not seeing the mark.

We drove about another mile and by that time it was pitch dark outside. I am fortunate that my night vision is outstanding. After another half mile or so, I believed that I found the landmark. I pulled the truck off the road and parked in front of the dead tree. I told Marci to stay inside the truck. I got out and looked around but saw and heard nothing. I felt confident this was the place though.

I stepped back inside of the truck and we waited. Marci fell asleep while I kept watch. After several hours, I heard some noise then I heard a baby crying. I knew it was my family. I got out of the truck and in the process, woke Marci. She followed me out of the truck. In the distance down the road, I saw my father. He noticed me immediately. He motioned for Zelda with my sister to follow him. When they made their way to me, I escorted them to the back of the truck. I opened the back door and said, "Well, this is the best I can do." Wolfgang was pleased with the accommodations. I showed him the shipping container that would be their transportation. I didn't want to risk the chance of my parents being seen, so we had to use the container to keep them hidden.

We stood around for a few hours, trying to waste some time. Marci went back inside and fell asleep. Wolfgang proceeded to tell me about the history of this road. He told me that the Nazi's used this road before the war started to transport tanks and armored personnel from the nearby city. Over time, thousands of Jews were transported along this road to a concentration camp that was not too far from where we were standing. His voice trailed off in a disappointed tone when he told me that after the war, the enemies destroyed the camp.

As the night turned to the morning hours, we decided to go to the airport. Sonja told me that any time after six in the morning was good for departure. I woke Marci and told her to help me with Eva. I asked Wolfgang to jump inside of the truck and help me. As he did, he caused the truck to rock back and forth as he was getting settled. I followed him into the back of the truck and asked him if he wanted to travel with the shipping container standing up or on its side. He told me that he wanted to travel with the container standing up. He got inside by way of a door that was located on the side. It was difficult for him to position his large body in the doorway. After he was in the container, he approved of his temporary home. I knew he was very apprehensive about this plan, but we knew of no other way to get him and his wife to the States unnoticed.

I jumped out of the truck and walked over to my mother while my father was getting out of the shipping container. I suggested to my mother that Eva should be with us always, and not with them. I said it would be safer for her, especially on this ride to the airport. After a long moment of hesitation, Zelda agreed for us to take my sister from her. I took Eva from my mother's arms and asked if Marci could hold her on the way to the airport and again, after an uncomfortable length of time, she finally agreed. I gave Eva to Marci. Marci was great with her from the start.

Wolfgang helped my mother into the back of the truck. The shipping container had small holes in the top of the container and along the sides. Wolfgang and Zelda got inside and to my surprise, they both fit rather comfortably. I'd had Sonja pack some supplies like water and some food, telling her it was for us on our long trip home. I closed the door of the shipping container and asked them if they were okay. They acknowledged they were fine so I gently closed and locked the large door of the truck.

Eva, Marci, and I got inside the front of the truck. I turned the truck around and drove to the airport. Eva quickly fell asleep in Marci's arms while I called the phone number that Sonja gave me for our point of contact at the airport.

When we got to the airport gate, we had to wait for a while. I was nervous that they might want to view the contents of the truck. I had instructed Sonja to pay off the customs inspectors for me so we would bypass inspections both boarding in Germany and unloading in the States. I noticed an airport employee approach the truck. I rolled down the window and introduced myself. The man just nodded. He started to walk slowly back to the end of the truck. My heart was beating so fast that I thought it was going to explode. He looked around the back and side of the truck then came back to the driver's side door. He looked inside as best he could and said in broken English, "What is inside? What are you carrying?"

I swallowed hard and said, "I have furniture and some artwork that I bought." The guy stared at me for a while and smiled as he looked down at the clipboard he was holding. I was ready to make any moves necessary if he was going to ask to see what was inside. I would have hoped that Sonja would have done as I instructed in paying off the essential people. The guy pointed without looking up at me. He told me to follow a guy that was in a motorized flatbed cargo vehicle. I eased the truck through the open gates and followed instructions from the guy in the cargo vehicle. We slowly made our way to the jet. The jet was large and spacious. The trip was going to cost me a small king's ransom, but there was no other way to secretly deliver my parents to the States.

I stopped the truck and instructed Marci to distract the men on the flatbed. Marci stepped out of the front of the truck and bounced baby Eva in her arms. The guys looked at Marci who entertained them as a forklift came toward us. I instructed the driver to carefully pick the container up and place it inside of the jet. The shipping container was on what looked like a pallet for easy moving. The driver skillfully moved the large vessel and placed it gently in the cargo section of the jet as instructed. I tipped the driver heavily and he drove back to a garage in the airport. I quickly went inside of the cargo area of the jet and asked my parents if they were doing well. Wolfgang said they were fine. I quickly left them, and Marci and I boarded the plane with Eva.

It is amazing what money can buy, especially if you know the right people. After an hour, we finally took off and were in the air headed home. I felt a great sense of liberation as soon as the wheels were up off the ground. I looked over at my Marci and my sister. Our eyes met and we smiled as one. Not one word was said between the two of us. We had pulled this off.

It was a long flight home although we were fortunate to have a direct flight into Louisville. Eva was hungry, so we fed her some food and milk that Zelda had prepared for us. After she was fed, she slept. The sound and movement of the plane aided her sleep for most of the trip. When we landed, I made sure to supervise the shipping container as it was placed into the moving van. As per my instructions, the moving van came around the corner of the building and pulled up next to the back of the jet. Now we had to negotiate with airport security.

I noticed the tall, thin man with glasses that Sonja mentioned. He walked up to me and introduced himself as Al. He allowed us to bypass the inspection of our luggage, the rest of our supplies inside of the plane, and the shipping container. The airport people checked our passports. He told me that everything was good to go. At this point, everything went according to plan.

I looked over my shoulder and saw a large moving truck coming our way. The truck stopped close to the back of the plane. A man of small stature slid out of the front of the truck, went to the back, and opened the large door. Again, a forklift took the large vessel that was sitting in the plane's cargo area and placed it in the rear of the moving van. I closed the large rear door, shook Al's hand, and tipped him heavily. He seemed to be very nervous but happy that our transaction was complete. I loaded up Marci and Eva and the rest of our luggage into the front of the truck then got behind the wheel of the van. We were escorted by a small cargo flatbed vehicle as we slowly made our way out of the airport. As we got closer to the exit of the airport, the cargo vehicle pulled over and the driver waved us by. Finally, we were free from all possible obstructions. I found my way to the interstate and we were on our way home.

The drive home took about an hour. It seemed that we had been gone for a month. I could hardly wait to get my parents home. It was getting late in the evening. During our ride home, I called Carolyn at the estate. She was surprised to hear from me. I said we would be home in a few minutes. Carolyn asked, "Is Lewis still alive?"

I said, "We will talk about Lewis when I got home. Carolyn, I have something to tell you and you are not going to like what I have to say. I don't want you to be upset so please calm down and prepare yourself. I have my parents with me. They are going to live with us."

Carolyn gasped on the other end of the phone. She said, "Do what? You have your parents with you and you're bringing them here?"

"Yes, Carolyn. I don't want you to say anything that will upset them. They are going to live in the basement. I have everything set up for them. My father will have use of the laboratory and my mother will have a place of her own as well. Please… don't worry. They will not harm you." Carolyn didn't make a sound on the other end of the phone. I said, "I will see you in a few minutes and will tell you everything."

Carolyn said in a low whisper, "Lewis is dead isn't he?"

I said, "I am sorry, Carolyn. You and I knew that he could not last long in that cave. I will talk more about it when I get home. Goodbye, Carolyn."

When I hung up the phone, Marci started to laugh as she was holding Eva. She said, "So, are you going to tell her the truth or are you going to make up something?"

I said, "I don't know, Marci. I do not know what I am going to do."

Marci said, "Oh please, let me tell her."

I quickly said, "No, Marci. I still love Carolyn. I do not want to see her hurt. I will just tell her that he dead."

Marci said, "You know that Wolfgang isn't going to go along with any lies, right?"

I swallowed hard and said, "Yeah… you are right. I forgot about my father."

Marci eagerly said, "So please, let me tell her. I will be nice about it."

I said, "Fine, but please be nice about it. I beg you, Marci. Please be respectful to her feelings."

Marci smiled and said, "I will."

Of course, I knew she wouldn't, but what was I going to do? I could not really stop her from doing what she wanted.

We approached the front of the estate. I called Carolyn and she opened the gates. The large **S** slowly split in two halves as the gates opened and I slowly drove the truck up the long, winding road. I felt like I did when I first took my Marci to see the estate. Marci, as if on cue, said the exact same thing to me as we drove. The sun was now setting off in the distance as I pulled the truck to the front of the house. I parked the truck and got out, taking a good look around to see if anyone could see me. Thankfully, the estate is far off the road and we are well hidden from our neighbors.

I hurried to the back of the truck and opened the large door. I said to my parents, "We are home. We are safe here. There is no one around." Within a few seconds, I opened the door of the shipping container. Wolfgang stepped out of the vessel, followed by Zelda. She wiped her large wolf-like head with her hand. They were both glad to get out of their confided, cramped little space. My parents stood looking out at the lush green grass of my front yard. I said, "Do not worry. No one can see you. We are exceptionally well hidden. We live in a very private area."

Wolfgang was cautious as he slowly moved toward the opening of the truck. Zelda held back a little but followed her husband's lead. Wolfgang came as far as he could to the edge of the truck. He looked down and took his first step onto the bumper of the van. He let his body fall forward as both of his large feet hit the ground. He stood there taking in his new surroundings then turned around and helped Zelda get out of the van. She copied my father every step of the way.

I said to my parents, "I know this is all new to you. This is like the future to you. You are going to experience different sounds, smells and sights. Please do not be alarmed. I am here to help you. Please, I must ask that you not make a lot of noise. You might draw attention from the neighbors. I doubt you will, but just to be on the safe side of things. I have a lady that lives with us. Her name is Carolyn, the one I told you about a few nights ago. She has been with me since I was a little boy. I warned her that I was bringing you home, but I know that she is not prepared for what she is about to see. Please do not be offended, but your appearance is hard to accept for anyone who is not used to seeing the effects of the formula. Okay, are you guys ready?"

My father was scared, which was a great surprise to me. I could sense his nervousness. He knew that I sensed his feelings and he didn't like it when others had the upper hand. He put on a false bravado to reestablish his confidence and masculinity. I knew it was going to be difficult for a man who had had so much control over his personal environment for over one hundred twenty-five years to be taken out of that environment and thrust into a new and strange world. A world that was completely different from his wildest dreams. A futuristic world that was so strange that all his senses were operating at the highest level to process his surroundings.

We stepped away from the truck and Wolfgang walked out onto the grass, with Zelda holding his large, hairy hand. He bent his knees to stoop down and ran his long and thick fingers across the grass. He then made a fist and pulled up as much grass as he could. He stood up and looked at the evidence from this new, futuristic world that he now occupied. He brought the blades of grass with both of his hands to his muzzle. He smelt the grass and then allowed Zelda to smell the grass in his hands. Zelda smiled and moaned. Wolfgang turned to me with a smile on his face and said, "It has been almost a century and a half since we have experienced grass of this nature, a grass lawn from a real house. It has been years since we have experienced this pleasure."

I said, "Now you can experience this and much more every day for as long as you wish. I share this lawn, this grass, this house, and everything that I have with you guys." Wolfgang and Zelda looked at me and smiled. The power of the unspoken word is stronger than words spoken. That moment exemplified that fact.

I took my parents on a tour. They were amazed at the size of the estate, the grounds, and the architecture. Wolfgang and Zelda couldn't keep their eyes off the house. They first wanted to see the entire outside area, so I took them in the back. They loved the large pool, the perfectly trimmed lawn, and the thick woods that served as the perfect backdrop. I showed Wolfgang the lawn area where the grass was greener than the rest of the yard. I pointed out how it had grown over the years. We all walked to the spot where my adoptive mother killed herself. I told them that the formula that was in her blood went into the ground. This area of grass, once as large as a garage can lid, was greener and thicker than its surrounding area. Over time, this patch of perfectly manicured grass became larger and now encompassed over half of the back yard.

I walked them toward the four trees where my brother's body parts were laid to rest. I pointed out how these three trees had grown in just a few years compared to the other trees in the forest that had been there for decades. I showed them how tall the trees were and how thick the leaves were. Zelda and Wolfgang were very interested as they held onto my every word.

I showed them the grave markers of my adoptive family, along with Trevor's father. Wolfgang and Zelda looked over the valley of trees in the distance. They were very impressed with the grounds. After several quiet moments admiring the views, we headed back to the house. I noticed Carolyn was in the window of the kitchen, looking at us. When I noticed her, she quickly moved out of sight. I knew she was scared about meeting my parents and, of course, she was anxious about knowing what happened to Lewis.

After several minutes, we were at the back door of the house. I went in and Marci followed me. Marci held the door for Wolfgang and Zelda to enter. They slowly made their way inside. The opening of the door was very small compared to them. They stood in the kitchen area, admiring the latest futuristic appliances they had never seen before. They didn't say a word. Zelda loved the kitchen. It had been so long since she had seen a fully functioning kitchen. I told them I would help them get acquainted with their new, modern lifestyle.

Wolfgang glanced over into the great room. He then quickly walked toward the room. He said, "What is this room called?"

I said, "It is called a great room or a family room."

Wolfgang said, "It's very large. Nice."

We walked into the room together. Over in the corner was Carolyn. Wolfgang noticed her immediately. Carolyn was visibly shaken. I hurried over to her and said, "Carolyn, I want to introduce to you my parents. They will not hurt you."

Carolyn froze. She could not keep her eyes off Wolfgang. Marci came in with Zelda as Carolyn's eyes quickly glanced at Zelda holding Eva. Carolyn nervously said, "A baby."

I told Carolyn, "I want you to meet my sister, Eva. She is my parents' little girl. She is formed like me."

Carolyn's head was shaking in disgust and fear at the same time. She didn't know what to say or how to say it without offending the people in the room. Carolyn couldn't stop looking at Zelda holding Eva. I was concerned that her stares might cause a negative response from my parents. I attempted to distract my parents' attention from Carolyn. I said, "Let me show you the rest of the house."

Abruptly, Carolyn started to speak, "What is this? Who are you people? What happened to you? A baby! Is it normal?"

Without a second to rest, Wolfgang stepped toward Carolyn at breakneck speed. His large hand grabbed Carolyn's shirt and his large hand made a fist with Carolyn's shirt, intertwined with his long fingers. He roughly pulled Carolyn closer to him. Wolfgang said, "Normal? Is that what you said, woman? Normal. I would be more careful if I were you in choosing your words."

Carolyn didn't know what to say. She was shaking from fear. Wolfgang released his hold and walked away, never breaking eye contact with her. Then Eva started to cry. That broke the tension and Carolyn fainted. I was not able to catch her fall. I hurried toward her limp body, picked her up, and placed her on one of the couches in the room. Marci stood near Zelda and Eva during this whole time as she smiled and snickered through most of this stressful moment.

Marci took my parents and showed them the rest of the first floor and the upstairs. I stayed with Carolyn, and when she came to, I told her to keep her mouth shut and not to upset them. She cried hard in my arms. I knew this was upsetting to her. I could only imagine what she was going through. The shock of seeing seven and eight-foot-tall hairy, wolf-like creatures standing and walking in the house you have called home for decades is rather daunting. In addition, seeing and hearing a "normal" looking child they had created had to be confusing and disturbing.

After several minutes, Marci returned with my parents. Wolfgang said, "She showed us the spot in your father's library where you came full circle."

I knew what he was referring to – when I ate my first animal, a small dog named Snowy. I smiled at my father and he returned my gesture. I suggested my parents follow me to the basement and escorted them down the wooden steps. I first showed them the lab which was located on the right side of the stairs. The stairs lead to a wide landing with large doors on both sides. The left side was a suite made up of a bedroom, kitchen, bathroom, and a large family room. This was the area where Lewis had lived. The right side of basement was the lab area, complete with cells and the crematory machine.

I first took him into the laboratory. When Wolfgang's eyes first saw the lab, he was beside himself. He loved what he saw. I told him he could use it whenever he wanted, and that this lab is now part his. He was most impressed by the crematory machine.

Marci then added to the showing as she told him how we executed the bum and his three sons. Wolfgang was noticeably impressed. He loved the hospital bed and the cells with attached toilets. He called it a perfect place to conduct our kind of experiments.

After the tour of the lab, I said, "Now, let me show you guys your new living quarters. You have the rest of the house at your disposal, of course, but this is where I thought you would like to sleep and relax. A place you can call your own, so to speak. If you don't like it, I have many rooms upstairs."

As I was walking out, we noticed Carolyn standing next to the entrance. She was not happy. She was visibly upset. Her quivering voice shouted, "What happened to Lewis? Did you people kill him?" We didn't know how to respond, but Marci started to laugh. Her laughter was too loud and long for the situation. Carolyn's eyes instinctually moved to Marci and quickly became angry at her callousness.

Marci seductively moved toward Carolyn. I attempted to stop Marci, but she pushed me away. Marci angrily told her with a smile on her face, "He's dead. Wolfgang transformed him, making him perfect. Then the son of a bitch didn't appreciate the gift that was given to him. With Wolfgang's help, I killed him. I murdered your pathetic excuse for a boyfriend or should I say, your imaginary boyfriend." Marci laughed loudly and continued her rant, "He didn't know you even loved him. Oh, and by the way, he had a small cock!"

Carolyn said, "You bitch. Why are you such a bitch?"

Marci shouted, "You're the bitch! You tried to come between me and Garrison. I will never forgive you for that, you fucking cunt."

Carolyn angrily pointed to me saying, "He's evil. He has always been evil."

Marci said with even more anger, "He is not evil, you fucking slut!"

I had to hold Marci back with most of my might. She wanted to tear into Carolyn. I never saw Marci so angry. Marci screamed back, "Guess what! Do you know how I killed him? Can you fucking guess how I did it? We tricked him into thinking he was coming back home with us by forcing him to kill another man. Then after he did it, we nailed spikes into his wrists to a cave floor. I cut his fucking ears off, cut his tongue out of his head, and cut his little dick off. I then cut his ugly ass head off with an axe and kicked it after I separated the horrid thing from his body."

Carolyn suddenly came after Marci vigorously. She quickly hit Marci in the head as I was holding my love. I had to let her go and somehow, I grabbed Carolyn. Marci stormed back and started beating Carolyn in the head with her fist. I pushed Marci away while my father just stood there. I yelled at Wolfgang, "Can you help me?"

Wolfgang reached out and grabbed Marci by the waist. He picked her up like a small bag of potatoes and carried her to the other side of the room with Marci kicking and screaming the whole time. Carolyn just broke down in my arms, and within moments she was pounding me on my chest for release. She said while yelling and crying, "You son of a bitch. You let this happen to him. Why didn't you stop it? You wanted him dead since you killed your own brother. You evil bastard." I let her go and she ran out of the room and up the wooden stairs.

Marci was still upset and yelling, "Let me go! Let... me... go!"

Wolfgang let her go and she ran toward the door. I stopped Marci and tried to calm her down, but she was out of control. I held her arms tightly and attempted to look her in the eye. I said, "Marci! Marci! Calm down... Marci!" She started to struggle less. I said, "Calm down! She is gone. It is over. Let it go."

Marci finally controlled her emotions and said to me, "It's not over. This is not over. I hate that bitch!" I let my love go and she stood there breathing heavy. Her breasts were moving with every deep but short breath as strands of her golden hair fell out of place. Her eyes steamed with a hateful yet sexy passion. Suddenly, she started to smile, followed by a giggle. After a moment or two, she rolled her head back and laughed a little harder. Her eyes got large and bright as she looked at me lustfully. She said, "Jesus, I am so turned on right now."

Wolfgang smiled and looked over at Zelda. Zelda smiled at him and shook her large head in bewilderment as she held Eva closer to her large breast.

Chapter Five

As the weeks passed, Marci and I helped my parents adapt to their new world. We taught them everything; from the new appliances in the kitchen, the electronics throughout the estate, and, of course, the lab. Wolfgang and Zelda were a little overwhelmed with all the new technology that was available. One of the more difficult moments for my parents was watching documentaries on cable about the end of World War II. They couldn't understand why people made Hitler out to be a monster. They, of all people, believed that the human race needed to be pure. That was one of the main reasons for Wolfgang's basic existence under the Nazi regime.

My mother loved to read. When she was in the cave, she didn't have any books to read so when she came to our house, she was mystified by the countless number of books I had for her disposal. I could immediately tell how she missed her reading. It was hard to believe that for over one hundred years, she never read a sentence while she was in the cave.

Throughout her past life, Zelda would read anything and everything, but she especially loved horror novels. She always laughed at the ironic twists to the love affairs humans had with that literary genre. One of the first activities that she started when she moved in was to pick up a book and start to read books from my library. Of course, she could read at breakneck speed, and could finish a long book within a couple of hours.

Zelda also loved to cook. She wanted to cook for the family, but Marci couldn't eat some of the dishes that she prepared. This didn't offend Zelda. She knew that Marci couldn't eat uncooked meat from a wild animal, but she did eat some of Zelda's cooked meals. Since my parents and I don't eat cooked meat of any sort, the cooked meats were not appealing to us. This didn't go over well with Carolyn. In fact, Carolyn never ate with us. She thought it was disgusting. I will give

Marci all the credit in the world. She never missed a meal with me and my parents. My parents took notice of this fact right away and were appreciative of Marci's strong stomach.

Wolfgang and I spent a lot of time in my lab. We watched all the films on each one of the experiments that I had recorded for documentation purposes. Wolfgang was beyond impressed. He told me that I did things that he didn't even think about doing when he was experimenting with the Jews.

We spoke a lot about the past experiments that he conducted during World War II, many times at the dinner table. Marci always seemed to be extremely interested in hearing the stories. Wolfgang was getting very close to Marci emotionally. He was letting her in, which was very rare. Wolfgang told her that she had a personality that was rarely seen. Few people share her passion for life and death. She had a unique type of personality that was like a trained assassin or a person that doesn't show remorse for others' suffering. In fact, she enjoyed seeing others in pain. Wolfgang was good at reading people since he had a vast amount of experience in dealing with humans. He knew that Marci was special, and at times I think he was more impressed with her than with me. I was glad this was the case because if he didn't like her, she would be dead by now.

Marci would come down to the lab and just hang out with us from time to time although most of the subjects that were being discussed were too advanced for my Marci to comprehend completely. My father and I were discussing some figures from an experiment that I performed on the birth of the newborns from Mary, the homeless lady. Marci was sitting next to me, trying to take in as much information as possible.

Wolfgang started talking about Eva. My heart sank somewhat every time Eva was brought up in a conversation. I hadn't told Marci what my father wanted me to do to Eva when she got to a proper age. I was going to tell her, but I never made the time. As Wolfgang talked, the taboo subject started to rear its ugly head. We were talking about mating the two bums and then the creation of Eva.

Marci asked Wolfgang, "Why did your kids come out as the perfect image of a human and not pick up the traits of you or Zelda with the obvious transferred state of wolf-like features mixed with human features?"

Wolfgang said, "I actually don't understand that myself. I can see where the imperfect cell make-up of a non-infected subject would have a more severe reaction to a subject that is infected with the formula. The formula is attempting to correct the imperfectness of the non-infected subject and vice versa. The cells are... confused, for lack of a better word. They attack each other, and this causes a chemical reaction that changes the bodies' cell make-up, thus changing the physical appearance."

"Since Zelda and I both have the formula in our cell make-up, the formula recognizes and accepts the familiar cells when the woman's egg is fertilized. It was a shock at first when Zelda gave birth to her children and they all came out as human. The only theory I have is the basic innate cells, or DNA, is buried in all of us humans. I believe there is a particular DNA strand that cannot be altered by the formula. If this is the case, the more traditional physical appearance of a human is undisturbed."

"The formula only reacts when it is introduced to a subject that the formula doesn't exist in. The formula in a female subject basically recognizes the formula from a male subject. Semen is a carrier of the formula, but the formula from the women identifies with the familiar formula from the male's bodily fluids. The formula cannot and will not attack the cell make-up of each other. It will only grow and enhance the cells to make the imperfect subject, perfect."

Marci was impressed with his answers. She said, "When Zelda got pregnant, did you think you would have children that would come out like Garrison or did you think they might be like Adam?"

Wolfgang said, "To tell you the truth, Zelda getting pregnant was a mistake, or I should say an accident, that was not supposed to have happened. We went over one hundred years without getting pregnant. For whatever reason, this time was different. Zelda didn't know she was pregnant until a month after we had intercourse. She started to feel funny and felt movement inside of her stomach. I tried my best to examine her and I discovered multiple heartbeats. We discussed the situation and talked at great length about her pregnancy. I didn't want any children running around in the forest. Our life was simple and I enjoyed that simplicity. I didn't want to operate on my wife, especially not in the cave. The conditions were not sanitary. We decided that Zelda was to give birth to them and I was to kill the offspring. After I killed the babies, Zelda stopped me when I came to Garrison. I remember I had him by the leg and his body was up to my chest. I was going to throw him down on the ground and step on his head like I did the others. Zelda reached out to me and stopped me. I gave her Garrison and she told me she wanted to kill him herself. I left the room and I assumed that she killed him. Somehow, she wrapped him up in a blanket and took him out to the place where he was found."

I sat there listening to my father telling us this story. My heart sank at the thought of how close I was to death. I don't hold that against my father. For the first time in my life, I understood his position at that time. When my father finished his story, Marci asked him, "Then why did you have Eva? Was she the only one in the current pregnancy?"

My father, without blinking an eye, said, "When Lewis first came to see me, I was angry at Zelda for not disposing of the baby... Garrison. Then Lewis told me how remarkable Garrison was after he had grown up. I knew that if I killed Lewis at that time, I would probably have a lesser chance of ever seeing Garrison in person. I wanted to meet my offspring. So, I allowed Lewis to live. I knew he would come back. I can read people well. I know what they are going to do before they do."

"I was not surprised to see Lewis return, but I was a little surprised to see Garrison. I thought it was my child when I first saw him in the woods." Wolfgang looked at me and pointed his long finger toward my chest, "I tracked you and Lewis for a few miles before I made my presence known to you that night. I thought it was you. When I had it confirmed, I wanted to talk to you. After talking to you, I knew you were special. At that moment, I thought of mating with your mother again and hopefully having the same result... a completely normal looking, human offspring. I had little doubt that we wouldn't, but I had to know if we could create another child that looked completely human, like you. After the birth of the additional offspring, we decided to keep one girl and only one girl. I knew you would be back. I sensed it. I knew that you couldn't leave Lewis there, not knowing whether he was dead or alive. I also sensed the longing in your heart for closure. I knew you missed having a family – your natural born family, not some adoptive family that you experienced in your youth."

Wolfgang got up and continued, "I have an eternity to live my life. I have all the time in the world. Being in that cave for so long a time makes a person wonder. I wondered if I had stumbled onto the answer of eternal youth by accident. That perfection can only be created.

Obviously, complete and total mental and physical perfection cannot be achieved by way of the formula only. It changed me physically. But you, Garrison, came out perfect, both mentally and physically. So, I wanted to see if my theory, that we discussed in the cave, would work."

Marci said, "What theory?"

I straightened up and cleared my throat. Wolfgang knew at that moment I hadn't told Marci what my father's plans were. Wolfgang looked at me and back at Marci. I just sat there wishing the subject hadn't come up. Wolfgang knew I wasn't going to volunteer any information, so he said, "So, Garrison didn't tell you our plan?"

Marci looked over at me with a slightly mad look and said, "No. He did not." Her icy stare was difficult to experience.

Wolfgang said, "Well, our plan is simple. It is our theory that both Garrison and Eva are perfect in almost every way, or at least as perfect as a human could be. I started thinking – what if those two perfect humans would mate and have a child? Our theory is that their child would be perfect as well. The offspring would have the same formula and cell structure as Garrison and Eva, so the chemicals and cells should not attack each other. It is our hope that the offspring would come out like them or more refined, if that is possible. Thus, we have a new species that is created – the perfect human species. It is what my Fuhrer had always dreamt about, the perfect human. I think I have finally done it; I have created the eternal fountain of youth in my children."

Marci just sat there in shock. She didn't know what to say. She looked at me again with a look that I had never seen from her toward me – anger. She said, "So, what the fuck are you going to do with your sister, Garrison?"

I just sat there, growing more uncomfortable by the moment. Wolfgang's face turned very serious. Even he felt the anger in the room. I looked at my Marci. She was hurt and angry at the same time. I had to say something so I said, "When we were in the cave, my father broached the idea to me about Eva and me mating, thus creating a child together. In theory, Eva should bear a perfect child with no effects of inbreeding. I am not looking forward to the act itself, but in the name of science I believe that the deed has to be accomplished."

Wolfgang said, "There is no other recourse. The mating experiment must happen. Is there a problem, Marci?"

For the first time, my father called my lovely Marci by her name. Marci looked at him as if she was scared, but anger was still present in her heart. She said in a broken voice, "I... it's not every day that you hear that your love has decided to fuck his own sister. That is not something you just accept lightly." Marci's eyes looked angrily into Wolfgang's. Wolfgang snarled and then let out a low growl, but Marci didn't look away. She said in a hateful voice, "So, is that supposed to scare me?"

As soon as those words came off her lips, I quickly jumped from my chair and grabbed Marci. Wolfgang lunged toward her and his open mouth was inches from the back of my neck. Marci was not afraid, she was angry. I said, "Stop it! Stop it, you two. There are other ways around this."

Wolfgang took his large hand and grabbed my shoulder and spun me away from Marci. He pulled me toward him and said, "There is no other way!"

Marci went between us and placed her hands on both of our chests and tried to separate us. She said, "Get back!"

I said back to my father in great haste, "Yes there is! We don't have to mate! We can use my semen and inject it into her ovaries. I do not have to have sex with her."

Wolfgang said as he released me, "Fine. As long as the experiment takes place."

I said, "The experiment will take place."

Marci's face was now one of concern. My father released his hold on me and I stumbled back a few feet. Marci came over and hugged me. I said to her, "I am sorry, Marci. I should have told you our plans. I will not keep another secret from you again. But the only worry on my mind when we were in Germany was getting my parents back home. I am sorry."

Marci started to cry. She said, "I am sorry. I just got jealous. I am so sorry, my love."

She then turned and looked at Wolfgang. She went over to him and went to hug him. His large hand reached out and stopped her. She attempted to move it but to no avail. He quickly glanced at me and I squinted my eyes at him as if to say, let her go. He acknowledged my facial gesture and moved his arm down to his side. Marci then quickly went to him and put her arms around him. Wolfgang didn't know what to do. Marci said, "I am sorry, Wolfgang. I just get emotional at times. I am sorry." Wolfgang then did something I never thought he would do. He slowly moved his hand up toward Marci's back and gently hugged her. I had never seen my father display any form of emotion until that moment.

I wanted to speak but I allowed the moment to continue for a while. Then I said, "Well, that experiment is a while off. When it happens, Marci should assist me in my sperm donation."

Marci then laughed as her head was buried in my father's massive lower chest. Wolfgang snickered and put both his hands onto Marci's shoulders and pushed her away from him said, "I am sure you will do a good job at helping with the donating of your boyfriend's sperm." We all laughed, and the air was once again clear in the room.

I was concerned how Marci would react. I would have wanted to present this information to my love while we were alone. Wolfgang's personality doesn't include much compassion toward others' feelings. Marci and I left my father in his lab as we went upstairs for the night. When we got to the great room, Marci turned around and said, "Don't ever keep things from me, Garrison, especially when it comes to your sex life."

I said, "Yes, Marci. I understand. I should have told you sooner. It will not happen again. There are ways around this situation. I would never cheat on you, especially with my sister."

Marci smiled and put her arms around my neck. She said, "It just bothered me, but I understand that you have to do what you have to do." She then smiled at me and jumped into my arms and wrapped her legs around my waist. She said, "Wasn't it fun? Wolfgang was about to kill me. I was so scared." She threw her head back and laughed hard. Then she tossed her head back, inches from my face. With a stern look she said, "Imagine if he would have bit me? I would live forever. I would be perfect like you."

I quickly said, "Marci! Stop it… get off me."

Marci struggled as I was trying to get her off me. I finally succeeded, held her by her shoulders, and said with some anger, "Listen to me, Marci… listen to me! You never want him to bite you. Never. You do not want to transform."

Marci quickly became sad and said, "I know, but I just want to live forever and be perfect." Moments later, she smiled at me and said, "Come on… all of this excitement has turned me on."

I said, "Marci, go upstairs and take a shower. I need to go over some experiments with my father. I will wake you up in the morning. Please."

She gave me that sultry look and purposely walked as sexy as she could as she walked away, without losing eye contact. Then she started laughing and threw her head back to allow the long, flowing locks of golden hair to fall on her perky backside. As this lovely figure disappeared from my sight, all that was left was a remarkable aroma that her body gave off. I heard her lovely and confident footsteps on the hardwood floor as they made their way to the bedroom.

I stepped toward a small bar area in my great room and poured myself a large glass of whiskey. I heard heavy, dominant footsteps coming toward me from the hallway. Wolfgang entered the room and without looking, I poured him a large glass of whiskey. As he approached, I turned and offered him his glass. He smiled, took the glass from my hand and said, "You have a very secure and spicy woman on your hands, Garrison. She was afraid, but she controlled her fear and stood up to me. I admire that in a human, especially in a woman."

I smiled and said, "She is the love of my life. You can see why I have worked so hard and sacrificed so many animals and humans to control the formula. I was going to tell her about the Eva experiment, but I just never got around to it."

Wolfgang smiled and said, "She took it rather well, I think." He looked outside in front of our large palladium window and gazed upon the treed area of our property. He said, "I am hungry."

I put my drink down and I said, "Well, let's find us some dinner, shall we?"

We walked out of the house, past the large swimming pool and onto the perfectly manicured green lawn. The experience we just encountered rekindled our senses to a high level. The smell, the sound and the sight of our backyard oasis was sensory overload. We walked deep inside the forest, taking in all its beauty, like someone would seize the moment in capturing the essence of the aroma of a fine wine before their lips touch its imprisoned container.

Wolfgang and I admired the beauty of nature. Without a word being spoken, we strolled through the trees and brush, enjoying our experience. Wolfgang broke the silence and said, "I am worried about what might happen in the future between your girlfriend and that old woman."

I stopped abruptly and said, "You sensed it as well? I know my love quite well. She has had an issue with Carolyn ever since she tried to push her away from me. Marci has never forgiven her for that." Later that night, Wolfgang and I caught a few birds and feasted well.

As the weeks passed, my parents were becoming more self-efficient amongst their new and very different way of life. Carolyn, though, was not the same person as I knew her during my youth. She had changed. For over twenty years, Carolyn was like a foster mother to me. She loved me. We grew closer during our time in Boston when we shared an apartment throughout my college days. She gave me my space, of which I will be forever grateful. The issue I had with Carolyn was that she didn't accept my experiments on animals and humans. I recognized this was a problem for her, but you would think she would be more understanding of my cause and focus more on the greater picture, so to speak. I forgave her ignorance, but what I couldn't forgive was when she told Marci to leave me and not come back, or when she said I was a monster. This was when my feelings changed toward her. From that moment on, our feelings changed for the worst toward each other. Now I sensed that she wished ill will to all of us, and that unsettled me.

Since my parents first entered the house, I sensed her built-up anger toward me, and pure hatred toward Marci. She feared my parents, and Wolfgang used it to his advantage. He used her like a slave by ordering her to do chores for him. Carolyn was a good person whose world had been turned upside down over the past few years. A part of me understood her side of the issue. She loved Lewis but lacked the courage to tell him. Now he was dead. She hated her life when my parents moved to the estate. They were a constant reminder of what was taken from her life; the man that she loved was gone, and that she had never seized the opportunity to tell him how much he meant to her. She blamed herself for not telling him her feelings. She thought if she would have said something to him that maybe things would be different today. Maybe he wouldn't have gone on that last trip to Germany. Maybe they would have left the estate and started a new life together. Regret is one of the worst enemies for all humans.

One quiet night as the dew started to develop on the plush green grass of the estate, my love found her way to bed deep into the night hours. My mother was in the basement reading a book like she had done since she had arrived in the States. Wolfgang and I were in the foremost back section of the property. Carolyn, though, was up and had been all night. Carolyn was a hard woman to read. I never sensed her loving Lewis, which came to a big surprise to me. I never understood why I never noticed that. Maybe it was a lie. Maybe she never had any feelings for Lewis. If that was the case, why would she be so emotional over Lewis's death? I understood her being upset at the fact that he died, but to lie about loving him would be strange. So that couldn't be the case. She must have cared for him deeply. It seemed that after he left and she thought she would never see him again, that is when she knew herself that she loved him. I spoke to Wolfgang about this issue and he seemed to think that was the case. She just realized that she loved him when she knew that she could no longer see him. I would assume that happens in many relationships.

As the night passed, Carolyn was still up pacing back and forth in the large bedroom that she had called home for over thirty years. Her heart was beating fast and her legs were growing weak. She decided to sit herself on the side of the bed to rest her aching legs. Her knees were bad and had caused her a lot of pain over the past few years. She was a little dizzy from all the endless pacing. She had conflicting thoughts ranging from evil doings to mindless, childhood pranks. Mixed with these feelings were also feelings of anger. She felt hatred that she had never felt before.

Carolyn then got up from her bed and went to her bathroom. She quickly opened the drawer and looked around. She came across many items, but nothing captured her interest until she found a pair of scissors. She thought to herself, *The scissors are sharp and could cut through clothes and hair with ease.* She picked up the scissors and practiced using them. The sound of the blades sliding past each other made an eerie sound that was disturbing to Carolyn. She quickly stopped and looked around to see if anyone was around. Of course, no one was there in her room. No one could hear the scissors, but like all animals that are ready to stalk their prey, the senses are keener and more alive just before an attack. They are more aware of their surroundings.

Carolyn took her worn and somewhat crooked feet out of her slippers and took her robe off with great haste. Even at her most mature age and potbellied figure, she wore a silky negligee, both top and bottom halves. She walked with great haste to her door. As quietly as she could, she opened the door, making sure her scissors were well hid. As the door opened, all three hinges squeaked. The blood was racing fast throughout her body. She poked her head out from the door jam and looked down both sides of the hallway. No one was out there, and not a sound was heard. She opened the door to allow the rest of her body out, and suddenly the end of the scissors knocked against the door. She stopped and in a controlled panic, she looked around and listened to see if anyone heard the confounded noise.

Carolyn had thought about killing Marci months ago, but she didn't have that in her. She couldn't bring herself to kill anything, much less another human being. Carolyn didn't like Marci for two reasons; she was not only a bitch to her but in her mind, she took me from her. Carolyn loved me and thought of me as her own child. As I grew up, my interest toward Carolyn grew from dependency to a mere friendship. When Marci came on the scene, I all but totally ignored Carolyn. Carolyn was jealous of Marci and that was the root of the issue between the diva and Carolyn.

Marci never liked Carolyn, and at that moment, she wanted to push her out the door and attempt to turn her feelings toward me. Marci thought that Carolyn didn't like her, thus she was always trying to throw a wedge in between Marci and my relationship. Contrary to Marci's belief, Carolyn did like Marci. She was just concerned over Marci's safety. She didn't want Marci to get involved with the family more than she already was.

Carolyn waited for the courage to come from within. She quietly moved down the hallway. After each passing step, she increased her speed until she got to Marci's bedroom door. Carolyn's heart was about to explode. A thought just occurred to her; *What if Marci locked the door?* What would Carolyn do? If she would awaken Marci, what would she say? Carolyn looked at the doorknob and took a deep breath. She closed her eyes as if that would give her more support. When she opened her eyes, she carefully attempted to open the door with her right hand. The knob was moving. Carolyn knew that she would be able to get inside. She slowly moved the knob until it could move no more, and she gently pushed the door open. Slowly, inch by inch, she coaxed the door open further. Carolyn stopped and peeked her head around the door. She saw Marci lying on the bed, covered by her silk sheets. Carolyn breathed heavily. Each breath was a strange breath of delight. Carolyn never felt so alive and her senses had never been heightened to this level in her life. She was worried that the sound of her heartbeat would awaken one of life's most beautiful creatures. She opened the door another foot and stepped inside. Carolyn could feel the beads of sweat that formed under her arms moving down her side. She had never been so nervous in her life. She walked as softly as she could toward the side of the bed.

There was enough moonlight outside that made its way into Marci's room for a person to make one's way through the room. Carolyn saw Marci sleeping quietly on the side of the bed closest to the door. Her head was lying softly on her pillow as her right hand was lying next to her golden blonde hair. Her left arm was alongside her curvy hip, and Carolyn noticed the single silk sheet that was covering the perfectly formed body. Marci's large and perky breasts formed a sexy silhouette. Carolyn's anger grew as she looked down on Marci sleeping.

Carolyn looked at Marci's long, flowing blonde hair that covered the pillow. She moved closer and as quietly as she could, she opened the scissors. The sound of two metal blades sliding against each other made a horrific but equally beautiful, steely sound. Marci adjusted her head from side to side and wet her beautiful lips while making a slight smacking sound with her tongue as Carolyn looked down at her, scared out of her mind. She slowly moved her left hand and went under Marci's hair that was lying on the pillow. Carolyn gently and slowly moved her hand, collecting as much hair as possible between her thumb and forefinger. Carolyn carefully collected enough of Marci's hair and she gripped the hair with her hand, making a fist. Carolyn moved the scissors toward Marci's hair. She wanted to cut off a large portion of her long, flowing, blonde hair. Carolyn wanted to hurt Marci but not permanently or physically hurt her. She wanted to get back at her. Marci loved her hair and used her hair to entice Garrison sexually. This bothered Carolyn to no end. As soon as Carolyn brought the scissors closer to Marci's hair, Carolyn's thigh lightly bumped the side of the mattress, causing Marci to slightly open her eyes.

Marci saw a figure in front of her and her natural reaction quickly took form. Marci's right hand grabbed the closest thing to her, that being Carolyn's arm, the arm that held Marci's hair. Marci's other hand came flying out from under the silk sheets and she grabbed Carolyn's other arm. One of Marci's large breasts were now totally exposed. Carolyn was shocked at first, but she attempted to cut some of Marci's hair. The scissors opened and closed as fast as Carolyn could work the instrument, but much to her dismay, no hairs were touched. Marci's heart was racing. She was still confused as to what was happening. With her right hand, she instinctively grabbed Carolyn's hand with the scissors. Carolyn then lost her balance and fell on top of Marci's naked breasts. Marci fought with all her might to pry the scissors out of her hand. Carolyn needed more leverage, so she got on the bed with Marci and threw her leg over Marci and straddled her.

Marci grunted, "You fucking bitch. You are trying to kill me! Give me those god damn scissors." She tried with all her might to pry the scissors from Carolyn's hand. The ladies had both of their hands on the scissors. As they struggled, the ladies held their arms out straight, clasping each other's hands. Marci moved Carolyn over to her side as the end of the scissors scraped the bed's headboard. Marci's legs and lower body were now free and as she gained leverage, she pushed her hands down on the bed, pinning Carolyn's hands over her head. Marci got up on her knees, all the time her large breasts swayed from left to right, her hair flowing over both of her perfectly tanned shoulders. Carolyn's eyes found Marci's breasts and for a moment she loosened her grip ever so slightly on the scissors. She then attempted to regain control, but it was too late. Marci's focus on the task at hand and her strength were too much for Carolyn.

Marci leaned into Carolyn and grabbed the closed blades of the scissors. At that moment, Carolyn stopped struggling. She knew it was over, but for some reason she didn't care. Carolyn's eyes were firmly focused on Marci's breasts that were only a foot away from her face. Marci, with one final pull on the scissors, took them from Carolyn's hands, causing Marci to pull back from Carolyn.

Marci said, "'You fucking bitch! You tried to kill me! I ought to fucking jam these god damn scissors in your fucking head! Really? A pair of scissors?"

Carolyn laid there staring at Marci's breasts, and after a moment of thought she reached for Marci's right breast. She touched the nipple and Marci slapped her hand away and said, "What the fuck!"

Carolyn looked into Marci's eyes and ran both of her hands up Marci's long and muscular thighs. Only getting to Marci's thin waist, Marci took her left hand and stopped one of Carolyn's hands, but Carolyn's other hand went up and touched Marci's breast again. Marci was confused and suddenly she realized that maybe Carolyn was not after her life. Carolyn smiled as she rubbed Marci's breast. Marci, with the scissors in her hand, pushed Carolyn's hand away from her breast.

Carolyn began to weep and said, "I am so sorry. I wasn't trying to kill you. I just came in and I wanted to... I don't know... you hurt me so and I just wanted to get back at you. I had the scissors and I wanted to cut some of your hair... just to get back at you. I would never hurt you with those scissors. I am so sorry."

Carolyn's eyes went back to Marci's breasts and with both of her hands, she grabbed Marci's breasts. Marci was in shock and as she lay on top of this sixty-plus year old woman massaging her breasts. Marci was trying to comprehend what was happening. Part of Marci was so pissed off she wanted to kill her, but the other part of Marci was enjoying the feel of having her breasts touched by another woman. Marci had never had a sexual experience with a woman, and she was still turned on from her encounter with Garrison in the great room. It was standard practice for Marci to be awakened by Garrison in the middle of the night for sexual favors, favors that Marci loved to give out to her love. But this experience was new and something strange to her. Marci sat on Carolyn while still holding the scissors. Then she threw them down on the floor next to the bed.

Marci regained her thoughts and wanted to have fun with Carolyn. Marci smiled at Carolyn while her breasts were being explored from every angle by Carolyn's hands. Marci allowed this to continue. Marci said, "So, you're a fucking lesbian?"

Carolyn was now extremely turned on. She was totally captivated by the moment. She said, "I don't know, but over the years I have always found you so beautiful. I... I loved Lewis, but I desired you."

Marci smiled and tossed her head back. With both of her hands, she pulled her hair back and ran her hands through her hair. Marci said, "If you wanted me then why not just ask me? Why did you want to cut my hair off?"

Carolyn said, "Because I didn't want Garrison touching you. I wanted you. I want you for myself. I love you and I want you so much. I wanted Garrison not to find you attractive."

Marci didn't like what she was hearing, but she wanted to have fun with Carolyn and was enjoying the sexual experience. Marci smiled at Carolyn and slid her half naked body down her. She moved her hands over Carolyn's breasts and gently squeezed them through the negligee. Marci took a firm grip on both sides of the negligee top where the small, thin straps met the material. She pulled the two areas of the top away from each other and ripped the negligee top to expose Carolyn's breasts. After several tugs, the top was completely torn in two. Marci took her hands and cupped each breast and brought them close to each other. She moved her thumbs up the underside of her breasts and worked them toward Carolyn's nipples. Marci softly rubbed the nipples at first and then she rubbed them harder. Marci bent down and let her long blonde hair fall on Carolyn's chest as Marci took one nipple in her mouth. She sucked softly then moved to the other nipple and sucked hard.

Carolyn was in great pleasure, moving around on the silk sheets uncontrollably. Marci moved her right leg off Carolyn and moved her hand down Carolyn's stomach. Marci's hand went under the small panties and reached Carolyn's vagina. Marci placed one finger inside and then two, then rubbed them the length of her vagina. Marci spun her body around and took off the panties and continued to rub Carolyn's large, meaty slit. Marci giggled as Carolyn played with Marci's ass. Marci said playfully, "Do you want my pussy? Hmmm? Do you want to taste my little pussy?"

Carolyn moaned and said nervously, "Yes... yes I do."

Marci slowly took off Carolyn's top and panties. Carolyn's wetness was now running down the inside of her thighs. Marci moved her body up toward Carolyn's face, hiked her right leg up, and looked down at Carolyn's wanting mouth. Marci said, "But first you have to earn my pussy."

Marci started to play with herself. She rubbed herself fast, stuck a couple of fingers inside of her, then pulled her fingers out and placed them on Carolyn's mouth. Carolyn opened her mouth and sucked Marci's juices from her fingers. Marci smirked, and a small chuckle came out of her mouth. Marci said, "Does that taste good? Now for you to get all of my pussy, you have to eat my asshole out."

Carolyn looked mortified but was willing to follow instructions. Marci repositioned herself and placed her asshole toward Carolyn's face. Carolyn nervously licked it while Marci was saying, "What a good little bitch you are. Come on... eat it." Marci increased her pressure on Carolyn's face until Carolyn's tongue made its way up Marci's asshole. After several long moments, Marci moved off Carolyn's tongue and straddled her upper face. She played with her pussy just inches from Carolyn's mouth. Marci quickly grabbed Carolyn's hair but instead of pulling her head toward her vagina, she pulled it back into the mattress.

Marci finished her orgasm, which was not a quiet one. Her juices squirted hard in Carolyn's face. When Marci was finishing her orgasm, she moved down Carolyn's body and let loose of her hair. Suddenly, Marci punched Carolyn as hard as she could in the nose. Blood immediately went everywhere. Marci got off Carolyn as fast as she could. She went over and picked up an alarm clock, lifted the clock over her head and smashed the clock into Carolyn's head. It took one try and Carolyn was out cold.

Marci got up from the bed and stood at the side of the mattress. She said, "Yuck, you are disguising old woman. I never want to get as old as you. Ever. Your fucking body is disgusting." Marci went to get to a bathrobe. As she was putting on her robe, she thought about what she was going to do with Carolyn. Marci started to worry about what I might do when I found out what had happened, and she started to panic. She decided to take the silk belt from her robe and tied Carolyn's hands with one end, and the other end of the belt she tied up her ankles.

Marci hurried and got dressed in shorts and a short sleeve shirt. She ran out of the room, closed the door behind her, and stormed downstairs. She hurried around the corner of the stairway and made her way down the long hallway. She entered the basement area and went inside the lab. She called for Wolfgang, but he was not in the lab. She went out of the lab and knocked on the open door to Wolfgang and Zelda's suite. Zelda heard the footsteps before Marci entered her suite. She heard the panic in Marci's voice.

Zelda said, "What is wrong, woman?"

Marci said, "Where's Wolfgang? Where's Garrison?"

Zelda said, "They are outside."

Marci ran out of the room and up the stairs to the main floor of the house. She turned right and ran into the great room toward the kitchen door. She stopped herself abruptly. She didn't know what to do, but she knew she couldn't tell me at this point. She didn't want to.

Marci stood there, collecting her thoughts. Part of her wished she wouldn't have done the sexual act to Carolyn. She was so afraid of upsetting me and that it might affect our relationship. Marci quickly ran back toward the stairs to the second floor, but before she could get there, Zelda was in the great room.

Zelda said, "What is wrong, Marci, are you hurt? Do you need some help?"

Marci thought for a split second and, still in a panic, she said, "Yes... yes you can help me. Please follow me."

The two ladies went up the steps and down the hall. Zelda was so confused and was generally worried about Marci's state of being. Before they could get to the door, the two ladies heard Carolyn screaming for help.

Marci looked back at Zelda and said, "Okay... this just has to be between us girls... okay?"

Zelda was perplexed and said, "What are you talking about?"

Marci said in a panic and with some anger, "Just... help me, please."

Marci opened the door and Carolyn screamed even louder. Marci hurried and found Carolyn's panties that were lying on the floor. She waded them in a ball and forced them into Carolyn's mouth. Carolyn was screaming though the silky panties. Marci turned and looked at Zelda. Zelda couldn't keep her eyes off Carolyn's naked, bound body.

Zelda said, "What in the hell is going on?"

Marci went over to Zelda and said, "Look... it's difficult to explain but... well... we... you know."

Zelda then gasped and said, "Where you two making love to each other?"

Marci said in a disgusting tone while rolling her eyes, "Aaaaa, no! The bitch came in my room and tried to attack me with scissors. We fought, and I hit her with the end of the clock and knocked her out."

Zelda looked down and said, "Why is she naked?"

Marci started to sweat and feel very warm as her blood pressure was increasing. She said, "Because she attacked me naked."

Carolyn was now moving around on the bed, trying to get free and was screaming as loud as she could through the panties in her mouth.

Zelda looked at Marci with a sheepish grin and rolled her eyes and said, "Come on, Marci, you can do better than that. You know I can sense you lying to me. You had sex with her. Just admit it."

Marci jumped up and down a few times while moving her hands in a panic, "What am I going to do? Garrison is going to kill me when he finds out what we did. I don't want to lose him, I can't lose him."

Marci started to cry uncontrollably. Zelda firmly said, "Now shut up. Control yourself. Let me think about this." Zelda stood there, trying to come up with a way out of this, but there was no way out of it. Zelda said, "You know you are going to have to tell the truth. Garrison will sense anything. He will sense your stress and, of course, she is going to talk."

Zelda's ears moved in the direction of the backyard. Marci noticed the movement of the long, wolf-like ears that sat high on Zelda's head.

Marci started to cry and said, "They're back aren't they? They're back. Oh my god, they are back!"

Zelda said, "Shut up! Just shut up! God, you are annoying. Just tell him the truth."

Marci said, "Yes... yes... just tell him the truth. Fuck!"

Marci stormed out of her bedroom and ran downstairs as Zelda followed her. Marci raced down the steps and jumped off the staircase with three steps to go. She ran down the hallway and into the great room. She stopped abruptly when she saw both Wolfgang and I as we entered the room. We both had blood around our mouths and hands. I was a little embarrassed but quickly noticed Marci's worried look. I said, "Are you okay? I am sorry you must see this. I will get cleaned up as soon as I can."

I started to walk out of the room when Marci said, "No! Garrison, I have something to tell you."

Marci looked back at Zelda for support and said, "I did something that might make you really upset with me."

I said, "What? What happened?"

Marci started to cry and told me the truth. She told me the whole story and held nothing back. I was calm. I didn't know what to say. Marci had never had any lesbian experiences before, at least not to my knowledge. I never sensed her ever being interested in a woman. I felt in my heart that she was just toying with Carolyn, but the act got a little carried away. I said, "Well... this is a lot to take in. I have to ask, are you a lesbian?"

Marci acted a little put off and said, "No! No, I am not a lesbian. I was just playing with her. She attacked me with a pair of scissors. She said she was going to cut my hair off and I thought she was going to use them on me to kill me. As we struggled our bodies rubbed against each other and I was so horny for you I just kind of lost my mind. I am so sorry, Garrison. You know I would do nothing to hurt you. I would never cheat on you and I know this doesn't look good, but she never touched my pussy."

Wolfgang then laughed and said to me, "You have a nympho on your hands, Garrison."

Zelda gave Wolfgang a disapproving look, and he quickly stopped laughing. I said, "Well, I was afraid that she might attack you one day. I didn't think you would have a sexual adventure with her though."

Marci started to cry. She didn't know what to do next. I said, "Let's go up and see Carolyn."

We went up together and as we made our way into Marci's bedroom, Carolyn was on the floor, trying to get loose. I was embarrassed for Carolyn, and I untied her and reached inside of her mouth and removed her panties. Carolyn immediately got up, and as fast as she could, went after Marci. With all her might, she initially tried to grab Marci by the throat. Marci fought with her arms and Carolyn grabbed Marci's shoulders and pushed her heavy body into Marci's. Suddenly, the two ladies were on the floor.

Marci's attitude quickly turned to anger. She said, "Get off me, you fat bitch. See... see what she is doing to me? She is attacking me again, this time in front of you guys."

I reached out and took Carolyn by the shoulders as Wolfgang took Marci by her waist, and with little effort, he picked her up and held her close to his chest with his large arm. He positioned Marci to his side. Marci's arms and legs were moving around in midair as Wolfgang held her by her waist. Carolyn was screaming and reaching for Marci. It was apparent to all that these women didn't like each other.

After a several long moments, I brought Carolyn under control. I took her out of the room and walked her down the hall to her room. Carolyn, still naked as the day she was born, said, "Garrison, she is crazy. Don't you see it? She hit me, she attacked me, she... she played with my vagina. She is a disgusting person."

I stood there listening to her and said, "But you went into her room. You are the one that first attacked her with a pair of scissors."

Carolyn said, "But I just wanted to get back at her. She is such a bitch."

I stepped away from Carolyn and walked toward one of the large windows in the bedroom. I said, "Carolyn... tell me the truth. Do you love me?"

Carolyn stood there and said, "Of course I do. Why do you ask me that kind of question? I have always been there for you."

I walked closer to the window and looked outside. I stared at the perfectly green, thick lawn. My eyes went over to the spot where my mother killed herself. I cast my eyes on the four large trees that dominated the scene before my eyes. I said, "Why did you ask Marci to leave me, to get as far away from me as possible? You know I love her more than anything in this world. I think you even called me a monster of some sorts. Why?" Carolyn didn't know what to say. "Don't lie. I know everything, I sense everything. You love someone in this house more than me. You love Marci, don't you? You want her for yourself. That is why you went into her room with those scissors. You wanted her gone. You could not stand that I was having her, and you could not. I always wondered why you stayed and watched us when we fucked a few times. Most people would leave the room or get away from the action as fast as they could. But you always lingered. Why was that, Carolyn? I will tell you why. You are a fucking lesbian and you wanted Marci. Didn't you?"

Carolyn's rage was now boiling over inside of her. I said, "I sense your hate now. I feel your distain for me."

Without notice, she ran toward me and attempted to hit me. I stopped her with my arms and threw her down on the hard floor of the bedroom. I walked toward the door as Carolyn got up again and ran after me screaming. I held her arms again, trying to calm her, but this time to no avail.

Wolfgang and Zelda heard the commotion coming from Carolyn's room. Marci, by instinct, ran out of her room and down the hall. Marci heard Carolyn screaming and went inside of Carolyn's room. There she saw me holding Carolyn's arms up over her head. Marci went behind Carolyn, grabbed her by the waist, and pulled her from me. Marci had Carolyn in a bear hug and was screaming at her, "You like this, don't you? You like me holding you like this, you fucking tramp." Marci looked at me said, "See, see what I was saying? She is a tramp. All these years she wanted to come between us. She did tonight... I will give her that... but this bitch will never come between us again, my love. She wanted me all for herself, but she knew she couldn't have me."

Carolyn was screaming and trying to get away. I watched the scene and even though I knew Marci cheated, I knew in the back of my mind that Marci was just playing with Carolyn, tempting her to set her up for a massive failure. I trusted my Marci so I said, "We need to do something with Carolyn. We cannot trust her now." Carolyn was yelling and pleading for her to be let go. Down deep, she knew she was in deep trouble.

Wolfgang stepped toward Marci and Carolyn and said, "Let me take care of her for the night." With those words, he grabbed Carolyn and flung her over his broad shoulder. Carolyn was kicking and screaming for him to let her go. Wolfgang turned and walked out of the bedroom, down the hall and went down the stairs. Zelda quietly followed her husband. Wolfgang took Carolyn and locked her up in one of the cells in his lab.

I turned to Marci and walked over to her. Not a word was said. I reached around her and took a good grip of her beautiful hair. I roughly pulled it, jerking her head back. Marci was scared and surprised, but she didn't say a word. I sensed fear in her soul. I pulled her hair back even further, exposing her neck to me. I used my other hand, placed it on her ass, and squeezed hard. I felt her breathing heavy with anticipation of the unknown. I brought my mouth just an inch away from her neck. Marci was indeed scared out of her mind. I sensed her confusion. The rough sexual play versus the anger that she thought I had for her.

I started to lick her neck multiple times. I brought her closer to me with my arm that was behind her, holding her hair. I took my other hand and started to unbutton and unzip the short shorts that she was wearing. She started to moan. Unexpectedly she said to me, "Come on… bite me… make me into one of you. Come on, baby. Just do your thing. I want it. I want it badly."

I pulled even harder on her hair, causing her to moan even more. She was enjoying it. I said, "Damn it, Marci, you know I will not transform you."

Marci said as best as she could with her head back as far as it could go, "I want it. I want to live forever. I don't care how I look. Do you care how I look?"

I paused and said, "Marci, I love you and I do not want you to change, but I don't want you to die either. I am not finished yet with my experiments."

Marci then started to laugh and said, "Why don't you experiment on Carolyn? You know you can't trust her anymore. Experiment on her." Marci continued to laugh the best she could.

Before I knew it, I had two of my fingers inside of her. She was clinching down on them with great force as she was squeezing and pulsating on them. I said, "I used to love Carolyn, but that love has faded. Do with her as you wish."

I brought her head up and I looked into her eyes. Marci made a "woop" sound and laughed. I said, "Did you like your experience with Carolyn?"

Marci smiled and said, "You got me all hot, and you know I love your long fingers." Marci closed her eyes and tried to think clearer. "When I woke up, I thought I was going to die. Then I realized she just wanted to pull some stupid sophomoric prank by cutting my hair off to get back at me. She wanted me... like I want you. So, I wanted to play with her and it just went too far. I hope you understand... don't you?"

She came closer to me, wanting to kiss me, but I spun her around and threw her on the bed, face first. I quickly pulled her shorts off, exposing her perfect ass to me. Marci was wearing no panties. I took my manhood out and told Marci to beg for me. Marci purred and moaned like I had never seen her do before. She was about to explode without me even touching her. Her continuous begging and pleading were making it hard for me to keep from exploding as well. I teased her with the head of my manhood and that sent her into an orgasmic convulsion. When she was finished, I rammed myself deep inside of her as far as I could go. I made love to her as hard as I could. In fact, I was to a point of it hurting her but she was enjoying it. When I was close, I pulled out and finished on her ass. I watched my sperm shoot out, up the middle of her back, down to the crack of her ass.

I then stuffed myself inside of my pants. She continued to arch her ass toward me, wanting more. Her fingers found her vagina and she was playing with herself in front of me. I walked out of the room with her pleading for me to come back. I said, "Do not let the Carolyn thing ever happen again." When I left, Marci rubbed herself into another orgasm.

The next morning, Marci, with her hair tied up in the back, made her way down to the kitchen. When she sat down next to me, she smiled and said, "I am so sore." My parents were in the room and both laughed. Marci asked them, "So, how is our little lesbian?"

Wolfgang said, "She fell asleep crying. We need to feed her."

Marci quickly said, "So what are your plans for her?"

Wolfgang said, "It is not my place to determine her fate. That is up to Garrison."

I said, "I do not care for Carolyn any longer. You guys can do what you wish with her. I cannot trust her any longer. I told Marci last night that she is yours."

Marci said, "So, what are you going to do with her?"

Wolfgang liked the fact that Marci asked him what his next move was regarding Carolyn. For him, it was a sign of respect. He said, "We first need to feed her and then we'll figure out what to do with her. I have some ideas. What are yours?"

Marci smiled as she looked at me. As her eyes moved to Wolfgang's she said, "I don't think keeping her alive would be a smart decision. What do you guys think?"

I looked at Marci, sadly lowered my head, and said with a heavy heart, "I do not trust her any longer. We cannot afford to have her go out on her own. She will call the authorities and attempt to make trouble for us. I think she must be eliminated."

Wolfgang shook his head in agreement. He said, "I agree. She is too much of a risk. She must die."

Marci smiled and said, "Then we are in agreement. The bitch dies, but I want to ask a favor. I want to be the one that kills her."

I looked a Wolfgang and raised my eyebrows at him for his approval. Wolfgang nodded at Marci. She said, "Awesome. Thanks so much."

She got up, walked over to the counter, poured out some cereal in a bowl and covered it with milk, smiling at me the entire time. I thought to myself, *My Marci is the sexiest woman I have ever met.*

Chapter Six

E va, during this time, was experiencing the same rapid growth as I did at her age. Eva was now three months of age. She started to walk and was trying to form words. I was a huge help to my parents during this stage of Eva's development. Wolfgang and Zelda read all of Lewis's reports and various doctor reports of mine when I was that age. We all assumed that Eva's growth rate would correspond with mine.

Eva was stunningly beautiful. We shared the same deep blue eyes and had the same blonde hair. She had a perfect complexion. She was strong and full of life. She rarely cried after we brought her to the estate and out of the cave. Even at a few weeks of age, she didn't like the cave that she was born in nor being transported from Germany to the States. Like me, she had bouts of growing pains which caused her to cry from time to time, but she never once got sick.

Wolfgang didn't run tests on her every day. Wolfgang loved his Eva and wanted her to grow into a powerful woman. He did take some blood samples and tested her hand-eye coordination, among other tests, but while he would test her, he caught himself smiling at her. For the second time in Wolfgang's life, he loved something more than himself or his work. His first love was Zelda and now it was Eva.

My father admired me and cared for me deeply, but I sensed that he never truly loved me, not like he loved Eva. He knew he couldn't keep this secret from me, so he was just brutally honest with me. I appreciated the frankness and grew to accept this as a fact. I did hope that in the future, his admiration for me would turn into love, but I understood. I still felt that I was lucky to have a father like Wolfgang to learn from and to have someone of his stature to share ideas of what I possess. Very few people on this planet understand what I experience every day of my life. It is nice to have someone that I can share my issues and experiences with occasionally.

Zelda, though, loved me. Like any mother, the bond between mother and son was strong and that was certainly the case with us. I loved my mother. We shared many stories about my adoptive mother, Adelle. I showed her pictures of her and told Zelda of her personality. Adelle was a sad woman, but before adopting me, she had great promise. She was smart, talented, and caring. It was a shame that my adoptive father didn't appreciate her for what kind of women Adelle was when they first got married.

Marci and Zelda became extremely close since my parents started living with us. Marci would take care of Eva any chance she could get. Wolfgang was very grateful for Marci and her help with Eva. Marci was becoming more accepting of the fact that one day I had to impregnate Eva with my sperm. I could sense that down deep Marci was not only upset at the eventual act but she was jealous of Eva and Eva's future child. Marci knew that she had no choice and had to accept the fact that Wolfgang and I were in control of Eva's future. But those issues were in the distant future. What lay before us was the Carolyn issue and what we were going to do with her. She was gone mentally, and she couldn't be trusted any longer. Her service to me was ending.

I must give Lewis credit that he understood, when he was alive, that eventually he would no longer be useful to me. He knew that he was just a pawn in my ultimate game of chess where I place people in my life. He knew that he was important but not critical to the end result or to the exploration of the result.

The morning after the Carolyn fiasco, Zelda made Eva and my Marci breakfast. As Zelda got more comfortable, she began to cook extremely delicious meals for the family, most notably for Marci and Eva. My parents, Eva and I maintained our usual diet of live animals, but out of respect for the house and Marci, we only ate outside. We did eat vegetables and such, but the smell of cooked meat was repulsive to my parents. I didn't have a strong stomach for cooked meat either and Eva refused to eat any kind of cooked meat.

After breakfast, Wolfgang went to his lab. After several minutes, I accompanied Marci to Wolfgang's laboratory. As we entered the entrance to the right of the stairway, we immediately heard Carolyn crying out for help. Marci was anxious and wanted to see Carolyn behind the bars of the cell. As we walked around the corner of the hall, we entered the lab. Wolfgang was standing in front of the cell. When Carolyn saw Marci, she immediately stepped toward her and grabbed the bars of the cell with her hands. Carolyn stood there, naked, shaking from being cold through the night. There was dried blood on her body and her hair was a mess.

Carolyn said to Marci, "You asshole. Get me out of here. You set me up, you bitch."

Marci smiled and looked over at Wolfgang. Wolfgang didn't move his head but glanced at Marci with his large, yellowish, bloodshot eyes. Marci said, "You brought all of this on yourself, bitch."

Carolyn retorted, "Why do you have me in here like some animal?"

Marci said, "Because you can't be trusted."

Carolyn knew the history of this area of the house. Her fears were now being realized, that she might be a part of something unnaturally evil. She wanted out, so her attitude changed very quickly. She quickly changed to a more apologetic mood.

Marci began to walk, in a sexy way that only she could fabricate, down the barred cell wall of Carolyn's new room. She ran her left hand and fingers across the bars and said, "So, Carolyn. When did you know you were gay? Come on. Be honest with me." Carolyn released her grip on the bars and folded her arms over her large, hanging and out of shape breasts. Marci asked again, "Come on, Carolyn. Tell us. When did you first know?"

Carolyn walked toward Marci and said, "When I was in grade school. I always noticed the girls and not the boys. When I got into high school, I noticed them even more, especially in gym class. I didn't want anyone to know so I tried to play it off as I was straight like everyone else. I went to college and studied to be a teacher. Before I knew it, I was in my thirties and not married. My parents and my friends tried to fix me up with guys, but I just never had time for them. I was always busy with school and teaching. When I got hired on here, I dedicated myself to the Seawick family." Carolyn turned and gave me a dirty look then continued, "I even spent a handful of years in a strange city for this family. I always wanted a child, but I knew I would never be able to have one. I thought about going through the act with a stranger or whatever, but my friends would talk and I didn't want that for me or my child. Then you came around. I tried to keep my eyes to myself, but it was hard to do. I knew what was going on in this basement, this so-called laboratory. I have seen so much evil and hideous creatures that were formed down here, both animals and humans alike. When I noticed that you were being drawn into this family deeper and deeper, I just had to try and save you from him… them."

Marci acted like she cared by creating the most serious and concerned look on her face. She said, "So you thought it was in my best interest for me to leave the only man or, for that matter, person that I have ever cared for." Carolyn knew at that moment that she was in too deep and might have said too much.

Marci walked toward Carolyn, and this time used her other hand to run her fingers across the bars of the cell. Marci said, "No one wanted me either. I stayed in the orphanage for most of my childhood." Marci looked up and then down the bars of the cell. She continued, "I had some foster parents, but they only got my hopes up. In the end, they didn't even want me." Marci, with an icy stare, looked at Carolyn who was now visibly nervous. Marci continued, "So, when I found my Garrison, you wanted to keep me from the only person that has ever cared for me, the only person that has ever wanted me or loved me. Why? Because you liked my tits?"

Carolyn was violently shaking from fear. She uttered, "No. That is not necessarily true. I cared for your safety. I knew the longer you stayed here, the more you would be in danger. From him! His experiments, his way of life, his obsession with you is not natural."

Marci smiled at me, winked, and said, "He loves me." Carolyn stopped talking. She knew Marci was too far gone from reason now. I knew it as well. I knew it before she did. I am the only one that has ever truly loved Marci. I can't understand why I was the only one. She was the most beautiful woman I had ever seen. She was sexy and physically attractive beyond the imagination. She was smart and had a strong personality. Maybe that was the problem. She was too perfect, too strong, too amazing for people to understand her. She intimidated people with her beauty and confidence.

Marci looked back at Carolyn and said, "So, did you want me anytime I was here at the house? Did you ever lust after me? Hmmm. Now tell me the truth."

Carolyn lowered her head and said, "I found you very attractive. Okay! You're sexy. You're beautiful."

Marci threw her head back and laughed hard and loud. That long, flowing blonde hair just avalanched off her shoulders and down her long, silky back. Marci collected herself, looked at Carolyn who was getting angry and said, "So you want me now, don't you? Come on.

Admit it in front of everyone here. You just want to fuck me, don't you?" Carolyn was now screaming. She wanted to hurt Marci. Marci walked over to the cell and stood there, just inches from the bars. Marci said, "Come on. You want me. I know you do. Come and get me."

Carolyn turned to her right and was going to walk away, but the anger she was experiencing inside was hard to overcome. She knew she was not going to ever be allowed to step outside of the cell as long as she lived. In fact, she knew that she was not going to live much longer, especially in her current, human state. Carolyn knew from past experience that they had plans, terrible plans for her. She was scared, lonely and hurt, especially hurt that Marci was making fun of her. She poured a small part of her heart out to Marci and Marci just stomped all over her feelings. She felt embarrassed and belittled. Suddenly, Carolyn stopped and without looking, turned as fast as she could toward the bars of the cell. She slammed her body into the bars and quickly attempted to get her hands and arms out through the bars to get to Marci.

Marci backed up a foot but didn't seem too surprised by Carolyn's reaction. Marci grabbed Carolyn's flailing arms. One by one she secured them, and with all her might, she pushed Carolyn's arms as hard as she could up against the bars, interlocking them over Carolyn's head. Carolyn's body was pressed against the bars and part of the front of her body was now up against Marci's. Marci was face to face with Carolyn, with only the bars between them.

Carolyn was screaming, "Get off me, you fucking whore! Get off me! Let me go!"

Marci was struggling to keep hold of Carolyn's arms through the bars. She pushed Carolyn's arms up from the elbows, pinning Carolyn's arms against the bars. Marci smiled and let Carolyn yell at the top of her lungs. Suddenly, Carolyn began spitting in Marci's face. After three times, Marci positioned her left hand under both of Carolyn's elbows to help lock her into place on the bars of the cell. Marci took her free hand, reached through the bars, and grabbed Carolyn's hair at the back of her head. Marci pulled Carolyn's head right in between the bars and the two woman's faces were just inches from each other. Marci said, "Don't do that, bitch." As she said that, Marci went at Carolyn's face and placed her lips onto Carolyn's. Carolyn struggled as best as she could, moving her head from side to side, but Marci's strength was just too great for Carolyn. With all of Marci's might, she pushed Carolyn's face into the bars as hard as she could until it was hurting Carolyn.

Carolyn stopped struggling as Marci continued to press her lips on Carolyn's. Marci then backed off and took her tongue and licked Carolyn from her chin, over her lips and up to the tip of her nose.

Marci looked over at me with that seductive look in her eyes. For some strange and unexplainable reason, I was enjoying the scene and Marci knew I was. Marci was putting on a show for Wolfgang as well. It was weird, different, and perverted. This was only Marci's second lesbian experience and she was enjoying the seductiveness of the moment. Marci turned her head toward a scared Carolyn. Carolyn didn't know what was going to happen next, but in a strange way, she relaxed and stopped struggling. Marci let loose of her grip on Carolyn's hair as she lowered her hand down over one of Carolyn's large breasts, playing with her large nipple. Carolyn was breathing heavy with sexual excitement. Marci started to kiss Carolyn on the lips and Carolyn was returning the gesture. Marci gently relaxed her grip on Carolyn's trapped arm and with that hand, Marci found the other breast.

Marci slid down a couple of feet and took one of Carolyn's nipples in her mouth. Marci licked and sucked, soft then hard. She kept Carolyn guessing as to how hard or how soft she was pleasuring her. Carolyn started to moan louder as Marci brought her hand down between Carolyn's legs and placed a couple of her fingers inside of Carolyn while her lips and tongue were still on Carolyn's nipple. This time, Carolyn was pushing her own body as hard as she could against the bars of the cell. Carolyn glanced at me and Wolfgang while this was taking place, but she was beyond caring at that moment.

Marci stopped licking and sucking her nipple and rose to meet Carolyn face-to-face. Carolyn opened her mouth and offered her tongue to Marci. Marci smiled and suddenly, without warning, spit directly into her mouth. Carolyn was surprised but she continued to stand there as Marci continued to touch and play with her vagina. Marci then spit again in Carolyn's mouth and the third time she spit in Carolyn's face.

Marci started to laugh and said, "You enjoy this don't you. You love to be whored out like a fucking prostitute that you are in front of men." Marci removed her hand from Carolyn's vagina and wiped it over Carolyn's face. Marci took both of her hands and made a fist and as fast as she could, she came down on both of Carolyn's breasts. The sudden blow of both fists surprised Carolyn as she stumbled back from the bars. Marci's demeanor completely changed from a sexy vixen to an almost sadistic, possessed demon. Marci reached for Carolyn through the bars, but Carolyn was out of reach. Carolyn held her large breasts and was in a great deal of pain. Marci was trying so hard to reach her through the bars, I thought Marci was going to hurt herself.

Marci angrily backed away from the bars. She quickly looked at Wolfgang as she was wiping the saliva from her mouth saying, "I want inside. Get that cell door unlocked."

Wolfgang smiled and said, "So, what are you going to do after I open the cell?"

Marci said, "You'll find out. Please just open the damn thing."

Wolfgang laughed and walked over to the keys lying on his lab desk. Marci went and got Wolfgang's all wood chair. She looked for some rope and when she couldn't find any, she asked for some. Wolfgang rooted around and found her a long piece that was to her liking then walked toward the cell and unlocked the door. Marci hurriedly walked inside, dragging the chair with her. As she went inside, Marci took the rope in her hands. She looped it a few times and without warning, started whipping the rope on Carolyn's body. Carolyn raced over to the cot and curled into a fetal position.

Marci said to Wolfgang, "Pick her up and put her in the chair." Wolfgang went over to Carolyn and with little effort, picked her up and placed her in the wooden chair. Marci said, "Now hold her still." Wolfgang held her down as Marci took the rope and tightly tied her ankles, legs, waist, and shoulders to the chair. She wrapped the rope around Carolyn and the chair, making sure each pass was tight so Carolyn couldn't get loose. Marci quickly wrapped each wrist with the rope and tied her hands behind her back.

Carolyn was screaming to be let go. She was scared, cold, and very concerned about what Marci was going to do to her. Wolfgang stepped back and went to the cell door. Marci went to the other side of the cell, trying to collect her breath as she looked at me for several seconds and gave me a wink. I looked at Carolyn as she was struggling to get free. Her face was bright red, and saliva dripped from both corners of her mouth as she struggled to get free. As old as she was, I was concerned that she might break some bones because she was struggling so much.

Wolfgang slowly walked toward where I was standing without saying a word. He turned around and stood next to me as if we were watching the sunset in my backyard. Marci noticed that she was on display. We both sensed her confusion. Marci didn't know what to do.

She stood there, leaning against the bars of the cell, trying to collect her thoughts. She watched Carolyn as she attempted to free herself from the ropes. The chair, which her naked body sat in, was moving about on the cold tiled floor, making short, annoying scraping sounds. Her constant groaning and grunting was getting on Marci's nerves. I sensed her anger starting to intensify after each passing sound.

Marci pushed herself off the bars with her muscular rear. She walked seductively over to Carolyn then squatted in front of her and just stared into her eyes. This bothered Carolyn as she was cussing at her the entire time. Carolyn said, "You fucking bitch, get me out of these ropes." Marci just smiled as she tilted her head from side to side like a small, playful puppy would do, listening to their owner. Marci looked down at Carolyn's open legs and looked at her vagina. She raised her eyes upward to Carolyn's breasts then stood up and walked closer to Carolyn. Without any warning, Carolyn spit in Marci's face. Marci was surprised as she backed away, wiping the spit from her face as she stared at Carolyn. Carolyn said, "Get me out of this chair!"

Marci quietly walked out of the cell as she continued to wipe the spit off her face. Carolyn continued to yell, "Where are you going? Untie me, you bitch." Carolyn looked over to me and said, "Garrison! Get me out of these ropes." I just stood there and said nothing. Marci glanced at me then walked past me while she went to the end of the lab table.

Without looking at Wolfgang, Marci said, "Wolfgang, when we were at your house, you mentioned an experiment that you hadn't tried yet. I would like for you to conduct an experiment on Carolyn." Wolfgang turned and continued to listen. Marci said, "Have you ever injected the formula or whatever you call it into a dead corpse before?"

Wolfgang said, "No. I have not."

Marci said, "What would happen if you did? I guess I respectfully have to ask as well… why you didn't."

Wolfgang smiled and lowered his head. He said, "I never was interested in raising the dead to life."

Marci said, "Would you be interested in seeing what would happen with that bitch in there?"

Carolyn started to cry and said, "Please! Please! I beg you. Don't turn me into a monster!"

Wolfgang didn't like to be called a monster. The room went eerily silent. Marci said to my father, "Would the formula that you or

Garrison have in your body, would that bring a person back from the dead?"

Wolfgang looked at me said, "I guess it would, but the formula would have to be injected as soon as possible. The formula doesn't work with cold blood."

I interjected, "Correct. The donor of the formula must be alive, and the body temperature must be at a high level, along with the high adrenaline levels as well. The subject's blood must be warm and the blood must be flowing to get to the correct areas of the body. What I mean is, if you would inject the formula into a cold, dead body, the formula would cool and would be ineffective. Therefore, the injection must be done and done quickly, probably as close to the heart as possible, I would think. It is a very interesting experiment, one experiment that I never really considered."

Marci smiled and winked at me. I acknowledged her with a smile. Carolyn continued to beg for her life and for us not to perform any experiments on her. Marci said to Wolfgang while Carolyn was ranting and raving, "Can I have some fun before the experiment begins?"

Wolfgang said, "Be my guest. You intrigue me with your love for torture." Wolfgang looked at me and said, "Impressive. Again, where did you find her?"

Marci laughed and answered for me, "I appeared before him as a dream, as a visionary angel of love, lust and desire." She looked at me and smiled, then a huge laugh erupted from her beautiful mouth. As she continued to laugh, she went through a few drawers of Wolfgang's lab table. She rooted around and discovered a pair of scissors. Marci picked them up and moved the blades back and forth. She started to laugh a little too hard for the situation. She quickly turned and jogged back to the cell entrance with the scissors in her hand. Her breasts moved up and down with every hurried step she took. Marci went inside of the cell and without much notice, walked over to Carolyn and grabbed her hair with her left hand. Carolyn was trying to move about to free herself, but her bondage was too great for her efforts. Marci moved to the side of Carolyn's face and pulled her hair back, exposing the front of Carolyn's neck. Marci said, "So, bitch. You wanted to cut my hair off, huh? Well, let's see how you like it when someone cuts your fucking hair off."

Carolyn said, "No! No! Please don't."

Marci took the scissors and immediately started to cut Carolyn's hair. Large chunks of loose hair fell to the tile floor. Carolyn was screaming and Marci said, "Shut up. God, you are so loud for an old bitch." Marci worked fast and cut most of Carolyn's hair off, as close to her scalp as possible. When Marci was finished, she stepped back and laughed, all the while busy playing with her long, golden locks of hair. Marci said, "Wait. Wait a minute." Marci hurriedly went out of the cell and retrieved a small mirror. She went back to the cell and showed Carolyn her new look. Carolyn was crying and cussing up a storm. She was at the point of anger, but it was somewhat controlled with a mixture of fear. Fear because she knew what was coming and it probably would contain a great amount of pain. She knew that she didn't want to anger Marci further, in horror of potentially intense pain. I sensed that Carolyn knew she was going to be turned into that horrid "monster" that she had always feared. I sensed that she quickly came to some revelation of acceptance that she had to endure her lot in life at that point. She had no control over what was going to happen to her, and her heart was racing so fast that I and my father could hear each pounding heartbeat.

Marci, with the scissors still in her hand, took the closed scissors and rubbed the cool blade over Carolyn's nipple. Marci slowly moved the blade up and down until the nipple was hard. Marci said, "You like that, don't you? You are still a dirty little bitch." Carolyn moved as best as she could, trying to move herself from the cool blade. Marci moved around to the back of the chair and with both hands, she grabbed Carolyn's breasts. Marci moved her hands to the front of the nipples and pinched them with her thumb and index finger. Carolyn couldn't move, but it was noticeable that she was getting a little aroused. Marci removed her hand from Carolyn's right breast while she sped up the massaging of Carolyn's left breast. Marci watched Carolyn as she was increasingly getting aroused, and when Carolyn slightly closed her eyes, Marci took the open scissors and as fast and as accurate as she could, she snipped at Carolyn's nipple. Blood started to flow as Carolyn let out a blood curdling cry. Marci quickly stepped back from Carolyn and watched her wiggle around in the ropes as she screamed in pain.

Marci laughed and walked out of the cell. As she walked past Wolfgang, she said, "So, you must infect her before her blood cools, right?"

Wolfgang acknowledged her statement with a nod of his head. Wolfgang said, "It must be quick, right after death."

Carolyn then screamed, "Noooooo! Please! Don't turn me into a monster!"

Wolfgang looked at Carolyn and snorted. Marci went over to the laboratory table and opened a few drawers but couldn't find what she was looking for. Marci's mind was racing as she was at a loss as to what she was going to do next to Carolyn.

Marci felt that she was slowly beginning to disappoint Wolfgang, something that she didn't want to do. Marci was, more than ever, trying to gain Wolfgang's total approval and acceptance. The best way to Wolfgang's heart was to not be afraid, be strong, and show no compassion for human life. This is what drove Wolfgang throughout his life. He loved to see others in pain. He loved to see others suffer. It was in his makeup since he could remember. Wolfgang told me that he sensed the same traits in Marci that he saw in himself. A part of me was at first disappointed to hear my father say those words to me, but the other part of me admired Marci's more sinister side. Marci is a good woman, but she had a very vindictive side when she got angered, and when she didn't like someone, she let them know it in no uncertain terms.

Marci told me when we first dated that her time as an orphan taught her how to be strong and how to take care of herself. She had gone from one foster family to the other, and no family took her in permanently. This had always bothered her and made her emotionally hardened toward others. So, as more families came to foster her, she was not as warm and nice as she should have been, so many people thought she was a problem teenager. At that point, Marci just stopped trying to get adopted by a family because it was just too late for her. On top of all the baggage that she carried with her was the fact that she felt abandoned. Her birth parents gave her up. I understood what that felt like, which is the main reason we connected from the start of our relationship.

As Marci was looking for something, anything to use on Carolyn, Wolfgang felt sorry for her. He understood and sensed her frustration. He walked over to where Marci was standing and said, "Marci, you need to think about this as an experiment. The objective is to learn, not to torture, to experiment, not to kill. The formula reproduces destroyed cells, skin, organs, and tissue. It repairs what is broken and enhances what is strongly present. It improves what is strong in character to the subject. Thus, in this case, it would be interesting seeing if a damaged organ or a damaged area would be repaired if or when the subject is brought back to life. I must admit, I am looking forward to such an experiment. This is something I wanted to attempt, but I didn't want to wait for the results. I had more pressing concerns at the time. I did attempt this experiment on a few animals but never on humans."

I interrupted my father and said, "So you experimented with bringing back animals from the dead?"

Wolfgang said, "Yes, we did but we never had any success. The issue, as I look back on this now, was the blood was not at the right temperature for the formula to process the dead cells into living cells. At the infancy of the formula, I didn't take into account that the blood had to be at a certain temperature for the formula to work. After the war, I still performed experiments, but I was never interested in raising the dead as much as I was interested in stopping the mutation process. Now I believe I have found a way to stop the process naturally with you and your sister's child down the road. If there is no mutation, we are onto something big. If not, we are back to square one."

Marci looked at me and I felt the jealousy pulsating through her veins. The thought of someone besides her having my child didn't set very well with my love, but she knew that experiment had to be conducted in the distant future.

Carolyn heard every word of our conversation and both my father and I sensed her fear. Carolyn was trying to hold back the tears, but that was a lost cause. She knew she was about to suffer mightily and the fact that she might come back from the dead as a monster that she had always feared scared her like no other time in her life.

Wolfgang abruptly came upon an object in the drawer. He picked up a pair of pliers and looked at Marci. Wolfgang said, "This item used to be a form of persuasion during the war." Marci smiled and walked over to Wolfgang and took the pliers from his large hand. Marci shook her head as if in agreement but with a subtle hint of topping that mode of torture. Marci reached for a small hammer and a screwdriver.

Marci said, "So, experiment with the broken, not just to torture."

Wolfgang smiled and nodded. Marci jumped a few inches off the floor and laughed. She ran over to Carolyn as Carolyn started screaming at her at the top of her lungs. She had screamed so much that she was becoming a little hoarse. Marci stepped inside the cell and went behind Carolyn, dropping the pliers and screwdriver onto the title floor. Marci took her left hand and reached up under Carolyn's chin, roughly pulled Carolyn's head back, and without warning gripped Carolyn's jaw as hard as she could. Carolyn had her mouth closed as tight as she could. Marci said, "Come on, bitch, open your mouth." With Marci's right hand, she quickly took the hammer and proceeded to land the first strike on Carolyn's lips.

Carolyn tried to move away but the rope had her fastened to the chair like glue. Carolyn screamed, and Marci again came down with the hammer on another tooth that was now not hidden by skin. Marci repositioned her hand on Carolyn's jaw in such a way that her thumb and first two fingers kept Carolyn's mouth open ever so slightly. Marci hit another tooth and then another. After five strikes, she stopped. Carolyn was in total misery. She spit some of the broken teeth from her mouth onto the floor as a pile of blood flowed in her mouth. Carolyn was coughing loudly as some of the pieces of her teeth went down her throat. Carolyn made the most hideous sound as she screamed, and her eyes were closed as tight as they possibility could be.

Marci looked over to Wolfgang for his approval, and he smiled and nodded his large head. She looked at me and knew this scene was bothering me. Marci's smile soon turned to a frown. I didn't want to ruin this moment for Marci, so I smiled back. She bent down and picked up the screwdriver, quickly grabbing Carolyn's head and holding it in her lovely arm. Carolyn's blood dripped onto Marci's arm as she took the Phillips screwdriver and placed the end of it into Carolyn's ear. Carolyn was trying to move away, but the ropes wouldn't allow it. Carolyn's body was beet red from stress, pain and trying to get loose from the ropes. The ropes dug into every place they touched Carolyn's naked body. Marci was careful not to go too far into Carolyn's ear canal. Suddenly, Carolyn screamed louder as we all assumed that Carolyn's ear drum was busted. Marci released Carolyn's head and stepped back.

Carolyn was in so much pain it was almost unbearable to watch. This was the lady that was my nanny growing up, but mostly she was my friend. I didn't have many friends growing up, but Carolyn was always there for me, from a very young age to my post collegiate days. But she had turned on me; she even turned on the love of my life. I was at a point now that I could never trust her again. So even though what I was witnessing saddened me a little, a part of me was also enjoying the experiment. I knew what Marci was doing. Injure the subject in many places and then after death if the subject rises to life, we will see if the injured places heal. Also, how long would those areas take to heal and at what stage would the injured areas heal? Would they heal before or after the mutation and, speaking of mutation, how far would the mutation process continue? This was a first, trying to bring a human back to the life. The unknown is great, but the main mystery was would the mutation be fully complete as it was with my parents or would the mutation stop and only go half or a quarter of the way? These were the questions that we all had and were eager to find the answers to.

Marci went over and picked up the pair of scissors that she had lying on the floor. I noticed the look on Marci's face, which was a look that I had never seen before. The passion, the obsession and total hatred that filled her soul was shining through her intoxicating eyes. With her pupils beaming with excitement and her mouth slightly open with a vast anticipation of a small glimpse into the future, she opened the scissors. Marci held Carolyn's head with her freed hand, pushing it toward the shoulder. Quickly, Marci opened the scissors wide and pushed them against the top half of Carolyn's uninjured ear. With a quick and strong squeeze from Marci's hand, the scissors cut into Carolyn's ear. It took Marci a few tries, but after several attempts, the top half of Carolyn's ear fell to the floor.

Carolyn felt the incredible sting on the side of her head. With so many painful areas on her body, she didn't know what hurt the most. Blood was everywhere on Carolyn's tied up, naked body, as her nipple, mouth, inner ear and now her outside ear were bleeding profusely. Marci attacked Carolyn again, but this time she pushed her head down to her chest and started cutting from the ear lobe and made her way up to the back part of the ear. Again, the loose appendage fell to the floor. Marci's hands were covered in blood and Carolyn was almost unrecognizable in her new appearance. She screamed out in so much pain, but now her voice was cracking and getting hoarser from the constant yelling.

Carolyn's face was covered in blood. Her mouth was open but little sound was coming out. She had screamed so loud for so long that her voice was almost completely gone. She didn't want to move a muscle because the more she moved, the more it hurt, but she had to move. She wanted to run away from the pain, but the ropes prevented her from moving.

The look on my lover's face during this exercise was stimulating. She had the same look during our lovemaking.

Marci looked at the blooded body that was now shaking uncontrollably in the chair bound by the ropes that had made their way into her skin. Marci walked out of the cell, making her way to the lab table. She said to Wolfgang, "Do you have any acid that I could use?" Wolfgang quietly pulled open a drawer and handed her a bottle of highly concentrated sulfuric acid. Wolfgang instructed Marci to use gloves when handling the product. After Marci put her gloves on, she walked over to the subject. Carolyn started to move and jerk even more, digging the ropes deeper into her body. Marci slowly unscrewed the cap and as she gradually walked toward the subject, she smiled. Marci slowly tipped the bottle over Carolyn's struggling body, and after a few drops hit the top portion of the exposed leg, the acid started to burn away some of the flesh. Marci walked over to the other side of the jolting subject and repeated the same procedure on the other exposed leg.

The smell of burning flesh filled the area. Marci was having the time of her life and was careful not to splatter any of the acid on herself. Marci walked behind the chair and carefully poured a generous portion on the subject's neck. As the acid poured down part of Carolyn's back, the flesh started to bubble and then smoke appeared. The subject was past the point of losing all control of her emotions and physical being. Her eyes and mouth opened as wide as they could, looking straight up from her imprisoned chair of torture. Suddenly, Carolyn started to make choking and gagging sounds and a horrid look formed on the completely blood-covered face. Her body shook and went into a convulsion. A last gasp of air left, and her body went limp. Carolyn's head fell quickly forward.

Marci looked at Carolyn and screamed, "No! You stupid bitch! Not yet! You are not supposed to die yet!"

Marci quickly looked at Wolfgang with great horror on her face, knowing that it might be too late to infect the body with the formula. Wolfgang moved with great speed toward the opening of the cell. He quickly made his way to the dead subject. Marci stepped back, still holding the open container of acid, and yelled, "Hurry! Before it's too late!"

Wolfgang glanced at Marci and quickly looked at Carolyn. Wolfgang made sure not to kneel or place his hand on any acid, either on the floor or on the body. With his large hand, he pushed the subject's limp head back. He knelt on the side of the body and opened his mouth as wide as he could. Marci said, "Hurry, Wolfgang!" I looked on from outside the celled cage, knowing what my father was going to do. Wolfgang roughly moved Carolyn's large, free, hanging breast to the side and thrust his open mouth onto the side of the subject. His lower teeth pierced the skin while his upper teeth clamped down toward the middle of Carolyn's chest. Wolfgang's plan was to bite as close to the subject's heart as possible to get the formula working as fast as it could, and the fastest way was through the blood flow. To get the blood flowing inside the body was to get the heart to start pumping blood. Also, one of the warmest part of the human body just before death is near the heart, at the center of the body.

Wolfgang didn't release his bite on the subject. He pressed hard enough to make sure his teeth were deeply embedded into the skin. Wolfgang felt and heard a few ribs break, and was mindful not to cause too much damage during the bite. After a moment, which seemed like minutes on end, Wolfgang released his bite on the victim. Carolyn sat there in the chair; her head was back and to the side, and blood was dripping out of every angle from her head. The acid continued to burn the flesh.

Marci said, "Did you do it? Did you get to it in time?"

Wolfgang said, "I don't know, Marci. I have never attempted this on a human. I don't know if she will come back to life or not. Help me get this thing untied."

I ran toward the cell to assist. Marci ran out of the cell, and as she passed me, she gave me a high five. She found a sharp knife in one of the lab's drawers then hurried back and started to cut the ropes from Carolyn. When she was freed, Wolfgang picked up her body, walked out of the cell, and headed toward the hospital bed in the other cell. Wolfgang roughly laid the specimen on its back and quickly put straps over her body. Marci helped as much as she could. The straps went under her breasts and pelvic area while the feet and hands were bound as well. Wolfgang worked fast and didn't utter a word.

When the subject was secure, Marci said, "So, why did we tie her up?"

Wolfgang said, "Because I don't know what she's going to be like or what she will do if or when she is back from the dead."

Marci said, "Do you have any idea when that might be?"

Wolfgang said, "I don't know."

Blood was still oozing out of the specimen, collecting between the rubber lining and the injured areas of Carolyn's body. Wolfgang quickly jumped on top of the body and lay naked on the subject in hopes of warming the blood.

Wolfgang said, "Garrison, get some blankets. Marci, start rubbing the body, starting with the face and working down to the shoulders. We have to get the blood temperature up."

Marci's blood-stained hands went to work. The more she rubbed, the more blood oozed out of the injured areas. Marci said, "Is she losing too much blood?"

Wolfgang said, "Right now we just need to warm the blood or the formula will not react with the blood."

I raced like a madman and looked for blankets. I found some in the closet and ran as fast as I could toward my father. Marci took the blankets from me and Wolfgang rose up as she placed a blanket on Carolyn's chest. Wolfgang then lowered his massive body down on the subject to continue the warming procedure. Marci went around the body and placed a blanket on her legs. Wolfgang and Marci worked well together. Marci was nervous, and Wolfgang sensed her feelings.

Wolfgang knew that Marci wanted to live forever and through all of what she demonstrated in front of Wolfgang, he knew that she was serious in her endeavor. Marci had impressed Wolfgang from the first time they met. He sensed the immense passion that she had in her soul and the equal fervor that burned for his son. She wanted life and wanted to experience life forever. Throughout all his victims that were a few lifetimes ago, he never experienced anyone that wanted life as much as Marci. Thousands of young and old, women and men my father killed, and most of them begged for their lives and for survival, but none of them verified the absolute unpolluted obsession that my Marci had toward the ultimate goal that is innate in all humans — to live as long as one could.

Marci stood at the end of the subject, holding a blanket around Carolyn's head. She had the most intense look on her face. My heart was beating fast as well. We were at the forefront of something that nature had never seen. To have the ability to re-create life, to bring the dead back to life. If this was possible, discovering the mutation secret of the formula might be within our grasp. So many possibilities were riding on this experiment. If we could bring the dead back to life and if the formula could repair what killed the body to start with, this opens another potential breakthrough in a most mysterious, unchartered new world. Then if we could dream a little and this experiment could link us to a chemical makeup that would prevent the physical change from the formula, our goal would be achieved sooner rather than later.

For Marci, this experiment was the last hope beyond all hope for her to stay young forever. She didn't want to wait almost two decades to see if the experiment with my sister worked. That would have my Marci twenty years older than she is now. That was unacceptable to my love.

I cannot recall exactly how long the subject was dead, but it had to be at least ten minutes. Wolfgang was still on top of her, trying to warm the blood. Marci was at a point to where she was yelling at the corpse, even slapping her bloody head a few times. Suddenly, Wolfgang pushed his upper body away from the corpse in the attempt to get off the body.

Marci's eyes closely followed his movements and she asked, "What are you doing? Why are you getting up?"

Wolfgang said, "We have failed. It has been too long."

Marci didn't like what was coming out of my father's mouth. Marci grew angry and said, "You are just going to give up? Get back on her!"

Wolfgang shook his large head as he placed his enormous right foot on the floor. Marci, out of rage, reached out to stop my father from getting his feet on the floor. As Marci lunged forward, Wolfgang's large hand quickly wrapped itself around the thin, fragile wrist of my love. My heart almost stopped. Wolfgang looked deeply into my love's face and shook his head. He said, "We were too late. Maybe we cannot bring the dead back to life."

Marci's eyes welled up, and tears began to fall down her cheeks. Marci struggled to free her hand from my father's and in her most horrid rage, took her freed hand, made a fist, and came down on the chest of the subject. The blow was so hard you could hear the blow from the punch around the lab. The body seemed to make a slight exhaling sound. Wolfgang would not let go of Marci's other hand. He started to get angrier and said, "Look... calm down, woman... it's over!"

Marci, with a crazed look on her face, violently shook her head and yelled back, "It's not over until I say it's over! Let me go!"

With all her might, she pulled and pulled to get out of Wolfgang's grasp, and before I knew it, Marci took her freed hand and attempted to hit Wolfgang. Wolfgang's natural instincts sprang into action and he quickly grabbed the freewheeling hand by its wrist. Wolfgang angrily said, "Stop it!"

Wolfgang looked at me. I went toward them and said, "Marci, control yourself!" Marci slowly stopped struggling, looked at me with that fiery passion, and I could sense her regaining control over the anger. My love finally controlled herself so I took her upstairs and she cleaned herself up. The rest of the day was depressing. Marci was saddened by the results from the experiment.

As a couple of weeks went by, Wolfgang administrated tests on the subject. He noticed something was strange with the daily results, but he kept this secret to himself. He monitored the body every waking hour during those two long weeks. He second guessed himself over and over, trying to understand what he might have done wrong. Did he bite the subject too quickly or not quickly enough? Was the temperature of the blood too low for the formula to react properly? But Wolfgang had a feeling about this subject, so he kept it in the lab.

Marci and I went downstairs to visit Wolfgang. Wolfgang wanted to move the body off the bed to better clean her. She had been lying in the same pool of dried blood for almost two weeks. As I stood there about to help my father, we heard a noise. The most wonderful and beautiful noise I had ever heard in my life. Marci was confused at first. She took her eyes off me and looked at Wolfgang. Wolfgang's long, pointy face had a look of amazement on it.

Marci slowly lowered her eyes down toward the subject and again the body made a slight sound, just one small cough. Marci moved further to study the body. The eyes were still open, with a glassy stare as blood covered the face. Marci moved closer to the head to see if it would make that cough sound again. Marci got closer, almost willing it to make a sound. Marci said, "Come on, make—" and before Marci could finish her sentence, the body coughed hard, causing a thick glob of coagulated blood to flow from the mouth of the subject. Suddenly, the subject coughed again, and this time blood sprayed out of its mouth and covered Marci's face. The subject was trying to breathe. Wolfgang quickly moved over and pushed Marci back as she was still in shock and disgust over the blood covering her face.

Wolfgang ordered for my assistance. I was already standing next to the body and Wolfgang told me to help him move the head over to the side. He told me to lift the bed as much as I could toward him, and I did as instructed. I saw the blood pouring out of the mouth of the subject as she continued to cough up more of the blood that was in the back of the throat and lungs. As the moments passed, the coughing continued at a more rapid pace, and at that moment we knew we had done something that no man had ever done in the history of mankind. We brought the dead back to life. Now the body was gasping for air. The eyes still didn't blink and no limbs were moving, only the chest and throat moved. I gradually moved my side of the bed back down as slowly as I could so as not to disturb the subject.

Marci moved around to where the head was located, and she said in an excited voice, "She's alive! It's coming back to life!"

Wolfgang had a forced smile on his long muzzle and he struggled to say, "She's alive but the formula is trying to repair the body. Notice the face is not moving, nor the limbs. The only area that is moving is where I bit her. Hopefully the formula will travel throughout the body."

Marci looked at me and said, "We did it!" in a loud and high-pitched tone as she reached up and put her arm around the large shoulders of my father and gave him a hug. She reached out and we held hands. I looked at this most perfect creature with blood splattered over her face and hair.

I said, "Let's back away and let my father work."

We stepped back, and the body was now breathing. This bought a smile to Wolfgang's face. "I think it's breathing now on its own." I looked down at the disfigured head. The facial expression did not change. The eyes stared straight ahead and blood covered every inch of that placid face. The hair was missing in large clumps and the ears were cut off. All of this was done by my love's scissors. Her mouth was open and if one would look closely, the tongue was just a small stump inside a very bloody mouth. All you saw was this blooded head making a strange gasping sound as it struggled to breathe.

Marci went upstairs to clean herself while my father and I stayed with the creature. Wolfgang was very proud of this successful experiment. The formula can bring the dead back to life as long as the blood is still warm. How warm is unknown, and obviously the normal body temperature is optimum for the formula to work, but when the body is cooler than normal, there is a point or a limit in which the formula will not react and produce life.

Wolfgang took many blood samples from all over the body. I categorized all the samples and made notes as they were handed to me for observation. After a week and a half had past, the creature started to move its hands and one foot. The eyes started to move, then the mouth, and then the head in short, stunted movements. The creature started to moan, and we knew it was in agonizing pain, but we didn't want to disturb the formula's path of taking over the complete area of the body. Marci came down to check on the creature periodically, but she was tired and I talked her into getting more rest.

As the days passed, we cleaned up the creature as best we could. After an additional week, the creature started to regain all movements of its extremities. We tested its sense of feeling over every inch of its body and we concluded that the body was in the same condition as it was just minutes before death. The creature's memories started to come back to her, you could see it in her face. It was difficult for her to talk because her tongue was cut out, but even without that issue, she seemed to have problems with even attempting to speak.

We kept the body alive with IV fluids, and after each passing day, the body seemed to get stronger. When the bleeding stopped, we saw the healing start in the damaged areas of the body. As the days went into weeks, the creature started to develop control over her voice box. We explained what had happened, but many of its thoughts were unclear. We knew she was scared and we believe she knew what had happened.

During this critical time during the experiment, I had asked Marci to help with Eva. Marci grew to love Eva greatly. Eva made great strides since her time at the estate. She started to learn how to crawl in just under two months. In my spare time, I went back through Lewis's notes and other documentation they had on me when I was first born. I shared the information with my parents and, of course, with Marci. If what we predicted for Eva's future was correct, she should follow the same path as what I experienced as a youngster.

Marci would, from time to time, visit the creature. Several weeks after the rebirth, we allowed Marci to watch but not antagonize her in any way. We kept the subject in the cell and after some doing, we got her out of the bed. The subject had trouble standing at first, but after a few days she was able to stand with some assistance. We kept the subject on a chain with the same metal neck collar the homeless people wore years prior. During this time, you could see some transformation starting to occur. Like with all my experiments, I videotaped every second from the cell room. The subject could speak but was very confused. It was like she knew what she was doing and where she was, but she would go in and out of this state of confusion. We believed the brain was damaged during the length of time the subject was dead, although we expected the formula to correct the mental damage.

The formula was correcting some of the damaged areas even a few weeks into the experiment. The tongue was becoming more rounded, and the ears were healing faster than normal. The tongue, nipple, ear, and the outer areas that were cut were starting to have a more rounded edge than the flat or jagged edges as it was in the beginning. The skin and muscle were building so it would form into a more curvature shape. This was beyond our understanding, but it was amazing to watch. We took picture after picture and documented everything we could. The burnt crevassed areas caused by the damage from acid exposure were healing as well.

After four or five weeks, the creature started showing gradual signs of sharp pains. After several days, the pains started to increase in both severity and frequency. The creature would periodically cry out in blood curling screams and moans. During this time of the experiment, my father and I decided it would be best to restrain the creature on the hospital bed with the straps. The subject was now able to speak with some clarity, and she begged for mercy many times during the day. We believed the pain was coming from the healing and tissue growth around the affected areas. From time to time, the subject would "space out" for a moment and then come back to cognitive awareness.

After strapping the subject in the bed, we continued to feed it regular food which we started around week five of the subject's new life. We did allow the subject to move freely in its cell for hours at a time every day, but when we could not supervise the specimen, we strapped it down on the bed. The creature seemed to be worried. Wolfgang and I were careful to never mention the transformation process. We didn't want to further upset the subject.

Another week passed, and the creature continued to complain about the rapidly increasing sharp pains throughout its body. Most of the pain seemed to come from the legs and arms. I noticed more hair was developing on the entire body. During this stage, the subject's memories were clearer, and it was sharper. The tongue and ears were at full size. As predicted and expected, those areas totally re-grew its once lost assets. The subject's mind was more aware than any time since its new life. It could also remember most of the events from the prior life.

We had numerous conversations about Lewis, Trevor and the subject taking care of me when I was younger. It was strange and very different. It was not really Carolyn speaking. Something was different about her, like she was in a small trance-like state but not aware of it, if that makes any sense. Her mind seemed to operate a little slower than in her previous life, but after numerous tests, that didn't seem to be the case. In fact, when we gave her a standardize test that I pulled off the Internet, she completed the test at a rapid speed and scored very high on all the tests we administrated. She used to be a teacher in her past life, so this was in line with the characteristics of the formula. It tends to accentuate the person's strengths at very high levels and elevates other underperforming areas in a person. At the end of the day, there still seemed to be a fog or glassy stare in the eyes of the subject. When Carolyn was alive the first time, she did have a stare about her, but this time the stare was more prominent. Again, maybe this was part of the formula and a normal reaction, but it was a moment of concern for us, especially with this being the first time we had ever re-created life from the dead. Either way, we believed this was a positive sign.

The transformation was going according to plan. It takes about three months for the process to run its course to completion. This area of the progression is when my mother decided to take her own life. We wanted to be careful and not have history repeat itself, so we decided to closely monitor the subject. We kept her in chains instead of the bed. We wanted her to have more movement in the cell.

At that point in time, the subject's ears, nipple, and tongue grew back to their normal size. The skin was completely free from the acid burns and the hair grew back thicker. Its speech took some time to fully develop, but as stated before, the formula accentuates the traits and characteristics of the previous state.

We continued to keep Marci's time with the subject limited. The subject rarely brought up Marci, but it did have long conversations with me about the past. From everything that I could deduce, the subject's memories of her past were intact and clear.

As the days passed, the pain in the extremities started and increased throughout the days. The subject grew very upset, knowing full well what was about to happen to it physically. We tried to calm the subject down but at times, had to use sedatives to help reduce the stress. The hair on the body was now in an advanced stage of grow. We kept the subject naked, since it was used to not wearing clothes. Throughout time, the bones in the legs and arms started to grow faster than the muscles and skin around them. The skin was stretched to a point where no wrinkles showed. The skin was pinkish in color and at times turned red and, in some places, turned blue, as bruising became easy. Even the slightest touch would cause the skin to bruise.

As the days passed, the pain increased. The bones grew more, and one of the leg's skin broke just under the right knee. The head grew large and at one point we thought the skull would break through the skin, but it never did. The fingers, hands, and arms all grew faster than the muscles and skin. It had an awful time handling the pain. At first, the pain would come and go, but at this point the pain was constant. We asked the subject to describe the pain and the only answer we could get was a constant, almost extreme burning feeling. The subject complained that the skin felt as if it was going to rip off the bloated extremities. There was a constant feeling of twisting, popping, and movement in the arms, legs, and fingers. Its bones constantly ached at the end of transformation.

My father and I took meticulous notes on every word, feeling and description the subject was attempting to describe. My father consulted with me every night, telling me that his transformation, as well as my mother's, had many similar traits. Wolfgang admitted to me that he wanted to kill himself because of the pain. He remembered slamming his body into the wall of the cave a time or two because of the intense pain the formula caused. He told me that Zelda cried most of the time that she was awake in her last month going through the transformation. He said your mind goes through this incredible stage of feeling absolute abandonment, which is so true because no one had experienced this feeling before, not from start to the end of the transformation. He had wondered if the formula would kill them during the process. He said conquering the fear of death and abandonment was the toughest part, but after the process was completed, he had never felt better in his life.

I had to stop for a moment and think about what my father was professing. He said, "I know what you are thinking, Garrison. I… we… abandoned you in that forest. You must have had strong negative feelings toward us while you were growing up. Yes?"

I stared at my father and said, "Yes, but I was too busy living my life and trying to understand why I was so different from the others in my family and why everyone treated me with distain. Only my adoptive mother, Adelle, treated me like a real person, but in the end, she turned on me as well. Then I think about my Marci. She was abandoned as well. To this day, she doesn't know who her parents are or who they were as people. I think her situation is more distressing than mine."

At that point, my father and I grew closer and we started to understand each other more. Then our attention fell to the subject. She was now screaming and moving around on the floor of the cell. We continued to monitor her by taping every second of the day and taking still pictures of all parts of her body at certain times of the day. We ran the pictures and the results through the computer and tracked her physical changes. As predicted by my father and by the well documented notes of Lewis, the body started to enlarge. Every aspect of the body was growing.. After a couple of painstaking weeks, the subject was mentally and physically exhausted. At times, the subject would fall asleep from pure exhaustion. Often the subject would collapse, which caused more bruising to the skin, and sometimes the skin would rupture or split. After several hours, the wounded area would grow back and heal itself.

The last week or so of the transformation was the most drastic. The head changed its appearance quickly. The nose area of the subject quickly developed a muzzle, which seemed to happen overnight. This was a very painful experience for the subject. The teeth first fell out and then the second set of teeth came in over just a couple of days. When the muzzle developed and started to grow out, at times you would hear the popping and cracking of the muzzle moving outward from the face. During this stage of development, the ears and head expanded. The legs, feet, arms, hands, and fingers all started to grow larger. The subject was in intense pain and discomfort.

Almost to the day, we came upon a full three months which was approximately ninety-one days. The subject suddenly stopped moaning and moving around uncontrollably, and just lay motionless. We had seen the end of the transformation. The subject looked like my parents and Trevor, Lewis, and the old man in my father's cave. It woke up from the floor of the cell and attempted to get up. The coordination was not completely there, and it stood approximately seven feet tall. Apparently, the size does vary from female to male subjects; again, the females seem to grow up around seven feet while the male subjects grow to eight feet and several inches or so. The burnt areas of the body were completely healed and there was no evidence of the burns in those affected areas.

The creature got up but was shaky at first and stumbled into the bars. I told it to be careful and not try too many sudden movements. The creature spoke well but, of course, had the strong hissing or lisping sound at the end of its words. My father said this was due to the fact that the mouth was narrower than what the mind was accustomed to, therefore, it takes a few months to get the words out of the mouth clearly. He said when he is angered, the slight lisp comes back from time to time.

Unannounced, Marci suddenly appeared just when the creature was standing for the first time. Marci was shocked at what she saw. I sensed that she admired the creature and, in her eyes, the thing was beautiful. This somehow made my father and Zelda feel closer to Marci. They sensed and knew that Marci not only appreciated and respected them but wanted to be like them. The mutation didn't bother Marci, she was focused more on the end game than in the present state. She wanted immortality and to be closer to perfect than she could ever obtain in her "normal" state of being. She stood there admiring the creature. Marci admired the long locks of gray hair that were coming down from its wolf-shaped head. The creature had a large belly, like the previous being, with large, thick legs, while the shoulders were narrower and looked disproportionate to the rest of the body. The feet and hands were small but the arms and legs were long. Marci's eyes couldn't leave the head of the creature. She found the wolf-like muzzle just amazing. She couldn't believe that this was, at one time, a human being. She could still see the former human trapped inside of this amazing creature's body.

We didn't want to anger the creature, so Marci's presence was not viewed as a positive situation. I looked back at Marci, but our eyes didn't meet because her eyes were fixated on the creature. Suddenly, it looked at Marci and I sensed anger. The creature fell trying to come over in the general direction of where Marci was standing. Marci spoke, "That's okay. Take your time to get used to your new body."

The creature moved its large head up. Its yellowish–gray, bloodshot eyes squinted, and its mouth curled up on both sides while its nostrils flared. The creature said, "You... fucking... bitch. Look what you did to me, you cock sucking, mother fucking bitch!!!"

Marci was shocked at the reaction which was puzzling to me, but I think Marci was more interested in the development of the most newly created and close-to-perfect creature that had been transformed. The creature continued, "I am a freak now," and suddenly the creature started to cry.

I ran over to Marci and pushed her out of the lab. I told her to give her some time and not to come down here until the creature was more stable. Marci wanted to stay but after I insisted, she left the lab and went upstairs. Wolfgang attempted to control the creature, but it cried uncontrollably for hours until it fell asleep for a couple of hours.

We ran numerous tests on the creature over the next week. It finally developed its coordination and was fully functional, physically, as my parents. We had great concern that the creature wanted to kill herself before we were ready for its life to end.

The creature wanted to die. It didn't want its new form. It begged to be killed. This upset my father to a point that he had to quietly collect himself. To him, his state of being after the transformation was a blessing, something that was a special and wonderful gift that only a very few should experience. It angered him that such a gift was being rejected by, at one time, in my father's eyes, such a pathetic human.

Chapter Seven

Marci helped take care of Eva during the creature's transformation. During this time, Eva had many painful nights. She would cry suddenly and then stop as fast as she would start. From all accounts, this was normal and what happened to me when I was Eva's age. The only solid documentation on me when I was a baby was my blood type, which stayed in a constant state of change. Eva's blood type was the same. One day it would be B negative, and the next day it would be O positive.

Eva was now about six months of age. She started to walk in the later part of her third month. After only working with her for a week, Marci got Eva to walk. After only stumbling twice, she got the hang of walking in less than a day. Eva was an amazing child. It was hard for Marci and Zelda to keep up with her around my large house. She was also speaking several words clearly during this time of her early development.

Eva's senses were just like mine; off the charts. She heard everything inside or outside of the house. Marci would take her in the stroller for long walks around the estate. After a few weeks, Marci came to us very concerned. Marci noticed the anomaly that when she pushed Eva in the stroller near the forest area of the estate, there was an abnormal reaction from the animals. Birds seem to be louder and would fly away more than usual. Squirrels would run as fast as they could up trees. When Marci told us this, we all just laughed then told her that I had the same experiences when I was a child. When I went to the zoo, the animals had a negative reaction to my presence, and would be more upset and hide or attempt to get as far away from me as they could.

The best way we could explain this to Marci was that animals have a higher level of scent and their senses are more advanced than humans. They can sense danger and, of course, with our propensity for wanting to eat them, they obviously sense this feeling, thus they are alarmed when we are in their presence.

Zelda and Marci taught Eva as much as they could, but you can only teach children like my sister and I so much. I realized at a very young age that I absorbed everything that was told and shown to me. It got to a point where everything was just repetition. I only needed to be shown something once. If someone were to repeat the same lesson or instruction, I quickly became bored.

Marci would practice her violin while Eva played either by herself or with Zelda. Little did I know at the time, but Zelda had a beautiful soprano voice. I was shocked when I first heard her sing to herself one day while she was cooking dinner for the family. Wolfgang told me that she would sing daily to him when they were living in the cave. Zelda's voice was strong but soothing and could reach levels that most operatic performers could only dream of reaching. Eva seemed to really like hearing Zelda sing. Marci loved Zelda and as each day passed, her admiration grew for the perfect creature. Marci had many talks with Zelda about her condition and said on many occasions that she envied Zelda's perfection. Zelda saw a lot of herself in Marci, and my mother told me many times that she was just like her over a century and a half ago.

Zelda, in her most distant past, studied voice and opera at the Hochschule fur Musik Carl Maria von Weber in Dresden, Germany. I was surprised to learn this about my mother, but I learned of her talents when we brought her to the estate. Many nights she would sing various arias from different composers as her voice resonated throughout the house. On some occasions, I would play the violin while my mother sang. At times, I would have Marci play the violin, and I would be on the piano while my mother would unleash that beautiful and powerful voice of hers.

My mother was well educated, and in addition to her musical background and instruction, she had also studied to be a teacher. She came from a very affluent family in Berlin, taught at a very young age how to be a debutant. Zelda had her pick of the gentlemen in her inner circle. Her flawless shaped body, with her long, flowing blonde hair kept her popular at school. She had the most striking blue eyes that a person had ever seen. Zelda, on a multitude of occasions, said that Marci's eyes always reminded her of hers before the transformation. She had stood five feet eleven inches in height and had very broad shoulders.

She ran track for her high school, as well as her college. She made straight A's but was a little on the wild side. She would get into trouble at school, mostly because many of the other girls were jealous of her, and she knew it and used it against them.

My parents met at a political function in 1930. Zelda told me it was love at first sight. At that time, Wolfgang joined the Nazi party, and because of his academic background, he quickly moved up the organization. Wolfgang was a tall, strong, broad-shouldered beast of a man. He stood six feet, four inches in height and weighted over 250 pounds. My father came from a very poor family of six siblings where he was the only boy. Wolfgang was a very smart kid at an early age and he knew it as well. He often talked down to his friends and even teachers. Through the years, he was picked on, and many of his classmates and neighborhood kids would pick a fight with him. Wolfgang was strong and large for his age, and many times he would win the fights that were forced on him. He grew to despise many of these kids, as well as their parents. He was smarter than most of his teachers and many of them either felt threatened or jealous of Wolfgang.

Wolfgang's personality developed into a spiteful and socially awkward type. His anger grew mightily during this time. He rebelled against all forms of authority and his anger especially grew toward the affluent. Many of the businesses in his poor neighborhood were owned by people of the Jewish faith. Wolfgang hated the fact that many of them didn't struggle financially like his family did. In my father's youth, he believed in socialism. He once believed that all people should be on the same social and economic levels from their early beginnings. This belief of his soon changed as he grew older.

Wolfgang enrolled at Heidelberg University and had a very productive first year academically. He was drawn to and had a great understanding of chemistry, and the subjects in that field came easily to him. Many of his professors quickly took notice of his brilliant young mind. He tested out of many classes, and after a few years he quickly mastered all his chemistry courses. While Wolfgang was there, he befriended one of the head professors in the chemistry department named Hans Wundrak. Hans's interest was in the field of genetics. This field of study was also of great interest to Wolfgang, and although genetics was relatively new at the time, the Germans made great strides in the field.

In 1931, Hans was offered a position in the Nazi party as one of their lead scientists on a special, top-secret project ordered by the Fuhrer himself. Hans hand-picked my father to be his lead and only assistant. The purpose of the project was to develop a potion or formula that would stop the aging process. Hitler wanted to find and control the fountain of youth. As the project developed over time, it branched out and incorporated genetics. During this time, my father further pledged his allegiance to the Nazi party by becoming a member.

Hans and Wolfgang's ideas were to genetically change the human condition so the aging process wouldn't exist. The project was top secret, beyond all reasonable understanding. Hitler was also obsessed with the idea of having the power to alter the genetic make-up of a human and to be able to destroy the imperfections of the human. He fantasized about the notion of creating the ideal master race, before, during or even after birth. Unfortunately for Hans, he died suddenly of a heart attack, leaving the entire project at the feet of my father.

Adolf Hitler loved my father. He used my father's past to fuel and control his passion. He knew that Wolfgang wouldn't think twice about killing another man or women if he could get away with it. Over the years, he killed thousands of people, mostly Jews, throughout the 1930s and early 1940s. He conducted numerous experiments on them and other subjects, trying to find the perfect solution to the potion that he discovered and what we now have today, Formula L. Even after I got to know my father, he showed not an ounce of remorse toward the thousands that he killed, nor the thousands that he tortured through experiments or for his personal enjoyment. At that time, Wolfgang only loved two possessions in his life – Zelda, and his work.

My parents dated for a short time and instantly fell in love. Both had strong personalities, and together they fed off one another. Within months, they quickly married but had no children during the war years. It was not an easy courtship or marriage for them. Zelda's parents didn't approve of Wolfgang or his family. They wanted more for her. They wanted her to marry someone of equal social quality.

Wolfgang's parents didn't approve of Zelda's family because of their hatred toward people with money and power, which her family possessed. As the years passed, Zelda was disinherited from the family fortune, so she developed a great hate toward her parents.

Wolfgang's family never accepted Zelda, which created even more tension for Wolfgang. Wolfgang's disappointment grew to utter hatred for anyone with the last name of Von Ritzmitter, so he disenfranchised himself from his entire family.

My mother loved Richard Wagner's music and usually sung his arias. She would sing only in her native German tongue. Zelda detested everything about the French and had issues stomaching the Italian operas. She loved Wagner because of his emotional connection with the more grandiose god-like or supernatural characters that he used in his operas. She also loved the tension in the composer's operas. She often compared his music to lovemaking. The build-up of anticipation of the main focal point was the main interest for Zelda in Wagner's works. Zelda also played the violin rather well but wasn't considered professional in that field.

My parents told me many interesting tidbits of their life during World War II. When my father worked for Adolf Hitler, he and Zelda were invited to many of Hitler's parties at his vacation residence at Berghof in Obersalzberg of the Bavarian Alps. Hitler spent more of his time here during World War II than any other place, and it was widely known as his headquarters. Wolfgang and Zelda had the honor of being invited many times to this most honored place.

Hitler also loved Wagner's music, so Hitler and Zelda had a lot in common from the start. Many times, Hitler would ask Zelda to sing a few of Wagner's arias. Zelda would never disappoint, and from my father's accounts, she was outstanding every time.

Hitler had great admiration for Zelda. Zelda, because of her beauty and being well endowed with a full figure, made friends easily with men. She was physically bestowed in her youth, and she kept her marvelous physique into her later life. Hitler spoke more to Zelda than he did to Wolfgang. Wolfgang so wanted to please his Fuhrer that at times he overstepped his boundaries with him. Wolfgang wanted to talk about his formula to Hitler, but the Fuhrer grew increasingly disinterested in the imperfect formula. He was only interested in Wolfgang creating a formula that didn't have the transformation effects. Hitler only wanted results, perfect results. He wanted to achieve immortality and that was his only goal for my father. Often Hitler would dismiss my father openly, which hurt him greatly.

Eva Braun was extremely jealous of Zelda. She noticed Adolf's stares and attention toward Zelda at the parties and meetings she attended. Eva attempted suicide in August of 1932 to gain attention from Adolf. It worked, and Adolf started paying more attention to her.

But Eva was uneasy whenever Zelda was in the room with her love, as his attention was always swayed toward Zelda. This would infuriate Eva, but she had to be careful. She feared Adolph and didn't want to confront him, fearing for her life. Zelda, on the other hand, didn't fear Adolph; in fact, she feared no one. Wolfgang thought that was part of Zelda's hold on Adolph. She was a strong woman, both physically and emotionally. She had a sturdy core that was built to conquer and devour fear. She feared only death. Zelda was unlike any woman of that time and was in total control of her life. She had to possess these many traits in her persona to love and associate with a man like my father.

In May of 1935, Eva made a second attempt on her life. From that moment on, Hitler and Eva were a tight pair. Adolf was so in love with his Eva that he couldn't bear the thought of losing her. There were times when Adolf's eyes wandered, especially for my mother, but Adolf was careful not to upset his Eva.

Wolfgang knew of this at the time and did nothing about it and, in fact, he encouraged Zelda to get closer to Adolf. Of course, Wolfgang had to be careful not to let the relationship get out of hand. Wolfgang loved Zelda and he loved his work as well, so he was caught in the middle, so to speak. He didn't want Adolph to take both of his loves from him; he wanted to be Adolf's friend. Like so many Germans at the time, he admired and worshiped the man. To this very day, my father and mother speak highly of Adolf Hitler.

Speaking to my parents about a historical figure was surreal. They would speak of him as if it were only yesterday. It was so hard to believe that all their history together took place over a century and a half ago.

Marci listened in and participated in many of these conversations. When we were alone, Marci and I would talk with astonishment about the stories that were told to us. Like little children huddled around a campfire, our imaginations ran wild as our hearts pumped faster than normal as the stories unfolded before our eyes. No one alive today has ever lived to tell about these special tales. No history books ever recorded the absolute truth about what happened during that time. I will say that at many points during their stories, I sensed there was something they were not telling us and, of course, they were on to my hesitation. Not one word was spoken about my uncertainties or my level of uneasiness that I could sense. No need to bring up any subject matter that wasn't worthy of discussion or of material interest to us at that time.

Wolfgang said to me on many occasions that Marci was like my mother in her day. The fire, the passion and sheer, constant presence of the macabre made her very poignant to my father. Zelda knew this from the first time they met. She told me that it was as if she was looking in a mirror when she saw Marci. I expressed these observations to Marci who was honored by the comparison.

Little Eva had grown so fast in such a short period of time. In a few years she would be ready for school. The rapid growth that she would experience over the next few months would be hard to accept. I understood more than anyone the pain that she would go through. Sudden and sharp pains would strike her body without warning then suddenly the pains would disappear. She'd had these pains since birth but soon she would be old enough to remember them.

I had great concern about the potential of Eva biting my Marci. After all, Eva was just a child and kids will be kids. She was no different than other kids her age when it came to anger or lashing out at someone. Marci was at a point in her existence that I believe she would let Eva bite her just so she would have the opportunity to live forever, but oh, what a price she would have to pay. Sometimes those thoughts lingered in my mind, and like a cancer, it would eat at my soul.

Chapter Eight

Months passed after the transformation, and the creature felt better about her situation. The formula has many blessings and it was up to us to discover what those blessings were to the creature. It didn't take long for us to discover that it loved to read and learn. Being a former teacher in her previous life, we knew this would have great appeal to her. It read and studied nonstop for hours on end. It was taken aback by the ease at which it read and how much information it retained. It had the ability to read pages upon pages and could recite word by word what was just read. It was happy for the first time since its change.

The reading and studying developed quickly. It requested more difficult subject matter and reading material. Hours upon hours it would read and study. It also had an extreme interest in women. It would masturbate at any time, even in front of us, while looking at pictures of women in magazines that it requested. My father thought it was one of the most interesting things he had ever seen. At first, it was shy and would go over in the corner of the cell to play with herself, then as time went by, the creature didn't care if we knew what she was doing, much less try to hide it from us. We knew that it was getting more enjoyment from the fact that we were watching.

One day Marci witnessed the act by accident and she thought it was extremely funny. The creature hated Marci, for obvious reasons. Its memories came back in stages and the creature remembered its past with Marci. It also still found Marci physically attractive, even in the creature's altered state of being. Marci knew how to get in people's heads, and she was an expert at persuading people to get what she wanted out of them. Marci used this skill to her full advantage with the creature. Marci would coax the creature into touching herself by wearing tight fitting clothing, and many times would remove an item of clothing bit by bit until the creature couldn't control her lust for Marci. Many times, she would masturbate in front of my love.

Marci would belittle her, which excited the creature even more. Of course, she noticed that fact and played the role strongly. She would order the creature to do things to herself. The creature hated the fact that Marci had so much control over her, but they both knew the creature wanted Marci sexually. She always wanted Marci, and this sexual desire was not lost in the formula's alteration. This brought up an interesting subject matter for me and my father's research. I asked my father if he found human women still attractive. I wondered if he found them more attractive than his wife's altered physical state. Wolfgang found this issue very interesting and was completely honest with me. He said he found both equally attractive.

The subject of sexuality was a difficult subject for me to speak about with my father, and his brutal honesty sometimes didn't help the situation. He told me that he found Marci overwhelmingly attractive and would love to have sex with her. He assured me that he wouldn't, but for the sake of the conversation, that is what he told me. He said that he found Zelda's appearance attractive as well. Both were equal in his eyes. He did state that he never had any homosexual tendencies or thoughts in his life. The thought of homosexuality disgusted Wolfgang before his transformation, and his thoughts about the subject of homosexuality was even more disgusting to him after his transformation. Of course, this would make sense since the formula heightens your senses and plays upon your strongest traits and improves those traits. This all became more understandable. Wolfgang's past desires for human women was still present in his mind but the altered state of his lovely wife was also attractive to him because his altered state is the new Wolfgang, so to speak.

In the creature's case, she was homosexual as a human, so it made sense that she would still find human women attractive today. What we found interesting is that the formula corrects mistakes caused by deformities in the host's cell structure. Therefore, in a twisted way, at least in this case, the creature's past homosexuality apparently was not a correctable mistake that the formula needed to make. The ears, nipple, hair, and skin all grew back, but the homosexual feelings stayed the same. Interesting.

As the days passed, Wolfgang and I had to decide what we were going to do with the creature. We ran many experiments on it and logged in every aspect of information that we could muster. We needed to eliminate it, but we were wondering about the method of extermination. The creature knew its life was ending, but it didn't want to die at this point. It felt better physically, knew more, and reasoned better than at any time in its previous life. It is interesting seeing the mental process of going through the transformation. In the beginning, it didn't want to transform, during the process it wanted to die, but now after the transformation it wanted to live.

I often wondered if Adelle would have accepted her fate for a couple of months longer before she killed herself in front of me? Would she have wanted to die after her transformation? Down deep in my heart, I believe she would have eventually accepted her metaphorizes. Oh, what could have been. I do truly miss my adoptive mother, and although she turned her back on me in the last moments of her life, she was usually there for me. The choices we make today certainly effect the aftermaths of tomorrow, which always had me contemplating about my Marci and the formula. I can't let her ever go through the transformation. Her beauty would be destroyed, and I don't know if she could handle the physical change. Then I think about my own feelings. Maybe I am the one that had the problem, not her. Maybe I don't want her to change. Maybe I wouldn't find her attractive after the change. I couldn't live with myself if I would end up rejecting her sexually after her transformation.

I bring this thought up because one of the most important crossroads Marci and I had in our relationship happened during this experiment with the creature. We were at this local restaurant that we often frequent, and during our dinner, Marci unexpectedly brought up the subject again of wanting to be transformed. Marci wasn't nervous nor was she angry. She was just matter of fact; more than normal in her tone. She said, "Garrison, we really must talk. You know I love you and I want to spend the rest of my life with you. We are made for each other. I feel that you believe this as much as I do. I have never loved anyone more in my life than you. I never met my birth parents since they abandoned me like you were abandoned. I admire you in so many ways, but when you wanted to seek them out, wanted to meet them face to face, that really impressed me and got me thinking. When I was there and saw your forgiveness of them, my heart skipped a beat. I could never find that much forgiveness in my heart for my birth parents. I was alone all my life. I always wanted a family but after ten, twenty, thirty different families would come and interview me like I was some fucking dog or job candidate, you tend to grow very cold to people after they all turn you down. Was I not pretty enough? Did I say something wrong in the fucking interview? Why didn't anyone want me as their daughter? I never understood that, and it hurt me." Marci began to cry, which was a rare event.

I sat there almost in tears myself. I didn't know what to say. The love of my life was pouring her heart out to me and I didn't know what to say. After several moments I spoke, "Marci, I love you. I have loved you from the moment I saw you in that theater. I do not understand why no one wanted to adopt you, but you have my heart, my soul, and my life. I am yours."

Marci cried even harder, and after a few moments she collected herself. She angrily wiped the tears from her eyes with both of her hands. The sweet, innocent, and vulnerable love of my life suddenly changed before my eyes. Marci hated to ever let her guard down or to let her emotions get the best of her. She looked at me with the most sincere and steely gaze that I have ever seen from her. She began to speak the words that I didn't want to hear, "Garrison, I want to make this perfectly clear to you. I want to be like you. I want to be like you parents." She leaned closer to me as her breasts pressed against the table. All of this was perfectly orchestrated by my love to get my attention. "I want what Carolyn has. I want to be perfect. I want to live forever. I want to be transformed. I have seen the formula's power and I'm willing to accept the pain of the transformation. I am at a point where I don't care about my appearance. See, you just don't know how lucky you are to be so perfect, to not ever worry about growing old or being sick. You know, you understand… you live perfection every day of your life." Marci's voice grew louder and more passionate. "I want to feel that way. I want to be with you forever. Don't you want that as well?"

So many thoughts were running through my mind. I thought, *Wow, there is no way I am going to change her way of thinking on this issue.* At that moment, I knew my Marci was at that crossroad in her life and in our relationship. My head was spinning as my heart was burning with anguish from the fear of losing my love forever. I had to say something.

I said, "Yes. Yes, I want the same as you. I want you to live forever with me. I just…" My feelings got the best of me and I had trouble speaking. I quickly regained control of my emotions and continued, "I have to be honest with you. First… I cannot bear to see you in pain. You will suffer through the transformation."

Marci quickly answered me, "I am prepared for that, my love. I know it will be tough on me and for you, but I am willing to do this for us."

I said, "I know. It is just difficult."

Marci looked down and said, "My biggest fear is not the pain or my transformed state. My biggest fear is would you still find me attractive? I mean, sexually attractive." She looked up at me to see my reaction.

I said, "You will change not only physically but mentally as well. Yes, it might be difficult at first, but my greatest concern is will you be the same person inside as you are now? That is my greatest fear."

At that moment, our hearts fell. We didn't know what to do. Marci wanted this. She wanted the perceived image of my perfection. But she knew that she might not be the same person as she once was and that scared her as well. We agreed that her aging over time would be difficult for both of us to accept. Her eventual death was not an option to either one of us, but what a price we must pay for immortality.

After dinner, we drove back home and I put Marci to bed. I walked outside and there was my father, out in the very back of the grassed lawn. He was just a few yards inside the treed area. He was directly under one of the four trees growing over Adam's remains. I approached him rather slowly as I took my time. He was eating a deer. His large hands held the deer in front of him, with the tail and head of the animal draped over his outstretched hands and arms. He opened his large wolf-like muzzle and bit directly into the side of the dear. He pulled mightily with his strong jaws and tore a good bit of meat from the side of the animal. He looked at me while he ate as I finally made my way to him. Without saying a word and without taking his eyes away from me, he lifted the corpse of the deer toward me. I looked at him and tears developed in my eyes.

I knelt toward the neck of the deer and paused for a few moments. Wolfgang sensed my issues as he asked, "Women troubles?" I nodded yes. He said, "So, your woman wants to transform. Are you going to allow it?"

I said, "I don't know if I have a choice."

Wolfgang said, "We all have choices. The issue is can we live with the choices we make? Sometimes it's best if you eliminate the issue before it becomes a matter of choice."

I looked at him and said, "That is not an option."

Wolfgang nodded and said, "I know that. So, what is your problem? Looks to me that you have already made your choice. You are worried about whether she will love you the same. Or is it that you might not find her sexually attractive any longer? Maybe her new look might repulse you. See, I know what you are thinking. I had similar thoughts regarding your mother." He looked down at his meal and took another huge bite out of the deer. He looked at me and said, "Eat before the blood gets too cold."

Those words, 'Before the blood gets too cold' resonated in my soul for a while as I remained kneeling in front of the animal. I ran my hand across the non-disturbed area of the fur, just below its neck. I said, "Before the blood gets too cold, Father?" I looked at him and our eyes met. He was confused. He nodded as if to say, 'so what' or 'yes' as he kept looking at me. I said, "I only bit one human in my life and that was Trevor. He turned normally, as we expected. He basically turned into your transformed state of being."

Wolfgang nodded his in agreement. I said, "But I have never bitten into a dead animal, or a dead human for that matter. You did with Carolyn and she turned into basically Mom and your current state."

Wolfgang said, "Correct, but you have not brought a human back to life as I have. So, now I am thinking what you are thinking. Maybe the formula that you have in your body might cause a different change in the new host. The basic chemical structure of the formula changes ever so slightly from current host to the receiving host. In theory, there should be some form of change from your bite compared to mine if we brought the human back to life."

I said, "I think so. Right? There should be a different physical change in the transformation. The transformation will still take place, but I wonder how much of a change compared to your experiment with Carolyn." I thought aloud, "I do not know if that is a good or a bad thing," as I looked into my father's squinting but interested eyes.

Later that night, I stayed outside and roamed through the forest area. I was alone and I needed to be in such a state of existence. Another unknown in this endless charade of god's punishment to me for being his most perfect humanoid prodigy. *Why does everything have to be so unknown and complicated for me in this life of infinite time? Why such a price, god? Are you there? Are you listening?*

God, if you exist, your idea of creation of the human species is completely different from my conception of what the human state should possess. I know that it would annoy you if I used my power to create my own human race, now wouldn't it? I have the power to start a whole new species of animal that the history of the world has never seen. Even though we only have a short time after death, we have the power to bring the dead back to life.

A man can talk himself into anything when he is at his wit's end. Maybe that is where I am at this stage of my life. If I want my Marci to live with me forever, then there is no other possibility. You leave me no other choice. To do nothing is not an option. I can correct what you broke, what mankind has broken through his inferior state of existence. Throughout these thousands of years, man has struggled to do only the mundane tasks of everyday life. I conquered tasks and have mastery over many of them in my short time of existence. My father spent most of his adult life working on the secret of everlasting life and he discovered the fountain of youth. Many humans died an agonizing and unthinkable death in the pursuit of the human's ultimate goal since the beginning of time. Everyone wants to be younger in age and appearance. Few want to die. Most humans will go to the most drastic edge of pain to buy a few weeks or months of life. For me, life is everlasting, a goal that I was blessed with since birth.

Many nights, while the world sleeps, I imagined the future for me and my sister, Eva. If what my father thinks is true, our child will be as perfect as us. If this does indeed happen to come true, Eva and I will be able to start a whole new species of anthropoid beings. I just hope that we produce a normal-looking and functioning human. Then I wondered if the new being might be even better than us, a more perfect version of Eva and me. But these needs are down the road.

Now my issue was what would happen if I were to bring my Marci back from the dead. What kind of effect would it have on her physically and mentally? How much would her body transform? This new avenue of adventure was not one that I wished to travel, but I knew I may not have a choice in the matter. Marci was going to go through the transformation one way or another. I knew I must come to grips with the idea and take an educated chance on what I thought was best for my Marci.

Chapter Nine

The creature continued to read and learn. Its appearance had not been altered since the transformation. It was hairy and didn't want to wear clothes. Its sexual craving was still extensive. Marci and the creature were always at ends with a constant exchange of bickering between the two. Wolfgang had to control the creature at times during their arguing by going into the cell and roughly grabbing her and forcefully placing her on the floor. He put extra chains around her wrist, which turned the creature on. Many times, it pawed out in the attempt to touch Wolfgang in his private area. Wolfgang found the creature disgusting and told her so on many occasions, but it never seemed to stop the creature from being sexually aroused. Wolfgang ended up placing chains around her ankles and wrists. Its neck chain was always around her neck and that was attached to the concrete wall of the cell. Wolfgang added an additional chain that wrapped around its waist. It hated to be treated like an animal, but in a twisted way, the creature found it sensual. I never would have guessed that in its past life she loved sex as much as it did.

One day, Marci was in the lab with us. As usual, she wore a short skirt with no panties. She would purposely bend over numerous times and show her private areas to the creature. This would send the creature into a frenzy. It would try to force itself not to look, but the power of its sexual side forced her to. Marci drove the thing crazy. We told Marci not to aggravate the creature since we wanted her as calm as she could be. It made it easier for us to run tests on the subject. We also wanted the creature calm because it was easier to deal with through the night.

Marci was becoming more difficult to control. I hate using the word control, but in the beginning of our relationship, I would make strong suggestions and Marci would follow those suggestions toughly.

As our relationship developed and we become closer, the sex increased to a level of unrelenting passion. Marci couldn't get enough sex to satisfy her. She would fuck until she was physically exhausted. She became more independent in our relationship and told me that only I had control over her and that she would never let or allowed anyone to control her life.

All Marci wanted to do was torment and tease the creature. That passion grew into her daily discussions of how she wanted to murder the thing. Of course, the creature knew its life was going to be short-lived anyway but hearing it from the person that it hated the most was not easy to come to terms with.

My love was becoming restless and bored. Her mood changed over the weeks to follow. She was withdrawn during our dates. The only activities that got her out of her funk was sex with me, her tormenting the creature and, of course, the time she played with Eva. As time passed, Marci developed an even cockier attitude, but she knew she was the inferior one of the house.

Eva was growing smarter by the day, and my parents and I were always a constant reminder of Marci's imperfections. Of course, the creature was also a constant reminder of her inferiority. Occasionally, the thing would taunt her. It knew how to get on Marci's nerves. Many times, they almost came to blows where I had to hold Marci back from attacking the creature.

In our downtime, Marci would play her violin alongside me while my mother sang certain arias. I didn't pretend, out of respect for Marci, that I needed to look at the notes. I would glance at them once and it was burnt into my brain forever. Marci would fail many times, trying to hit the correct notes, and that greatly upset her. She often would throw a fit and the discussion would always turn into an argument about how she was never going to be as good as me or 'them' as she called my parents.

Adding to Marci's stress was Eva's sudden burst of pain that caused her to cry uncontrollably. Many nights, Marci would go without sleep tending to her needs, trying to comfort Eva in the best way she knew how. Zelda was also concerned about Eva's pains, but as Wolfgang and I explained, it was part of the process of what she had to experience. The pains would eventually go away.

I showed my parents countless reports that Lewis had written on me during my time at Eva's young age. I still remember those pains when they occurred. I never slept much as a baby or toddler, mostly because I only required a couple of hours of sleep, not to mention, the pains kept me up. When the pains hit, they were usually confined to one area of my body, like my arm, leg, or my side. The worst pains were in my head and in the back of my neck. Sometimes the pain would be all over my body and at times the pain would be so intense, I had difficulty in locating where the pain was coming from. I knew what my sister was going through. Many times, I would hold her tightly, but sometimes that would make her cry even more. Then, without notice, the pain would go away quickly, with no lingering pain. It would just disappear, and sometimes faster than when it came on. According to Lewis's notes, there were times when I would go days without any painful attacks.

Life sometimes can be difficult, and during some of those most difficult times is when life usually becomes more interesting. After all that happens in our lives, I wanted my world to stop moving and reshaping before my eyes. From the time that Lewis and I went on our trip to Germany to the creature's experiments, it seemed that in that short span of time was a lifetime of events. I wanted a more stress-free life.

My parents were home with us, my sister was in my life now and my Marci was safe, if she didn't upset my parents in any way, which seemed likely at that point. Still, the thought of her doing or saying the wrong thing at the wrong time placed fear in my imagination. There was always that chance that her life could be in danger. The creature lurking in my basement occasionally sent chills down my spine. I always had the fear of it getting loose and killing whatever was in its path. At times, I wanted to take my love and run away from it all, but I loved my parents too much for that to ever happen. I could never abandon my parents like they abandoned me. They, like I, would live forever so we are forever linked as one.

My finances were going well. The bulk of my fortune came from mining gold, which added to my real estate ventures, and that led into buying up various arrays of different companies from diverse sectors across many industries. I took over my conglomerate with the intention of attempting to retain and improve my vast fortune to be as recession-proof as possible.

One day, I called in some favors at one of the local jewelry stores that I owned. I ended up creating an engagement ring for my Marci. It was spectacular. I had a massive diamond placed in the middle of the ring while many other fine diamonds surrounded its corners. The finest platinum formed the ring that held the diamonds in place. The total cost was extraordinary for its time and for such an item. Many kings and queens would have grown jealous over the piece. I know that Marci and I never talked about getting married, but we never made our love official with a ring. I thought now was a good time to start with the journey of having a symbolic reference of our relationship, even though we're not going to marry.

I took Marci out on a date at the finest restaurant the city had to offer. Afterward, we went to the Kentucky Opera and watched a Puccini opera, 'La Boheme', which was one of Marci's favorites. After the opera, we went backstage and met with our friends from the Orchestra, and we introduced ourselves to many of the performers in the opera. Marci was very content. She was stunning. She wore a long and perfectly fitted, low cut dress that highlighted every inch of her beauty. She looked flawless. Her hair was golden blonde, but this time she wore it up. A few hairs graced her face that set off that perfect and seductive look that she had possessed since day one. She had a confidence that I had not seen in a while. I sensed in her that she didn't have a care in the world. She was more than content, she was truly happy. I had not sensed nor seen that in my love in quite some time.

Marci struck up a conversation with the conductor, Nicolas Swartz of the Kentucky Opera. She complimented his skills as a conductor and his visualization of what the composer had in mind. Marci said, "I love when conductors orchestrate the original version of what the composer wanted from the start. In my opinion, no one can perfect the original version of any composition. Only the composer knows in his mind what is perfect and how it should be played. No one should step in and alter what the creator wanted when he created the work. To change the opera, you change the entire intent of the piece of music. It would be like someone walking up to a Picasso and editing his painting. If that were to happen, it would be regarded as a ruined Picasso. Right? If Picasso wanted to make any changes, he would have already done so during his creative process creating the work. Music is no different."

Nicolas nodded but tended to disagree. He said, "But some composers would welcome the artist to change a phrase, a note or tempo to fit a certain mood of the conductor or to the skillset of the orchestra."

Marci quickly said, "But if the orchestra is not skilled enough to play a certain passage, either they should be replaced for better musicians or the conductor should move to an easier piece of work. Perfection is the goal for music. No mistakes. Of course, unfortunately this is impossible, right? Perfection cannot be achieved." She looked over at me as Nicolas followed her brilliant, deep blue eyes, Marci continued, "Unless you are Garrison Seawick. Now this is perfection, both in his performance and in his aura. Don't you agree?"

Nicolas smiled at me and said, "How lucky you are to have such a beautiful lady admire you the way she does."

I said, "Yes, I am lucky. Very lucky, but perfection is not everything..."

Marci interrupted me and said, "It's the only thing. Right, my dear? It's the only thing that matters because perfection, created by man or woman, is the direct adversary of God. Right, Garrison?"

I smiled and said, "Yes. I assume that to be the case."

Nicolas was bewildered, then Marci raised her hand and bent her wrist toward Nicolas. Nicolas, like a scared young teenage boy about to experience his first kiss, nervously but gently took Marci's fingers in his hand and laid his lips on the back of her hand. Marci enjoyed having one of the most important men in the room feel so nervous, to basically push him out of his comfort zone, and to force him to act the way she wanted. Marci's confidence made her more attractive than I have ever seen her. She knew she was able to control anyone in the room, she had that much assurance that night.

We made our way around the room and met most of the people that were present. I heard numerous conversations. Many whispered and some came out and asked me if this was my love interest. All I said was, "I am the luckiest man on the face of the planet to have found my soulmate."

Marci's smile was large, passionate, and sexy beyond all reason. I sensed that Marci needed to hear me tell others that she was my partner in life. She knew it from the heart, but she needed to hear it from my mouth to others' ears. That was her confirmation, especially in the presence of this group of people, this group of people who were living Marci's dream, the dream to be in an orchestra, to be the best out of a large section of people. For the first time, she was happy and not angry or envious. She was at peace with herself. That impressed and pleased me.

When I brought my love home, Marci got out of the car and walked seductively toward the back of the estate. I turned the car off and followed her. She looked back at me with those intoxicating deep blue eyes and slowly but methodically unzipped the back of her dress. I watched her lovely hand travel down to her backside as I enjoyed the most perfectly shaped and very athletic back that I had ever seen. That night, my love didn't wear any bra or panties. As she walked, she moved a certain way that made the dress just melt off her perfect body. She stopped, moved her right leg out and dropped her arms down to her side. The dress fell to her thin waist as she stopped the dress at that point. My heart skipped many beats. She looked back at me and smiled.

She threw her head back and laughed aloud while she took her right leg, picked it up and stomped hard on the cement floor of the pool area. Her dress, that cost thousands of dollars, fell helplessly to the ground. With one slow movement, she walked out and away from her dress. The only man-made article of clothing on her perfect body was her four-inch high heeled shoes. She slowly and seductively walked over to the back of a chair that was near the pool. She bent over slowly as she grasped both arms of the chair. She again looked back at me, smiled and ever so slightly, moved her rear from side to side. Her backside was pointing out and begging to be touched and used.

Marci picked up the chair and deliberately placed it facing me. She slowly moved around the side of it, bent over and sat down. She crossed her legs and placed her hands on the arms of the chair. Her bare breasts stood perfectly still. She gently bit her lower lip and said, "Now take off all of your clothes." She looked at me and said strongly, "Now!" I did as I was instructed. She told me to kneel before her. As my knees felt the cement, I knew what I was supposed to do. She moved her body forward and placed each leg on the top of the side of the chair. I then performed oral sex on this most lovely and intoxicating creature.

The night was filled with lovemaking and was not only confined to the chair. Our ventures were in the pool and on a sashay lounge chair as well. My love moved in directions that I didn't know was possible. I stood in the middle of the shallow end of the pool as my love wrapped her legs around the small of my back. My hands held her ass as her arms moved in all directions. One moment they were wrapped around my head, the next moment she was bent backward as her back hit the water. After our climax was over, we staggered out of the pool and she picked up her dress and shoes. When we went inside, my mother was there in the kitchen with my father. They both smiled. Marci smiled at them and didn't say a word, she just kept walking out of the kitchen. I fumbled to get my pants on, the whole time all I heard was my parents' loud snickering. I looked at them and rolled my eyes as my father laughed hard. I made my way upstairs to my love.

The next morning, Marci took her time getting downstairs. It was strange but not one word was mentioned about what they saw that night. As we ate breakfast, which consisted of chopped, raw deer legs that Zelda fixed, my Marci entered the room. She smiled at everyone and made her way toward me. She bent down and opened that lovely mouth of hers and as our tongues played with each other, my father said, "Do you have to do that at the dinner table?"

Marci playfully said, without looking at Wolfgang, "I bet you enjoyed our show last night. Did you take notes?" Wolfgang smiled and let out a hardy laugh. Marci reached for one of my chopped-up deer legs. I smacked her hand and said, "Marci! You cannot eat that, you will get sick."

After breakfast, Wolfgang, Marci, and I made our way into the basement to check on the creature. It was not happy seeing Marci. It seemed every passing day that the creature's hate for her grew. The tension was easy to sense. Marci hated the creature but at the same time admired her fate. It could live forever. It could perfect what it excelled in in its former state of being. This is what Marci admired.

The creature hated Marci's beauty. Before her transformation, she wanted Marci sexually because she had been a closet lesbian, with bi-sexual tendencies, throughout her life.

After the transformation, that passion toward Marci was even more intense than before. Mixed with those feelings of desire was the creature's utter jealousy of Marci's beauty and the love she had toward Lewis. She saw so much evil throughout the decades but kept so much of her thoughts in because she had no other choice but to do so. She couldn't or wouldn't leave. She knew that if she left the family, she would probably be murdered before she could get out of the door. Now it is a character of that evil story. It was the product of its own innermost feared evil.

At first, Marci didn't say a word to the creature upon our visit. Marci didn't have to; she just looked at her and winked. It set off the creature to almost uncontrollable levels. It said, "You piece of shit. I heard you last night. Even from down here in this fucking cell I heard you and Garrison having sex. You are such a tramp. Do you not have any shame, you stupid bitch?"

Marci just laughed as she covered part of her face with her hand. The creature moved over toward me and said, "What happened to you, Garrison? Why did you let this tramp into your life? She's not worthy of you."

I said, "So, you want me to leave her so you can have a chance at her yourself?"

The creature got angry and rushed the bars of the cell, pressing the entire front of its naked body against the cold steel. It reached out and attempted to grab me. Marci said while laughing, "Pipe down, you pathetic piece of garbage."

The creature said, "Fuck you, bitch."

Marci said, "Just shut the fuck up so we can think how we're going to kill your ass." Marci walked up to the cell and said, "I hope I get the honor of killing you myself." Marci looked at her with those beautiful blue eyes as she cast them up and down the creature's naked body. Marci said, "I hope you have a long, slow and painful death."

I stepped in between the two and asked my love to step away. I heard the creature move away from the steel bars. The chains gave her movements away. Marci said, "So, when are we going to kill the cunt?"

I said, "Marci, just go upstairs. There is no need to get yourself aggravated. Come on… please go upstairs."

Marci looked at me and said, "Okay" in a sexy way. She smiled and started to walk away. Suddenly, we all heard the creature slam her naked body against the steel bars again. Marci quickly turned her head from being slightly startled. Out of nowhere, a large, heavy, and thick book came flying out of the creature's hand. The book hit Marci's forearm as she quickly put her arm up to protect herself. This enraged Marci. She said, "You fucking shit head." She began to walk toward the cell and suddenly, out of the corner of my eye, I saw something in the creature's hand. It had a silver-like shine to the object. Before I could say anything, the creature rose its hand and arms up and quickly flung the object toward Marci.

I attempted to shout out, but I had no time. I saw the object in the air, headed toward my love. Marci had no time to react. Before I knew it, my love's head jerked back and Marci let out a blood curdling scream. I raced to my lover's side as fast as I could. I heard in the background the creature said, "Yes!"

Marci was bent over screaming, and as she straightened up, I saw a metal object which looked like a steak knife. It was lodged in my Marci's eye. Marci held the injured part of her face with one of her hands, and with the other she grabbed the knife and quickly pulled it out of her eye. Blood was everywhere. Marci was screaming in pain but also in great anger. The creature was laughing uncontrollably.

Wolfgang quickly moved over to the pulley and started retracting the chains into the wall, which forcefully moved the creature slowly back as it fought the chains every step of the way. The creature lurched, jerked, and tugged at the chains with all her might. Meanwhile, Marci was now in tears from the pain. It was a perfect throw by the creature. How she got ahold of that knife was beyond my comprehension at that moment.

Marci held her eye with both hands. Blood was starting to seep through her fingers. I quickly picked up my love and carried her upstairs. I ran as fast as I could while I carried her through the house. Zelda saw us and asked what happened. I said nothing to my mother as I raced out to the car and placed Marci in the seat. Marci was crying hard but was also very angry. I drove as fast as I could to the nearest hospital. When we arrived at the emergency room, I got her out of the car and proceeded to carry her inside. I yelled at the top of my lungs for help. A small army of hospital workers came to our aid. The medical workers took her back as I attempted to tell them what happened. I told them that someone had thrown a knife at my fiancé's eye. I was stopped abruptly by some guy in hospital scrubs telling me I had to wait out in the lobby. Marci was screaming for me and I told her I would wait for her and I loved her.

I went back to the lobby and was forced to speak to a bunch of people. Some took my insurance information while others asked me if I had something to do with her injury. I was confused and angered at the surreal moment. After what seemed like days, the doctor came out and told me the horrible news. Marci had lost her sight out of that eye. The knife cut her optic nerve and it was unrepairable. The eye itself should heal but it would never look like the other one. I asked if I could see her and they let me go back.

As I approached the bed, Marci moved her head over to see me and she started to cry. I said, "Marci, I am so sorry. I don't know what to say, but I am here for you."

Marci said, "Please keep loving me."

I said, "Marci, I love you more now than I have ever loved you before."

Marci said, "I am now a freak."

I said, "No. You are not a freak. You will get past this, I promise you. You are not alone. I am here for you. You are still my girl." Marci just cried, and the doctor told me that I better leave.

I stayed the night and the couple of days that Marci was in the hospital. When Marci was discharged, she was depressed. She felt disfigured. She was at a special moment in her life just before the incident. She was happy and very content. She was at peace like I had never seen her before. It was like she had come to peace with her demons. The world that was there just days ago was now destroyed.

I sensed her depression, but I also sensed her anger, her anger toward the creature. I was very concerned. I knew I had to keep an eye on my love. I knew something had to be done right away with the creature because if not, Marci was going to do something to it. My concern was that the creature would hurt her further. Of course, Marci thought she was prepared, but the formula made the creature better, her senses and reflexes were just too advanced compared to Marci's. I think down deep in Marci's subconscious mind, she knew this to be the case as well, and that knowledge further depressed and angered her.

When I brought Marci home, my parents met us at the door. Marci had a bandage wrapped around half of her head and covered her injured eye. Marci's eye was hurting her, we could all sense it, but as soon as we entered the house, Marci started to speak, "Just take me to that bitch. I have something to say to her."

Wolfgang stepped in front of Marci and said, "Marci, I think it is best that you leave the creature to us."

Marci said loudly, "Get out of my fucking way!" as she started to cry because of the pain. Wolfgang looked at both of us, but he didn't move. Marci said, "Wolfgang, get out of my fucking way. I am going to kill that bitch." Wolfgang stood there, not moving a muscle. I placed my hands on my love's shoulders. Marci quickly moved away from me and slapped at my hands. She said, "Get off me. Leave me alone and tell your father to get out of my god damned way."

Wolfgang started to speak, "Marci..."

My father was abruptly interrupted as Marci screamed, "Get out of my fucking way!"

Wolfgang hung his head slightly, moved his large frame out of her path as he raised his arm as if to show her the way to the basement. Marci angrily looked at him with her good eye and said, "And you think your fucking Jews died a horrible death... you have not seen pain. You are going to have to redefine pain after tonight!"

Wolfgang stood there with his arm still held out, growing more impressed with the frail human that stood before him, and his admiration was at its highest level for her.

Marci walked fast as she made her way to the stairs. She walked through the door on the right at the bottom of the stairs. My father and I quickly followed as Zelda tagged along behind us. As soon as we got in the lab, the creature was laughing and saying, "How's your eye, bitch? How many fingers do I have up?" Marci was beyond upset as she ran toward the cell. I raced with all my might and somehow got between the creature and my love. Marci started fighting me to get to her. The creature kept talking and making fun of her. It said, "Come on, Cyclops, let me take the other eye."

Wolfgang had the creature sitting on its cot with the chains pulling its head and lower back to the cement wall of the cell. Its hands were shackled on the main chain around its waist. It smelt terrible as it was sitting in its own waste. Wolfgang had not washed it since the attack.

The creature continued to talk and now it was directed at me. It said, "I bet you don't want to fuck that freak anymore, huh? You're not the only freak in the house anymore. Oh wait, your parents are even bigger freaks than you or your imperfect whore."

That moment is when Marci completely lost it. She ran toward the cell and tried to get inside but Wolfgang had the cell door locked. Marci was possessed. I have never seen her so upset. It was very frightening. Marci was screaming and making no sense as to what she was saying. The creature kept mimicking her every word. I was very upset myself so I looked over at Wolfgang and said sharply, "Open the cell door now."

Wolfgang smiled and said, "This ought to be fun to watch." For some reason, that pissed me off even more. It was like this was a funny scene to him, but for us, it was beyond just revenge. We needed to hurt this creature and make it wish it was dead. My hatred for this thing was close to the hatred that I had for Adam.

As Wolfgang went to get the key, Marci hurried around the lab looking for something, anything, but at the same time, it had to be the perfect item for which she was searching. Meanwhile, the creature kept talking and yelling to make sure it was heard. One insult after another came from its mouth as the words cut directly into the core of Marci's insecurity. It was a nonstop rainstorm of offences, each one making Marci's anger grow beyond human belief.

When Wolfgang opened the cell door, Marci quickly went in behind him. She attempted to push him out of the way, but my father was too large to be pushed. Marci made her way around him. I wanted to be in front of her, but I failed in that attempt. Marci had an object in her hand, but I couldn't make it out what it was from my vantage point.

The creature's muzzle was open as wide as it could get. Its head was firmly resting on the cell wall, unable to move its head a quarter of an inch from the wall. The creature was growling and saliva was dripping from its many long, sharp teeth as its breath passed through its flaring nostrils. Marci stood in front of the creature as it continued to howl and growl at her. Marci unraveled a long, curled up piece of wire, quickly uncoiling the wire from her hand. She attempted to place the wire over the muzzle of the creature, but it kept moving its head from side to side. Wolfgang came to Marci's assistance as he took hold of the creature's head and forced the muzzle shut. Marci quickly wrapped the wire around the muzzle a handful of times. Wolfgang then took over. He continued to wrap the wire around several more times. The creature couldn't open its mouth. Liquid of some sort was flying out of the nostrils and saliva continued to drip out of the mouth and onto its naked breasts.

Marci looked at the creature with her one eye and said, "You fucking bitch. You took my eye from me, now I am going to take your fucked-up life from you, but it is going to hurt like a bitch, you pathetic, god damned old useless bitch." Without warning, Marci lunged forward and placed as much pressure as she could on the creature's furry forehead. With Marci's other hand, she quickly straightened her fingers and thumb and went for the creature's eye. The creature moved her head to the side to avoid contact from my love's lovely hand. Marci blindly searched for the eye as the creature's face moved closer to the wall.

Marci pressed harder against the creature's head and finally, after some effort, she found the eye. She moved her fingers across the eye as the creature closed its eyelid as tight as it could. Marci pushed her forefinger and index finger into the corner of the eye socket as hard as she could. The creature moaned hard through the procedure as it attempted to move its large head from Marci's pressure hold. Marci pressed as much of her weight against the creature's head that was firmly pressed alongside the cement wall. Marci's fingers made their way past the eyelid and they felt a warm and slimy feeling as they went deeper into the socket. The creature exhibited great pain and discomfort. The wire that was wrapped tight around its muzzle was now making way into the hairy skin as small drops of blood started to form around the wire. Marci's fingers went inside the eye socket, and after going an inch deep, she curled the ends of her fingers to get a hold on the back of the eye. After some probing, Marci quickly pulled the eye from the eye socket. She adjusted her hold on the eye and with a firm tug, she pulled the eye out of the creature's head.

I noticed the creature's body was dripping with perspiration. Marci moved off the creature with her right hand incased in blood. Marci didn't say a word or even have a reaction. She just stepped backward and continued to look from her one eye at the creature in extreme pain. The creature's freed head was moving from side to side, trying somehow to ease the pain. It was moaning and snorting as it attempted to scream. Wolfgang and I just stood there, watching the entertainment. Any feeling of remorse or sympathy toward my once close nanny was absent from my being. The feeling I had was hate; pure hatred in my heart toward this pathetic living being. It had disfigured my love. Marci's eyes were so intoxicating to look at, and now one of them was gone. I love my Marci with all my heart, and to me she was still as beautiful as ever, but to see my love in pain and to lose a part of her senses was something I had trouble accepting.

Marci continued to stand there, watching the creature attempt to move about in pain. The blood was still dripping from her fingers. I walked toward her and Marci said, "I am not done, Garrison. Don't interrupt us."

I bowed my head and stepped back. I motioned to my father to leave them alone. Wolfgang and I stepped out of the cell and I saw Marci moving closer to the creature. I sensed that Marci was in great pain. Her eye was hurting her greatly, but this didn't stop her from continuing what she had to finish for herself. Marci quickly left the cell and ran over to the closet door in the lab. She brought out a large leather bag that made some clinging noises as she carried it back to the cell. Marci placed the bag on the cement floor, peeled the zipper back, and brought out a long, heavy metal wrench, which she must have gotten from my workbench in the garage. I sensed that she'd had this planned many days or even weeks before her being attacked by the creature. The premeditated torture of the creature was all orchestrated in my love's mind and there was no way I could or wanted to stop my love from her utmost required pleasure.

Marci took the large wrench in both hands and said as she raised it in the air, "You hurt me, bitch, I am going to hurt you even more. You have been a pain in my ass since I met you. I hope this hurts you really bad." The wrench quickly came down on the edge of the creature's knee. We could hear the crunching sound as the heavy metal weapon hit the edge of the knee. The creature attempted to scream, but once again the wire that kept the muzzle closed prevented the scream from performing naturally.

The creature twitched and tried to move out of its chains. The more it moved, the more it hurt, especially the injured knee. Marci looked at the pained creature and started to laugh. She went over to the leather bag and brought out wire cutters. The instrument was large, made for heavy-duty cutting. Marci took the apparatus and roughly placed the tool on the creature's muzzle. Without care, Marci started cutting the wire that contained the muzzle and, while during so, cut the surrounding tissue of the creature's lips. After several cuts, the wires were cut and the muzzle was released from its wired trap, but the wire was still imbedded deep into the muzzle's flesh. The creature started to scream and suddenly started moaning loudly. The wire started to slide through the indentions of the muzzle. This was obviously uncomfortable for the creature, so it clinched its teeth forcefully to prevent more unnecessary suffering. It snarled at Marci, as blood from its one eye made its way down the side of the creature's face and shoulder area.

Marci looked at the creature's hands. The wrists were shackled and linked to the restraint that was around its waist. Marci took her foot and pressed one of the wrist shackles against the creature's leg. She quickly attempted to place the wire cutters around one of the creature's fingers, but the creature quickly made a fist with the hand. This enraged Marci, so she went after the creature's feet. Marci braced the nearest foot with hers and placed the wire cutters on the little toe. With little effort, Marci squeezed the handles and the toe was severed from the large foot. The screaming started up again and Marci quickly moved to the next toe and then the other. Within moments, Marci had cut off four of the toes. The creature was bucking in its restraints.

Marci's injured eye continued to pound away with shooting pains, I could tell from the way she was acting. I quickly stepped inside of the cell and asked her to stop. I told her that I would finish what she started. Marci suddenly started to cry. I held her tightly and told her that I loved her. I motioned to my father to step inside and take Marci. As Marci was being escorted by my father out of the cell, the creature started pleading with me to kill it. It wanted to die and end the suffering. Marci looked over at us as she walked away, and she yelled strongly, "Don't kill the bitch. Make her suffer, Garrison!"

I acknowledged her request. Marci wanted to stay, but her pain was great and she needed her pain pills. Wolfgang said he would take care of my love. When they walked around the corner of the lab and disappeared from my sight, I felt extreme hatred in the bowels of my being. I had to keep myself as calm as I could, but my senses were on overload. I heard and smelt everything in that room. The smell of the creature's blood was so strong to my senses that I could almost taste it in my mouth.

I couldn't look at the creature, even though it was pleading to me to kill it. I said nothing for a while then I spoke during one of its many pleads. I said, "You took my love's eye. You hurt my Marci. You have been very... difficult during our relationship. You know that nothing is more important to me in this world than my Marci. I love her with all my heart. I do not like when things hurt the ones that I love. You of all people should know that considering our background. Why in the world would you want to see something that I love suffer?"

The creature said through its muttering from the pain, "Yooooou are unholy. I couldn't let you mate and create something even more unholy than you but... I loved you, and the only way was to get her out of your life. I would deal with you later. I was going to kill you, Garrison. I hate myself for even thinking of such a thing, but I was going to kill you for the sake of humanity." The creature started to scream loudly from all the pain that it was under.

I calmly walked out of the cell and went over to one of the drawers in the lab. The creature was screaming, "Don't leave me here to suffer. Just kill me, you bastard. If you had any heart as a human, you will kill me now."

I picked up a knife from one of the drawers. I walked inside the cell and went over to the leather bag that was on the floor. I looked through the bag and a smile developed on my face. Inside I saw a drill. Next to the drill were large drill bits that were lying loose inside the bag. I took out the drill and one of the larger bits. The creature started to cry, followed by loud screams for help. I told the thing to shut up, but it ignored my demands for silence. I quickly enjoyed listening to its cries for help. Like a lone operatic voice in a theater singing its tale of sorrow, it sung so loud and strong that I began to appreciate the music it was making.

I placed the bit inside of the drill and tested to see if the tool worked. To my excitement, it did. I walked over to the creature and without saying a word or even stopping for a moment, I pressed the lever all the way down to make the drill spin as fast as it could. I pointed the spinning bit at the left breast of the creature and quickly plunged the bit deep inside of the fatty flesh. The creature's screams were almost intoxicating to my ears. I then lifted my finger from the lever and the drill stopped spinning while inside of the fat pile of blubber. I gently pulled upward on the drill and the flesh around the bit pulled with my tug. The creature was howling, spitting, slobbering, and trying to catch its breath during her performance. I pressed down on the trigger to start the drilling process again, but this time I buried the bit inside the quivering mound of flesh and I instantly pulled the bit out. Blood poured from the hole that I made in its breast.

I examined the specimen and focused on the inside shoulder about an inch from the shoulder socket. I pressed the drill bit onto the hairy skin and pressed down on the trigger, causing more beautiful noise from both the machine and the creature. The mixture of the two juxtaposing sounds made for an interesting tune. The creature pleaded with me to stop. She mixed in her desires of wanting to die from time to time during her insane ranting.

I was with the creature for many minutes, too many to count in my mind. I lost track of the count after so much noise, mixed with this newfound pleasurable music that I'd created. I generated over twenty twisted holes of pure pleasure in this most wretched being. The loss of blood was great, but the formula created new blood as fast as it was losing the old. I cast my eyes down upon this body of work and saw blood mixed with sweat over most of the hairy body of this creature that was in excessive discomfort. Its eye had that crazed mixture of pleads of mercy and loathing, along with a mixture of desire for escape while simultaneously experiencing a desire to accept more in the hopes of death. What a wonderful paradox I created for my senses to enjoy.

I took a small break from this procedure and searched through the drawers of my father's desk in the lab. I came across a large hunting knife that my father and I used at times to gut some of our prey, namely deer. The knife was very sharp and had a large curve to the blade. I picked up the knife and made my way over to the creature. It was still active in its bound chains but seemed to be slowing a little as the torture progressed. With its one good eye, it took quick notice of the sharp and shiny steel blade that made its home in my hand. My senses were overly stimulated. I heard, smelt, and saw everything. I even heard the creature's heartbeat increase in rhythm the closer I approached its miserable body.

A strange sensation flowed through my veins. I hadn't experienced that kind of awareness in quite some time. I could almost taste the sweaty perspiration mixed with the iron-like aroma of the exposed, half-coagulated blood from the specimen. I bent down in front of the chained creature and placed the knife just below the broken knee cap. I looked at the coarse hair that was about an inch long and rather thick, and gently slid the knife down the front portion of the leg as a few hairs came off the leg. I repeated the procedure, but turned the knife upside down and went against the grain of the leg hair. The creature was not pleased and begged for me to stop.

I looked at the creature's large and hairy face and said, "Be still and try not to move." I quickly looked down at the leg and repositioned the knife in my hand to have the blade face down. I again started just below the kneecap, but this time I bent the knife at such an angle as to force the blade into the skin, just enough to peel the flesh from the incased leg muscles. I slowly slid the knife into the leg, but the creature moved and started screaming. I was upset at its movement, but the cries of predetermined pain were pleasing to my ears. I took a firm hold of the ankle and placed the blade into my first cut in the flesh. I quickly slid the blade down the leg, attempting to peel the flesh from the leg. To my amazement, the flesh came away from the leg rather easily. The slightly abrasive flesh peeled in long, one-inch wide, uncurled strips as I moved the blade under the tissue. At times during the peeling, I went a little too deep but generally I was impressed by my blade work. I proceeded down the leg and ended at the ankle. I took another swipe next to the peeled area and shed another strip from the leg.

The creature was screaming so loud that my parents, along with Marci, came down from upstairs. My father was impressed with what he saw. He said through its screams of anguish, "Very impressive, Garrison." Marci was in shock, but a smile formed on her most perfect face. Her good eye was feeling heavy from the pain medicine that she was under, but she didn't want to miss this most exciting endeavor. I continued to strip the skin from the lower portion of the leg until half of the skin on the leg was peeled away. The creature's voice was now cracking as it was losing its voice. At first, the screams were so loud but now were mostly air passing through the mouth and the clinched teeth of this most unfortunate animal. Every move the creature made sent shockwaves of pain throughout its large body.

I stood up and looked at the bloody mess of this ungrateful animal. I could see some of the muscle that was exposed on the leg of the beast moving as it attempted to twist in the chains because of the intense pain. The legs of the beast were actually muscular whereas the torso of the creature was mostly fat. The arms were filled with lots of extra blubber as well. I decided to see how deep the fatty tissue was surrounding the stomach area. I quickly took my hunting knife and firmly made a cut into the flesh, just under the breast bone, and I continued to cut to several inches below the naval. This created a whole new set of sounds that filled the room. I only went into the fleshy fat about an inch then made another pass through the open slice and went another inch deeper. It was difficult to move the knife cleanly because the creature kept moving and jerking the entire time.

After many attempts, I finally came to the end of the fatty blubber. I would guess the creamy color of fat was a good five inches deep. During my cutting, I accidently cut a few of the muscles that wrapped themselves around the stomach area. When I looked down, I saw the large incision that measured about a foot and a half in length. I had Wolfgang take pictures of the most incredible discovery. I used my hand to press into the stomach of the creature. The area was soft and very buoyant to the touch. In its previous life, the creature was always fat from the shoulders down to its stomach but always had rather thin and athletic-looking legs.

The creature was still shouting and crying, but the sound it made grew muffled. Its constant screaming forced the voice to give out inaudible sounds. I looked at this horrible thing and thought, *Oh what pain this creature must be experiencing at this moment.* I looked in its eye and the small limited view to her soul was a fear of living, not of dying. It wanted to die to make the pain to stop. I wanted it dead so I could move on, but another part of me was enjoying this playtime with the creature.

The constant lower tone of moaning was interrupted by my love's intoxicating voice. Marci said to Father, "Wolfgang, I have a question. Of course, I know you don't want to do this, but what would you think this thing would taste like if you ate it? I mean, would that be cannibalistic to you? I don't mean to be offensive, but I just don't know. I was just wondering."

Wolfgang said with a smile, "I never thought of the idea, Marci. I personally wouldn't consider it cannibalism. This thing is not as pure as Zelda or myself and certainly not as pure as your lover here." Wolfgang pointed at me and winked. Marci walked over to the cell in a slow and seductive walk. Her eye was still pounding from her attack but the painkillers were making her words and actions seem to be in slow motion.

She said, "So, I wonder how it would feel to have someone with big, strong and powerful jaws just tearing into and ripping the flesh and meat off your body? Especially on someone that is confined and couldn't fight back. That would be very hot to watch, if you ask me."

Marci looked over at Wolfgang and smiled. Wolfgang laughed and said to me, "I think your woman is coming on to me, Garrison."

I smiled although I was uncomfortable with Marci's actions, but I knew that she was not herself because of the medicine. Marci continued, "So what does an animal taste like?"

Wolfgang stopped smiling and said, "I would not suggest eating it because your immune system is not capable of battling the potential parasites, germs or diseases that you will attract. But for us and your lover over here, we can eat any animal live or dead. We prefer a live and naturally warmed body. The coldness of meat or flesh is not highly desirable to us. We like the texture of the muscles, and the aroma of the fur. I personally like when I bite into the flesh. My teeth tend to float or slide across the flesh until they penetrate."

I added my thoughts by saying, "When I experienced my first animal feeding, it was a little dog. This feeling of wanting to eat it, hungry to taste it, and the pure passion of wanting to kill it, came over me like a warm blanket on a cold night. That feeling was a cross between loathing and obsession. I felt a great desire that I had to kill it, a fascination that filled my awareness and brought me to a transformed state of mind where the only thought I had was the animal before me. My sense of smell and taste was so keen that I could detect the slightest scent or aroma on the animal from its innermost parts."

"I could smell its breath and could taste what it last ate. I could feel what it felt. Usually it was fear, which produced the most intoxicating aroma. Then when you attack the animal, the struggle that it puts up is almost sexually arousing. Not in a physical way, but the mental climax during sex. The way the animal moves as your mouth and teeth are into the animal is just astonishing, but it is short-lived because obviously the animal dies quickly in your hands and mouth, which is another mind-altering level of pleasure."

Marci looked at me with a desired look that possessed her perfect face. She stood there listening to every word that came out of my mouth. Wolfgang smiled as he looked at the chained specimen. It had a horrid look on its face. It uttered something, but at this point very little sound was coming from its mouth. I could obviously sense what my father was thinking. Even Marci sensed it. She beheld me with that lusty façade that she habitually revealed. Whenever she wanted something, all she had to do was give that certain sultry look and she normally got what she wanted.

Wolfgang placed his large hand on my shoulder as he walked past me. He gently pushed me toward the creature. Part of me felt, during my torture process with the creature, sexually aroused. I realized how strange that sounds, but the cries of the creature are what I found pleasurable. When I focused on my innermost psyche, it appeared logical to comprehend. Sexual pleasure can be derived in many forms of foreplay. We play off our partner's interest. With my Marci, her most preferred form of sexual foreplay is to be in control. She prefers the more dominant form for her sexual arousal or release but so do I. We therefore take turns during our sexual adventures.

My father and I each took a stool as we went inside of the cell. We went to opposite sides of the creature's legs. I followed my father's lead. We sensed what we were going to do without saying a word. My heart was pounding hard inside of my chest. The smell of fear the creature was excreting, as the sexual scent that Marci was giving off, was almost too much for me to handle. My father sensed these feelings as well. We both looked at Marci who by now had her body pressed against the bars of the cell, her hands grasping the iron bars like she was holding on for her life.

Almost simultaneously, Wolfgang and I lifted the creature's legs. Wolfgang had the leg that was peeled. The blood had somewhat clotted and was sticky to the touch. The creature was attempting to move and free herself from the chains that bound her soul to the most unpleasant task of being the main event of her anguish. The creature's eye was moving all around the room, trying to figure out how to prevent what was going to happen, while its mind bordered on the unthinkable and the unnatural. Within seconds, my father and I opened our mouths wide and struck down on the target in front of us with experienced quickness and snake-like form. Part of me was disgusted and repulsed by my action, but the other part of me enjoyed the pain that was caused.

I struggled, as I usually do, with getting my teeth into the flesh. My father had no issues or problems with his portion. His muzzle and teeth were formed perfectly for such biting action. Out of the corner of my eye, I saw my love. I wanted to make sure she was enjoying this performance since this was all for her viewing pleasure.

Marci's eye never wavered from our biting attacks. I saw my father rip his portion of flesh from the leg he had in his sharp, massive teeth; the portion of muscles and fleshy, meaty tissue in his teeth, pulled and rip down a good part of the creature's leg.

I had to readjust my bite often until I finally created a break in the flesh. I pulled with all my might. I went back and started another bite, trying to make a large, open wound. I didn't want to chew the tissue and I noticed my father didn't either. He was ripping the flesh from the leg bone and spitting the meat out onto the floor.

The creature, with her silent screams of whispered torment, had never felt this much pain in her life. To remain in a semi-motionless bound state while two people bit into the lower parts of its legs, had to be a difficult experience. The body tensed up to a state that I had rarely seen. Not since the liberating torture of my brother had I experienced such fear and agony.

I sensed that this feat brought back many fond memories to my father. He loved torture and seeing people or animals in pain. I believe he was born with these feelings, but some of his fellow Nazis had to learn this different form of pleasure. They grew used to the victim's cries for mercy, and for others, the byproducts of torture, like the audible sounds the victims made, had little if no effect on the one administrating the pain. For my father, he was one of the rare individuals that enjoyed the screaming, the discomfort, and the extreme pain that the victims bellowed from their mouths, for my father viewed most people as sub-human. In his mind, many of the humans that he killed were not worth the effort to keep alive. He felt that he was doing society a favor by killing them, thus eliminating them from the upper crust of the purer human race. He was a true and proud disciple of the only pure race of Hitler's version; the perfect Germanic race.

My father and I kept biting, pulling, and ripping as much tissue as possible. Our goal was to reach the bone and expose as much of it for our and Marci's pleasure. After much work, I made my way to the bone. After several minutes, I made my way down the front portion of the leg. My father had more success and was almost finished with his task. He, at one point, was chewing his portion and after several moments looked at the creature and spit part of its chewed leg up on her bare chest. He just laughed and continued with the task at hand.

Marci was in a trance and part of the reason was the effect of her painkillers that aided her in enjoying the scene before her. I quickly took note of my love moving her hips from side to side as well as pressing them hard against the steel bars of the cell. The short, tight sundress she was wearing moved with her body in perfect harmony. Wolfgang and I looked at each other at the same time, knowing full well that Marci was on the edge of an orgasm if she continued. This made both of us work even harder on picking the leg bone as clean as we could.

I still had more work to do on my leg. Wolfgang even added to the excitement by snapping his side of the leg off from the kneecap. It was rather easy to do since all the tendons and muscles were gone. I had more trouble separating mine. I had to bite off the remaining muscles that were holding the lower leg on the body. After some intense chewing, my portion broke away from the body as well.

I noticed that Marci looked the creature in the eye most of the time and only allowed herself to look away to the creature's devoured legs. Marci ran her tongue alongside a most fortunate steel bar, knowing full well that she was pretending it was my manhood. As she was licking the bar, her eye finally fell on my face and graced my eyes with a most surreal scene. Marci released her right hand from the lucky steel bar and seductively slid her dominant hand down the side of her curvy, luscious body. Her hand found the bottom portion of her dress as she snaked her hand up her thigh. She fingered herself to immense pleasure and after several moments, she had her release. She pounded her body against the steel bars until her pleasure subsided. She opened her eye and looked at me, and with great effort, she peeled her succulent body from the bars. She almost stumbled as she weakly walked to a chair next to the lab table. Undoubtedly, between the pain medicine and her newly experienced orgasm, she needed to rest from the excitement.

The creature was unable to speak or to make any loud sound. The only noise that was coming from her mouth was the breath that was passing through her clinched teeth, caused by the excruciating pain her entire body was experiencing. Every passing second she wished was her last. My father and I stopped gnawing on her lower legs. His side was mostly clean with the total bone exposed. He held his portion up right by the meaty ankle like he was holding a torch. I held my lower leg with both hands and turned mine around like someone would when eating corn on the cob. I roughly threw my portion of meat down as my father followed my lead. We both looked at the creature who looked like it was on an airplane that was about to crash land into a building. Its eye stared straight ahead as it seemed to focus on some object across the room. Somehow, we sensed what it was thinking, that if she took her eye off that object, the pain would increase somehow. I looked over to where it was looking and noticed it was the crematory machine. I instantly looked at my father and we smiled in unison.

I got up and walked over to the lab area to find the key to the lock on the chains. I told Marci, who was sitting down in a chair touching herself as she was smiling at me, "Marci, would you like to participate in ending this creature's life?"

Marci seductively said, "Yeah."

I retrieved the keys to the locks and walked over to the creature. I unlocked the numerous locks that were holding the chains together. The creature didn't move because any time it would, the pain would grow in intensity. The creature's plan was to move as little as possible.

I said to the creature, "If you want to end your suffering, you have to make your way to the crematory machine." The creature finally took its eye off the machine and glanced at me for a few seconds. Its eye was saying that it was impossible to do such a task. The movement alone would send shockwaves of pain throughout its pathetic body.

Marci got up and walked over to the crematory machine and opened the hatch. She said to the creature, "Come on! Crawl over here and get your fat, wretched, disfigured body in here and then all of your pain will go away."

The creature didn't move a muscle. It was afraid to move. Marci was noticeably frustrated after several additional attempts to see the creature crawl to its demise, so she went to retrieve a mop. She took the handle off the head of the mop. She rooted around the drawers on the lab table and pulled out some duct tape. She walked over to the cell and picked up the bloody hunting knife that I used on the creature. Marci laid the stick and the hunting knife on the creature's bed. She pulled a large piece of duct tape from the roll then placed the knife next to the end of the wooden pole and wrapped the two together with the tape. After many feet of tape, Marci had made a spear-like weapon, and she was proud of her creation.

The creature watched every second of the weapon being assembled, and in the back of its mind, it knew what Marci was going to do with it. Marci told us to step out of the way. She approached the creature with that smile that only Marci could produce. She shouted at the creature, "Come on! Get up, you lazy fuck!" She took the self-made spear and roughly poked the blade about an inch into the side of the creature's upper leg. The creature looked down and covered her new wound with her one hand. This movement caused more pain than the creature first feared. Its legs were throbbing in pain and the ends of her knees where the lower legs were once attached, felt like they were on fire. The creature looked around since it knew that it had to move or Marci would continue to poke her with the hunting knife. No telling what else Marci may have done if the creature hadn't obeyed her commands.

The creature had no choice but to bend over to her left side and use her weight to help her body fall out of the chair. The pain and the cramps that were forming in her lower back and upper leg areas made movement difficult, and the dried blood didn't help the situation. As the creature forced itself to fall out of the chair, it caught itself with its hands, breaking its fall. The exposed area just below the knees where the lower legs once called home, hit the floor, causing more concentrated pain for the creature.

Marci continued to yell at the creature. Tears of pain dropped onto the cement floor from the creature's good eye. The creature had to find some relief, so it fell on its belly to help ease the pain from the severed lower legs. Marci took the wooden shaft and struck down hard on the creature's back, not cutting the creature this time. Constantly screaming, Marci ordered the creature to crawl toward the crematory machine and that would be the only way her suffering would cease. The creature used her forearms to crawl several feet, but every inch was a torturous undertaking. Marci continued to beat the creature's back with the wooden shaft but suddenly, without warning, she took the shaft and sliced back with the edge of the knife. The cut was about two feet in length. After Marci made her swipe, she controlled the shaft and plunged the entire knife inside the buttocks of the creature. She pulled the knife out quickly, raised the shaft over her head, came down with the shaft, and created another slice on the back of the creature. This slice came across the previous cut, which made the symbol of a cross.

Marci noticed what she did on accident and laughed hard at the symbol. Marci said, "If only you could see what I am seeing. You are like… carrying a cross on your nasty back." Marci continued to ridicule the creature. Marci's words were cutting and deep rooted in pure hatred, saying, "You wear the mark of Christ, you pitiable creature of God. Crawl on your belly like a serpent into the fiery flames of hell. Crawl on your fat, disgusting belly into the metal chamber that is your salvation from your current hell. God does not make it easy on us, now does he? Now does he? Answer me, you pathetic being of your new God!"

Marci took the wooden shaft and swung with all her might, hitting the back of the being's neck with the wrapped area of the instrument of persuasion. The being attempted to speak. Marci looked down at the being's mouth as it attempted to speak the words… "God have mercy on me. Please help me." Marci repeated these mouthed words of the being for us and mocked her faith in some being that it doesn't know exists.

The being fell face-first onto the cold floor of its current hard and bloody world. Its neck and head had now joined in with all its other pains. Together, the pain became an unimaginable heartbeat of one inescapable, painful torment during this long journey into hell. Entrance into hell is the only salvation for the being made by the new god. The god that many feared over a century ago, a god that was here physically before the being, the god that created her and gave her actual life after death. Even with all those facts available to the being, it still prayed to another unseen god. How pathetic.

I stood there before this being, watching it struggle, praying to a god that ignores its cries for mercy, and at the same time it fails to acknowledge the actual god that created it that was standing in the same room as the being. In a twisted array of events, I found myself admiring the being's desire to endure more pain in exchange for preconceived peace and a pain-free new life. Again, for so many, the main and sometimes only purpose in life is to die so one could spend its eternal life with their predetermined vision of god, a god that is only taken on faith, but not on fact. I thought, *How pitiful but touching that a human's faith can be so gullible, so naïve and so trusting to an idea that, for the logical thinking person, there is a good chance this deity will not exist.* I stood there in pure astonishment at this being's faith. I wondered if the being believes it will be saved through its own painful death. It really makes me question the intelligence of cognitive, functioning intellectual beings.

I watched the last living being from my youth crawl its way toward its only refuge. Not one time did this being ask for help from its known creator, who stood a few steps away. He stood by a machine that would cause even more pain for the being to undergo. One could only induce that this being didn't want the blessing any longer. It didn't want its current state of change. The creature knew its legs wouldn't grow back, and that we wanted it dead.

My father gave it life and it still didn't want everlasting life, it wanted everlasting life from a god that it had never seen and only existed as a fairytale character made up in its mind. A god that's story had been passed down from generation to generation, and this being wanted that mythical storied god over what is real that stood before it in real life.

I played this scene out in my mind. I knew what the being thought, and rightfully so, that its life would eventually end. It knew that its time on this world was extremely limited, but it didn't even one time ask for its life to continue. The being didn't appreciate the blessing that my father bestowed on it, even though it knew it was an experiment. To call out to some fictional god for its mercy and to ignore its true creator is unimaginable to me. It didn't deserve to live.

My father stood a few yards away from the scorching, metal machine, a type of machine that he had seen and used too many times to count. I sensed excitement in my father's soul, an excitement that he hadn't experienced in a long time. I said to him, "This brings back a lot of memories, does it not?" Wolfgang smiled. I sensed that his excitement was more than just watching a body burn into ashes. No, what he was feeling wasn't the pending death of his creation but the development of a human that he thought disappeared over a century ago. My father didn't like this new world that he lived in and had been introduced to since his arrival to the States. He couldn't understand this country's acceptance of so many ethnic groups of people, ethnic groups that he deemed as sub-human. My father believed the formula offered hope for a potential master race in the future. A dream that he thought was dead after the war.

Marci was the only person, besides myself, that gave him comfort and reminded him of a time he cherished long ago. He felt only Marci understood what a blessing the formula was, and the fact that she wanted to transform was impressive to my father. He knew that she was willing to give up and sacrifice her most perfectly-formed human body. To trade that flawlessly body for one that would be deemed as a monstrous one to all who inhabit this planet, for the ability to be close to perfection as a human could get, was refreshing to him. Marci wanted perfection, not in human form, but in god-like form, both in mind and in spirit. Marci admired the transformed body and all its voluminous physical and intellectual nuances. This is what my father and I admired most about Marci. Her desire for perfection was so great that she was willing to give up believing the god concept that she was taught throughout her life. She was starting to understand that it was based on unfounded truth. She was willing to embrace something different, which was intoxicatingly inspirational.

Marci stood a few feet from the crawling being, listening to it pray to its unseen and deaf god. The being started to pray, "Our Father, who art in heaven..."

Marci yelled, "Shut up! It cannot hear you because it doesn't exist! I have prayed to that made up character for years and not one... NOT ONE... family wanted me. Not one family took me into their home and called me one of their own. I even had men try and rape me. I had little boys play tricks on me, call me names, and told me they didn't want me as part of their family, some trying to rape me. I prayed many days, weeks, months, years, and not one time did anyone come to my rescue. Then one day I got lucky. I met a man that loved me, wanted me, and worshiped me as I do him. I followed him all through my teenage years, admiring his greatness as a musician and as an intellectual. Then he comes into my life and you, you pathetic piece of shit, tried to come between us! How the fuck dare you. Fuck you!"

Marci's anger level was high. She took the wooden instrument which she'd created into her hands. She jammed the end of the spear into the side of the being. The entire knife disappeared inside of the being's fatty side. Marci pulled it out and stabbed her repeatedly. With all her might, she repeatedly stabbed the being as fast as she could in a small area of the side of the being's stomach. Marci took her spear and gouged the device down on is lower back and buttocks area. The being quickly stopped its praying and replaced those prayers with cries of pain.

Marci continued to scream at the being and told it to crawl toward the machine. The being desperately tried with all its might to make its way across the floor to its final destination. After several minutes of struggle, the being finally got to the crematory machine. The hatch was open, and the creature crawled to the front of the machine. With all its might, it raised its right arm and grabbed the lower portion of the opening of the machine. Without notice, Marci took the hatch and quickly slammed the door on the fingers of the being. Marci had closed the hatch with her entire upper body weight. The door of the hatch was extremely heavy and closing it with that amount of force cut the being's four fingers from its hand. The being screamed in pain.

Marci closing the hatch door even surprised my father and I. Wolfgang was so impressed he started to laugh and said, "Now Marci, that was not very nice." Marci smiled as she enjoyed the pain that she had caused on the being laying on the floor. The creature held its fingerless hand as tight as it could, trying anything to stop the pain from pulsating through its large body.

Marci reopened the hatch door and said, "Now I want you to stand up on your little nubby knees and walk yourself into your salvation." The being shook its large head to acknowledge that it couldn't possibility do what was order of it. Marci again called the order out to the being. After several attempts, Marci walked over to the being, pushed her face down with her foot and plunged the shaft directly into the middle of her back. The hunting knife was so sharp that it made its way clear through to the front of the being. Marci tried with all her strength to lift the being up on the nubs of her legs. I had to help my love. I reached down and took hold of one of the being's arms. I heard my father moving around behind me and he assisted me with the other side of the creature. We lifted the large mass of flesh up as Marci helped. She twisted the shaft about ninety degrees so the shaft wouldn't slide out of the being.

Wolfgang and I placed the thing on its knees, causing more extreme discomfort than I could imagine. Marci yelled, "Now walk inside." The being didn't move so Marci pulled back on the shaft and we helped the being slide its upper portion of the legs across the floor of the basement. The being was in so much pain that it lunged forward so that half of its body was in the machine. With its one good hand, it pushed itself into the chamber. When all its body was inside, it started to cry and scream loudly. Never in my life had I seen someone in so much agony and wanting instant relief from its suffering.

Marci screamed at the top of her lungs, "You are going to burn now, bitch!" Marci slammed the hatch shut and locked it. Marci looked inside and watched. The being was tossing from side to side, and every now and then you heard her fist hit the inside of the chamber. Marci stood there, admiring the pain the being was under. I looked at Wolfgang and wondered what we should do. Wolfgang smiled at me and shook his head as if to say, *This is your girlfriend's show and you need to stay out of it.* We both stepped back a few yards to give Marci some space. Marci turned and looked at me and smiled then started to laugh. She laughed as though she was mad, crazy mad. Marci pounded on the door of the machine to mimic the being's actions.

After several minutes of his insane torment, Marci went over and started to fire the machine up. Marci only turned the knob a quarter of the way. Inside, the chamber grew hot. You could see the fire come out of the nozzles. The air inside was miserably hot. The being looked around and had to be wondering when the machine would go full blast. Marci teased the creature and wanted to see just how much the being could take. The hair was burnt off the body as the skin turned red and started to blister in many places. The open wounds took on a brownish look and, in some areas, turned black. At this point, the being was forced to move and before we knew it, the face of the being was against the glass of the hatch. Marci got as close to the glass as she could to make sure that the being saw her, but upon closer inspection, the good eye of the being had been cooked. Marci screamed at the being saying, "Fuck you! Fuck you! Take that, you bitch! I hope it hurts so bad you would peel your own skin off."

At this point, the being died from a lack of oxygen. I told Marci that it was dead, but Marci was having trouble with the truth at that point. She still thought the being was alive. After a minute or so, Marci concluded the being was dead so she turned the furnace of the machine to full blast. In a short time, the only thing left of this miracle of nature would be its ashes.

Marci grew quiet and had a look of sadness on her face. She turned toward me and started to cry. We embraced, and she said to me, "I hated that woman. I just hated her. Now she is out of our lives for good."

I said in response, "Yes. She is gone. It is over now. It is over." As my hand stroked my lover's back in an effort to calm her down, a part of me grew sad as well. Not for the same reason as my love. My Marci was coming off a euphoric high. My sadness was that this was the end of any live connection to my childhood, another reminder that no one truly loved me in my life besides my Marci. My adoptive parents feared me, Lewis used me, and Carolyn stayed around for the paychecks. Loren loved me, but we never had the closeness that I craved or desired in my life. But now a new chapter in my life had begun, and hopefully it would be better than the previous years.

Carolyn burned, and the body turned into ashes. Wolfgang cleaned up the mess, throwing the ashes into a large garbage bag in the trash. The next morning, I wheeled the garbage can out to the end of the street and walked toward home. Not a tear developed nor an ounce of sadness crept up on my senses. I felt complete satisfaction because my Marci was completely happy.

Chapter Ten

$\mathcal{S}$everal years after the extermination of Carolyn's life, the world started to settle down for me and my family. Marci ended up with a black patch that covered her injured eye. She grew to like the look but having only one eye at this point in her life made playing the violin even more of a challenge for her. Marci was so upset over having her skills even more eroded, causing her to give up playing the violin many times, but each time that she quit, she ended up going back to playing her beloved instrument. Her anger and resentment increased toward her inability to even play as well as she could before losing her eye. Marci continued to practice, but despite her frustration over her injury, she never gave up trying to achieve her ultimate goal, which was to play for the Louisville Orchestra.

Marci was more obsessed with wanting what Carolyn briefly possessed. Of course, saying to my love that there was no cure for the physical transformation was running thin with her. She would have moments of either great despair regarding the issue or expressing her displeasure in uncontrollable acts of rage. She would at times lash out, throw things, break things, or storm out of the room in a fit of fury. Many times, I would find her walking in the back yard or in the forest, crying softly. She was getting older and she wanted to stop that natural progression from happening.

Marci would only eat vegetables along with fish or chicken for her meals. She did everything humanly possible to stay as healthy as she could. She exercised several hours a day to stay fit and she got so incredibly well-developed that her body was exceptionally muscular. She looked as sexy as she had ever looked. She never lost her figure and, in fact, her body got curvier. She liked the way she looked because she had control over her body.

My parents were understanding the modern world, but they couldn't accept the multinational and cultural relationships of the time.

They were forced to tolerate the new world, even though they didn't agree with its politics or lack of its ethnic cleansing. They learned much during this time. Their minds were like sponges, soaking up everything they heard, read, or saw.

Eva was growing as fast as expected. When she was just a little older than two, I pushed every subject on her. I encouraged her to read everything. I had been taught by an early age that an open book is an open mind. I wanted to push Eva in her studies more than I was pushed by my parents. Since we all knew what Eva was capable of, we knew how hard to push her academically. Wolfgang and I used all of Lewis's documentation that he and other doctors had compiled on me when I was Eva's age. I could have been pushed harder and I should have been exposed to more experiences than I was, and I didn't want us to make that mistake with Eva.

At age three, she mastered many skills like advanced hand-eye coordination, talking, thinking independently, mathematics, problem solving and high-level reading. She mastered all school work that Zelda and Marci presented to her. They helped her study every day. Eva was eager to learn everything. All she wanted to do was read, study and figure out how things worked or how things came into existence. She questioned and wanted to understand everything and all the aspects of every subject she studied. Her favorite subject was anything related to science. It didn't matter if it was chemistry, biology, or physics. Eva loved everything about science.

Eva was a beautiful little girl. She was athletic and didn't have an ounce of fat on her body. Besides excelling in academics, she had incredible hand-eye coordination, just like I had at that age. At this point in her life, she had shown no appetite toward live animals.

Eva grew twice as fast as other children her age. She still experienced multiple painful attacks during the day, but as the months passed, her sharp, sudden pains decreased the older she got. Her rapid growth didn't take away from her little girl charm and sass. She had long, flowing, curly blonde hair that grew down to the small of her back. She possessed a flawless, cream-colored complexion. She had the most stunning blue eyes that pierced through you. Many people thought she was the biological daughter of me and Marci.

It was very difficult to think about everything, but one topic that we as a family had to discuss was Eva's future. Since she looked like a normal human, we could bring her out into the world, unlike my parents. The only option our family had in explaining Eva to the world was for Marci and me to adopt her. I sensed some jealousy that Marci had toward Eva, but I believed it was more envy than jealousy. Marci envied Eva and her gifts, the gifts that only her and I shared. Oh, my parents had gifts as well, but they didn't look human. The only two people in this world that had these gifts and looked human were Eva and me.

Because of my wealth and influence, I had many friends throughout the city, and some of my friends were in government positions. I had some of my associates take care of all the legal issues with Eva's existence. It was rather difficult to explain a person that just appeared out of thin air. We used some of our contacts in Germany, through a company that I owned based near Berlin, to create a birth certificate and all the basic information that a young baby would need when born in Germany. I made sure that this information would be very difficult to trace. We took the identity of an orphan child that just recently died. I had them change some of the information, and through some private donations of monetary value, I had adopted this dead child with the name of Eva Rein. I called in a few favors and had an individual show up from the adoption agency and have Eva's information transferred to the United States.

After a few months, I was legally Eva's father, and we changed her last name from Rein to Seawick. Within months, I went from a single person to a father of one. My Marci was there every step of the way. Not once did she interfere with the adoption process. Marci loved Eva and Eva viewed her as her second mother.

Eva knew that she had different looking parents. She never confused the fact that Wolfgang and Zelda were her biological parents. Eva often asked why she didn't look like her parents, and Wolfgang always told her the truth and she seemed to accept what was told to her. With her extensive mind even at the tender age of three plus years, she completely understood. We repeatedly told Eva to never speak of her natural parents to anyone outside of the family.

We sent Eva to a small private school, the Louisville Collegiate School. Collegiate was similar to the school that I had attended when I was young. We wanted Eva to be able to associate with kids that are more normal. Of course, the kids that she encountered were from wealthy parents and many of these children were highly gifted. Eva was the youngest in the class. The teachers put her through a battery of tests and she had perfect scores on all the tests that were administrated to her. Eva blew the minds of her teachers and proctors. We even hired many educated professionals to teach her at the estate. Eva couldn't get enough of school and teaching. She was a like a sponge to water; she soaked up so much information it was stunning to witness. Her intelligence level was the same as mine but because of our academically assertive ways with Eva, she was more advanced than I was at that age.

During this time of Eva's rapid change and growth, we discovered that not only did she excel in academics but in piano as well. I was playing the piano when Eva walked up to the bench and sat next to me. She watched as I played. I was playing with no notes in front of me but as she watched my fingers move, she quickly studied my every movement and the corresponding sounds for each ivy key that I touched. I had her play a little on the keyboard and she was hooked.

I had to make sure that when we had visitors over to the house that my parents wouldn't be seen. Normally they would reside in the basement when our visitors or friends came over to visit.

I brought in a good friend of mine who was an expert pianist, and she trained Eva for about a month. Her name was Katherine Hertage. Eva's unearthly ability to catch on so quickly to the instrument astonished Katherine. Katherine was so excited to have witnessed such a wonderful prodigy at such an early age.

Eva, at the tender age of three, had a vocabulary that was well beyond her years. It impressed Katherine who wanted to be her full-time teacher. I talked it over with my family and we decided to hire her as Eva's private piano teacher.

The subject of marriage between Marci and I had never come up over these past few years. So many other issues presented themselves in our lives that our marriage was always placed on the back burner. We always felt that we didn't need a piece of paper or some Justice of the Peace to tell us that we were married. We already made the vow to each other over the passage of time. We decided to never officially marry.

My relationship with Marci never wavered or changed. Our sex life was fantastic and, in fact, was getting better and even more frequent, which I didn't think was even possible. Marci's sexual appetite was borderline nymphomaniac. I sensed Marci was very worried about growing older and that she didn't want her body to grow less attractive to me. She didn't want to lose me as a lover, which is why she tried so hard to make love often, to keep my interest in her at the highest level. Of course, I spoke to her about this issue and reassured her that I would never leave her just because she had grown old, but these facts fell on closed ears.

Marci ceased trying to persuade my parents or me in transforming her. I found it a little strange that she just stopped talking about the issue. A part of me was clinging onto the belief that she had given up on the subject, but the other side of my intellect knew that she wasn't going to give up that easily. I didn't know what to do because my hands were tied. Marci knew full well that there was no cure for the physical change that would take place if one of us would infect her with the formula.

Marci's personality had developed through the years since I first met her. In the beginning, she had this quiet confidence about her. As time passed, she developed into a more open person whose personality grew more aggressive daily. When she first met Wolfgang in Germany, it seemed that something had developed her personality into an extreme sadist. To this day, I cannot pinpoint why my love's personality developed in that way. Sometimes in life, either through an experience or some sort of revelation, we discover something about ourselves, something that we never knew existed. For some, they find peace and comfort in wanting to help others in need. Some people find restitution in their later years when they discover they are about to die and they gain a new perspective on life.

For my Marci, she discovered that she didn't really like many people. Many times when she had encountered people, they ended up hurting her. She always felt unwanted and unloved. She never lacked confidence, but she lacked someone loving her. When our paths crossed, she discovered a person that loved and desired her, someone that wanted her was now in her life. She loved that feeling and when she first discovered someone wanted to take that feeling from her, she just lost her sense of normalcy. Her deep-seated passion took over her senses. She liked when her blood flowed faster through her veins as it pumped into her heart, causing it to beat faster. It made her feel more alive than at any other time in her life. It was like what a runner feels during or after a run. The runner's high, so to speak. For Marci, her high was anything that made her adrenaline increase. It awakened the deepest part of her psyche, causing extreme pleasure to many parts of her senses. Wolfgang told me that it was a rare trait that Marci possessed. He said that few had it in their repertoire of emotions.

I understood Marci like no other human I had ever met because I accepted her unconditionally. How so? Because I am just like her. I had never felt more alive than when I first bit into that little dog, when I bit my father, or when I tortured my brother to his death. It was equivalent to an overly sustained orgasm. A mentally simulating pleasure that shakes the core of your soul, strokes it, and massages it to a point of constant waves of heightened tension that begs for release. But the closer you get to the release, you intentionally hold back and slow it down to avoid lunging into the abyss of devilish desire because at that point, you are fully aware that the moment of pleasure will soon dissipate.

So often in life, the art of the hunt is greater than the capture. The longer you stalk your prey, the more enjoyment you receive, not only after the kill but the time leading up to and including the kill. That is what makes the slaughter so enjoyable. Feeling, seeing, and hearing your prey struggle for survival is intoxicating. Only my father understood the intense pleasure that one derives from this dubious psychotic behavior that one allows themselves to playfully explore. My father and I derive great pleasure from all our senses and that is why Marci is so fascinating to us; her pleasure is not as great as ours, yet she still craves the desire to torture, rip flesh from the bone, slice, dismember or dig out a piece of her prey, all in the name of personal enjoyment... pleasure.

Marci had become more evil and somewhat distant. I think she had become more cerebral, thus extra aware of her surroundings. Living with me through the years and with the addition of my parents, had conditioned Marci to think, see, hear, and react to her environment more like how we acknowledge the happenings that surround our lives. Many call it learned behavior. Marci's eye, head, and ears were more alert than before we met.

Whenever I walk outside, my senses take everything in at once. I can convey my current surroundings, quickly process what makes up my environment, and I act accordingly. For example, when I walk outside, I hear and feel the wind. I can automatically determine which direction it is coming from. I notice the different scents that the wind carries, like freshly cut grass, flowers, or the wood from trees, etc. My eyes notice the wind by which way the trees and their leaves sway or which way the blades of grass move, or which direction plants move. As I walk, I feel the terrain under my feet, I quickly conclude whether the surface is uneven, uphill, or downhill. My mind processes the vast multitude of information very quickly. It naturally collects and analyses this data and my physical body reacts accordingly, either by natural or controlled impulse.

All humans have this power, but not to the extreme extent that I possess, and many humans just don't pay attention to what's going on around them. It's impossible for someone to walk up behind me without me knowing. I hear and smell them before they even make their move. What a beautiful gift I possess. I have my parents to thank for this advantage.

Many times late at night, I find myself outside, either walking the well-manicured lawn or walking through the area that I refer to as the forest or treed area on my land. This area has been there since my grandfather built the estate. Over the years, this area has grown thick and lush. I naturally created some pathways that I used over the years to either explore or just take a leisurely walk. I also used these pathways when I was in a hunting mood and hungry for live meat. My parents used these pathways and created others. This area backs up to a larger forest area which eventually funnels down into a ravine where a large stream of water flows and makes its way down through a smaller forest area near an upscale neighborhood.

Marci and I have always been members of the Louisville Opera. One of Marci's passions, besides the violin, is singing. She had a beautiful voice but not on the concert level ability that one needs to perform on the opera circuit. My mother has a wonderful voice and, of course, thanks to the formula, her voice is pitch perfect and flawless. Marci had always admired my mother's voice. Again, another haunting example of perfection that stared in my Marci's face, another constant reminder of her imperfections.

One special night, Marci and I had a romantic dinner at one of the top ranked restaurants downtown. Afterward, we attended a Bellini Opera, 'Norma,' which highlighted the soprano voice. It was a moving opera for Marci, one which she loved deeply.

Opera always moved Marci to tears. She loved the interplay of the violin section, which was her dream job, and the performing singers.

The marriage between the violin and the human voice was intoxicating for her. We sat there listening to this wonderful Opera and in the middle of the performance, Marci leaned over to me and said, "The violin is this inanimate wooden object that lays dormant in suspended time until a talented creature caresses it with its hands and fingers, strokes the heart of the instrument with a long, stringed shaft, making sounds that could only imitate the voice of a singing angel." She looked over at me and placed her hand on the upper inside of my leg and said, "It's like us making love. Is it not?"

I gazed upon my smiling lover as she stared into my eyes. I felt a smile develop on my face, anointing her statement with full agreement. Like so many times in the past, at the end of the opera we made our way backstage. We met many members of the orchestra and the performers in the opera. Marci loved meeting everyone. She fit in so well. Ever since I can remember, Marci always stood out in public. Her tall, thin but shapely figure seemed to force whatever she was wearing to melt onto her perfect figure. She moved with style and grace and held this inaudible command over a room. Her hair was pulled up and rested on top of her head as that golden blonde hair sparkled in the artificial light. Her bangs were neatly placed as they gently tickled her forehead, and her skin was flawless from head to toe. Her body teased the onlooker by hiding behind expensive cloth, but the areas where the skin was exposed radiated a sexual appeal that no man or woman could resist observing. I don't give that god of others much credit but with this creation, he certainly outdid himself, which makes me sad at the same time. He tends to destroy his perfect creations long before their time is finished on this planet. This knowledge haunted me each passing day and slowly ate away at my essence. Why can I not preserve this most beautiful creature? Time stands still for me, why not for her? It is not fair at all.

Later that night, Marci was frisky on our drive home. The minutes seemed to be like hours on the way to our estate. As I reached the front entrance of the gate, my Marci started to kiss me on my neck. As we made our way to the garage, I quickly parked the car. We kissed for a few moments then Marci lead me toward the backyard. Before we made our way to the deep green lawn in the back of the house, Marci reached for a dark red blanket that she had placed there before we started our evening at the Opera. Marci was notorious for many of our unplanned sexual encounters, but from time to time she would preplan our evenings.

As we walked toward the backyard, she silently handed me the blanket. As she turned her back to me, she seductively walked past the pool. The moon was full, clear, and bright, casting a dim light on every item on our property. The moonlight highlighted her golden curls, the curves of her body, and the muscular structure of her bare back. Her plunging V neckline exposed almost half of her breasts to the light of the moon.

Not a cloud could be seen in the night sky. The wind was gently blowing, but the night air had a certain heaviness with a slightly musky fragrance that came from the nearby trees. The moonlight tried to penetrate the tall trees that surrounded the back area of the property while the lush green grass was awaiting our nightly ballet amongst the stars. Marci glided like a ballerina across the cement floor guarding the pool. Her hands went behind her back, and with ease, her fingers found the zipper in the lower part of her dress. She continued to sway her shoulders from side to side, allowing the dress to naturally fall toward her hips. In one quick and tantalizing movement, the dress fell to the ground, and without missing a step, Marci literally walked out of her dress. Her naked backside was exposed to the night air. She wore nothing under her dress. This was all preplanned.

Marci stopped, bent down, and reached for something on the ground. She quickly looked back at me with her luscious ass pointing toward me, when suddenly her right hand whipped across her body. I quickly saw an object coming toward me. I moved my hand up to the side of my head and caught the rock that she'd slung toward me. I looked at Marci and before I could say a word, she started to laugh. Her eye sparkled in the moonlight as laughter rolled out of her mouth. She said, "That never gets old." She straightened herself and walked toward the four trees that we'd planted over the remains of my dead brother.

Marci stopped walking, extended her arm, and pointed to an area on the ground. Without any hesitation, I laid the blanket out as smooth as I could. Marci was facing me with that sexual but sadistic smile that she possessed. She said, "Take off all of your clothes." I did what she demanded, although I felt somewhat uncomfortable at first as I quickly removed all my clothes. She stood there, one hip higher than the other as her arms rested on both sides of her long, curvy body. Every so often she would move her hips to transfer her weight, but she never took her eyes from my body. I finally removed my clothes and after she seductively observed me, she began to walk toward me. She said,

"Don't you dare move." She reached her hand out and took hold of my manhood. Her grip was warm to the touch. The mixture of her soft fingers with her nails that gently dug into my skin, caused me to grow longer.

Marci studied my chiseled face as she pushed my manhood downward. I knew what she wanted. I knelt before her as she took my head in her hands. Without any instruction, I took the first nipple in my mouth. I sucked and licked the breast as I listened to her make seductive moaning sounds that were music to my ears. I paid homage to the other breast and repeated the same ritual. I licked every inch of her massive breasts.

After my love had enough of my tongue, she backed away, turned her back to me and slowly bent over. She looked behind her and stared at my face. My eyes were forced on the perfectly formed private area between her legs. I dove my face into her backside, enjoying and tasting every inch and inhaling all her aroma. My tongue probed and licked every inch of her as she continued to moan in pleasure. Every so often, she spread her cheeks with her own fingers for me to have better access.

I continued to lick until I felt her warm foot on my chest. Marci pushed me backward. I braced myself with my hand as Marci turned around and her other foot came in front of my face. I licked the sole of her foot. Marci lowered her foot and quickly pushed it into my chest again, but this time I fell on my backside. She walked toward me and straddled her legs over my chest. She slowly lowered herself and sat on my face. I pleasured her as best I could. I never stopped licking, sucking, and mouthing at her vagina. Unwillingly, she started to move herself from my mouth and she slithered down my chest. Her pussy slid across my stomach and just before her hips got to my manhood, she raised herself just enough to where the head of my penis just barely rubbed the outside portion of her vagina.

In one nonstop motion, she took her vagina and placed it on my testicles and rather forcefully moved up my shaft. The head of my manhood quickly discovered her opening and at that point, Marci forcefully pushed her cunt over my manhood, squeezing it as it entered her. At that point, Marci lost control. She had to finish what she started. She moved up and down as I lay there pounding as hard as I could. I watched those beautiful breasts sway back and forth in the moonlight. I watched them collide with each other. Her nipples were as erect as I have ever seen them. After several minutes, Marci's body tensed up and she let a scream, then a moan escaped from her mouth. She continued to bounce on my cock as her hands rubbed up and down on my chest. At that moment, I couldn't last any longer. I quickly pulled out and exploded an unusual amount of cum on the outside of her pussy, which made her moan even louder. After seven or eight powerful spasms, I placed my cock inside of her and continued to pump her until she started to cry, which she does many times during our sexual encounters.

When we stopped our lovemaking, Marci remained on top of me. She looked at me with the sweet but sadistic smile that she normally has on her face. She slowly removed herself from me, standing up and stretching her arms and body upward to the moon. My Marci was so unpredictable that at times she even she surprised me. She walked away from me toward the area of the property where my family members are buried. I sat up on the blanket that we had made love on and admired the silhouette of the most wondrous creature that I had ever met. This moment was one of the happiest times I had ever experienced.

Marci reached the family burial site which was located at the top of a sharply descending hill that made its way to a valley filled with trees and a small steam that flowed through the middle. Marci walked in front of the tombstones and stopped at Adelle's grave site. My adoptive mother's grave was small like the others but wider. We didn't want to obstruct the view of the landscape that overlooked the valley of trees, which that is why the tombstones are not large. She bent down and reached for something in front of Adelle's tombstone that was out of my direct line of sight. I heard something move across the thick blades of grass in front of the grave marker. Since I can see well in the dark, as my Marci stood up, I saw she had something large, what seemed to look like a knife. The knife had a large blade that captured a few of the moon's glows as the blade moved in her hand. Instantly, my heart started to race.

Marci's back was still to me and all I saw was her naked body with a machete in her right hand. She took a deep breath. As she turned toward me, she moved the end of the machete across Adelle's gravestone. The reflection from the moonlight was captured from time to time as she finally faced me. This most beautiful and perfect creature was looking directly at me with a most wicked smile. Then the majestic creature spoke, "Don't come any closer, baby." I was sitting on the side of my hip with one hand supporting my weight. I moved to my knees as

I knelt before my goddess. My heart felt as if it was pounding out of my chest. Suddenly, my mind became clearer. Marci said, "I want this to be the most perfect night of all nights. I had so much fun and enjoyed every minute that we shared together."

Marci walked a few feet closer to me as my heart began to pump faster. My eyes kept darting from her face to the sharp machete that was in her hand. I couldn't help but notice her constant turning of the instrument in a clockwise movement as the wide side of the shiny new blade would catch the moonlight. I was afraid to move. The movement paralyzed me. Marci was in total control. This was her moment and I couldn't move or say anything in fear of jeopardizing it, thus disappointing her. My mind was numb yet racing at the same time. I had no clue as to where this was going. My first thought was that she was going to throw the machete at something to prove to me that her hand-eye coordination was improving or that she was going to kill an animal that she had trapped somewhere; these were my thoughts, my only thoughts, at the time. She stood there with a calm and innocent smile. Her eye was swimming with love and a controlled anticipation.

My stunning creature looked at the machete as she turned the blade in her hand. She continued to look at the blade as she rolled it back the opposite way. Then she looked at me while her head was cocked to the side. She seductively moved her head as she looked deeply in my eyes with that controlled and passionate smile of hers. My love repositioned her grip on the handle of the machete as she calmly moved her arm and the knife in front of her. She quickly held the handle with her other hand. I was afraid to move. I said, "No! No! Don't do it!" My heart felt like it was in a freefall as my senses were on fire.

Marci said, "I love you, Garrison, more than you will ever know. I have always loved you. You are the only person that loved and wanted me. For that, I am forever in your debt. I could never repay you for what you have given me. You gave me attention, hope, love, and encouragement. I never want our love to die. I want to live forever and share eternity with you. Save me and make me into a better person. Make me perfect like you. I want you to be my creator, my one and only god. Give me eternal life, Garrison. Resurrect me, my love."

Marci smiled at me. I noticed her knuckles turned whiter as she grasped the handle as tight as she could. Her eye never left mine and my worst nightmare suddenly became reality. Marci plunged the sharp end of the blade into her heart. I heard one of her ribs break as the steel shaft penetrated her most passionate heart. I will never forget the look she had on her face. Her smile quickly turned to a surprised look, as her mouth opened wide and her eye squinted from the pain. The power of her thrust caused the blade to go through her body and come out of her back. What followed next was a sharp and quick scream from her mouth. It was suddenly silenced by the pain that filled her body as she stood there motionless for what seemed like eternity. She managed to look at me one last time and a sudden smile came upon her face as she looked to be at peace with her decision. Her intoxicating stare was broken as she fell to her knees. Another scream formed from my love that just broke my heart. She closed her eye once more to confirm to me that the pain was unbearable. She attempted to catch my eye one last time, but her life was quickly fading. Slowly, her lifeless body fell on its side.

I screamed, "Noooooooooooo!" I got up from my knees and ran over to my love. Before I could get to her, my Marci's life was expired. I knelt in front of my love, tears flowing down my cheeks as I felt my body starting to tremble. I smelt death, the death of the only person that I had ever truly loved in my life. I suddenly heard something coming toward me. It was my parents. Wolfgang and Zelda were running as fast as they could. All I heard were their heavy footsteps. Wolfgang said, "What happened? Are you all right?" I said nothing. When Wolfgang got to the horrid scene, he understood what my love did. Wolfgang looked at me as any sorrowful father would. I was devastated. I couldn't control my senses. My tears were falling unlike any time that I could remember. Wolfgang said in as soft of a voice as he could, "You understand she did this to force your hand, right? You have a decision to make. Do you want to bring her back to life or let her die?"

I looked at my father and said, "I don't know what to do."

Wolfgang said, "Do you want me to infect her?"

I quickly shouted, "No! Leave her alone!"

Wolfgang calmly said, "You know you have to quickly make your decision. Her blood is running colder by the second. You must infect her while her blood is at a certain level. The longer you wait, the more of a transformation she will experience."

I again shouted back at my father, "I know all of this, god damn it! God damn it! I... know all of this."

Marci knew this was the only way for her to ever experience perfection in her mind. She needed to force me to infect her with the formula. She knew her kind of transformation would be unknown. She didn't know what she was going to turn into, but she didn't care. I cared because I didn't want her to change. I wanted her just the way she was, but of course that wasn't going to last forever. What a decision that was before me. I heard my mother say, "Garrison... Garrison... she wanted this. You know that. Save her. She wants this." I looked up at my mother as more tears formed in my eyes and I was crying uncontrollably. I quickly controlled my emotions as best I could. I looked down at my poor Marci.

My love had forced my hand. After everything my love said and did, how could I not attempt to bring her back to life? I saw the effects that Wolfgang's bite had on Carolyn's transformation. I didn't want the same to happen to Marci. Wolfgang sensed my thoughts and confusion. He said, "Garrison... we spoke of this a while back. You need to introduce the formula you have in your system to her body if you desire a different outcome than the last human subject."

I said, "But I never brought anyone back from the dead, either human or animal. How do I know this will work and what kind of change would she undergo?"

Wolfgang said, "It might not work, but you have to try if you want her back from the dead. The longer you wait, the lesser your changes are in your desired result."

I knew my father was right. I had to bite into my Marci. I had to at least try to save her. It is what she wanted. I only wished that I had experimented on a subject before this situation had to become reality.

Wolfgang was staring at me. He again spoke, "Garrison, you need to act now if you want to bring her back to life." I knew I had to act as soon as possible. The seconds that passed in my mind felt like a hammer banging away inside my head. Time was getting out of control for me and I had to decide. I had to save my Marci. I looked down at my love and carefully pulled the blade out of her. The blade slid out easier than I thought it would. I quickly bent down and positioned my body so my mouth was adjacent to the slit of the wound. My senses were lite up like a Christmas tree and I felt the adrenaline flowing throughout my body. I heard and felt my heartbeat, and at one point I thought my heart was going to jump out of my chest. Adrenaline is the carrier for the formula, so I wanted to make sure that my adrenaline was pumping in full force.

I opened my mouth and slid my front teeth into the long slit of the wound then reluctantly closed my bite. I felt the bottom portion of my teeth bite into the lower portion, just under the wound. I could feel the adrenaline flowing inside of her, but I was wondering when I should stop. Suddenly Wolfgang yelled, "Stop! Not too much. You might not bring her back if you inject too much of the formula."

I immediately opened and removed my mouth from my love. I said, "Is that enough? Was that long enough?"

Wolfgang said, "You never can tell. It depends on so many variables. I have been testing some dead animal subjects from the forest that I captured and killed. Some of them came back to life and some did not. Some changed their form drastically and some didn't even resemble their original form. Too much or even too little of the formula can be devastating. It is impossible to measure because the formula is coming from inside of your teeth. You can't extract that from you because the temperature change would destroy the integrity of the formula that you possess in your body. There are three main factors. The length of time and temperature of the subject's blood just after its death, the temperature of your fluids that was injected, and the amount of the fluid, all determine the type of transformation the subject will undergo, if they even come back from the dead."

I looked down at my love who lay motionless on the cold, hard ground. I felt her blood on my lips, mouth, and chin. I wiped Marci's blood from my face as I smelt her essences. I knelt there, crying uncontrollably. Never in my life have I cried so hard for so long. I looked at my love who was staring up at me with that lifeless eye and blank expression tattooed on her face. Wolfgang broke my trance with his large hand on my shoulder. He said, "Let's get her inside."

I moved out of the way as my father picked up Marci's lifeless body. Seeing her arms, legs and head being tossed around in all directions as she was carried inside caused my sadness to worsen. Zelda opened the door of the house for Wolfgang. As I followed them, I tried to get my emotions in order. We made our way into the lab area and Wolfgang gently placed Marci on a hospital bed and wheeled her inside of the cell. He could sense that I was upset at first, so he reassured me that he had to keep her locked up in the cell. I understood. Zelda went to clean Marci as I retrieved the silk sheets from her bed. Marci loved the silk sheets. I brought them down to the cell, and Wolfgang picked up her body as I placed them on the hospital bed.

Marci's body lay motionless as my mother cleaned her. My father instructed me to always keep the cell door locked. After they left me to go upstairs, I broke down again. I sat by her side and never left it for hours on end. I constantly talked to her in the hopes that maybe it would bring her back to me. I touched and rubbed her skin in an attempt to accelerate her resurrection. I begged for her to wake up, but not once did I ever pray to God. I would never give him that satisfaction.

The days were long, and each day melted into the other without warning. Marci's body was still hard, and it was now starting to smell and change color. It had been several days since her death. At this point, I was starting to lose all hope, but as my father pointed out, it took a while for Carolyn to come back to life.

I cannot tell you how long I stood there by her side, thinking about all the wonderful moments we had shared together when she was alive. I didn't remotely entertain myself with the idea that those moments would ever happen again. I lowered my head and walked out of the cell. I locked the cell door and continued to walk toward the hallway to go upstairs. Then I heard the most magnificent sound behind me. I heard something that sounded like an exhaling of breath. I quickly turned and looked at my love, hoping against all hope that the noise came from Marci and not from something else. I raced over to the cell door and fumbled with my key, trying to open the cell door. I finally opened it and quickly went to the bed. I looked over Marci's body, keeping my attention on any potential movement or sound that she might make. I thought my ears were just playing a cruel trick on me and that the noise didn't come from her.

I looked at Marci for a while and she didn't move, nor did I hear any noise from her. As soon as I stood up and was about to walk away again, I heard her faintly inhale. I looked at her mouth, and her chin quivered slightly. I held my breath. I couldn't have taken a breath if I'd wanted to. I didn't want to miss any part of this phenomenon that was about to take place before me. I almost jumped out of my skin when I saw my love's head move to her side ever so slowly. I wanted her to take another breath; I would have given my own life to have made that happened. Tears were forming in my eyes, and I quickly wiped them away as fast as I could in fear of missing any further movement or sound that Marci might make.

Without forewarning, she took a deep breath. The sound was hauntingly beautiful. Her mouth opened wide and then she exhaled the breath. She was trying to breathe. I couldn't believe what was happening before my eyes. I caught myself mimicking the breaths that she took. I noticed her lips quickly jerking in small movements then she had another labored inhaled breath and this time the lips, mouth and head moved in unison. After several seconds, she let the air out of her lungs. The air passed through her mouth in a rough and forceful exhale. Her eye didn't blink and the only movement that took place was from her lungs and face.

I bent over and got just inches from her face. I said softly, "Come on, Marci. Wake up. Breathe for us. Breathe. In and out. Breathe, my love. You can do it."

Suddenly, her breaths were more rapid but still forced. She had to force herself to breathe because it wasn't coming naturally to her body. It was like she was teaching her body how to breathe again, even though she was unconscious. Her lungs moved faster in an up and down motion as the air poured in and out of her beautiful and sensual mouth. I then simultaneously saw and felt her right arm move against my chest. I quickly moved back in fear that I interrupted her process. I looked down and her arm stopped moving. Suddenly, it moved again and then quickly relaxed. Her feet started to jerk and twitch, then her other arm moved. At that moment, I noticed her breathing was more constant and not as labored. The color of her skin was changing from a grayish color to a more natural color.

I heard large and heavy footsteps running down the hallway toward the lab. It was my father. He ran into the cell and looked at the situation before him. He was overly excited to see Marci coming to life. Marci's arms and feet seemed to rest for a moment while her body was trying to regain more control over her breathing. Wolfgang and I looked into her eye, which remained lifeless. Her injured eye had no pupil, but it looked straight at us while her good eye was looking in another direction. After a few moments passed, her body seemed to have complete control over her breathing.

My Marci was breathing naturally and nothing was forced, but she was not cognitive at all. She didn't respond to anything, not our voice commands or our touch. Wolfgang ordered me not to talk and let him control things for the moment. I backed away and allowed my father to oversee my love. Wolfgang was pleased to see what was taking place. He administrated many tests, drew blood, and listened to her heart for hours on end. He kept track of her IV and made sure she was getting enough nourishment. For the first time in a decade, I was exhausted. I went over and sat in a chair next to Marci. I laid my head down on the bed next to her arm and fell asleep from pure exhaustion.

After a few hours, I finally awoke. Wolfgang told me that everything was processing well and the only thing we had to do was to wait. The formula needed time to work into her bloodstream and revive all her organs. This process needed time.

The next day, Marci's movements were more rapid and fluid. She started to move her arms and legs while she was still on her back.

The following day, she moved her head and neck with more articulacy and that triggered louder sounds coming from her throat area. The next day, Marci gained additional control over her facial movements, and she started to reach out with her arms. She even bent her legs by drawing her feet up the silk sheets. Before long, she could control her arms and hands. After several attempts, her hands made their way to her head. She cupped her face with those long fingers. She held her hands over her for a few moments, and another wonderful moment happened – she smiled.

My heart soared with joy in seeing that smile of hers. She started to speak as best she could, but only grunting and heavy breathing sounds were coming from her mouth. I looked at her and immediately her facial expression changed. I could sense that she could see me or at least see an image before her. Wolfgang came over and put a light in her eye. The eye twitched and the pupil dilated a little. We asked her many questions and it seemed that she was attempting to respond through her grunting and moaning noises. I could sense that it was aggravating her not to be able to verbally communicate. We told her not to strain her voice and to relax. We told her that her voice would return eventually. She nodded to acknowledge to us that she understood.

Marci kept pointing to the ground while she moved her arms and drew her legs up. She wanted to sit up on the edge of the bed. I told her to take her time and that I would help her. I wrapped my arms around her and sat her up. She drew her legs up as I spun her around and let her legs dangle off the side of the bed. Marci looked at me and smiled. She started to move her head from side to side, up and down, and in circles. She then stretched her arms out and was moving them around. It looked as if her arms had gone to sleep and she was trying to get the feeling back.

Wolfgang was impressed and told us that at that moment, Marci was more advanced than Carolyn was at this point of her transformation. Marci still couldn't speak, but Wolfgang was not concerned about that. Wolfgang continued to administer countless tests on Marci, both biological and physical. He compared that data to Carolyn's and the numerous dead animals that he had brought back to life over the past several months. The data suggested that I had injected just enough of the formula into Marci and that hopefully her transformation would not be so intense and extreme.

During the time of Marci's after death experience, I kept telling her numerous times what had happened, and it seemed each passing day that she understood more of what I was explaining to her. Wolfgang, Zelda, and I spoke to her as often and as long as we could to help her brain repair itself and to assist in its development.

Eva wanted to see Marci, but Wolfgang and Zelda told her it was too soon. Eva was very disappointed, but we didn't want to disturb Eva emotionally. Zelda kept her from coming down to the basement although it was a difficult task keeping her away and answering her questions about what happened to Marci. Eva was very close to Marci and loved her very much.

A couple more days passed, and Marci was grunting and making all sorts of sounds. Each passing day, the sounds were getting closer to forming words that were somewhat recognizable. We attempted to start with simple words and regularly repeated them to her. She tried to form the words, but it was difficult for her to process what was forming in her brain and transfer those thoughts to her tongue. My father kept reminding me that when a subject is brought back from the dead, it takes a while for the formula to correct what was once dead. Speech and hand-eye coordination are the two areas that take the most time to repair.

It wasn't too much longer that Marci started to form words. At first they were slurred and not in a sensible order, but at least she was speaking words. One moment I will never forget is when my love spoke directly to me. Her eye looked at me and she struggled mightily to stay focused on my face. She sometimes had trouble staying focused or still at times. She didn't have full control over her body, even at this point of her conversion from death to life.

As she looked at me, she attempted to speak. Her lips formed a word and she spoke to me for the first time by saying, "Aaaaa... aaaa laaaa laaaaaavvvee." She had to rest for a moment and then she started again with other words, "aaaannkkk... yuuuu." My heart beat wildly. My Marci was talking to me. I knew what she was saying. It was one of the most beautiful moments in my life. I felt tears pouring down my cheeks. I needed to hear her say that she was thankful, but if truth be told, it was I that was the most grateful. I knew she understood that she was now alive. She spoke to me in ways that no one could. My senses knew that she was able to understand what had happened to her.

I knew she'd had a traumatic experience, but what concerned me now was the future — how much change she would experience and hopefully the right amount of the formula had been introduced into her system. Too much of the formula would dramatically change her physically, but at this point, that couldn't be determined.

After several more days, Marci's speech pattern improved and became clearer at a rapid pace. She started to put words together to form coherent sentences. Wolfgang and I told Marci everything that happened from the moment just after our lovemaking to the present. Marci seemed to grasp, understand, and recall the moment just before she died. As part of our multitude of tests, we asked her many questions and she responded to all of them. Sometimes it took her longer on some of the questions, but she understood what had happened and what was about to take place to her body. I sensed that she was mentally prepared for what would eventually happen to her physically.

Marci wanted to get out of the bed and walk. We slowly moved her legs off the bed. They were weak and out of shape. My parents and I had worked her leg, arm, and neck muscles from the moment that she came back to life. It was important to keep the muscles moving to prevent them from deteriorating. In addition, Wolfgang said that moving the body's extremities would help increase the blood flow, thus the formula would move quicker throughout the body, regenerating cells.

Wolfgang and I helped Marci off the table by supporting my lover under her arms. Our goal was to get her to stand. We gently picked her up from the bed without allowing her feet to touch the ground. We wanted the blood to rush down to her feet and make sure she was used to the feeling of the blood flow. We slowly lowered her to where her feet made contact on the tiled floor. At first Marci cried out in pain. It hurt her. The combination of the blood flowing to her feet in a rapid fashion and the texture of the tile was strange to her at first. After several attempts, we got her to put her full weight on her feet.

Marci wanted to see if she could stand on her own. We slowly released our support from her arms. At first, she was a slightly dizzy and almost fell several times. Wolfgang instructed her not to look down and to keep her head up. She stood there a few moments and we could sense that she had forgotten how to walk. I bent down and moved one of her legs forward, then did the same with the other leg. I repeated this procedure many times until she started to remember how to walk.

After a few days, Marci was able to walk without any trouble. She started to get full use and control of her fingers, toes, and other parts of her body like her mouth and tongue. Marci's appetite was also starting to develop. She wanted us to take the IV out of her arm so we started slowly with the food. First, we fed her fruits and small vegetables. After a few bites, she looked at me and smiled. Again, it was a beautiful moment that we shared together. It was like she was her old self again. It was a strange feeling, but it was like training an adult baby and giving her experiences for the first time.

Marci was rediscovering what she once took for granted. After several feedings, she looked at me and pointed to her mouth and said, "I want meat." Wolfgang ordered Zelda to cook up some deer meat that we had stored in the freezer. Marci ate a few bites of the meat and politely pushed the plate away. She looked at us and said, "Sorry, but meat is too done. Raw meat, please?" Wolfgang quickly added that it was too early for raw meat and that it would be very harmful to her.

After a week, Marci's life was getting better and more productive. Her body was getting stronger. Her coordination was getting better at a swift pace. She took long walks on the grounds and she even worked out with some light weights. I would take her in the car for long rides in the country with all the windows down, listening to music. I played the violin and the piano at her request. Zelda would sing arias throughout the day. We, as a family, all helped to stimulate her brain and make her whole again.

We constantly tested her memory. Overall, she remembered most events that took place in her previous life. She remembered our moments together as a couple, which pleased me to no end. At the beginning of this horrid episode in my life, I was haunted with the fear of my love not remembering me or the love that we had together. After all that had taken place, I had my doubts, but when she recalled our life together, I felt more positive about the future. Wolfgang assured me that if Marci could recall her memories now, she should retain them after her transformation. The only problem we had with Marci was that she didn't like to be held under lock and key in the cell. She understood why we had to take precautions, but she thought it was excessive.

Marci had now been alive for just over six weeks. In the middle of the night, she ran into the great room with a smile that lit up the room. She said, "Garrison, I am feeling sharp pains in my body." Then she pulled at her hair and said, "Look, some of my hair is falling out. Oh, this is just wonderful, my love. It is finally starting. I am finally going to be perfect like you." I knew this moment would come, but I wasn't fully prepared for the reality that was setting in at that moment. Marci looked at me and said, "You are my creator. You know that don't you? You created me. Soon, my love, we will live forever."

I was speechless. I didn't want to dampen her excitement, but I knew that she was in for a great deal of agonizing pain over the next month and half. I told her, "Marci, you know that you will suffer significantly over the next month. You will feel pain like you have never felt before. I just want to prepare you."

Marci said, "I know, my love. It's not wonderful, but I can take it." She then started to take her clothes off and before I knew it, she was naked before me. It had been so long since we'd had intimate relations. We made love like there was no tomorrow. After our sexual experience, I took her down in the basement and locked her in her cell.

The next day, all four of us sat down at the kitchen table to discuss the realistic and potential changes that would happen to Marci's body. We knew the transformation was in its beginning stages, what we were mostly concerned with was how much of a transformation Marci would experience. Wolfgang went over all the possibilities that he could think of and offered his expert opinion on how long and how much of a change would occur. But after all the data that my father had before him, the essential point was that there was no way to tell how much Marci would change physically. It was up to nature now. The amount of formula that I bit into Marci was the main determining factor, but there was just no way to tell if I introduced too much or too little of the formula. Marci was very worried after our meeting. It wasn't my intention to worry my love, but I didn't want her to be totally surprised as to what might happen.

As the days passed, we continued to monitor Marci closely. We had taped everything to this point and we would continue to record in the future. We administrated countless mental, physical and blood tests that Wolfgang had at his disposal.

As the days progressed, Marci's pains became sharper. At first, Marci loved to feel the sharp pains because she was excited for what was coming, and she knew the formula was working its magic. These pains would hit her without warning and then leave as fast as they came.

After several straight days of these sharp pains, the pains started to become more severe. Marci's joy quickly turned to grave concern. She tried to hide her worry and pain from us, but when the pains hit, she couldn't hold back the screams and cries of desired relief.

A week passed, and we entered the eighth week of the transformation. Marci was miserable. The pain in her legs, arms, back, head and neck were now starting to really hurt her. What was a sharp shooting pain at first now developed into a constant piercing agony. More hair on her head fell out, and she lost all hair on her arms and legs, as well as her pubic hair.

As the days passed, the pains, especially in her legs, became so debilitating she was resigned to her bed. The legs and arms were growing at an alarming rate. We could see that the skin and muscles were pulled so tight that she wasn't able to bend them. The skin turned pink and red, and at times would turn white from the constant growth taking place in her body. Wolfgang and I were very concerned, although not surprised, over these results.

The concern we had was if the bones grew too fast for the skin and muscles to adapt to the new length, it would just split the tissue and the subject would die. This was what happened in countless experiments that Wolfgang conducted on the Jews in his concentration camps. Even animals experienced this problem. Too much of the formula will cause too rapid of growth for the tissue, and basically the body's skeleton would just rip out of the body. Marci knew all of this and she was very worried about her life. We were all worried, wondering if I'd injected just the right amount of the formula for the proper bone growth to take place inside her body.

The continuous ebb and flow of bone growth verses tissue expansion and new growth was maddening. To see my love experience this pain and for me to deal with the emotional trauma of the unknown was unsettling, to say the least. From all early indications, there was enough tissue for the expanding bone growth to prevent a total and complete rip in the tissue that could be fatal. Marci's suffering increased exponentially as the transformation progressed. I stood there with my father looking at Marci while she lay on the bed. She was noticeably shaken because of the pain she was experiencing. She had at least six inches of growth in just her arms, back and legs alone.

The next section of her body that experienced massive growth was her head. After the growth of her extremities and her back, Marci's body didn't give her a break from the growth and the pain from the formula. Her head caused her intense pain, more so than the other parts of her body. I felt so sorry for my love. She would lie on her back and all she did was move her head from side to side and cry the entire time. She let out the most incredible and unsettling screams that I had ever heard. It was difficult to watch and experience. I saw her lying there, and without warning her head would shake violently. I saw the head swell before my eyes. After several hours, her head began to swell to an enormous size. At the same time her head was expanding, her back started to hurt again. She was in so much pain that she could hardly move, it was beginning to be more of a struggle to talk, and it was especially difficult for her to keep her thoughts coherent. I could sense that Marci was questioning, or rather regretting, the transformation process, but obviously we were at a point of no return.

Marci's head continued to swell so bad that you could hardly distinguish her eyes, nose, and mouth. The swelling pulled the skin to such a degree that at times some areas would split open, only to be quickly closed within a few minutes. The constant breaking down of the tissue and the regeneration was unbearable for my Marci. I could only imagine the pain she was experiencing.

Wolfgang was concerned with Marci's labored breathing. He knew that throughout a transformation, when the subject looks and feels the worse, that is when the formula is creating the physical change is made to the body.

Wolfgang examined her skull and, like some sort of black magic, after the swelling, the skull would expand and make the swelling subside. This eased some tensions that we had during this process.

Marci was in such excruciating pain that she couldn't communicate with us any longer. Also, what was complicating this situation was Marci's back was growing and there was a small bump forming where her tailbone was located. She screamed like I have never heard her scream before and I hope I never hear again. It just broke my heart to hear her in so much pain. Throughout this stage of the process, her back did bleed some from every bone in her back growing and stretching. As soon as an area on her back tore, in just minutes the tissue would repair itself with a rapid growth of skin and muscle. During this same time, the bump on her tailbone was developing into a tail. At first, the section of her lower back looked like an overly enlarged cyst that protruded through the skin, then the tip of the tail broke through the infected area. The sheets were soaked in blood from both the skin splitting on her back as well as her tailbone area.

This time of nonstop, unbearable pain pushed Marci past the brink of exhaustion. Not only could she not sleep, but she couldn't rest. Every part of her body hurt from either the skin being ripped open in small contained areas to the actual bones increasing in size and girth. She tried to lay still but the pain was too intense. The tail kept her from lying flat, and she had to move her hips to the side, but because of her limited mobility, that was becoming a difficult task for her. We propped pillows up under the right side of her body in an attempt to alleviate pressure on her tail. Her newly formed tail was sore to the touch and grew at an alarming rate. Near the end of the tail's growth, Marci was able to lie on her back again. The tail grew downward, almost parallel to her legs, and was not curved up like some animals' tails would grow.

Wolfgang continued to video tape this transformation. In our downtime, we went back and reviewed every second of the tapes. At this stage, Marci's head was twice the size as normal, but her head was narrowing in width and becoming straighter on the sides. The top of her head, as well as her chin was rounding. The head was in the form of a capsule. She had lost all her hair and her back continued to grow, and its increased size was averaging about an inch of growth every couple of days. The head continued to grow longer and deeper in dimensions.

The next stage the formula attacked was her eyes. More pain and suffering besieged my love. At this point, both her physical body and her mental consciousness could no longer accept the pain. She passed out from pure physical and mental torment after she hadn't slept in over a week. Wolfgang said this was normal and it was a body's way of trying to shut down from all the pain.

The most interesting of all the changes were occurring to her injured eye. This was the stage that Wolfgang was the most interested in observing. The formula started to work its wonders on the eye until it developed and healed to the same shape and look as her good eye. The formula somehow used the DNA that still existed in the host, forced the body to reproduce that lost or injured organ, and within days or hours, it repairs or grows that organ.

Marci's head continued to grow longer and deeper, and at the same rate of growth, the shape of the eyes grew larger and more oval, which deeply concerned us. We took videos and broke the feed down into still pictures, frame by frame, during the metamorphous. We compared the pictures in sequence and what we captured on film and still frames were extremely disturbing. Each passing hour, and in some cases minutes, the head and its features were noticeably changing.

Marci started to grow bleached white hair on the top of her head, and it didn't grow on the sides or the back of her massive head, but the hair grew at a frightening rate. At times, when you watched closely enough, you could see the hair grow, then the next few minutes it remained the same length. We had never seen anything like this in our previous experiments. Even Wolfgang was shocked and surprised.

As Marci's legs, arms and back continued to grow, you could hear the bones and cartilage move. At times, they would make popping and cracking sounds. Every so often, we would hear a few bones break in two, but then they quickly regrew into their new shape. We didn't want to disturb the growth. During each of the different stages of the transformation, Marci would lay there in her blood-soaked silk sheets. She would focus on a spot on the ceiling above her in the attempt to take her mind off the pain and to catch her breath.

Marci's hands began to grow longer and wider. Her boney fingers, with a muscular look, grew to abnormal lengths, almost twice the size as before the transformation. The knuckles were large and prominent, and the fingertips came to a well-defined point, causing the fingernails to have a triangular shape to them. The fingernails were black, which prominently stood in contrast to her ultra-white flesh tone.

Her feet grew longer and wider, and after the growth period, they were three times their original size. Her feet were slightly larger in proportion to the rest of her massive body. Marci didn't end up taller than Wolfgang or Zelda, but she measured out at seven foot, three inches in height. Before the transformation, Marci was five feet eleven inches tall.

The head was long and had a capsule shape. It was rounded at the top and the chin was not very pronounced, giving a more curved look in that area of the head. We measured the head length to be about sixteen inches long and the width to be approximately nine inches. The nose was flat with only a small rise from her face. Her two large nostrils each measured an inch and a half in length. The oval-shaped eyes were large and were located over halfway down her head, dominating the face. They measured about three inches in width and five inches long. The sclera was as black as the pupil with a hint of blue. The pupils were cat-like in shape. From a distance, the entire eye looked all black, but up close, if the light hit the eye a certain way, you could see the pupil.

Her mouth was wide and large, and her tongue was long, but narrow and very flexible. Marci could move her tongue like a snake could contort its body. The only hair that appeared on her body was on her head. She possessed not one hair follicle on her arms, legs, or pubic area. She had no eyelashes but did have eyelids. Her porcelain white hair was long and thick. The hair started rather high on her head, making for a very long forehead in both actual size and presence. Her hair flowed down her back and stopped at the top portion of her buttocks, and her ears measured about six inches in length. The top part of the ear had an extremely pointed shape, whereas the bottom part of the ear was more of a standard human form.

Marci's breasts grew to an enormous size with large and very prominent nipples. The breasts were wide, perky, and firm to the touch. Her ass was nicely developed, large, firm, and muscular, but not out of proportion to the rest of the body. Her skin color was extremely pale and complimented her long, white flowing hair. At first glance, she had a ghostly appearance to the eye of the observer. This was interesting to Wolfgang and he had no rational explanation as to why Marci's color was so white. She had lost all the pigment in her skin and hair.

My lover's neck was long but thick. Her waist was tight and very muscular. Rolls of muscle were interwoven throughout her stomach. Marci had a strong and tight core in her previous life and as expected, most of what was dominate in your previous life gets accentuated in the host's new life. Her legs were thick and long, with large muscles dominating every inch of her legs. The arms were well defined, and the biceps were not bulging but the entire arm was well-developed.

Marci's teeth were large and long. There were small but noticeable gaps between each tooth. The front teeth came to sharp points at the end of each tooth, and her gums were overly developed, probably to compensate for the large teeth. Marci's upper teeth had two incisors that were longer than the rest of her upper teeth, and when she closed her mouth, the two incisors protruded from her mouth. She also had two of her lower teeth that were a longer and sharper than the others. Her lips were modest in size and shape, which was surprising since she had very pouty lips in her previous life.

Marci's tail grew longer and thicker. The tail grew downward past the back of her knees and was very thick near her back and tremendously strong. The girth of the tail gradually became thinner toward the end of the tail and at the end it came to a point. The tail was as white as the rest of her body. This new addition was very surprising to us. We were not expecting her to grow a tail.

During this entire process, Marci was under constant, intense pain. She never had a moment's rest, her body in constant painful changes. Every inch of her body was either moving, popping, stretching, burning, or bulging from the rapid growth she was undergoing. Many times during her change, she wanted to roll up into a fetal position, but either her body wouldn't let her because her joints wouldn't bend or she couldn't because of the pain or exhaustion, or a combination of both.

When the transformation was complete, Wolfgang and I stood back and admired the newly-formed body. We both sensed that Marci was finished evolving. At first, I was saddened that my love was so disfigured but at the same time I was happy that she was at least alive and well. Also, having the knowledge that she should live forever with me had completely satisfied the greatest need in my life.

Marci seemed to be happy that she was alive, but I wondered how shocked and upset she might be at her newly-formed appearance. Hopefully over time, she would accept her appearance and maybe even eventually like her new look. Marci would discover another world that she could only imagine existed. Marci wanted this, and she remembered that she desired this change. This little fact would go a long way in her acceptance of her new form.

During this juncture, we needed to let nature take its course. Marci required time to adjust to her new and improved body. We didn't have to start back at ground zero like we did when she came back to life, but she needed time for the formula to heal her, both mentally and physically. Her thoughts were confused at times, and she needed to learn how to walk and move in her new body. She had to adjust to her larger, heavier, and thicker body. She had to learn how to speak and to move her newly formed tongue, mouth, and vocal cords. Like any animal born in the wild, it takes some time to adjust. In Marci's case, she had to put everything together so the whole was working with the numerous parts to create one functioning unit. This took time and patience.

Wolfgang said the formula would correct anything that was not exactly perfect as the formula constantly repairs what needs to be corrected in the host's body. Wolfgang and I had to keep a close, observant eye on her after I brought her back from the dead. Not only from a historic prospective but from a caring prospective.

There was a chance that Marci wouldn't have even come back from the dead, not to mention to be able to survive the transformation. Wolfgang and I were concerned if enough or even too much of the formula was injected into my love. At this stage, the danger was over. After the physical change had taken place, the formula would only make Marci a better, healthier, and stronger being. Now the only question was how much of a mental change would have taken place. This was now my new nightmare. Would my love even remember me? Would she have to fall in love with me again or would she even be interested in me? Would she find me attractive? Then I wondered after the initial shock has passed, would I find her physically attractive again? How much of her personality will have changed? These thoughts were just as distressing as not knowing if she was going to survive the conversion.

As Wolfgang and I stood back and looked at this amazing form before us, we were both in awe and wonder. Her new form and looks were beautiful but disturbing at the same time, a cross between a being of amazing wonder to simply a terrifying sight that graced our eyes. Her look was so intimidating, but when you studied her body, you had to come away impressed that something like a few drops of some strange liquid could create such a magnificent creature.

Wolfgang told me that from all early indications, Marci was going to be fully functioning physically in a matter of hours. Wolfgang said that from his data, not only on himself but on Zelda, we could expect about a twenty-percentage change in her personality. He reassured me that the core of her personality should still be intact, but there would be some slight to even major changes in certain areas of her character.

When Marci started to be more coherent, I spoke to her and slowly tried to get her to communicate with me. Marci was confused at first, but quickly seemed to understand what I was saying and what had happened to her. I know my love well, and from the look that was buried inside of this new face, I knew she understood that something happened to her body. I sensed and saw concern, anxiety, and nervousness on my love's newly designed face. She wanted to speak, but her face was in a frozen state. I told her to rest and that soon she would slowly regain more movement in her body and body functions.

After several hours had passed, I heard a groan struggling from my love. My eyes studied her entire body and I noticed her fingers starting to move slowly. She was trying to adjust to her new body. From our indications, she had a small degree of pain which we assumed was created from the stiffness of her joints. She tried to move her paralyzed body, with each new movement causing various grades of discomfort.

As the hours passed, Marci could move all her fingers and both hands at the wrist, as well as her toes and ankles. Her face began to show more movement in the lips and cheeks areas. Her large black eyes moved ever so slightly, and she could now control her large eyelids. She would slowly open her eyes and then close them, each time with greater speed. It was an amazing sight to witness these large black eyes open and close. Wolfgang tested her eyes to see what he could find. As he shined the light in her eyes a few times, she finally started to react to the brightness.

I talked to Marci throughout this process. I could sense that over the past several hours, she could hear me. I had no idea at the time if she could understand me, then after countless questions, there came a point when Marci started to understand what we were saying. We asked to her blink once for yes and twice for no. After a long series of questions, Wolfgang and I felt comfortable that she understood what we were trying to communicate to her. It was at this point that I started to explain everything that had happened to her. From early indications, it seemed that she understood what I was saying to her.

As the hours passed, Marci regained additional movement over the once paralyzed areas of her body. She also gained control over the areas that she was able to move at the start of her new life. She started to move all parts of her body, and at first it was slow because she was trying to adjust to her new body. Her face also started to develop more of a personality by way of facial movements. The scene was surreal and unbelievable that something so large, so different, so perfectly formed was regaining control of her new life.

Late at night, I was by Marci's side and I heard more groaning. She was trying to speak. Her mouth would open and close as her eyes seemed to follow in unison. Then she started to move her hands from the bed. She was bending her arms and in slight, small jerking movements, she lifted both arms off the bed. She then laid them down as if to test rest them. Then she brought them up further. After several attempts, she finally lifted her arms up and moved them closer to her face. For the first time during her new life, Marci finally got to see a part of her new body. She brought her long, porcelain white hands, jerking slightly after each passing inch, near her face. I could see the first reaction on her face. She knew that she was going to change physically, but I knew she wasn't expecting this much of an alteration. I noticed large tears were developing then falling down the sides of her face. Her lips were quivering and she was franticly trying to form words to describe her feelings. Nothing was coming out of her mouth but groaning and grunting noises. She moved her hands around from side to side as she laid there looking and studying them. What a shock this must have been to my love.

Wolfgang talked to her and said, "Marci, don't be too shocked at your appearance. Your skin is extremely white. You lost all pigment in your skin. Your body has grown and changed beyond your comprehension. You must accept your new body." Wolfgang and I were concerned about Marci's mental psyche then her physical body. I saw what just part of Adelle's transformation did to her, but I also saw what it did to others and they came through the change quite well. I knew Marci was mentally strong, but I was obviously concerned for her mental wellbeing. She couldn't keep her eyes off her hands, wrists, and forearms. She moved them back and forth from her face. She studied every angle then moved her neck ever so slightly. She suddenly lost control over her arms as they fell on her chest. Her arms were tired. After a few moments, she moved her hands along her breasts, slid them down her stomach, and then rested them on her sides. I could see a smile was trying to develop on her face.

After a good night of rest, Marci regained more control over her legs, arms, and shoulder muscles. She could move her head in at angles. She was slowly adjusting to her new form. Wolfgang and I took our time with Marci and we never rushed her in any way. This part of the transformation was out of our control. She had to regain use her of body, but it would take time. I stayed by her side the entire time, talking to her and trying to comfort her in every way I knew how.

As the first day of her reborn life flowed into her second day, she started to move onto her side and then on her back. She would rest for a moment then repeat this process continually. She moved her legs up to her chest in a fetal position and then would stretch them out. She looked as if she wanted to get up. She placed her large hand on the bed, moved her elbow back, and tried to push herself to sit up. I said, "Marci, do you want to get up?" Knowing full well she couldn't speak to me, I could sense her thoughts. She tried so hard to get up and finally I had to help her. I placed my arm around her, pushed her, and gently placed her in a sitting position on the bed.

I then heard her make a noise. For the first time, she saw her new legs. Between her legs was her long and newly developed tail. She looked at her newly formed legs and tail, and after a few moments she made a gasping sound. Her hands started to move on the bed in the attempt to reposition herself. Her head moved from side to side. She looked at each square inch that was in front of her. The noises that came from her mouth were desperate sounds and cries for help. She was unquestionably scared out of her mind. I have never seen her this way. My heart just sunk as I tried to console her as best I could.

Marci suddenly took hold of my hand for the first time and squeezed it hard. I was in pain from her powerful grip, but I didn't allow myself to have any reaction. Her legs were moving and bending in front of her. She seemed to be in great terror, and without warning she quickly threw her head back and screamed, "Aaaaaaaaaaaaaahhhhhhhhhhkkkkkkk."

Wolfgang came running into the room and asked, "Is everything all right?" Not answering my father, I leaned over and got very close to my love's face. I said, "Marci! Marci! Stay with me love! I am here for you! I love you!" As long as I live, I will never forget that scream or the look she had on her face. It sent shivers down my spine. Her mouth was open as wide as it could go, and all her teeth were showing. Saliva was dripping from every long tooth. Marci kept her head back and for a moment no sound was made. Then she took a deep breath. I heard every long moment of that powerful breath then she let out another scream from hell. A desperate, lonely, and scared sound, the likes of which I had never heard. Her high-pitched screams of panic made me scared for my love's wellbeing. I pleaded and pleaded with her to control her emotions and to calm herself down. Nothing seemed to work.

After the second scream she took another large, deep breath and this time she moved her head back down and was panting as if she was hyperventilating. She looked everywhere around her in the most desperate horror I have ever seen. She moved her head toward me and looked right at me. Her breathing was fast and short. Then abruptly the corners of her lips turned upward ever so slightly. She moved her head and lips and finally she spoke, "Gaaa." She took a deep breath and said again, "Gaaaaaaa" in a more emphatic and forceful way. She drew another unfathomable breath and said, "Gaaaaaasssss... oooonnn"

Tears ran down my cheeks. My love spoke my name. She remembered my name! By the love of everything that is perfect and good, she remembered me. Oh, the relief that swelled over me was the most incredible feeling that I had ever felt in my life. She took her other hand and opened it in front of her. Her palm was facing down, and with a trembling motion she said, "Paaa. Paaaaaa. Fffff. Kaaaaa." While sobbing like a baby, I said, "Yes... yes, my love, you are perfect." Without notice, she bent her head back and let out another unholy scream as tears were just pouring out of her large black eyes. She caught her breath and another scream of release came from this powerful being. But this time it was not a scream of panic but of ecstasy, bliss, and joy – all in the purest sense of those words. I placed my love down gently on the bed as she continued to let out those horrifying screams of elation until she collapsed from apparent exhaustion. The next moment, all I could remember was falling to the floor. Wolfgang came inside the cell and helped me up. All I could say to my father was, "She remembers me. She is scared... but she is so happy." I felt lightheaded and suddenly, I collapsed in my father's arms.

Chapter Eleven

lowly, after several hours of rest, I heard my parents talking in the far corner of the room. My father had placed me on a cot after my collapse from apparent exhaustion. I got up and made my way to them. My mother, Zelda, met me half way and hugged me. She said, "I am so happy for you, Garrison." I quickly kept control over my emotions. This was no time for me to lose control of my emotional consciousness.

I asked, "How is Marci?"

Wolfgang answered, "She is still resting."

At this stage after the transformation, we needed to introduce Eva to the newly developed Marci. My parents and I were afraid that Marci's new appearance would significantly scare Eva. Eva had grown very close to Marci and had been demanding to see her. My parents had been preparing Eva for her inevitable encounter of the newly formed being. Wolfgang tried to explain to Eva about the formula and its effects on the host's body. We were forced to tell Eva about the formula because she was constantly asking why she looked so different from her mom and dad. Because of her familiarity with Wolfgang and Zelda's physical form throughout her entire life, she just accepted their appearance, but as the years went along, she posed more questions about the way they looked. Eva seemed to understand about her parent's history. Wolfgang continued to prepare Eva that Marci was going to go through a dramatic physical change and that Eva should not fear her.

Eva was wise beyond her years and we sensed that we could trust her with this private information. Wolfgang, even though he was Eva's father, was still a very demanding and intimidating figure, and Eva feared her father. Wolfgang had threatened Eva's life if she were to ever tell anyone about the family's secret. Wolfgang knew just how much he could push people and, in this case, he made no exception with his daughter. To help further aid Eva's meeting with the new Marci, Wolfgang showed her some photos of Marci. At first, Eva was shocked but after several minutes she seemed not to be afraid. With Wolfgang's training, Eva was surprisingly well adjusted with the contrasting differences between her parents' appearance compared to the humans that she saw on television and in real life.

Wolfgang and Zelda took Eva into the lab where I was sitting next to my love. I carefully leaned over and said to Marci, "Marci, Eva wants to see you. It has been a long time since she has spoken to you. We told her of your physical change, so please have some patience with her because it might be a shock when she first sees you." I was worried about Eva's reaction to Marci's new look and how it not only would affect Eva but how it might impact Marci's mental state. Even though Marci wanted this new and improved body, it was still an awesome challenge for a person to accept, especially when others might look at you as a freak.

I rose from Marci's side and unlocked the cell door. I saw Eva's little face with that long, flowing blonde hair bouncing around her shoulders. My parents carefully walked Eva around the corner of the lab. Her beautiful, piercing blue eyes immediately looked at the large figure on the hospital bed inside the cell. Eva said, "Is that Marci?"

I said, "Yes, Eva, come over here and let me introduce you to the new Marci." Eva ran over toward me and put her small hand in mine. We walked over to Marci's side. I said, "Marci is having some trouble speaking right now but she is awake."

Eva said, "Hi Marci!" Marci moved her head to the side. Eva screamed loudly. She backed up a few feet, but never took her eyes off Marci. After several moments, Eva composed herself.

I said, "I know it is a shock at first, but this is Marci. Soon she will be able to talk, walk, jump, and run around with you like she did before, only better."

Eva quickly broke her stare and looked at me and smiled. She said to Marci, "Sorry, Marci. You have big eyes. Your feet got big too. You grew a lot."

Marci moved a little and attempted to say something but all she could get out was, "Eeeeeffffaaaaaa."

Eva helped Marci by saying, "Yes, Eva! I am Eva. Keep trying and you'll get it someday. It took me a while to learn how to talk."

As the days progressed, Marci's speech, hand-eye coordination, and bodily movements greatly improved, and her strength rapidly increased. At this stage, she sat up on her own. The main issue that Marci experienced was getting used to her enormous size, both with her height and weight. When she sat up, she would sway from side to side from the fact that she felt top heavy. It was difficult for her to adjust to her new body.

When the time came for Marci to get on her feet, both Zelda and Wolfgang assisted her in this feat. I was a little undersized to help keep her from falling. When Marci's feet first touched the floor, she again yelled out in pain. Her feet were not used to carrying so much weight, and this part of her body also had to adjust to her new size. She started out shuffling her feet at first but after a few tries she was able to walk better. The steps that she first attempted were a tough go. Her feet were three times larger than what she was used to before her conversion, which made walking difficult. She had to lift her feet and legs higher than what she was used to. Another issue she had was her tall size and large amount of weight made it problematic for her to modify for the strange new factors now present in her life.

Marci also had a difficult time adjusting to her long tail. It was strong, and at the beginning she had limited control over her new appendage. She would whip the tail around her body and it would slap against her leg or her stomach. It would hit so hard it would leave a red mark, which was not a pleasant experience. At times, her tail would touch me and it would feel like being whipped harshly. After a few days, Marci was able to control her tail and use it as a primitive helping hand. She was able to wrap her tail around things, and after she learned how to squeeze her tail, she could pick up small items. She worked so hard in controlling her tail that after a week, she had total mastery of her new growth.

Once we re-established her physical motor skills, I worked with Marci's speech. We studied pronouncing the alphabet together, and Marci was quick to learn. Within a day, she was pronouncing all the letters correctly. We sounded out words that I picked out randomly in my head. The largest hurdle in these new tasks was Marci adapting to her new mouth, teeth, lips, and tongue.

Many living beings take for granted what they control over their bodies, both their physical and mental capabilities. For example, moving your leg without much thought but compare that easy task to someone who has a spinal cord injury that maybe for them the task would be laborious. Therefore, when Marci was forced to think how to use her mouth to form words, that exercise became very difficult.

Marci had large teeth and gums and it was difficult to close her mouth so her lips would meet. Because of this fact, she had to talk with her teeth and gums exposed, without her lips touching or moving in the way that she was used to in her previous life. She had issues with accomplishing that task, and it was not coming natural for her so that made her mispronounce some letters and words. In addition, her extremely long tongue was getting in the way of her trying to speak clearly. It took her a while to adjust to this new addition. After several days, her noticeable lisp improved. She had to learn to move her mouth and tongue in certain ways for the letters and words to come out clearly. When Marci mastered this task, she had a very distinct way of talking. Her words were very pronounced, placing emphasis on each syllable of each word. Many times, she would stress the last syllable of each word in an emphatic style.

When Marci mastered getting up, down and walking on her own, we took her outside. She loved the outdoors. The first time we took her outside was at nighttime. The moon wasn't out and the grounds were pitch black. Since Wolfgang and I could see at night extremely well, we wanted to see how Marci's night vision was compared to ours. As soon as we stepped outside, she described everything that she saw in the dark. Her eyesight was better than ours, which really surprised us. She told us that she could see just as well as night as she could during the day, the only difference was what she saw was darker at night.

We worked long hours on Marci's hand-eye coordination. This area of her development would come naturally to her with the aid of the formula, but we wanted to accelerate this process. Wolfgang had Marci pick up stones and throw them at trees, which served many purposes. It helped her by bending down and getting back up in a straight up position. It helped her adjust to her new height, weight, and girth, and it also assisted her coordination skills that could be used in hunting. Even though we don't call ourselves animals of the wild, we are basically bred to hunt, kill, and eat our prey.

We threw golf balls, baseballs, and eventually small rocks at her and forced her to catch them in either hand. We would throw small sticks at her and she would smack them down with her long tail. At times, she would pick up the stick and throw it back at us. She would use her tail for balance and even as an aid for helping her hands catch things. At times, when she caught an item with her hands, her tail would quickly come to assist.

We taught Marci how to run and how to change directions quickly while running. Marci had to step higher than normal because of her large feet. After several hours of practice, she would run through the forest and try to dodge trees, branches, boulders, steep cliffs, and downed trees.

Wolfgang, Zelda, and I worked constantly on further developing her senses. Again, we could have the formula take its natural course, but if developed, her senses and coordination would advance further and faster. We wanted to guide her to always be ultra-aware of her surroundings in her now long, endless life. Marci's senses were off the charts in sensitivity. She could smell, hear, and sense everything around her. We would have her close her large eyes and walk around the grounds, only being a slave to her hearing. This forced her to hear things that normally people ignore or tune out. We would toss golf ball or baseballs to her while her eyes were closed to force her to hear the ball while it was in the air, so she could catch them in flight. Marci was outstanding in being able to anticipate what was around her or what was sneaking up on her. We learned that because of her large eyes, she could position her pupils to extreme angles and could see approximately half of what was behind her head.

Marci had been on a diet of vegetables and cooked meat. Marci now hated cooked meat and at times, it made her sick to her stomach, but we wanted her body to further adjust to its natural changes before we started to feed her raw meat. Marci approached Wolfgang and I on many occasions wanting raw meat, a natural byproduct of the formula's symptoms. Wolfgang, Zelda, and I had set traps throughout the forest area in the back part of our wooded property. Some of the traps were metal and some were made from strong rope. Usually the traps were for large animals like deer, and some were for smaller animals like squirrels, possums, foxes and similar animals. Many times, we would hunt the animals and kill them by throwing stones, golf balls, or any sharp object toward them. We wanted to make it easy for Marci for her first time, so Wolfgang set a rope trap for a deer.

Wolfgang and I took Marci deep into the forest. She was very excited and could hardly wait to eat her first animal. My parents and I went over the parts of the deer and gave her an outline on how to first approach the deer and where to bite. We went over this information about other animals as well. We told her that we had set a trap down in a gully of the property. This area was heavily populated with deer and other animals. As we walked through the forest, we looked down the large hill and saw that we had captured a large deer in one of the rope traps. It looked to have just walked into the trap, so the deer was still very active. Many times, the deer would fight the traps, and in the attempt to free themselves, they would exhaust themselves trying to get out of the trap.

We made our way down the large hill, with Marci ahead of us. Her large feet made it easy for her to navigate her way through wooded terrain. For Wolfgang, the forest was basically all he knew. He spent most of his life living in the forest and that is where he felt the most comfortable. It took me a while to catch up with them because I only had a human body and it took me longer to get to our destination. Marci stood next to the deer but didn't touch the animal. Wolfgang walked her through the necessary steps and she followed them closely.

Marci knelt beside the head of the deer. It was moving in all directions, trying to get away. It was in total fear of not only Marci but the other two onlookers as well. Marci said, "This is incredible. I can hear its heartbeat. I can smell its fear. Its fear is so strong I can actually taste it in my mouth." She removed some of the rope around the deer's head and with her large hand, long fingers, and catlike reflexes, she quickly grabbed the deer's throat. The deer started to kick Marci and that upset her a little. She pulled the rope back off the front part of the deer but kept its legs tangled up in the rope. The deer kept kicking Marci's upper thigh. Although the deer had limited motion in its kicks, it was pissing Marci off. Marci said, "Stop kicking me, you fucking deer!" Then, without any warning, she placed her large muscular leg over the top of the hoof that the deer was using to kick her. She used her strong tail for additional support by placing her tail on the ground to steady her body. Marci tried to secure the deer's leg as best she could with her leg and then she quickly made a fist. She punched as hard as she could on the side of the leg, instantly breaking it in two parts. The deer let out a whimpering cry and moved even harder and faster.

Marci looked at the deer for several moments, not letting loose of her grip on the deer's neck. She placed her other hand on the hurt leg to keep it as relatively still as she could as she leant forward. I saw large drops and strains of saliva dripping from her large teeth. She opened her mouth as wide as she could and quickly bit into the deer's neck. Her teeth easily went into the deer's flesh. The deer's body shivered then tensed up as it was trying to protect itself from its inevitable death. After just a few bites, Marci was able to remove a large portion of meat from the deer's neck.

I watched her facial expressions as she was experiencing pure ecstasy. When the deer's life ended, she knelt in front of her kill and chewed on the deer meat. She lifted her head up, looking at the sky above. The light that passed through the leaves of the forest cast an eerie glow on her porcelain skin. She was savoring every bite. The deep red blood was very pronounced on Marci's face. I watched the stains of blood as it dripped down her chin, ran down her long throat, and settled between her large breasts. The sound of her eating was menacing as well. Powerful but precise bites dominated the air around this majestic scene. Then I noticed large tears swelling in my love's eyes and they poured down her checks. She finished chewing and swallowed hard. She looked at me and said, "That was so good. I can see why you guys love eating live, warm meat. I loved when I bit into the animal; the smell and the way it tensed up. It was just amazing. It was so erotic, I think I had an orgasm during my meal." I looked at my love and smiled. My love had not changed much after her conversion.

Wolfgang was very impressed with the way Marci ate the deer. He said, "Her bite is cleaner than mine," acknowledging that Marci's teeth were even better equipped at digging in and tearing flesh off the bone.

Marci offered a portion of her meal to us, but we declined. She continued to eat. At first, she made every attempt to be dainty, clean, and wanted to be precise with her bites. As she grew more comfortable with her consumption of the neck, she wanted to try a leg. She bent down and took a large bite out of the top portion of the upper leg socket and simultaneously took her powerful hands and tugged at the leg. Within a few seconds, she was successful at removing the leg from the deer. We were very impressed at what we were seeing since we didn't tell Marci how to perform such a maneuver. What we witnessed was the formula igniting a basic instinct that was hidden deep within her.

Marci took the leg in her hands and tore the flesh and muscles of the leg bone. She carefully removed the meat from the muscles, and after she thought there was enough there to eat, she started to eat.

Throughout her meal, she dipped parts of the muscles in the semi-warm blood of the corpse that lie before her. My mouth watered at the sight. The blood typically has an iron-like taste and when it mixed with the tissue of the muscle, it creates the most aromatic flavor that you ever put into your mouth. Combining that sensation with the natural earthy and musky smell of the animal made for a hallucinogenic meal that would transcend your senses into another world.

Marci knew her transformation was now complete. Finally, she could not only sense but comprehend what I had known all my life. Marci understood the desire for raw animal meat. It's not just the taste but the total sensory experience. She asked for this and at this moment, I was finally at peace for what I had done to my love. I gave her everlasting life. I gave her a new life that any human would find repulsive, but not my Marci. She was different. She was special. She was perfect for me in every way. This moment was her official coronation, which launched her new and improved life.

When Marci finished her meal, we walked back to the estate. In the distance, we heard, smelt, and saw Eva, who came running out of the house. Wolfgang yelled at her, "Get back in the house, Eva!" Eva stood there watching us come out of the tree lined forest and onto the perfectly manicured lawn made from Adelle's blood. She didn't move a muscle. Wolfgang again said, "Eva, get back in the house!" Eva walked toward us, disobeying our father's orders. My heart sunk for my sister, partly in fear of her disobeying our father, and partly for her seeing blood all over Marci. We all could sense each other's feelings and we knew that Eva possessed enough knowledge to know what Marci had done. Eva started running toward us and Wolfgang again yelled, "Stop, Eva!"

Eva finally heeded our father's command. Eva started with the questions. She said with a smile, "What happened to you, Marci? Are you okay?"

Marci said, "I think you know what happened. Don't play coy with me, Eva. You should not play those sorts of games with me." Eva knew full well that Marci had dined on some sort of an animal. This act was something that Eva had been wanting to do herself for a while now and her curiosity was running wild.

Eva and Marci were always close but after Marci's rebirth, they had grown closer. Eva was very instrumental in her continued development. Eva accepted her completely and never was scared or made fun of her appearance.

Eva said, "So what did you eat? How did it taste? How did you capture it?"

Marci was smiling and said, "It was a deer. Your father captured a deer for me."

Eva said, "How did it taste? Did it taste good?"

Marci opened her large eyes and said, "It was scrumptious."

Zelda quickly came out of the house and said to Marci, "Marci! Shut up! She is too young."

Eva continued to ask questions. She asked, "How did you kill the deer?"

Wolfgang was very upset and yelled, "Eva! Go to your room! Now!"

Eva gave her father a dirty look and stomped her foot hard on the ground. Wolfgang puffed out his enormous chest but before he could utter another word, Eva quickly turned and stomped away. She passed her mom and they exchanged evil looks as she made her way to her room.

Marci said to Wolfgang and Zelda, "I am sorry. I shouldn't have said anything."

Wolfgang said, "You're right. You should have kept your mouth shut. But what is done is done. She was going to find out eventually. We cannot keep anything from her. Her senses are too strong." Wolfgang walked away toward the forest and said in a passing voice, "I am hungry. I will be back in a while." Zelda closely followed Wolfgang into the forest.

I retired to the great room and started to play my violin. Marci headed upstairs to her room. As she walked down the hallway, she heard a strange noise coming from Eva's room. Marci walked up to the door and knocked. Marci heard someone running inside the room and after several moments, Eva opened the door. Marci could sense something was in the room. Eva knew that Marci smelt the guest, so she quickly reached out and grabbed Marci by her long arm and pulled at her to come inside her room. Marci slowly walked inside as Eva quickly but quietly closed the door behind her. Eva said, "Now be quiet and don't say anything to my parents." Without any warning, a slight purr came from behind the closet door.

Marci quietly said, "Do you have a cat up here with you?"

Eva smiled widely and said, "Do you want to see him?" Marci nodded and smiled back.

Eva went over to the closet door, opened it and there was an adult cat with a rope around its neck. It was too scared to hiss as it stood there and made no attempt to protect itself. Eva picked up the cat and held it closely to her chest with both arms wrapped around the cat's body. It was scared and tried to run away from Eva but her grasp on him was too tight. Marci asked her, "Where did you find the cat?"

Eva said, "I found it in the yard walking around. I went to pet it, but it hissed at me and ran away. This happened every day for a week so I put out a bowl of milk in the garage and waited for it to come by. One day, it did and as it was drinking its milk, I tried to throw a box over it. I missed it many times, but I had it cornered in the back of the garage, and finally captured it. I found some rope in the garage and placed it around its neck for a leash. When my parents were in their bedroom, I carefully brought the cat in my room. It doesn't like me. It constantly hisses at me and wants to run away."

Marci was confused. She didn't know what to do. She didn't want to lose Eva's trust, but she also didn't want to keep this from Wolfgang and Zelda. Marci was careful not to discourage or sound accusatory to Eva. Eva said, "So, Marci, how was it? What was it like? What did the deer taste like?"

Marci said smiling, "I don't think I should be having this conversation with you, Eva." Marci stood there looking into Eva's eager eyes.

Eva said, "Come on. Tell me." Marci noticed Eva's fingers were attempting to stroke the cat but it was difficult for her since the cat was fighting her every step of the way, trying to get loose from Eva's grasp. Eva said, "So, how do you do it, Marci? Where should I bite?"

Marci knew she should stop Eva, but she was caught up in the moment as well. Marci said, "I started at the neck, but your mouth might not be strong or big enough for a clean bite. You must get your teeth into the skin of the animal. If you bite going with the grain of the fur, your teeth might slip a little, causing a clean bite. You need to pull back the fur or tighten the skin up around the neck to get a deep bite."

Eva looked at Marci as she quickly lowered her head near the cat. The cat let out a loud hiss. Marci reached out and took hold of the cat. Her large hand was under the cat's jaw and untied the rope. When the rope hit the floor, Marci methodically used her fingers to part the fur and expose as much skin as possible around the cat's neck. Marci said, "Okay, see how I did that? Now bite into the neck, but do it hard and forcefully, and make sure you break the skin. Don't stop in the middle of the bite. Just bite down hard and try to force your upper and lower teeth to touch toward the end of the bite."

Eva positioned her mouth to the cat's neck as it continued to make haunting pleas for help. Eva opened her mouth and quickly drove her teeth into the cat's neck. Eva did as instructed and continued to bite hard. The cat screamed and tensed up. Eva was surprised at the rush of adrenaline that was now pulsating through her veins. Eva's senses were lit up. She heard the cat's heartbeat, and she smelt the cat's fear and desperate plea to get away. She savored the musky animal smell of the cat.

Eva had trouble getting her teeth to break the skin. The cat's hair was silky and her teeth slid a little and disrupted the bite. She lifted her head back and went after another bite, and this time she finally broke the skin. It was Eva's first taste of an animal. She felt the warm blood on the lower gums of her mouth. Eva moaned from the physical, mental and auditory pleasure this experience was giving her. Soon she felt the warm blood on her lips and felt the blood as it made its way down her chin. The cat jerked in great pain and continued to make strange sounds.

Suddenly, Eva and Marci heard Zelda at the bedroom door. Zelda attempted to turn the door knob, but it was locked. Zelda said, "What's going on in there? Eva! Open this door now!" After several moments passed, Zelda's strong hand twisted the doorknob, breaking the lock, and she swung the door open. Zelda caught Eva taking a bite out of a cat with Marci holding it for her. Zelda's emotions were at a fever pitch. She yelled at Marci, "What are you people doing? Why in the hell would you teach her this at her age?"

I stopped playing my violin. I placed the instrument down and made my way toward the stairs. I heard Wolfgang behind me as his large feet and heavily framed body ran behind me. He passed me and went up the stairs in just a few strides as he made his way to Eva's bedroom. Zelda continued to yell at Marci, "She is way too young to learn such things."

Marci said, "What's the big deal? She will end up eating animals at some point in her life, so why not teach her now?"

Zelda said, "This is not your daughter! You don't make these kinds of decisions without consulting me!"

Without any notice, Eva attempted to take another bite out of the cat. She bit down on the open wound. Zelda screamed, "No, Eva! Stop it. Give me that fucking cat!"

Wolfgang yelled, "What is going on in here? Eva! Stop eating the cat. Marci, put the damn thing down now!" Wolfgang's voice was filled with anger. He said, "She is entirely too young for this. She is not ready. You of all people should know this."

Marci answered back, "So what is the big deal?"

Zelda screamed and said, "She... is... too... young!" Zelda let out a growl, showing her large white teeth as the saliva dripped from a few teeth. You could hear the saliva hit the hardwood floor, making small splat sounds. Zelda reached out and grabbed the cat from Marci's hands.

I raced as fast as I could and when I got to the entrance of the bedroom, I quickly went to Marci, took her by the arm, and pushed her toward the door. I said, "I will take care of Marci."

By the grace of all that was good, Marci quietly let me take her out of Eva's room and we went into her room next door. I cleaned Marci up and told her not to do that again. She apologized to me and said she knew she had made a mistake.

Meanwhile, Zelda and Wolfgang told Eva that her system was not ready to eat live meat. Wolfgang went downstairs to get some medicine to administer to Eva so she wouldn't get physically ill from any parasites that the cat had in its system. At this stage in Eva's life, the formula probably would have destroyed any foreign substance that was in her body, but Wolfgang didn't want to take any chances.

Zelda looked at the cat and noticed it was still alive. It was trying to get away from all the strange beings that were in the room. Zelda took the rope leash and tied it to Eva's bedpost. The cat's lungs were expanding and contracting rapidly from its pain. Zelda led Eva to her bathroom and cleaned her up. Wolfgang came back to Eva's room and gave Eva a few shots, which she didn't like one bit. He knew the medicine wouldn't really help Eva because the formula would attack the medicine, break it down in her system, and render it useless to her body, but Wolfgang wanted to impress upon Eva how serious the situation was, although we all knew that Eva sensed what was going on. Wolfgang was calmer and told her that someday, when she was old enough, she would be free to eat all the animals she would want, but at this stage of her development, her system was not mature enough to properly handle this form of eating.

Eva wanted her cat to be kept alive. Eva said, "Please don't kill it."

Wolfgang said, "But you tried to kill it yourself. What does it matter to you whether it lives or dies?"

Eva just shrugged her shoulders and said, "I just want it alive. I promise I won't eat it."

Wolfgang, out of morbid curiosity, picked up the cat and took it downstairs. He placed it in a small cage and attempted to nurse the cat back to health. Wolfgang was curious to see if the cat would change. Wolfgang's first thought was that the formula, even though it in her system, might not be mature enough to cause a physical change in the cat. He knew that Garrison was a few years older than Eva when he bit Trevor and changed him. Wolfgang wanted to see what would happen to the cat.

Later that night, Marci apologized to my parents and to Eva. Wolfgang accepted the apology but told her not to go behind their backs again. Marci agreed.

Eva never suffered any side effects from biting her cat. Wolfgang and I had to reinforce the incredible responsibility that Eva must shoulder. We must contain the formula to ourselves. If Eva's cat would have escaped and he went out on his own and mutated, after his mutation process, he would eventually pass the formula on through biting another animal. If that animal would survive, it too would mutate, and the process would continue. This was a lot for a young little girl to comprehend, but we had no choice but to tell her because she could have caused a major problem for many animal species, including humans.

Wolfgang and I kept close tabs on Eva's cat, who she named Midnight, over the next few weeks. We kept Midnight in a crate made for a large dog. We placed the crate in one of the cell rooms in the lab. We would lock the cell door every time we entered or left. It laid around for a couple of days without moving around because of the large wound on its neck. We handfed the cat during this time. The cat was in obvious pain, but we didn't give it any medicine in fear that it might counteract with the formula in some unexpected way.

I was about five when I bit Trevor and the formula was strong enough in me to change a grown man. We had been monitoring Eva since she arrived at the estate, and her vital signs and growth patterns mirrored what Lewis had on my early records. Of course, we had more data on Eva at her young age than we had on me. Wolfgang's theory was that the formula needed time to adjust to its host for it to take on its full effectiveness. He thought the time was not long enough for the formula to be fully developed in Eva's system as it was when I was five years old. Either way, we knew the cat would probably change, but to what extent?

Around day three after the bite, Midnight started to show uncharacteristic signs and traits of a typical cat. The cat shook violently at times and then it would lie perfectly still. After several hours, the cat was in extreme pain, cried out relentlessly, and would stretch its paws out like it was reaching for help. As the hours passed, events became more interesting. The cat's body started to swell. Throughout the swelling, portions of the cat's body would swell up and then decrease. The body of the cat looked as if small balloons were under the fur, inflating then quickly deflating. The cat was in tormented pain throughout this natural progression of the formula. At this point, it was obvious that the formula was in full force in Eva's body. Now the question was how pure the formula was at this stage of her development. I had my own theory that the formula was already developed. If that were to be the case, then when I was her age, I possessed this same power. Maybe the formula doesn't develop in our systems, it is just there, the same chemical structure no matter how long the formula has been in the host. Perhaps my father was incorrect in his assertion.

The transformation continued in front of our eyes. Midnight suddenly shed all its hair in a matter of a minute. The skin was very white and looked bloated, and the blood-colored veins were pronounced throughout the body. At times, the veins would enlarge to a point where they would seem to burst then the next moment their size would retract. The cat continued in this state for an hour until the cat's skeleton structure started to increase in size. The skin around the bones were pulled so tight that it started to split in thirteen different areas of the body. As soon as the slit in the skin would develop, it would heal just as fast. Blood covered most of the cat's body and the floor of the crate.

The neck grew faster than other parts of the body. The head changed its form and increased fourfold. The head was completely round. The eyes were large and pink in color while the slit in the eye was light green. The nose never protruded, and only two holes made for air passages. The ears grew long and pointy. They were positioned on the side of the head with the end of the ear pointed backward, parallel with the cat's back. The tail grew twice the length of the legs. The girth of the body increased to three times its normal sized body. Its chest and stance resembled a Bulldog but with longer legs. The feet were large with long, prominent toes. The toenails grew out about an inch, which made the toes look even larger.

After Midnight's transformation, it slowly got onto its feet. It shook it body, and as it did, it fell. After several minutes, it staggered to its feet again. It looked at us and made the most interesting sound. It opened his mouth, which was filled with teeth, and let out a growl that was loud and low in pitch but resembled a goat.

Wolfgang and I studied Midnight's teeth. Wolfgang held the cat down and I took many pictures and videos of Midnight's mouth. There were three rows of teeth on both the upper and the lower gums. Everyone was razor sharp. The tongue was long, thin, and forked at the end. It was very snake-like in appearance and structure. Midnight had an enormous appetite. It loved meat, rodents, and bugs. We made sure to always keep it on a leash.

We introduced the new and improved Midnight to Eva and Marci. Eva fell in love with Midnight. She didn't bat an eye or was even the least bit disturbed by Midnight's appearance, although Midnight wasn't kind to Eva. It growled at her and made Eva very upset. Wolfgang had Midnight on a leash while it growled and snapped at Eva. Eva ran away to the far side of the lab. Marci tried to calm Midnight down but she had the same luck as Eva.

Midnight was growling, hissing, and trying to get loose from the leash. It wanted to attack Marci. Wolfgang and I didn't have this experience. Maybe it was just used to us. I heard the small, dainty footsteps of Eva coming up behind me. I turned and noticed Eva was hiding something on the side of her leg. She quickly ran toward Midnight. Midnight was growling harder and louder than ever and suddenly Eva raised her arm. She was carrying a metal level. She quickly swung the level across her body and hit Midnight on the side of its face. Eva readjusted her grip and with both hands, swung the level back the

Kevin C. Popp

other way, hitting the cat in the middle of its head. Midnight moaned as its body slid back a few feet. Eva swung the level again, hitting Midnight on its side with great force, causing the cat to slide a few feet to its right. I quickly raced over and grabbed the level from Eva. Wolfgang tightened and shortened the leash in fear of Midnight attacking Eva. Eva looked at our father and said, "Father! String him up by his neck. I need to say something to him." Wolfgang looked bewildered, but a smile came across his face.

Midnight was whimpering on the basement floor as Wolfgang pulled the cat toward him by way of the leash and reached down with his large hand and fingers and grabbed Midnight's collar. He lifted the cat up from the ground, its legs dangling in the air. Eva looked at the hurt and helpless cat, walking uncomfortably close to it. Wolfgang said, "Be careful, Eva. Not too close."

Eva looked at our father and said, "Don't worry, Daddy. I will be careful." Eva came closer to Midnight, who was now swinging from his collar. Eva said, "Midnight. You are my cat now. You will never try and hurt me again. Do you understand? If you do, I will kill you." Eva batted her deep blue eyes at Wolfgang and said, "Please let go of him now, Daddy." Wolfgang slowly lowered the cat to the ground. Eva went over to pet the cat, but Wolfgang jerked on the leash to keep the cat away. Eva said, "Stop it, Daddy." Eva placed her small hand on the white skinned cat. Midnight was coughing and shaking from being choked and beaten then lowered his head and stared at the ground. His only movements were him trying to clear his throat so he could breathe. He shook from fear, but as Eva petted his back, he quickly stopped shaking. He slowly moved his head up and licked Eva's hand. Soon Eva had total control over her new pet.

Chapter Twelve

Marci wanted to start playing the violin like she did in her previous life. She had utmost confidence that she would reach perfection. I told her that it would take some time, especially now that her arms and neck had changed in length and size. Marci picked up her old violin and drew on her instrument for the first time since her rebirth. As expected, she was out of tune. She had major issues dealing with her new body, which created new positioning for her violin. She became extremely frustrated. I reassured her that it would take time but one day she would be able to play perfectly. At least in the beginning, I was hoping that to be the case since the formula usually highlights and expands your past talents.

One day, Eva stood watching Marci in the large great room playing the violin. She was very interested in the sound it was making. Eva took quick notice that I helped Marci with her playing. She also noticed that her big brother was very good at the violin and the sounds that I was making were prettier. Her majestic head moved from side to side, trying to digest every sound this wonderful instrument was producing.

I asked Eva if she would like to try her hand at playing the violin. She said, "Yes, I would like to play." I went upstairs and brought out the very first violin that Trevor and Adelle had bought for me. It was a miniature violin, but its sound was greater than its size. I brought the violin downstairs and introduced it to Eva. When Eva first laid her magnificent eyes on this instrument, she instantly fell in love with the small wooden string contraption. I held the violin with great reverence and I said, "Eva, this was my very first violin. I played for hours on this instrument. My mind was lost for hours on end and I enjoyed every second of the many struggles I had trying to perfect the pitch on every note I played. You will experience the same trials and tribulations, but some day you will play perfectly." I extended my arms and presented the violin to her.

Eva walked closer to the outstretched violin, and as gently as she could, she placed both hands on the device. This was the first time she had held any musical instrument. She brought the violin up close to her nose and inhaled its scent. She was a very happy little girl at this point. I handed her the bow. She took the violin in one hand and the bow in the other and quickly placed the violin on her shoulder. It was like she had done this exercise thousands of times. She placed the bow on the strings and ever so slightly, she moved the bow back and forth on them. She closed her eyes and enjoyed the sounds that she created. I sensed that is why she loved the violin so much, being able to create something from nothing. I know this concept well. I sensed her love for this most reverent instrument. Of all the repertoire of musical apparatuses, her love for the violin was something innate. I understood more than anyone; after all, we are related and are so much alike.

Eva began playing the violin virtually nonstop. I gave her many lessons and pointers on what and what not to do. She was far advanced from where she should be at this point, but this was totally expected. I did my best in instructing both Marci and Eva. It became abundantly clear that Marci was becoming jealous of Eva, not only of her ability to play the violin well but of her beauty and the attention that she was receiving from everyone in the family. After several weeks of constant practice, Eva was more advanced than Marci, which made Marci very upset. She thought she would be further along in her skills at this point, but she was still having difficulty adjusting to her newly formed body. Her arm, neck and hand length were problematic for Marci to master. After additional weeks of hard practice, Marci started to get accustomed to her body, and her hand-eye coordination was improving. In just a couple of weeks, Marci's playing surpassed Eva's, and this was the most needed confidence builder that Marci could receive. She gave up a lot to experience the gift of perfection and everlasting life.

Marci and Eva pushed each other. They loved each other so much, but Marci had a jealous side to her whereas Eva's personality was more into herself and not really caring what others thought. She was so good at everything that she never really had anyone to compete with her.

Marci was still new to her improved body and still growing into her personality. It was a large adjustment for my Marci. She had to teach herself and relearn everything she had learned in her past life. Once she mastered a task, then she had complete control over it.

I noticed that Marci needed more attention, so during this time I spent as much time as I could with her. Marci's jealously subsided and she seemed to accomplish more in a shorter time span. It was difficult trying to teach two people. I knew that at some point, I needed help. I loved Eva very much, but there was nothing or anyone in this world that I loved more than my Marci. I needed to spend more time with the greatest miracle man had ever seen. Marci and I spent more time together and just like the many years in her past life, she was always honest with me. Marci had known for many years now that at some point I was going to eventually mate with my sister. Marci was a naturally jealous and possessive person. Growing up as an orphan, she was poor, unloved, and unwanted. The few possessions she had, she'd cherished significantly. When it came to emotional relationships, she had never truly loved people. In the early stages of her youth, she had gotten attached to foster parents only to have them call the orphanage to take her out of their lives. After so many failed relationships, one tends to grow hardened toward people, and the door of close friendship closes quickly and rarely reopens. Only I had been fortunate enough to open that door to the most special human being on this planet. When I don't give her the attention that she deserves, it quickly annoys my love. This I understand completely.

Eva was becoming more restless. We knew that she needed to associate with more kids her own age, and we felt comfortable that she would keep her real birth parents a secret. She understood that she had to play along, that her relationship with me as her father had to be played out. Eva knew, even at this young age, that if anyone were to know about Wolfgang, Zelda, or Marci, that she might be taken from her family and never see them again. Therefore, after carefully considering many options, we started Eva in an advanced school. The most exclusive grade school in the Louisville area was a school called Cloverleaf.

Eva had to be tested to be accepted at Cloverleaf. I knew what was going to happen during Eva's testing since I had been through numerous tests myself. I prepared Eva as well as I could. I met with the teachers and, as expected, they wanted to test Eva with advanced placement tests. Eva took the tests, and she not only scored perfect scores on all the tests but finished the exams in record time. The school counselor said her test scores and the short time it took for her to finish the tests, had never been accomplished in the school's long, prestigious history.

The school board was so impressed with Eva's advanced intelligence that they wanted to have a meeting with us as soon as possible. This same procedure happened with me when I was younger, and Eva was more advanced than I was at her age. I believe that our intelligence level was the same, but my family and I had pushed Eva, whereas Trevor and Adelle had no clue about my intellect so they made no attempts to expand my intelligence when I was Eva's age. I didn't want to repeat that same mistake with Eva.

The members of the school board suggested that Eva not only skip a grade but several grades. They did have concerns about her youth and whether that would be a problem. I convinced the board that would not be a problem and had them ask Eva a multitude of questions about everything and anything. After the period of questioning was over, they all came away not only convinced that she was socially ready for advanced placement for her age, but that she might even surpass most students that were several grades in front of her. At the end of the interviews, the administrators were all more than impressed with Eva.

Eva was very young when they wanted to place her ahead of the most gifted children that were years older. We didn't want to place her in a grade that was too advanced for her age because Wolfgang and I wanted to have some control over her in the future. If she got out of high school too soon, who was going to go with her to college and babysit her? With the businesses that I had to manage, I couldn't possibly take years out of my life and live with her in some apartment off campus like Carolyn did for me.

When the time was right, we placed her in the fourth grade with all advanced students. Eva was not scared or intimidated with her new surroundings. At first, her classmates took some time accepting her but after several days, she was known for what she was by reputation – the smartest kid in the class. Eva not only stood out amongst her classmates academically but also in physical appearance and ability.

Eva's hair grew to extreme lengths. Her long, flowing, wavy blonde hair came down to the small of her back. Her complexion was flawless; not a blemish could be found on her skin. She was a head taller than any fourth grader, and her coordination skills were unmatched. She would play on the playground at school with breathtaking skills that no one possessed. When they played soccer, she would never miss kicking the ball. Almost every kick, her foot was in the middle of the ball. She threw a ball with uncanny accuracy and she caught almost every ball thrown at her. She was the boy's favorite on the playground.

Academically, Eva's classmates were in shock because of her extremely advanced intelligence. Many of her fellow gifted classmates never experienced or had been in the company of someone with that much more intelligence than themselves. I tried to prepare Eva as best I could regarding all these issues, from an intellectual and physical standpoint. I had gone through all these obstacles when I was her age.

Eva knew all the material the teachers taught. Her teachers were astounded by her intellect. As the fourth grade progressed, Eva grew bored and it was at that time I decided to hire a tutor for superiorly advanced children. I was given a short list of names to choose from. I interviewed only three tutors and decided on a lady by the name of Karen Stein, and offered her a healthy salary. I wanted her to teach Eva every other night of the week, and on the weekends. Eva wanted to learn as much as she could.

Karen accepted my generous offer. When I presented the information to my parents, they were not thrilled. They immediately pointed out that she possessed a Jewish name. Wolfgang said, "No fucking Jew is going to teach my daughter."

Zelda agreed with my father. I said, "Look, she is the best tutor that money can buy. She is a no-nonsense type of person that fits Eva's personality. I personally didn't consider that she was Jewish, nor do I even care. This is the twenty-first century and Jews are all accepted around the United States. She will be your daughter's tutor, teacher and friend."

My parents looked at me like I had three heads. Wolfgang wasn't used to someone speaking to him in such a tone, even from his only son. But over the years, living under my roof, his personality had changed a little and he was more accepting to harsher language thrown his way.

When Karen was present on the estate, Wolfgang and Zelda spent their time in the basement. Marci usually went to her room or followed Zelda to the basement. All three were extremely careful not to be seen or heard by Karen. The result would have been disastrous for all concerned.

Eva liked Karen from day one. After just an hour sitting with Eva, Karen had to speak to me in front of Eva. Karen said, "Mr. Seawick, in all of my years I have never seen anyone of this age this intelligent. Eva knows more at age four than most middle-aged adults. I have never seen anything like this in my life. What a brain your daughter possesses."

Eva was never one that needed to be showered by compliments, but Karen's words seemed to please her. Karen continued to teach Eva more complicated subject matters on a host of different academic material from chemistry to history, and from math to English. Eva digested all the presented material.

As the year proceeded, Eva and Marci's violin skills improved at an alarming rate. The further Marci improved, the more her enjoyment of playing the violin increased exponentially. She was so close to playing her most covenant instrument to perfection that she pushed herself harder to achieve her ultimate goal... complete perfection. This was one of the main reasons Marci went through the transformation; not only to live forever but to come as close to achieving perfection that most would deem impossible.

If there was a god, thanks to him, no human can be perfect, thus no human can create something flawless or immaculate. Thanks to my father, who is real, for he gave me the power to achieve almost impeccable, exact precision to accomplish any task to textbook completion. This power is what Marci was after since she began to understand the formula existed. It was her obsession to experience repeated flawless attempts. Having the ability to create any piece to a pitch and note-perfect sound on a small box with strings is what Marci found intoxicating. The added bonus was her additional gifts of increased knowledge on numerous academic disciplines, and extreme levels of heightened sensory acknowledgment of her surroundings.

My Marci was entirely content with her new existence, just as she had strived for throughout her previous life. She now possessed that unique ability of what I call, in its most rudimentary terms, achieving perfection or as close to perfection as humanly possible. She now possessed the ability to repeat, at a moment's notice, any task to perfection, where no mistake is made in an attempt of said task either before, during or after its completion. Being the only human on this earth that can endure this high level of precision on such a repetitive platform is truly a supernatural power that only some divine deity holds as its own. This immortal figure hides somewhere in the universe behind a mythical theorist story whose sole purpose is to deliver continuous pain century after century, millennium after millennium, with no true rational solution to an adequate and fair conclusion for all effected. What sick spirit would have its creations suffer so much for its own selfish pleasure? A true and most holy god would strive to create goodness, not evil, among its followers.

Nothing was more evident that demonstrated this fact than the first time Marci played a Mozart piece to absolute perfection. She stood before me as I reverently sat before her towering figure. She started with the fifth of Mozart's Violin Concertos. I had played the piece for the orchestra only and had many of these types of recordings. They are especially made for someone to practice playing with the orchestra when an orchestra is not available. Every note Marci played, every draw of the blow and every pause was perfectly played. She could not have improved on her performance. After the last note was played, she lifted her bow from the strings and stood motionless. She started to cry. Everything that she went through all through her previous life, and the pain and suffering that she experienced in her new life was just for the opportunity to have this moment. All her emotions came rushing together at once, a sensory overload for my love.

I understood that feeling more than anyone. This happens to us from time to time. You create something so perfect and you are so wrapped up in the moment that all five of your senses hit you at once. It is more powerful than any organismic experience one could imagine. At times, it becomes overwhelming to a point that you almost faint from such an experience. It is all inspiring and powerful. This was the reason Marci altered her physical appearance without having a shred of doubt.

Marci looked at me with those large black eyes of hers, tears flowing fast and running down her cheeks. She said, "My god," while looking and referring to me. "I have been waiting for that all of my life." This moment made her not only feel more alive than she had ever felt, but it made her feel more sensual, powerful and in control of her surroundings. That moment, playing the music of the greatest composer this world has ever heard to perfection, made her feel liberated. She had accomplished what she had always wanted to demonstrate – perfection.

Marci shared my passion of playing a work to perfection, the way the original composer wanted that piece to sound. He wanted to pull the listener into his world, where he controls everything and forces you to listen to his thoughts and what was going through his mind at the time that piece of work was created. Musical perfection is complete mastery and control, combined with majestic grace of a man-made instrument, trying to paint a musical description of utopia.

Only Mozart saw this in his head but very few, if any, had ever pulled back the hidden layers that are cursed with god's sabotaging hand at each turn and could experience his own private utopia. A place that god doesn't allow his faithful and stupid subjects to ever enter. Not until we came along. Not until my father discovered the secret to life – to live forever and experience perfection. To experience what god and only god created for himself. For this precious snippet in time, Marci was one of only five people that could claim they are god's equal.

I knew what my love desired after such an event. Her eyes looked at me with unlimited erotic desire. Her scent filled the air around us. Her aroma was musky with a slight fragrance of wet leaves that lay on the forest's floor. I stayed seated in my chair. Part of me wanted to run and part of me wanted her forbidden and altered femininity. I didn't know how to feel or react. Marci sensed my apprehension, and without a spoken word between us, she told me that she understood. Her appearance was much different than before. She knew that her physical appearance was off-putting for a normal sexual encounter. She had to seduce me psychologically before any physical contact would transpire.

Marci's extreme height caused her to wear a shirt that covered her large breasts, but her stomach was always exposed. She either wore short shorts or skirts. This evening, she was wearing a short skirt. Her feet were too large for any man-made shoes.

Marci and I hadn't had sexual relations since her death. Marci needed sexual release and affirmation that she was still a desirable woman. She stood before me and smiled. She slowly turned her large, porcelain white body away and laid her violin and bow down with the utmost reverence, as if she was laying a child down in its crib for the night. She slowly stood up and looked toward me. Her long tail whipped around her thigh and she placed the end of her tail on her muscular stomach. She raised her hands and placed them on her covered breasts. She massaged them, and after a moment or so, she pulled at her shirt. She said, "Do you want to see them?" She walked closer to me and continued, "I know you do. You have been looking at them since I was born." She raised her large head up and looked toward the ceiling. Her hands went back on her breasts and she said, "Oh, they feel so firm, strong, so tight." She lowered her head, stared at me, and suddenly ripped her shirt off with both hands, exposing her breasts to me. Her nipples were large and very pronounced. Her stark white skin danced before my eyes. Her long, silky, all white hair moved with her sexy shoulders. She moved her body from side to side, showing me every angle of her upper front and side torso. I began to ache with desire. Deep down I knew it was wrong and not natural, but my sexual desire for my love was greater than my self-control. I wanted to touch her, and she knew it. She was getting to me.

Marci moved her hands toward the back of her skirt. She slowly unzipped and allowed her skirt to fall down her long and well-developed legs. Her vagina was large and intimating, thus requiring more than just a normal male appendage to please her. She sensed that her appearance might be a hindrance for me to sexually perform like we had in her previous life. It was difficult to comprehend at first. I was scared that I might not enjoy the sexual experience and I didn't want to hurt her feelings in any way. The fact that Marci understood that it was a difficult situation for me made her less menacing. Instead of not being able to sexually perform, I found myself not able to take my eyes off this perfectly formed creature before me. This was still the love of my life, the woman that I had desired like no other.

Marci's sexual advances were well calculated and orchestrated. She made every attempt to seduce me into making unnatural love to her seem natural. She attempted to not show her large teeth and she lowered her eyelids to cover up half of her large eyes. I sensed that she didn't want me scared of her in any way. She stood before me motionless until she felt the moment was right then moved her hands up to her large breasts, massaging every inch of them. Her long fingers stroked her pearl white skin. She ran her fingers over her nipples, then began rubbing and pulling at them. At the same time, her tail moved across her stomach and she made it snake its way downward to her vagina. It was extremely erotic to witness. She pleasured herself with her tail before me. The tip of her tail went around the lips of her vagina then it found its way inside her. It probed, wiggled, and rubbed itself over, inside and around her opening. She brought her tail up toward her face, and with her long snake-like tongue, licked her juices from her tail.

I sat there about ready to explode. I got up from my chair and made my way to her. She was surprised at first as a smile developed on her face. I went immediately for her breasts and when my lips touched her nipple, Marci breathed heavily. Her hands went for the collar of my shirt, she ripped it in two, and tore it off me. I unbuckled my pants and removed them.

Marci's tail quickly wrapped itself around my penis, moving her tail in a stroking motion. I placed my hands on her hips, moved my hand down between her legs, and placed my fingers inside of her. After several minutes, we both climaxed so hard we hit the floor on our knees. She wouldn't let me go. I was forced to lie on my back as she moved on top of me and placed my manhood inside of her. She was warm and felt natural. She made it a point not to hurt me. As she was moving up and down on me, she bent down and looked at me. She said, "Oh fuck, I have missed you." She gently opened her mouth and her long tongue escaped and touched my face. She made her way down the side of my neck, licking in an up and down motion. Her tongue went on my chest and across one of my nipples. The sensation was out of his world. She then moved her tongue up my chest, along my neck and up under my chin. I couldn't speak a word. I had never felt so much pleasure in my life. She knew I was close to another climax. She took me out of her and placed her long fingers around me and finished me off. While I was climaxing, she threw her head back and moaned. Her long teeth were exposed, and during my climax, I felt large drops of saliva fall from her mouth and grace my stomach. No words could describe this most intoxicating sensation. I knew from that moment on that Marci's new look wouldn't be a hindrance to me. In fact, she was more desirable than ever. She knew that she had captivated me. Now our reunion was complete. Our lovemaking was even better than it was before her death.

Marci rose to her feet and looked down at me. She said, "You haven't changed, my love. You are the same stud I had in my previous life. But I think I am better than I was before. Do you agree?"

I laid there trying to catch my breath, and all I could muster was a shake of my head and saying, "Yes... yes... it is better."

Marci smiled and said, "I had no doubt." She closed her large eyes, took a deep breath, and said, "I can sense your candor, my love. I smell your sincerity." She turned, picked up her clothes, and walked out of the room, leaving me lying there on the hardwood floor, trying to recover. Little did I know that my parents were in the kitchen area and they heard and saw everything. When I came to my senses, I picked up my clothes and went upstairs with Marci. That night we continued to explore each other's bodies. Up to that point in my life, I had never enjoyed any sexual experience as much as I did that night.

This was a great time in my life. The only down part was not being able to go out on a date with Marci. Because of her appearance, our social life was no more. I ended up explaining to my network of friends that Marci and I had broken up and she left me. I said she went to another state to start a new life for herself. Many people were upset at the news, but all accepted my story as the truth, and I continued to live out my social life as before. I had many women ask me out on dates, and many older women were introducing me to others while I was out, either at the orchestra or on business meetings. I never lied to my Marci. I told her everything so there would be no secrets in our relationship. This infuriated Marci to no end. Part of Marci appreciated the honesty, but the other half of her didn't. But she would have sensed something was up anyway so why even try to hide it? I will say that after some of my potential encounters, Marci would always make it a point to be sure that no one could pleasure me like she could, and that was the truth.

Chapter Thirteen

va was far advanced at the violin at this stage of her childhood development than I was at her age. She was playing complicated and intricate works with relatively no mistakes made in her playing. Marci and I instructed her to the best of our abilities and she was flourishing under our guidance. The only issue that was developing was her attention to the utmost detail. We felt that she needed a new instructor that would give her new ideas to keep up her interest. Eva came to us and said that she wanted a new instructor. She felt she needed some distance from our teaching and she requested a different personality teaching her.

Eva got these ideas from watching recordings of me when I was her age. Eva enjoyed watching her brother perform on a big stage in front of a large crowd, and she had shown great interest in experiencing that for herself. She was obsessed with the idea of playing her violin for an audience. The combination of Eva watching my past recordings and the fact that I took her to many concerts over the past year at the Louisville Orchestra, fed her desire. Eva thought it would be incredible to perform on a large stage with the orchestra in the background. She wanted to feel that power over not only the orchestra but the audience. She craved attention and she needed to feel special. I understood this more than anyone since I was just like Eva at her age. I knew I possessed greatness and I wanted everyone to know it. The feeling of dominating the orchestra, the conductor, and the audience was a special feeling. Mastering the instrument is easy, it just takes time and the pleasure of that mastery is of indescribable pleasure to its creator.

I knew what made Eva tick. It was the creation of music. It was the creation of bringing a dead composer's music back to life. It was the ability to perform the composer's thoughts to nearly perfect precision. On top of this, having the opportunity to share your talents with others is truly a hallucinogenic experience that makes you feel like... a god.

I made a phone call to the music director of the Louisville Orchestra. I was directed to one of their best violin players that was willing to take on only superior students. Her name was Nancy Whitman. Eva and I went to meet her during one of Nancy's practices. I knew of Nancy, but I didn't know her personally. After the practice, I introduced Eva as my daughter. Eva always thought it was funny when I would introduce her as my daughter. She understood why I had to, but she always found humor in the situation.

Nancy was a warm and friendly person. She was very nice and respectful to Eva. I always appreciated people giving the benefit of the doubt and respect to young prodigies when asking someone to tutor them. In my life experience, I haven't found where many people were respectful to me and I had to prove my worthiness to them. I also hated those circumstances and found that to be very discourteous.

Eva spoke to Nancy in a respectful tone. Eva asked her, "May I play for you, so you can see that I am not here to waste your time?"

Nancy was very surprised and was now intrigued with Eva. Nancy said, "I would love to hear you play a short piece. Do you have a piece in mind?"

Eva said, "Yes, a bunch of Mozart pieces. I play a lot of Mozart."

Nancy smiled and handed over her violin. Eva looked perplexed. Nancy said, "I know this violin is larger than you probably have a home but let's give it a go, shall we?"

Eva shrugged her shoulders and started to play. Eva was anxious at first because she was trying to adjust for the large size of the violin, something she wasn't used to. After several moments, Eva mastered the size factor and started to play rather well. Eva played bits and pieces of Mozart's violin sonatas and concertos. She played a few short and longer passages in both repertoire but she didn't stop playing. She just continued to play one piece after another in non-stop fashion.

I looked around the room and only a third of the orchestra's members remained, and they all ceased putting their violins away or getting up to leave for their cars. After a minute, the entire room was so quiet that only Eva's playing dominated the room. Even the conductor of the Orchestra paused and listened. After five or so minutes, Eva stopped and said, "Shall I continue?"

Nancy stood there with her mouth open in awe. She said, "That is amazing control you have of the violin. Are you sure you need my help?"

Everyone in the room laughed, but not Eva. Eva said, "Well yes, I do need your help or someone's help. I am not perfect yet." Again, everyone in the room laughed. This bewildered Eva as to why they were laughing at her.

Nancy smiled and said, "Eva, no one is perfect, and no one will ever play the violin perfectly."

Eva said, "But... my father does."

Nancy's smile left her face and said, "Well, yes, yes your father is the best I have ever heard."

Eva said, "So teach me to be better. I can be perfect."

Nancy smiled and said, "Only God can be perfect, Eva."

Eva quickly said, "God is only jealous of people that can be perfect. I have no interest in what god does or is. I am only interested in playing the violin perfectly. I will someday. Just watch."

Nancy was surprised by the retort and was almost offended by Eva's response. I had to step in and somewhat defuse the situation. I said, "So, will you take on this challenge?"

Nancy, with a placid look on her face said, "Ahh yeeees. I will take on the... I mean, tutor young Eva. She has a very special talent." With that, we left and again you could have heard a pin drop in the room. Eva and I loved surprising people with her wit and brazen attitude.

The next day, Nancy came over to the estate and taught Eva, and they quickly became good friends. Nancy always respected Eva and treated her like a young woman. Eva appreciated the courtesy. As time progressed, Eva developed wonderfully and at a very swift pace. Eva was now to a point that Nancy thought she was ready to go on tour and demonstrate her talents. Nancy said that only I could rival her playing skills and admitted with great reverence to us that Eva had far surpassed her own playing skills and anyone in the Louisville Orchestra. This pleased Eva and made her very proud of herself.

One day the Music Director, Mike Sellers, called me and asked if Eva and I would play a Mozart piece for two violins. Sellers thought it was be a wonderful thing to see two prodigies of our time playing together on the same stage as father and daughter. We agreed, and the date was booked for the following year. In the meantime, Eva played at small gatherings at local churches or small concert halls. Eva didn't like playing in churches but her love of performing won out over her petty aversions.

Time passed quickly and now Eva was almost five years old, and our concert was fast approaching. The first time we practiced with the Louisville Orchestra was a special time for both of us. The members had heard about young Eva and wanted to see for themselves just how special of a violinist she was, as well as get the chance to hear my fiddling in person.

Eva was not as nervous as I thought she would be. We stood on the floor with the orchestra surrounding us, tuning their instruments, which really bothered Eva. She hated the sound of uncontrolled instruments being tuned up at the same time. It bothered her so much that she had to leave for a while until everyone was finished. She came back, and we began.

Eva and I had practiced the piece that we were going to perform at home, and we had supreme command of the work. During our first practice section, we were pitch-perfect and our timing was flawless. After practice, Maestro Sellers applauded and said, "In all of my years of conducting, I believe we just witnessed the perfect combination of two great prodigies playing at a level that very few have reached." At the end of rehearsal, Eva and I were bombarded with praise. The members of the orchestra wanted to meet us, especially the daughter of the great Garrison Seawick. Eva was officially considered the next amazing prodigy.

The opening night of our concert, Eva and I were getting dressed. Marci and Zelda were helping Eva with her dress. We left in the car and arrived at the Louisville Arts building. With our instruments in hand, we made our way to the backstage area. I was surprisingly nervous, and Eva was bouncing off the walls with nervous anticipation. Our adrenaline was pumping with full force in our bodies.

Just minutes before we were about to go on stage, I looked over to Eva who was standing there looking straight ahead at the stage door. I said in a calm but quiet voice, "Me too." I stopped and looked at her as Eva looked up at me with a bewildered look on her face. I swore that I heard her say something, but she hadn't. I said, "I am sorry, I thought you said something." I looked away, shaking my head. Eva looked at me strangely, almost in astonishment. I forced my attention to the door and heard in my head, "How did he know what to answer?" My eyebrows moved upward on my face. Without looking I thought to myself, "Did Eva say something or I am imagining that she did?"

Eva then spoke without taking her big blue eyes off me, "I know, I can hear your thoughts too!"

I looked at her and my heart was thumping a million beats a second. I thought without physically moving my mouth, "That is impossible. What I am thinking now, Eva?"

I thought about falling on the stage before we got to the platform near the conductor. Eva smiled at me and said, "Watch your step. Don't fall.'

I stood there in amazement. I was shocked. I was at a loss for words. I was hearing Eva's thoughts. I had never experienced this before in my life. I could always sense what people were thinking but I never heard or could read someone's thoughts. It was like our brains were connected, which, as I thought about it, I assume they were. This world has never seen the likes of the two of us. It would make sense that we were more connected than others.

Unexpectedly, Eva said aloud, "This has never happened to me before either... Dad." Eva smiled, knowing that we had something very special in common.

My mind was racing. I thought, *What a potential breakthrough.* This had never happened between us until now. It had to be the increase of adrenaline which caused the formula to heighten our senses to work at an even higher level. I had experienced many special events that the formula had blessed me with, but never this level of capability. I wondered if this was just a thing between Eva and me or could we read other's thoughts on a regular basis?

I immediately stopped thinking about what had happened and started to focus on the music that we were about to perform. We were going onstage in just moments. Then without warning, I heard Eva say in her thoughts, "I know you can hear me, Garrison. I agree, we need to concentrate on our music and not our new mindreading skills."

I smiled and thought to myself, "Good luck, Eva."

Eva responded, "Good luck, Garrison."

We both smiled and giggled. Without a moment to relax, the stagehand told us that we were on and the door opened for us. Eva went first, and I allowed her to walk ahead of me by several paces. When Eva first appeared, the crowd in attendance clapped loudly. When I made my entrance, the crowd rose to their feet and we were greeted with a thunderous applause. Eva thought, "Watch your step here." I laughed aloud, and Eva giggled. We were about to have the time of our lives.

As the crowd settled into place, the conductor looked at us and we gave the signal that we were ready. The air was thick and pungent. Eva and I sensed the tension from both the orchestra and the audience. The orchestra started the piece by our favorite composer, Mozart, the only double violin concerto that he had composed. He wrote better works, but this was the piece that we wanted to play together because it was his only work for two violins and orchestra.

Throughout the work, Eva and I were able to communicate to each other mentally. When the orchestra started the concerto, I gave Eva mental instructions as to when to start playing. I knew she was nervous because I not only sensed her feelings, but she told me in her thoughts. She didn't need for me to tell her what to do, but I wanted to help her. I told her when she should come into the piece and from that moment on she needed little help from me.

Eva and I played to our fullest potential. We played with great passion and love for the work we were performing and the moment at hand. We wanted to enjoy this unique experience with each other. This was my little sister playing a complex piece of music, standing next to me in front of a full house of strangers. She loved this experience. Eva reminded me so much of myself when I was her age. She was perfect in every way. She was so physically attractive that her beauty forced people to admire her unearthly attractiveness. Whenever she spoke, her voice was pitch-perfect, to a point where her voice would enslave your intellect to her every word and moment. This was truly a miracle of man-made nature. A man created us, not any god.

A man named Wolfgang created Eva and I from a complicated formula that bypassed god's little game called life, a limited game where only god controls the outcome, and you are just a meaningless buffoon that is placed on this earth only for his enjoyment. But my sister and I are different. Who knows what limitless boundaries we will explore in the distant future? That was the only reason I rejoiced at my moments of perfection, because this is my family's victorious moment over god.

As we played perfectly, Eva was having the time of her life. She didn't miss a note. The audience sat there in complete amazement as to what they were witnessing. Eva's playing gave her great pleasure and up to this point of her young life, she had never experienced such joy. I felt the same as Eva. During the Mozart piece, we connected with each other on a level that only my sexual relationship with Marci could

Kevin C. Popp

compare. We played as one person, one entity with the solemn purpose – to complete the work to near flawless perfection.

When the last note was played, the audience paused for just an instant, savoring every moment of the most perfectly played concerto that probably had ever been played. They didn't want the performance to end. They wanted to hear more notes, but that brief interlude between the last note and the anticipated applause was one of the most powerful feelings I have ever felt in my life. As we slowly lowered our bows, the thunderous applause began. Everyone jumped to their feet and clapped loudly. The entire orchestra clapped or waved their bows in the air in honor of Eva and me. The conductor looked at us and smiled and mouthed the word, "Splendid." Eva and I walked off the stage. The crowd cheered even louder for our return, and we had to make numerous curtain calls before we could officially leave the stage.

Eva loved the attention. I felt her excitement pulsing through her body. I read her thoughts on her enthusiasm of what she was experiencing. I understood exactly what she was going through since I had experienced the feelings and had the same thoughts as Eva. Although I was a little older than her, I was one of the few that knew what she was going through at that moment. Eva was carbon copying my young life musically, academically, and socially. I was never so proud or happier for her than at that moment.

After the concert, all the members of the orchestra met with her and lauded her with lavish praise. The local print and television media were in attendance as well. Many reporters from the major cities across the country were present. Audio feeds went out to countries overseas. The new Seawick prodigy had been discovered. I had extravagant praise heaped upon me as well. Many people even acknowledged that I had improved over the years.

The next day, Eva and I looked through all the major newspapers online. All were more than complimentary of us. Comments like what an amazing family, we were wonderful musicians, and that we were a very cordial family to the media. While we were sitting at the dinner table, I told my parents and Marci about my experience with Eva. I told them about Eva and I being able to read each other's thoughts. I told them that I had never had this happen to me before. I could sense people's thoughts but never actually read someone's mind.

Wolfgang was fascinated with our apparent skill. He could never read another's thoughts, and neither could Zelda or Marci. Eva told my father that she couldn't recall a time when she could read other people's thoughts, she only heard my thoughts on the night of the concert, so we could only read each other's thoughts. That day, when I told them of our apparent skill, Wolfgang instantly wanted to conduct some simple experiments on us. Eva and I agreed to join in the tests. Wolfgang had us sit in his lab and had one of us think about something as hard as we could, then have the other describe the other's thoughts. In the first few attempts, we both failed in our mindreading skills. He first started with us being in separate rooms, then in the same room, and then he sat both of us side by side. Still nothing. We could not read a word from each other's mind.

I told Wolfgang this apparent skill must be related to the amount of adrenaline that was produced when our senses were working on a high level. In other words, we needed to be either extremely stressed or overly excited to read each other's thoughts.

Wolfgang quickly wanted to run an experiment on us. He told us to force ourselves to get excited about something and see if we could recreate what we experienced the night before. We tried, but we still didn't have success.

Wolfgang left the room for a moment and came back. He retrieved Eva's cat Midnight. Eva said, "Aaah, Midnight. How are you?" Wolfgang walked over to a drawer in his lab and immediately pulled out a large knife. Wolfgang quickly walked over to us and placed the cat on the table in front of us. He grabbed Midnight's chained neck collar and held him almost six feet in the air. He took the knife and held it to Midnight's throat. Midnight made some of the strangest sounds as it was struggling to breathe. Eva yelled at her father, "Stop it! What are you doing? You are killing him!"

Wolfgang said, "I am going to kill your cat in front of you, daughter."

Eva yelled, "No! Put him down, now!"

Wolfgang screamed back, "Tell me what your brother is thinking right now! Tell me or I will kill it!"

My heart was racing. Marci was yelling, "Wolfgang! No!"

Zelda was in shock and got up as if she was about to come to Midnight's defense, but she stopped because she knew better than to interrupt. I quickly began to understand what my father was doing. I looked at Eva and thought, "Ask our father how many gold teeth he kept when he extracted them from the thousands of Jews he killed." Eva looked at me, her eyes got very large and she started to repeat what I thought. It was a few words off because she was nervous. Eva said, "How many gold teeth did you take from the Jews you killed?"

Wolfgang was stumped. He stood as still as a marble statue. He quickly moved his large head in my direction. I looked at Wolfgang and smiled without saying a word. I looked at Eva who was crying her eyes out and I thought, "Tell our father that he would look good in a dress."

Eva repeated what I said. I then thought, "Tell him that I will mate with you in the future."

I didn't want to spring that on her at this point in time, but that would prove to Wolfgang that she could read my thoughts. Eva didn't know what to make of my statement. She looked at me and said aloud, "What? Mate with you? Tell him I would mate with you?"

Wolfgang stood there with Midnight fighting for his life for release from its collared grip of death. Eva looked at our father and said, "Put my cat down now! I did what you wanted me to do!" Eva's cries now turned into anger. Wolfgang, who was in sheer amazement at what he had just witnessed, placed the cat down on the floor. Midnight ran toward Eva and they embraced.

Wolfgang said, "Amazing!"

Eva looked up at our father and said, "Please don't ever do something like that to Midnight again." Wolfgang lowered his head and walked out of the room. For the first time, I saw remorse in my father's actions. He knew he did a horrible thing, but his emotions had gotten the best of him.

I got up and went into the next room where Wolfgang stood alone. I said, "Father, are you okay? I hope that you understood what I was doing. I had to prove to you that Eva could read my thoughts and that she was not making something up. I am sorry about telling her about us mating at some point. I should not have said that to her."

Wolfgang acknowledged me and said, "I understand. This is amazing. I would have never thought this would be possible."

Before we knew it, Eva was behind us and she said, "What are you going to do to me, Garrison? Father? What is this mating thing about? I don't want to have a baby."

Wolfgang turned to his daughter. For the first time, I saw my father be a gentle father to one of his offspring. He knelt on the ground on one knee in front of Eva and asked her to come closer to him. Eva reluctantly walked over to him. Midnight wanted to get out of Eva's arms, but Eva held him close and tight. When Eva approached, Wolfgang said, "I am sorry if I hurt Midnight. I had to get your attention to see if you really could read Garrison's thoughts."

Eva interrupted, "But I told you I could. Why didn't you believe me?"

Wolfgang paused and said, "I am sorry for not believing you. I just need to be absolutely sure that you could. I am also sorry that you had to hear what Garrison thought about mating. I didn't want it to come out that way. I must be honest with you, Eva. I kept you alive for the possibility that one day you and your brother would mate and have a baby. For experimental purposes only, I would like to see how your child would turn out. Garrison and I believe that you guys would create the perfect human or, at least in theory, create a near perfect human. I will not force this on you if you don't want it. I know you are too young at this point so please don't worry about this. As far as I am concerned, this subject is closed until after you are older, much older."

Eva looked at Wolfgang with bewildered eyes. She was confused. She said, "So you did not want me?"

Wolfgang said, "I wanted a daughter from the start but after you were born I fell in love with you and nothing in this world will ever cause me to harm you. I love you, Eva."

Eva smiled. I stood there in astonishment. This was the same evil man that killed thousands of people and had no regard for human or animal life. This is the same man that had killed over a handful of his own children either by throwing them to the ground with great force or by smashing their young skulls in with his large feet. He knelt before his only daughter and poured his heart out to her. It was an incredible scene. I had to speak. I said, "Eva, I do not want you to be afraid of me either. I will never harm you. When the time is right and you are ready is when and only when that experiment will be conducted. It would be up to you. Is that okay with you?"

Eva looked at me and back at our father. She said, "Will it hurt?"

Wolfgang said, "No, it will not."

Eva shrugged her shoulders and said, "Okay. But only when I feel like it. I am not going to like that."

Wolfgang said, "Obviously."

Eva turned away and began to walk out of the room with Midnight firmly in her grasp. Before Eva left the room, she turned around and said to Wolfgang, "Don't ever hurt me again, Father, or anyone I love. You scared me, and I don't like that one bit." My father said nothing. Eva then turned around and left the room.

As the days progressed, we received many messages from other orchestras from all over the world. We heard from many newspapers that wanted to do a story on our family. Wolfgang was concerned about all the attention the family was receiving. I had many concerns as well. Many times throughout the week, my parents or Marci would be outside. Of course, I had state-of-the-art security around the estate, and my parents and Marci's senses would have detected someone if they were to intrude on the grounds. To error on the side of safety, I had our security amped up during this period. We had cameras located everywhere on the estate. We had to be a little more discreet when we went out at nights, but we felt safe for the most part.

During this time, Wolfgang and I had many conversations in his study about Eva and my ability to read each other's thoughts. Wolfgang wanted to explore this new potential breakthrough. Wolfgang and I attempted to experiment on each other in the attempt to read each other' thoughts. Zelda and Marci would join in these experiments as well. Eva also went one-on-one with each family member. None of us had any luck in reading the thoughts of our family members except for Eva. Eva could read a word or two of her parent's or Marci's thoughts, but she couldn't read more than a couple of words.

When Wolfgang and I were alone, he asked me if I could have ever read anyone's thoughts. I had to admit that my immediate thoughts were no, I never heard someone else's thoughts in my head, but when I thought about certain situations in my life, maybe without me realizing it, maybe, during certain stressful times, I did hear another's thoughts. I never had anything to compare it to, so whatever I heard in my head, I just assumed everyone else heard.

I told Wolfgang, "Father, I have been thinking about my telepathic experience with Eva. Many of the tough moments that I have experienced in my life, I tended to block out or refused to remember. But when I go back and think about some experiences I had, I think I have heard some people's thoughts. At the time, I thought it was my mind making up words, that my mind was reinforcing what I already knew or sensed. Much like if you are frightened and you heard something go bump in the night, you look over in the direction of the noise and your first thought is you see some figure, when in reality it is the outline or the corners of a piece of furniture in the dark."

I had obviously never told this to anyone, not even to Lewis. But when I was in the process of mutilating and killing my brother, I knew what he was thinking, but at that time, I didn't think much about it. I remember when Adelle held me while I watched Trevor die in front of us. I remember hearing something in the back of my mind. I thought it was something that I was imagining or made up in my own mind, but after what I discovered with Eva, maybe I didn't imagine it. When Trevor was bleeding out on this actual basement floor, I remember thinking, *Damn you, Garrison. This is all your fault. You caused this to happen to me. I never wanted you for my son in the first place.* I thought it was me thinking those thoughts, but I was scared, frightened because of so many events that were happening that day. Adam had bit my mother, and then he attacked my father who eventually died within minutes of Adam's attack.

I thought I was punishing myself for my father's transformation and his eventual death at the hands of my brother, even though Trevor created Adam with my mother. It was Trevor who created Adam... not me. It wasn't my fault. I had no clue who I was at that time; I had no knowledge of the formula, what it was, or its powers.

Trevor was looking right at me when he thought those thoughts. I was being held by his wife, my adoptive mother, while he was lying in a pool of his own blood. I felt the hatred in him, but I was feeling sadness because of his pending death.

I felt Adelle's heartbeat, I even heard her thoughts. She thought, *My dear, I am so sorry. I love you.* Of course, at the time I thought they were my thoughts, but ever since the other night, I cannot help but think that I heard my adoptive parents' thoughts the night of Trevor's death.

Wolfgang intensely listened to my every word. He thought it was fascinating and tried hard to completely understand what I was telling him. He said, "It makes sense that you and Eva could hear thoughts. The formula is at a high level in your bloodstreams. Zelda and I are just products of a transformation whereas you and Eva, by way of the formula, are full blooded and evolved human beings. The formula had time to mutate just enough to correct any barriers that might prevent you from certain tasks, like mindreading. Obviously, it is not perfected yet in either one of you since you cannot read minds on command. That is where you guys need to learn to use your anger or control your adrenaline glands to a point where you can call upon that power at a moment's notice."

My conversation with Wolfgang drifted my mind to mating with Eva. I reassured Wolfgang that we owed it, in the name of science, to following through on the taboo mating experiment. I knew I would go through with the experiment. I knew that down deep I am my father's son throughout. The same with Eva. She is just like me. We share the same parents and the formula; thus, we are one and the same.

Wolfgang and I would stay up late all hours at night and talk about what my child with Eva would be like. We talked about how we thought the formula would react to two perfectly normal looking and functioning humans having a child. Would any physical or mental changes occur? Would we produce a being with an even better mind and body than ours? This was the morbid experiment of all experiments and our answer to the now most important question; just how would that child turn out? If our baby turns out better than Eva and I, we could produce an entirely different race of better human beings. We could produce the perfect race of humans.

Wolfgang wanted us to wait. We all had time on our side. We needed for Eva to grow older. We also wanted her to experience the world through her studies as well as her violin skills. She was having fun and enjoying life. This was a good thing for us to witness and she needed this for her development into becoming a woman.

I didn't want to father a child with Eva. Wolfgang, Zelda, and I all knew that, but we knew that I had to do it for the sake of science and for the future of humanity. We all were apprehensive about this taking place in the distant future. The only major issue was Marci. Marci wasn't as accepting of this potential fact developing in front of her, and Marci was becoming more jealous of Eva. Marci didn't want to share me with anyone, not my time and certainly not my sex. She understood that the experiment had to take place, but she didn't like it one bit.

I had to talk about it again with Marci, I mean really talk about it with her so one day we sat down, and I said to her, "Marci, you know I love you more than anyone in this world and I would never want to make love to anyone but you. Down the road, in the future, Wolfgang and I need to see what Eva and I will produce for a child. This in no way will ever come between us. I will not let it. I just want you to understand this is not something I am doing to hurt you in any way."

Marci understood. She said, "I know, but I just can't stand the thought of your dick in someone else."

I said, "There are other ways of getting Eva pregnant, but I understand your concerns. I wouldn't want you to have sex with another man either."

When we ended our conversation, I knew Marci wasn't in any way going to let this issue rest any time soon. As soon as I left her bedroom, in a matter of minutes, Marci ran down the stairs and confronted Wolfgang in his lab. Without warning, she yelled at Wolfgang, "You fucking bastard! Why in the fuck would you put my Garrison up to such a task? Having him fuck his own sister? What kind of a monster are you? I will never allow you to do this to us."

Wolfgang was furious as he retorted, "Never allow me? I do what I want! It's none of your fucking business anyway. Just be grateful we allowed you to transform – and just stay out of our way."

Marci screamed, "Don't treat me like that, you fucking piece of shit!"

Wolfgang raced toward her and wrapped his large hand around her neck. Marci grasped both hands around his thick and powerful forearm in the attempt to free herself. Wolfgang shouted, "You stay out of our way, bitch!"

I ran toward them. I pushed as hard as I could against my father yelling, "Stop it! Stop it! This is my Marci you are choking! Let her go!" I looked in my father's eyes and the hate was terrifying to see. He pushed me back about five feet with his other arm. I said again, "Let her go, Dad. Please" in a softer voice. I never let my eyes escape from his stare. He let her go and pushed her onto the floor. Marci tried to get up as fast as she could. I immediately jumped on her and said, "Stay down! Stay down! Relax." Marci's heart was racing as I could feel the hate flowing through her body. For the first time ever, I felt Marci's hatred directed totally toward my father. My heart was racing. I sensed that for the first time Wolfgang was ready to kill Marci if she had made another advance toward him. There was no way I could stop Marci physically if she made her move.

I was struggling with Marci on the floor. She was being gentle with me in the attempt to not hurt me, but she wanted a piece of my father. Suddenly, one of the most amazing things happened – I could hear Marci's and Wolfgang's thoughts. I repeated what they were thinking. I started to speak their thoughts aloud and after a few moments they both stopped and redirected their attention onto me. I repeated what was on Marci's mind as she said in her thoughts, "If the bastard thinks he is going to go through with this, I will kill him." I then repeated Wolfgang's thoughts, "I should have killed the bitch before her transformation was complete." I repeated many other thoughts and described both of their emotions and what they were feeling. They quickly calmed down.

Wolfgang hurried out of the room. Again, my adrenaline was flowing at a high level. With the combination of my senses being overloaded and the stress of seeing my love and my father in a physical confrontation was just enough for me to be able to reproduce what Eva and I experienced at our first concert together. I said to Marci, "Look, calm down. He will kill you if you continue fighting with him. You are lucky you are still alive. Just shut the fuck up. Okay?" Marci was still furious, but she calmed down to a point where she was thinking clearer.

Marci and I got off the floor and I led her out of the room. Wolfgang was in his lab taking notes. Marci stopped and looked at my father. My heart skipped several beats. Wolfgang whipped his head around to see what Marci was going to say or do. Marci said, "I'm sorry, Wolfgang, for attacking you. It will never happen again. You just cannot imagine what I am going through. It's been hard for me. This transition has been harder than I thought it would be. I just cannot lose my Garrison, especially to another woman. This has been hard to accept. I will deal with it in a more appropriate manner in the future. Again, I'm sorry." Wolfgang looked at her and let out a deep breath. He turned around without saying a word and continued his work.

It took a while for Marci and my father's relationship to heal from that experience. The event was never forgotten but their relationship got on track mostly due to Zelda's intervention. Zelda knew her husband better than anyone and she had a way of calming him. Both understood their passions got the best of them. Wolfgang understood what he was asking and the pressure he put on our relationship.

As the weeks went by, Marci felt better about the experiment. She knew down deep in her soul that she had no say about the subject. She knew that she couldn't stop it from happening. She just had to accept as fact that the experiment must take place. She knew that making a deal with the preverbal devil had some pitfalls and she was now, more than ever, fully aware and accepting of those unpleasant moments. I also think it was more about Wolfgang's disrespect toward her, but as I informed and reminded Marci, my father doesn't care about hurting other people's feelings or what others think. Marci still couldn't totally forget the words that he said to her about how he should have killed her before the transformation. This was another reminder to Marci that another person in her life had little regard and less love for her. In a twisted way, that event was a positive for our relationship because only I had never let her down.

As the year progressed, Eva and I worked on controlling our mind reading blessing. We actually started to read each other's thoughts on a more regular basis, but it was a struggle for us and would take a lot out of us physically, mentally, and emotionally.

We were also careful not to overload Eva with unnecessary stress. We took our time and never rushed into anything including television and newspaper interviews. We limited her concert appearances as well. Eva wanted to play in all of them but we, as a family, thought we needed to limit her exposure to concerts as well as interviews. Eva only played in large concert hall settings a few times during the year.

Marci kept most of her comments to herself, and Wolfgang and Marci went on about their business as if nothing happened. This was a difficult time for Marci because I was not showing her enough attention. Marci was becoming increasingly jealous of my relationship with Eva. I knew my Marci; I didn't need to read her mind to know what she was thinking. She didn't want to share me sexually with anyone. I knew that she thought if I mated with Eva that I might mate with others. I reassured her many times that she was the only woman for me, but Marci was the jealous type. She couldn't help what she was feeling inside her soul.

In the face of all these events, Marci decided to be the best and the smartest in everything she attempted. She wanted to make herself more attractive to me, so I would give her more attention. I tried to tell her on numerous occasions that she didn't have to win me over by trying to prove to me that she was special. I told her that I loved her, and I respected her, but she just nodded. To her, she had to prove to me that she had more in her than just being great at the violin. She started to study and read about all types of subject matter, and she practiced harder to compete with Eva's abilities. She was fighting for my attention; not my affection, but my attention.

The problem for Marci was that Eva was just better than her. No matter how hard Marci would try, Eva's intellect was greater, and her violin skills were superior to Marci's. From Marci's point of view, the whole reason she wanted to transform was to be my equal and to experience perfection in extended bursts of time. But after her transformation, Eva was now in the picture and this was someone that was just better than her, and Marci knew it. Marci loved Eva with all her heart, but she was still jealous of her. She was jealous of her natural ability and her relationship with me. Marci was uncomfortable having to compete with Eva for my attention, which is something that Marci had never experienced before in our relationship. I admitted to my love that she was right.

I started to show Marci more attention. We made love more often, I would talk to her more and we would take long walks together. I helped teach her about many different subjects and I tried to explain, to the best of my ability, what I knew. I had a lot on my plate at this time in my life, so it was difficult for me to juggle my time between my parents, Eva, Marci, and my businesses. After showing Marci more attention, this seemed to alleviate most of the stress between everyone in the family. Over time, Marci started to come to grips with the idea of her eventually being a foster mother to her lover's and his sister's baby. Marci was more accepting of the untapped potential of witnessing the creation of the perfect child from two near perfect. The formula should 'self-correct' any mutation that might possibly develop during the contraception cycle. Therefore, any issues of inbreeding would be corrected by the formula mutating the genes, and the biological cells.

Over the year, Eva enjoyed her school and classmates. Eva made many friends at her school, and she viewed school as a social event. She knew the material, never had an incorrect answer to any question, and she aced all her exams. She got in trouble a lot for talking in class, especially to the boys. Some of which she was very attracted to and most of the boys all tried to get her attention. Outside of school, she worked hard playing the violin and we took a couple of trips to Europe; one concert was in London and the other in Amsterdam. We played together at these concerts and again we had rave reviews.

Wolfgang thought at this stage of Eva's development that she could start dining on live meat. Marci helped Eva to the best of her ability. Marci showed her the proper way to trap an animal. Wolfgang and Zelda taught the girls how to and where to bite each different animal. They taught them where to take the meat from those animals. They showed them places on the animals where the meat would come off the bone easier, as well as showing them places that were not good to eat at all. Marci and Eva would normally share a deer once or twice a week. They also ate squirrels, birds, rabbits, and raccoons. I would sometimes join in, but I normally left this time to Marci and Eva. I wanted them to grow closer, and I thought it was important for me to give them some distance from me.

Eva was a fussy eater. She was not as strong as the four of us in the family, thus, after she had the animal in her hands, she would try and start on one spot and after the skin was broken in that spot, she would rip the skin and fur back. Basically, she would skin the animal alive. She loved the way the animal felt in her hands as it would wiggle around in extreme pain. Sometimes she would hold the skinned or partially skinned animal close to her chest. Wolfgang would tell her to stop playing with her food and eat it, kill it, or give the animal to one of them.

Marci and Eva would sometimes play games with their animals and see which animal would stay alive the longest after skinning them or after eating portions of their animal. It was a game to them at first, but natural instinct took over after so long and both Marci and Eva developed a desire for live animal muscles. Again, the muscles are the best part of an animal but for Eva that part was very tough for her to eat. Over time, you eventually develop your jaw muscles to a point where they are strong enough to pull and eventually tear away from the body. After a while, you begin to develop your own personal way of chewing the muscles. At first, Eva and Marci enjoyed the meat of their prey and that portion of any animal was delicious, but the true delicacy was the muscles and tendons. The absolute most favorite part of any of these animals they caught were the eyes. Both of my girls loved the way the eyeball would pop inside their mouth and between their teeth. They loved the warm, gooey, and slimy feel in their mouth after they bit into the eyes. They enjoyed the way they tended to explode.

This was a wonderful time in my life. Even though Marci was still a little jealous of Eva and Eva knew of her jealousy, they were the best of friends. They acted more like sisters instead of an aunt and niece relationship. At that point in my life, I finally had the family that I had always wanted. I had a great relationship with my parents, one who respected me and the other who loved me. I had the most wonderful relationship with the woman of my dreams and I had a sister that I loved dearly. It was a stark contrast to what I had during my first ten years on this earth. Now I am the lucky one. I have parents and a sibling that will never die. That is the type of family that I had always dreamed of having and I helped bring everyone together. Then I have the love of my life, my Marci. Although she had to be changed, which was her choosing, she was still the same person that I first met.

I stand now in front of that storybook character that many call god. I am the one laughing in the face of the great disgruntled creature of the imagination of the weak. Now I have won over the fate of life. I had to make many extreme adjustments to my life and the people that inhabited it through the years. I replaced my adoptive parents and brother with better beings. I had replaced imperfection with perfection. I have unionized my real family into one powerful organization that was ready to change the world. It would take time, but time is what we had in my family.

I would help orchestrate a massive correction that would take place in the next few centuries. The human race must be improved; it must change its current course of continuously making the same repeated mistakes. If they don't correct their current path, they will soon die out. Many will die from mass self-inflicted extinction while others will die from disease or natural causes. Through their short lifespan on this planet, humans have found multiple ways to extinguish themselves in short phases throughout history. Then, after these phases of population diminishment, the great irony is they kept multiplying in numbers. Over long periods of time, humans overpopulated their species with substandard specimens. Our creator saw all of this over a century ago, and I am here to help him accomplish the goal that was first set in place by great visionaries of the past. I am honored that my creator is my father. Hail victory!

About the Author

Kevin C. Popp was born and raised in Louisville, Kentucky, graduating in the early 1990's from Bellarmine University with degrees in Business Administration and Accounting. After working a couple of jobs after college, in 1997 he found a great company in the Financial Securities market, working in the finance department.

Kevin grew up as an only child, living modestly. His parents saved every dime they made, but when it came to Kevin's basic needs, he wanted for very little. His parents were much older than most of his friends' parents, thus his grandparents were older as well. His mom and dad spent the majority of his youth taking care of their parents, so his entire youth was surrounded by grandparents' illnesses, hospitals, nursing homes and eventual pending deaths.

One of Kevin's childhood memories was a struggle to find time to be alone. He felt strongly that he needed that time to himself, even for short time spans. He would regularly take long bike rides through the neighborhood, ultimately taking him through a park that his neighborhood bordered on. At times he would think to himself about money, politics or the concept of God.

Kevin took up golf at an early age and played the game well, but not to the level that he desired. He always admired people that were great at something, venerating intelligent, athletic, wealthy and attractive people, both young and old.

Kevin had many obsessions growing up, including golf, stamp collecting, money, stock market and numbers. He grew up thinking he was poor, but actually the opposite was true. He always saved more than others. At the impressionable age of twelve, he invested in the stock market and quickly enjoyed making money.

Although very intelligent, Kevin never liked school, and constantly daydreamed, thinking about things that never occurred to others. His mind, even to this day, continuously ponders and worries about everything, planning out numerous courses of action for every situation that he attempts or is forced into doing.

As an adolescent, Kevin was starved for attention so he attempted to be the class clown, only to find himself a colossal failure in that role. One area of his mind that was not a failure was his imagination. His mind worked continuously, exploring many subject matters. The one motif that kept his attention was horror. He loved watching 'monster' movies, and found that he could stomach the most ghastly scenes that included demonic possession, dismemberment, and torture at a young age. His mind was fascinated with the macabre, both real and imaginary, trying to understand the complicated relationship between life and death and how God played His part between the two.

As the years passed, Kevin could no longer find any outlet to whet his appetite for this strange, dark world resting in the innermost parts of his brain. One day at work, he decided to write a book, and began creating an outline. Before he knew it, he had over five typed pages of notes. Creation, he loved that word! So he began creating a story, not about anyone in particular, but a story that he created from his imagination alone. He quickly found that he could create something by writing down what was in his mind.

Although certainly not the twisted, heartless monster you see in his books, Kevin says he sometimes has a dual personality, especially when he writes. While busy typing away, he loses himself in an imaginary world of a multitude of sadistic renderings, and his hope is that he is talented enough to bring his imaginary world into focus for all to see and enjoy. It is his goal, as the writer of this series, to disrupt not only your cognizant state of mind, but also your unconscious realm simultaneously. Like any great composer of music, artistry or writing, as you read his books, he wants you to experience what is in his mind and soul. He wants you to understand his repulsion and loathing for a portion of the human race, as well as the pursuit of perfection that is inside his being. He doesn't want to just scare you, he wants to firmly implant horrific torture scenes in your memories that will haunt you daily. He wants you to question the human race and the many gods they pray to. He wants to dominate your thoughts and force you to feel others' pain.